"Daddy, who's this?"

Longarm turned to face the open doorway. Two young ladies were standing in it, each one dressed in a long white frilly nightgown, their luxurious, straw-colored hair falling far beyond their shoulders, all the way to their narrow waists. They looked at least eighteen.

"Mr. Long, may I present Marilyn and Audrey, Emilie's sisters. The shy one is Audrey. The outspoken nymph is Marilyn."

Marilyn reached out at once and took Longarm's hand boldly. "Oh, Mr. Long, please do bring Emilie back to us! Emilie is a match for any man! But that's just it. She won't submit easily."

"Let's hope she won't have to," said their father . . .

. . . from Novel 4: . . . the Wendigo

Longarm shifted quietly to a more comfortable position, seated in the grass with the rifle across his bent knees as he chewed an unlit cheroot to pass the time and keep awake.

Somewhere in the night a coyote howled and once a train hooted far across the prairie . . .

Then he heard something.

He didn't know what it was, or where it was coming from, but he suddenly knew he wasn't alone on the lonely prairie. He strained his ears in the dead silence all around.

A big gray cat was walking around in Longarm's gut for some fool reason; he told himself he didn't believe in ghosts. Nobody sensible believed in ghosts, but then, nobody sensible was sitting out here in the middle of nothing-much after making himself a target for whoever might be interested . . .

◄─ TABOR EVANS ─►

LONGARM

DOUBLE #2

LONGARM OF THE LAW

J

JOVE BOOKS, NEW YORK

THE BERKLEY PUBLISHING GROUP
Published by the Penguin Group
Penguin Group (USA) Inc.
375 Hudson Street, New York, New York 10014, USA
Penguin Group (Canada), 90 Eglinton Avenue East, Suite 700, Toronto, Ontario M4P 2Y3, Canada
(a division of Pearson Penguin Canada Inc.)
Penguin Books Ltd., 80 Strand, London WC2R 0RL, England
Penguin Group Ireland, 25 St. Stephen's Green, Dublin 2, Ireland (a division of Penguin Books Ltd.)
Penguin Group (Australia), 250 Camberwell Road, Camberwell, Victoria 3124, Australia
(a division of Pearson Australia Group Pty. Ltd.)
Penguin Books India Pvt. Ltd., 11 Community Centre, Panchsheel Park, New Delhi—110 017, India
Penguin Group (NZ), 67 Apollo Drive, Rosedale, North Shore 0632, New Zealand
(a division of Pearson New Zealand Ltd.)
Penguin Books (South Africa) (Pty.) Ltd., 24 Sturdee Avenue, Rosebank, Johannesburg 2196,
South Africa

Penguin Books Ltd., Registered Offices: 80 Strand, London WC2R 0RL, England

This is a work of fiction. Names, characters, places, and incidents either are the product of the author's imagination or are used fictitiously, and any resemblance to actual persons, living or dead, business establishments, events, or locales is entirely coincidental.

LONGARM DOUBLE #2: LONGARM OF THE LAW

A Jove Book / published by arrangement with the author

PRINTING HISTORY
Jove edition / August 2008

ISBN: 978-0-515-14509-0

JOVE®
Jove Books are published by The Berkley Publishing Group,
a division of Penguin Group (USA) Inc.,
375 Hudson Street, New York, New York 10014.
JOVE is a registered trademark of Penguin Group (USA) Inc.
The "J" design is a trademark belonging to Penguin Group (USA) Inc.

PRINTED IN THE UNITED STATES OF AMERICA

NOVEL 3

Longarm and the Avenging Angels

Chapter 1

It was a Monday morning and it wasn't raining. The high, clear air of the capital of Colorado seemed reasonably fresh and invigorating as Longarm stood by the open window. Of course it was early in the morning, before the horse manure of a new day was pounded into its golden essence by countless hoofs, sending its pungent fragrance into the heavens to mingle with the coal smoke and soot that was already blackening every new building in Denver. But that was Denver after twenty-odd years—horseshit and coal smoke. And always from some place—he wished to hell he knew where for sure—came the smell of burning leaves.

As he peered down at the narrow streets, Longarm heard the bedsprings squeak behind him and knew the girl was waking up. He was naked and did not want at this moment to turn and face his guest. After all, he had to report to the chief in less than an hour.

He sneaked a quick look over his shoulder and saw that she had just turned over, drawing the sheets up around her naked shoulders, the luxurious spill of her auburn hair tumbling down over the coverlet. She was breathing steadily, which meant she might well be asleep still. But then you could never tell.

Longarm left the window, padded across the threadbare carpet to the dressing table, and peered at his reflection in the mirror. He was a big man, lean and muscular, with the body of a young athlete. But there was nothing young about his face. It was seamed and cured to a saddle-leather brown by a raw sun and cutting winds, both of which he had experienced in abundance since lighting out from his native West-by-God-Virginia. His eyes were a gunmetal blue, his close-cropped hair was the color of aged tobacco leaf, and he wore proudly and kept well-trimmed a drooping longhorn mustache that added much to the ferocity of his appearance on those few occasions when ferocity as well as firepower might be decisive.

As he loomed above the dressing table in the early morning dimness, he heard another squeak of the bedsprings behind him—and this time he knew it was for real. He turned easily, cat-like, aware as always that his movements had an almost hypnotic effect on others.

The girl—her name, she had told him the night before, was

Rosalie—had a foolish little Allen pepperbox in her hand. It was a relic, at least twenty years old and of such an ancient and uncertain design that it would often fire all six barrels at once. As Longarm loomed closer, she raised the pepperbox and aimed it at his naked chest.

"I'll fire!" she cried in a frightened voice. "I warn you!"

Longarm smiled and sat his naked rump down on the edge of the bed. "Ain't it a little late for you to be protecting your honor, miss?"

"But I didn't *mean* that last night! I didn't mean that to happen!"

"Didn't appear to me like you was acting, ma'am. Leastways, you sure put your whole heart and soul into it." He grinned at her past the wavering pepperbox. "Fact is, what happened between us was mighty nice."

She scooted up angrily in the bed and propped her back against the brass bedstead, the little gun still trained on Longarm's chest. "It was my body that betrayed me, Mr. Longarm, I assure you! My heart and soul had nothing to do with it!"

"Why don't you put that little toy down now, Rosalie? You got my attention, all right."

"No!" she cried firmly, steadying the weapon. "I am going to shoot you, Mr. Longarm! I am going to send you to your Maker!"

"Mind if I ask why? I didn't think I was *that* bad last night. And by way of apology, I might remind you of the number of drinks you insisted on buying for me."

"That's not the reason!" she fumed. "What I mean is, you were—fine." She became intolerably flustered at this point and her face went dark with embarrassment. "*That's* not the reason!"

"And what is the reason?"

"My brother! Merle Bond! You're the one that sent him to prison! You testified against him. I heard your testimony. I was in court. When you stepped off that stand, the judge had no choice but to sentence Merle to all those years! You did it with your testimony!"

"Why, thank you, Miss Bond. I'm glad you think so."

Her eyes widened in fury. She brought up a small, pink hand to steady the weapon and seemed intent on pulling the trigger. "How dare you say that!"

"That's easy, Rosalie. I believe in using the most direct route to wherever I'm going. Sometimes I might seem uncommonly blunt, but I don't mean any harm by it. I'm glad my testimony gave that jury the backbone to convict your brother. He is one mean son of a bitch, if you'll pardon the liberty."

"Oh!"

"I can't help it." He smiled sadly at her. "It's the truth and that's the long and the short of it. Wish it weren't, I surely do."

Tears welled in her dark blue eyes and began to roll down her fresh, round cheeks. There was nothing hard about her, he remembered from the night before. She was as soft and cuddly as a kitten—until she caught fire. And then it was all hands to battle stations and hang on for this one! The pepperbox trembled. She seemed determined to pull the trigger.

Longarm got up casually and looked down at her. Convulsively, she brought the weapon up again so that it was still trained on his chest. "I *am* going to shoot you!" she cried between clenched teeth.

"Then do it, Rosalie, and get it over with."

She closed her eyes and squeezed the trigger. As the tiny hammer came down on an empty chamber, Longarm reached down and gently but firmly took the weapon out of the girl's hand. She collapsed onto a pillow, her head buried in it, sobbing.

He watched her for a moment, then turned and walked over to the dresser and dropped the Allen beside the pile of tiny rounds he had taken from it the night before. He poked through the rest of the clutter atop the dresser, found his bar of soap, and brought it over to the washstand. Pouring water from the pitcher into the china basin, he dipped a washrag into it, soaped it, and began washing himself about the face, neck, and shoulders. He was in the midst of rinsing off his face and neck when he heard the sobbing subside rather abruptly, and heard the bedsprings jounce.

Reaching for a towel to dry himself, he looked back at the bed. Rosalie was sitting bolt upright, staring at him. She was still paying no attention to her nakedness, and this time he found it difficult not to notice her breasts. What was it that fellow Solomon called them—*like two young roes that are twins?* Well, maybe. And then he saw that she was looking, at him.

"Longarm?"

"Yes?" He finished with the towel and tossed it onto the foot of the bed.

"Would you come over here?"

With a sigh, Longarm crossed to the bed and sat down, facing her.

"You knew—about that gun, I mean."

"I found it last night while you were sleeping."

"You were just toying with me."

"I wasn't sure what you wanted."

"You weren't sure? You mean you suspected who I was?"

"I knew I'd seen you before somewhere and that it would be a good idea for me to remember. But like I said, I wasn't sure."

She closed her eyes, as if determined to keep her temper and remain composed. Opening them again, she said, "Those were terrible things for you to say about my brother."

"I just said he was a mean son of a bitch. And he was."

"He was just a high-spirited boy!"

Longarm nodded. "That's right. A high-spirited boy who robbed three stages, killed a driver and a shotgun on his third attempt, and later shot up a saloon, killing one of the bar girls. He resisted arrest and the posse that chased him to his hideout lost three good men. When they sent me after him, Rosalie, the price on his head was fifteen thousand—dead or alive. I brought him in alive. I didn't have to, but I did."

"And I should thank you for that, I suppose!"

"You can if you want. But maybe you already thanked me. Last night."

She tried to generate a head of steam over that comment, but couldn't quite manage it. And then her eyes dropped to that portion of Longarm's anatomy that made the most sense at times like this.

She looked back at him, her eyes softening. The memory of last night clouded her eyes, softening the anger she had tried so hard to retain. "Oh, Longarm," she whispered. "I'm so confused."

Longarm stood up. "Let's put it this way, Rosalie. You're a woman—one hell of a woman and that's nothing to be ashamed of. I can see what you planned, all right. You'd ply me with drinks, get me to take you up to my room, and then you would avenge your brother's life sentence. You've been reading too much of that Ned Buntline crap, if you'll pardon my bluntness."

She closed her eyes and shook her head. "Don't keep asking me to pardon your language, Longarm. I'm used to it by now. But of course you're right. I guess I was being overly romantic."

"And foolish. But I guess you loved your brother. And I guess that excuses it some."

"I tried so hard to raise him properly, Longarm. But when Mother died, he just went wild. I followed him out here, but he was determined to go his own way. And that meant guns. And robbing. And killing." She bowed her head and began to weep softly.

Longarm stood where he was, watching her, waiting. After a little bit, her crying abated and she glanced up at him. "Aren't you going to . . . comfort me?" She managed what she thought was a seductive smile, but it just didn't make the grade.

"Is that what you want, Rosalie? Comfort?"

She wiped her eyes. "I don't know. Last night, we—"

"Forget last night. You had a reason for coming up here and trying to tire me out." He grinned quickly at the thought. "How did you know I'd be the one to tire *you* out?"

She blushed and wiped tears from her eyes hopefully. "I tired you out *some*," she insisted. "But you were so—nice."

"You had a reason last night, Rosalie. What would your reason be now? I think you just better get dressed and go home and start thinking like a good girl again, and stop reading that Ned Buntline crap."

"You mean you don't—!"

"I mean I got a job to go to and you don't know me well enough to start bedding down with me on a regular basis. Not unless you're trying to gain instruction in a new line of work—where the only rest you get is standing up."

"Oh! You're so cruel!" She snatched up the bedclothes and covered her lovely breasts. "If you wouldn't just stand in front of a girl like that with nothing at all in front of you . . . !"

"Beg pardon, Rosalie. Guess that *did* sort of cloud the issue some at that." Longarm reached for his knit cotton longjohns. He pulled them on while standing up and then reached for his brown tweed pants. They were a size too small and he had his usual struggle getting them on. At last he cursed his fly shut and straightened, the pants as snug as a second skin.

"That's much better," Rosalie said. "I don't feel so threatened now." There was a hint of deviltry in her voice. Glancing quickly over, he saw the gleam in her eye.

"As soon as I leave here," he said, "I'll expect you to dress and go back home, wherever that is. Understood?"

"You're not married, are you, Longarm?"

"No."

"Engaged?"

"No."

"Well then, why do you want to get rid of me?"

"How old are you, Rosalie?"

She hesitated. "Twenty!"

"Closer to eighteen, I'd say."

"I'll be nineteen next March!"

"I'm close to forty," he lied. "You're young enough to be my daughter. Come to think of it, I must have some daughters around your age at that."

"What's age got to do with it? It didn't seem to be such a terrible nuisance last night."

Longarm sighed, bent over, and fished under the bed for his boots, then sat on the edge of the bed and tugged them on. They were low-heeled cavalry stovepipes more suited for running than riding, which was just what Longarm wanted. He spent as much time afoot as he did in the saddle, and with these boots he could outrun almost anyone.

But how was he going to outrun this girl? He stood up and turned to look down at her. She was still sitting up and holding the sheet over her breasts, but her shoulders were bare and her face was flushed. Her eyes . . .

"Damn it, girl! I don't want any! You got that?"

"You don't have to shout!"

"Yes I do, it seems like. Now listen here to me. I'm a lawman. That means I go most anywhere they send me. I'm here today, gone tomorrow. I find my loving where I can, and I don't look back. I'm not interested in paying for it, which means I can go without if I have to. What I don't want and what I will never want, as far as I can see, is a wife on my neck—or a girl sitting in some hotel room waiting on me! Now if you don't make tracks, girl, back to wherever you came from, I'll haul you in for attempting to shoot a peace officer. I've got your weapon here as evidence, and my testimony will be accurate. That means, Miss Rosalie, that I won't leave out a thing!"

"You wouldn't!"

"If it would knock some sense into that pea brain of yours, I would do it. Yes I would."

"Oh!" She glared at him. "Oh!"

He turned his back to her and put on his gray flannel shirt. He fumbled with the string tie, fastening it into a tolerable knot, then tucked the shirt into his pants. His gunbelt he had stashed under some clothes in the second drawer of the dresser. He pulled the gunbelt out and strapped it around his waist, adjusting it to ride just above his hips. The rig holding his double-action Colt Model T .44-40 was a cross-draw, and he wore it high. He drew the revolver smoothly, effortlessly, then turned about and leaned back against the dresser, his gun held out carefully in front of him.

Aware of Rosalie's eyes on him, he proceeded to inspect this most important tool of his trade. The barrel was cut to five inches and the front sight had been filed off. He didn't want the revolver's barrel to catch in the open-toed holster made of waxed and heat-hardened leather. Moving then to the bed and still apparently ignoring the girl, Longarm emptied the cylinder on the bedsheet at the foot of the bed. He dry-fired a few times to test the action, easing the hammer down with his thumb, as always, then reloaded. Before thumbing each cartridge home, he held it up to the window for a quick, minute inspection. He loaded only five cartridges into the cylinder. He didn't want to lose a foot jumping down off a train or a bronc, so he kept the firing pin riding safely on the empty chamber.

He holstered the Colt, and finished dressing swiftly. He took the change and his wallet off the top of the dresser and pocketed them, ducked into his vest and frock coat, dropped the pepperbox and its cartridges into the coat's right side pocket, then inspected critically his Ingersoll pocket watch. It was on a long gold-washed chain with a clip at the other end. He placed the watch in the left breast pocket of the vest, leaving the chain dangling. Then he reached in under the mattress at the foot of the bed and pulled out a stubby, double-barreled .44-caliber derringer with a small brass ring soldered to its butt. This he clipped to the loose end of his watch chain and dropped the pistol into his right breast pocket, allowing the chain to drape innocently across the vest front.

"You . . . had a gun there?" Rosalie asked.

"That's right. I would have had it under my pillow, but I wanted to leave you room for that pepperbox. I stashed my gunbelt and Colt in the drawer in case you proved more anxious to kill me than I figured."

Rosalie took a deep breath. "I've been very foolish, haven't I?"

"Yes."

"And this . . . isn't the beginning of anything, is it?"

Longarm shook his head. "Nothing personal, Rosalie. It's just the way I'm built. Some men are for marrying, some men are for . . ." He shrugged and smiled at her. "No hard feelings?"

She considered the question seriously for a moment or two, then looked him squarely in the eyes and shook her head. "I guess not. Just tell me one thing, Mr. Longarm."

"What's that?"

"Why is it that the ones who want to settle down are so much less fun than the others?"

Longarm laughed. "Maybe it just seems that way now. Just give yourself time. You'll find a man who's fun and who also wants to settle down. Just keep looking."

"That's what I've been doing."

"You've got some time left, you know."

"I suppose."

Positioning his snuff-brown Stetson carefully on his head—dead center, tilted slightly forward, cavalry style—he smiled at the girl.

"You need a shave," she said.

"I plan to get one from the barber," he told her.

"And you want me to dress and leave as soon as you are gone."

"My landlady—an understanding soul—will be up here in less than thirty minutes to make sure. She knows I'm a lawman working for the government and she is a great help." Something occurred to him. "Do you . . . need any money?"

"No. Didn't you say you never had to pay for it?"

"That's not why I asked," he said, with a gentleness that surprised even him.

She ducked her head. "I'm sorry. A train ticket back to Saint Louis would cost me more than I have left right now."

He nodded, took out his wallet, and dropped a twenty-dollar certificate on the bedspread. "I know the train schedule," he told her. "I'll have someone at the depot watching to make sure you're on that train for Saint Louis this afternoon."

She swallowed eagerly. "Is there one then?"

"There is."

"Thank you," she said, reaching for the certificate. "This is more than generous of you." She turned her face up to his, fully expecting a good-bye kiss, he realized.

He bent swiftly and kissed her lightly on the forehead, then swept past her to the door. Pulling it open, he turned to look back at her.

"Remember. I'll have someone watching that train. Be on it, young lady!"

There were fresh tears running down her cheeks as she nodded. Longarm pulled shut the door and hurried down the stairs to find the landlady. It was curious. He should have felt twenty dollars poorer and more than a little irritated. But he didn't. He felt good, in fact.

Longarm's shave took longer than he had expected it would. Glancing at his watch as he passed the U.S. Mint at Cherokee and

Colfax, he turned the corner and started for the Federal Building. Once inside, he strode through the lobby as swarms of officious lawyers hustled their legal briefs in one door and out another, talked excitedly in groups, or hurried upstairs and downstairs, sweating themselves into such a fine frenzy that their oil-plastered hair was already coming unstuck. At the top of a marble staircase, Longarm came upon a large oak door. The gilt lettering on it read: *UNITED STATES MARSHAL, FIRST DISTRICT COURT OF COLORADO.*

Longarm pushed the door open and strode into the outer office. The pink-cheeked clerk was playing with his typewriter. The newfangled piece of machinery raised a fearsome clatter.

"The chief in?" Longarm asked the clerk above the clatter.

The fellow turned. "Oh, it's you, Mr. Long!"

"That's right. Custis Long." Longarm grinned at the clerk. "You don't have to announce me. You just go ahead and play that thing. You sound great." Longarm started for the inner office.

"Just a moment, Mr. Long," the clerk said. "I believe Marshal Vail—"

Vail appeared in the doorway. There was a harassed look on his face. He growled, "Can't you ever, make it in here on time?"

"It's this damn clerk," Longarm said. "He makes me wait out here."

Vail glared at the clerk, who began to sputter indignantly. When Vail saw Longarm's sudden grin, his shoulders slumped and he waved Longarm past him. "Get in there, Longarm," he said, "and stop upsetting the clerical staff." As Longarm moved past him into his office, Marshal Vail closed the door and smiled sardonically at him. "You're not going to like this."

Longarm slumped into the red morocco leather armchair across the desk from his superior and tipped his head slightly as he regarded the marshal. "They want me to rescue Sitting Bull from the Wild West Show?"

Vail's eyebrows shot up a notch. "That wouldn't be such a bad idea, at that." Then the man moved behind his desk and began pawing through a pile of paper. "That might be a lot easier than this little job." He found what he was looking for and squinted at Longarm. "Ever been to Utah?"

"Sure. Remember that jasper I caught up with in Provo? Tried to get lost in a band of them Mormon night riders. What the hell did they call themselves?"

"Avenging Angels."

"That's right. Sounds like a Ned Buntline joke."

"They are no joke, Longarm." He looked down at the dispatch he had retrieved as Longarm took out a cheroot and stuck it into his mouth. He didn't light it, just began chewing on it. "Seems a bunch of Mormon fanatics somewhere in Utah have kidnapped a Mormon girl from Salt Lake City. The Mormon authorities have requested federal help in getting her back." Vail leaned back and looked at Longarm, just the trace of a smile on his pasty, indoors face. "I'm sending you. Washington wants the best man for the job." Vail shrugged. "What choice did I have?"

Longarm shrugged. "Who do I contact in Salt Lake City?"

"Wells Daniel. You won't contact him. He'll contact you. Stay at the Wayfarer. It's a new hotel. I understand it's reasonable."

"Who is this Daniel?"

"A high-muck-a-muck in the Mormon Church. That's all I can tell you. But you work through him."

"I've got the feeling you know a lot more you ain't telling."

"And if you notice, none of it's written down. This is a political hot potato, Longarm. As I understand it, there are members high up in the Mormon Church who are sympathetic to this kidnapping—or at least to the fanatics behind it."

"I see," said Longarm dryly, working, the cheroot about in his mouth. "So the federal government is called in to do the dirty work. I don't know if I like this so awful much. What can you tell me about the kidnapping?"

Vail shrugged. "I don't even know the girl's name. She was taken from her home at night and hasn't been heard from since. A note was left by the fanatics, but nothing's been heard from them either. She's supposed to be a very pretty young thing who'd make a fine addition to some Mormon's harem."

Longarm frowned. "From what I hear, those women are supposed to make a choice about joining one of those households."

"They are. This one, it seems, wasn't given that choice."

Longarm nodded and got to his feet. The thought of a young girl hauled off like that didn't set right with him. "You got my expense vouchers? I'll need a railroad pass, too."

Vail nodded. "See my secretary." He looked up abruptly at Longarm. "Oh. I almost forgot. You remember that punk desperado—Bond, Merle Bond—the jasper you caught up with last spring?"

Longarm grew suddenly alert, his teeth chomping down hard on his unlit cheroot. "I remember."

"Did you know he had a sister?"

"Not until recently."

"Well, according to Deputy Wilson, she's in town looking for you."

"That so?"

"Well, she's armed, according to Wilson. Armed and dangerous."

Longarm interrupted Vail with a wave of his hand. Then he took out the old Allen pepperbox and the cartridges and dropped them on Vail's desk. "Miss Bond is no longer armed. And tell Wilson to check the train depot tonight. I've already seen the young lady and told her to be on tonight's train for Saint Louis."

Vail got to his feet. "You mean you've already tangled with that girl?"

"I guess that's what you'd call it."

Vail's face went pale. "And you let her go?"

"She's just a kid, Chief. A foolish young thing with romantic notions about paying back those that testified against her brother. I disarmed her and got her promise. She'll be on her way back to Saint Louis tonight. Relax."

"For God's sake, Longarm! Before that foolish kid landed on your doorstep, she killed the poor son of a bitch in Cedar Creek who testified at her brother's trial—Amos Beedle, the stagecoach driver. He was number one on her list. *You* were number two!"

Longarm took a deep breath, his teeth clamping down hard, cutting through the cheroot. He spit the end into the wastebasket, then looked at Vail.

"I guess she won't be on that train to Saint Louis, then," he said. "Just the same, it might be a good idea for Wilson to check it out."

Without a word, Vail nodded. He was still standing, thunderstruck.

"By the way," Longarm asked, "what did she use to kill the stage driver?"

Vail slumped back down into his chair and nodded at the pepperbox. "She used all six barrels." He sighed. "At least you didn't give it back to her."

Longarm stuck what was left of his cheroot back into his mouth. "I'll go see about them travel vouchers and the railroad pass."

He turned then and made for the door. As he pulled it open, Vail cleared his throat. Longarm turned. Vail leaned forward onto his forearms.

"You take care of this business in Salt Lake City with a minimum of fuss, Longarm, and I just might forget to include this business with Miss Bond in my report to Washington."

"Chief?"

"Yes?"

"Have I ever asked you to wipe my ass before this?"

"Hell, Longarm, I was just—"

"Well, I ain't asking you to do that for me now. You hear? You want to include that there business with that little tramp, you go right ahead."

Longarm left then, slamming the door firmly behind him.

Longarm sat morosely on a faded red plush seat at the rear of the passenger car of the Union Pacific's Hotel Express. There was nothing luxurious about his accommodations, and Longarm's large frame was more than a little weary of the tedious ride. The coach was noisy, filled with smoke and with the stench of unwashed humanity. Looking about him, Longarm found it difficult to keep his temper at times. What he saw and what he heard made him stir restlessly in his seat.

His fellow travelers were not elegant, not by a long shot. They were dressed carelessly, sloppily, many times in ragged garments and more often than not clutching dirty bundles. Most of the men had revolvers stuck carelessly in their belts, a piratical gleam in their eyes. They were unshaven usually, some were bearded. Their talk was loud and filled with profanity that took no note of the women and children forced to endure their company. Those men with wives tried not to notice the language and the single men's insolent stares, lest they be forced to stand up to them and lose their lives in the bargain.

Salt Lake City was the next stop. They were only a few hours away, having passed through Provo less than an hour ago. It was close to three in the afternoon and the heat inside the coach made Longarm's skin crawl. Babies were bawling and the voices of mothers scolding their restless children were a constant irritant to all those in the coach without offspring.

The door to the coach opened and Longarm saw a bearded desperado step inside, pulling the door shut behind him. There was something particularly offensive about the man, something that sounded a deep warning bell within Longarm. Had he seen this man before? Did he know him?

The fellow lurched down the aisle, found an empty seat next to a drummer, and squeezed in beside him. The drummer had been dozing. He awoke with a start, began to protest the abrupt manner in which he had been joined, then immediately thought better of it as he took in his new companion. No longer casting about in his memory for some clue as to where he might have met the fellow before, Longarm smiled at the drummer's reaction.

He took out a cheroot, lit it with a sulphur match that he ignited with a single flick of his thumbnail, and turned his attention to the landscape stroking by the train window. They had left the Utah Lake behind and Longarm could see the towering, snow-clad peaks of the Uinta Mountains to the east. The grade was now steadily downhill, and he realized the heat would get progressively worse as they neared the Great Salt Lake Desert. Pine-covered ridges swept up to and fell away from the train as it racketed along. Great stretches of barren, uninhabited land met his gaze. Used to the long, arid stretches of the West, Longarm was nevertheless mildly depressed by this glimpse of Mormon country. Only a band of religious fanatics, he supposed, could make a land like this bloom. Or would want to.

A woman entered the coach. She seemed very tired and a bit desperate for a place to sit. She was a gaunt but attractive young woman; her head was enclosed in a severe, dark blue bonnet, her dress was heavy and extended down to her feet, which were encased in heavy black shoes, laced high and tight. She appeared to lose her balance for a moment, then began to move hopefully down the aisle toward Longarm.

She must have gotten on at Provo, Longarm realized, and had not yet been lucky enough to find a seat. He moved closer to the window, touched the brim of his hat as she met his gaze, and smiled. With enormous relief, she hurried toward him and the seat he offered her beside him.

As she passed the jasper who had entered the coach just before her, however, she let out a tiny cry. Longarm craned his neck to look and saw that the man had reached out and grabbed the woman by the wrist. She tried to pull away but the fellow just increased his pressure on the girl's wrist and pulled her back toward him. The man got to his feet as he pulled the girl to him and smiled. It was not a pleasant smile.

"Well, if it ain't Annie Dawkins!" the fellow exclaimed, his leering smile freezing the girl's feet to the floor, it seemed.

"Jason Kimball!" the girl managed. "You leave me be! I ain't a Mormon no more and you can't collect no more tithe from us!"

The fellow's leer deepened. "Why, sure I can, Annie. You is in arrears, you is! We'll just collect you and even up the books! How's that?"

The girl Annie tried to pull away, but the fellow had a firm grip on her arm and wasn't about to let go. Still holding onto her, he looked down at the drummer, who all through this had been trying to ignore the ruckus completely, his head turned resolutely while he contemplated the grim Utah landscape.

"Get up, drummer," the fellow ordered him in a harsh, grating voice that brooked no argument. "Me and my friend here wish to sit down in the same damn seat. Git!"

Longarm would never go looking for a fight; he would, in fact, leave an unfriendly bar rather than provoke a confrontation. A peaceable man who liked his solitude, he preferred always to mind his own business. But he was sorely tried at this juncture. The sight of this walking carrion manhandling the terrified girl caused his stomach to rumble dangerously. The fellow was nothing but a murderous, loud, profane old blackguard in an unclean shirt. His laugh was a demented horselaugh, and his walk was a buccaneer's swagger.

Glancing quickly about, Longarm noticed that there was not a single male in the coach who did not have his eyes averted. The children were all being forcibly made to look elsewhere and they were all uncommonly hushed. The sight of this universal cowardice caused Longarm to grind the end of his soggy cheroot, and at last, when he saw the quivering drummer sidling out of his seat to make room for the blackguard, he got reluctantly to his feet and started down the aisle.

The drummer was in the aisle when Longarm reached them. When he saw Longarm's empty seat, his eyes lit and he tried to move past Longarm to get to it. Longarm restrained him with a hand on his left shoulder and gently pushed him back and out of the way. Then he turned to the girl. Tears of anger and frustration were rolling down her youthful cheeks. She looked at him with wide, hopeful eyes.

"May I be of assistance, ma'am?" he asked her, lifting his Stetson slightly. "I saw you were looking for a seat."

Before she could answer, the fellow who had been bullying her spoke up roughly. "Here now, what the hell are you about, mister? You leave Annie be. She's with me now!"

"Why don't we leave that to her?" Longarm inquired, his voice gently conciliatory.

Longarm turned his eyes to the girl. "Would you care to join me, Miss—?"

"Dawkins," the girl said eagerly, wiping away her tears quickly with the back of her hand. "Annie Dawkins."

"Hey, now!" protested the bully. "You just stand back there, mister! Who says you can interfere, you dirty gentile!"

Longarm smiled at the man. "That's right. I'm a gentile. And what are you—a Mormon?"

The girl pressed anxiously toward Longarm. "He's—he's an Avenging Angel! Maybe you better not get mixed up in this." Longarm's quiet, almost gentle aspect had about convinced her that he was no match for this Avenging Angel.

"You heard her!" blustered the man, pulling himself up to his full five-feet-ten or so. "That's what I am, all right. So you better mind your own business."

Longarm smiled at the man. "You don't smell like an angel."

The fellow's eyes went hard. He reached his right hand up and began to tug on the handle of a big Colt he had stuck in his belt. Longarm slapped the fellow in the face with his left hand, drew his Colt with his right, and brought the gun's barrel up swiftly, catching the fellow across the side of his head. The Avenging Angel slumped back into his seat, glassy-eyed, his jaw slack, a broad red welt rising across his cheekbone.

Holstering his weapon, Longarm swiftly disarmed the man, then frisked him expertly for any hidden weapons. Finding none, he looked up and nodded to the drummer.

"You can have your seat back now. When this fellow wakes up, keep him amused with dirty jokes." Longarm grinned at the look of pure terror on the man's face.

Straightening, Longarm turned to the girl and tipped his hat. "My seat is this way, Annie."

Her eyes still wide—and a look of pure, undiluted gratitude filling them—she nodded, did a quick curtsy of a sort, then preceded him down the aisle to his seat. Longarm allowed her to get in first so that her seat would be next to the window. Longarm took from her the little carpetbag she had clung to all through this unpleasantness, and placed it in the rack over their seat. Then he sat down beside her and smiled at her kindly in an effort to quiet the young girl's thudding heart. Her face was flushed and it was obvious that she did not really know how to account for her good fortune.

For his part, Longarm did not know how to explain his own

lack of good sense. Twice now within two days he had allowed a pretty face to obscure his role as a law officer. He should have brought in that sweet little murderess when she pulled that weapon on him, ridiculous as it appeared to him at the time. And this most recent bit of gallantry did nothing at all to insure his quiet entry into the case of the missing Mormon girl. Every Mormon and gentile in this coach—and soon, he had no doubt, throughout the train—would be discussing in hushed tones the way he had rescued the Fair Young Maid from the Avenging Angel. Longarm might as well have entered Salt Lake City wearing a sign announcing his profession and his intent.

He sighed, stretched his legs as much as was possible, and took from his inside breast pocket a fresh cheroot. This one he was tempted to smoke, despite his vow to quit the filthy habit.

He spat out the stub of his previous cheroot and poked the fresh one into his mouth, then turned his head to nod at the girl. He didn't want his preoccupied silence to make the woman feel unwelcome.

"You can light that, if you want," she suggested. "I won't mind."

He smiled his appreciation, took out a match, and lit it with his thumbnail. As he sucked the pungent tobacco smoke into his lungs, he leaned back, placated somewhat.

"Perhaps I should explain," the girl said softly.

"That ain't necessary, ma'am," Longarm said.

"Call me Annie," she insisted quietly.

He smiled at her and took a deep drag on his smoke. "Annie, then."

Frowning, he leaned back in his seat. What was the matter with him? He could use any information he could get on the Avenging Angels, and this girl beside him might very well be a gold mine of such lore. Maybe he was getting old. He had never heard of senility setting in at his age, but he sure as hell wasn't acting very bright lately.

"Of course," he said, turning to look at her, "it did seem strange for a man to do something like that in front of so many people. Did he know you from somewhere?"

She nodded quickly. "My father drew a terrible farm in the lottery years ago. It was in southern Utah. Brigham Young told my father and the others to grow cotton there. But we couldn't. No matter how hard we worked. The soil was alkaline, and the grasshoppers and crickets were everywhere. We were lucky if we could grow enough food for our table."

She sighed and looked away from Longarm, her gaze following the shifting contours of the semiarid landscape. She was seeing it all again, Longarm realized, in her mind's eye. Talking about it had upset her.

"You don't have to tell me about it if you don't want to," Longarm suggested gently.

She looked back up at his face. "But I do. I owe you an explanation. You see, we did so poorly that we couldn't pay our tithes. So Brigham Young sent the Avenging Angels after us. And even then we couldn't hardly gather enough to satisfy them. So my father left the church."

"Did that help?"

She shook her head sadly. "They said he couldn't leave the church. They said they were excommunicating *him*. And so we lost everything."

"I'm sorry, Annie. What happened to your family?"

"I don't know what happened to my father. He rode out one night—to talk sense to those Avenging Angels, he said. He never came back. My mother just gave up after that and died soon after. My sisters—like me—have become fallen women." She bowed her head in her hands and wept softly.

Longarm said nothing and did not try to comfort her. Instead he quietly, patiently puffed on his cheroot, being careful not to blow any smoke toward her. At last she recovered her composure and looked at him.

"So you see, Mr. . . . ?"

"Long," he told her, smiling. "Custis Long."

"So you see, Mr. Long, you seem to have saved from that terrible man only a piece of soiled goods."

"Guess you've got a right to be ashamed if it makes you feel any better, Annie. But I always thought soiling came from inside."

She raised her eyebrows in surprise at Longarm's comment. Surprise and appreciation. "Yes, of course, Mr. Long. You're right. But there aren't many people in the Mormon community— or anywhere else, for that matter—who would agree with you. You have no idea how difficult they make it for a woman without a family or a husband. I tried to get a job as a seamstress in Provo and Salt Lake City, but since the Saints own all the establishments that use seamstresses and since my family and I were excommunicated . . ." She shrugged. "So I went to work for Ma Randle at the Utah House."

"A saloon?"

"Yes—among other things."

"I thought Mormons didn't drink."

"There are many gentiles living in Salt Lake City, Mr. Long. And many Mormons *do* drink. Have you ever tasted Valley Tan?"

Longarm shook his head.

"Wait until you do." Her eyes danced mischievously. "It is a kind of whiskey. Only the Mormons make it and we're the only ones who can drink it, seems to me."

"Annie," Longarm said, noting that the girl had recovered her composure well enough to handle tough questions, "what was that fellow going to do with you? He said something about collecting you and evening up the books. I assume he had some plan—some way of using you."

She shuddered involuntarily and nodded. "Yes, he did, Mr. Long. He would take me as his wife—or as one of his wives."

"I thought the Mormons could only do that if the girl was willing." He watched her narrowly.

"That's the way it *should* be, and that's the way it is, usually. But not for them—not for the Avenging Angels." She looked out the window of the coach. "They're out there. Everywhere. Waiting. Small colonies of squatters." She shuddered. "One of my sisters is with them. I haven't heard from her in a year." Then she uttered a bitter laugh. " 'Celestial Marriage,' Joseph Smith called it."

Longarm leaned back in the chair. He had almost finished his cheroot and he had just glimpsed a portion of the Great Salt Lake Desert through the coach window. He was almost to Salt Lake City, and Annie to the Utah House.

Not long after, the train creaked to a stop. As Longarm got to his feet and lifted down Annie's carpetbag, he saw the Avenging Angel she had addressed as Jason Kimball getting to his feet as well. Once in the aisle, he glanced in Longarm's direction. The look on his face would have curdled the heart of an Apache. Longarm just smiled at the man and nodded briskly.

Jason strode angrily down the aisle to the door of the coach, not at all gentle with those he brushed aside.

"You have made an enemy there, I'm afraid," said Annie, watching the man go. "But I thank you from the bottom of my heart."

"I wouldn't say any day of mine was entirely wasted, ma'am, when I gained an enemy of that stamp. When carrion like that starts thinking of you with any kind of charity, you ought to wonder what you're doing wrong."

The train jolted to a stop. He stepped back and let the girl precede him down the aisle while he followed, carrying her carpetbag and his own canvas gladstone. He could not help noticing her trim figure and the thick curls that coiled on her slim shoulders. Despite her severe dress, there was no doubt in his mind that Annie was all woman and he did not wonder at Jason Kimball's eagerness to take her into his harem to settle past debts.

Hell, Longarm told himself, *he wouldn't even need that much of an excuse.*

Now hold it right there, old son, he told himself somewhat sheepishly. *Just you back off. You've already muddied the waters enough. The chief told you to keep low—not to spend the taxpayers' money sparking a fallen woman with pretty ankles!*

With a sigh directed at the unsought complexities of a lawman's life, Longarm followed the girl from the train and was immediately engulfed in a tide of gushing femininity.

Three shrieking, delighted young ladies had darted across the platform to welcome Annie, and she was reciprocating their greeting most heartily. His face reddening to find himself in the midst of all this feminine chatter, Longarm put down Annie's carpetbag and tried to sidle out of the crush. But Annie reached out before he could get away and caught his arm.

Squeezing it fondly, she called out above the happy babble, "Thank you so much, Mr. Long. You are very kind!"

Longarm nodded his good-bye to her, aware suddenly of the curious, approving appraisal of the three young women, and pulled away. A tall, imposing woman close to her mid-thirties, with a handsome face and magnificent dark eyes, stopped before him. She didn't seem to have the bust her size would have deserved. Indeed, she was almost as straight as a razor. But her waist was slim, her hips ample. This was obviously Ma Randle, the owner of the Utah House.

As the girls moved off across the platform, chatting gaily, the madam's dark eyes regarded Longarm coolly. "Thank you, sir, for escorting Annie from the train. I trust you are under no misapprehension concerning Miss Dawkins?"

"You mean do I know where she works?"

"Yes, that's precisely what I mean. I own the Utah House and the adjoining facilities, and Annie is one of my nicest girls. I am very fond of her."

"Yes, I can see that," Longarm remarked. "She must be great for business."

"That is not my only concern."

"If you'll excuse me, ma'am." Longarm started to move past the woman.

"Just a moment. You don't understand. I simply wanted you to realize that if you do come to visit Annie at the Utah House, you are most welcome. Only I would hope you won't make a fuss if you find she is occupied with other . . . customers." She sighed. "Annie is very popular, and sometimes men who are taken by her make a fuss when they find her already with someone."

Longarm smiled in spite of himself. "No chance of that, ma'am. My expense voucher don't cover that expense, and besides, my interest in Miss Dawkins has just about evaporated." Longarm caught sight then of Jason Kimball standing with four other cutthroats on the far edge of the platform. They were dressed in the same nondescript fashion, falling somewhere between that of a pirate and that of a highwayman. They were all uncommonly interested in Longarm. "But you better keep those sharp eyes of yours peeled. One of them Avenging Angels over there—the good-looking one with all the hair—put in a claim for Miss Annie on the train. But I lost my head completely and went to her aid and assistance. Shoulda known better. Now if you don't mind, ma'am, I've got business."

Frowning, Ma Randle turned quickly to face Kimball and the men with him. Then she turned back to Longarm, restraining him with a gloved hand on his arm. "You mean that man was on the train? The one in the middle? And you tangled with *him?*"

"I just told you, ma'am," Longarm said patiently. "Now would you please unhand me? I really do have work to do—and you have four young ladies to escort back to your place of business." The five men, he saw, were walking toward them.

She let go his arm, as if she had touched a hot stove. "Of course," she said, stepping back. "Please forgive me for detaining you."

Longarm smiled, touched the brim of his hat to the madam, then crossed the platform to the few remaining hacks waiting and climbed into one rather beat-up old carriage. He gave the name of the Wayfarer—the hotel the chief had mentioned—to the driver. As the man cracked his whip over the backs of his horses, Longarm leaned out the side window to look back.

He was in time to see the five Angels piling into another carriage. In a moment it had started up and was following Longarm's. Longarm leaned back in the seat and frowned thoughtfully. He was sorry he had been so short with that madam, but he had seen at once what was happening. As the crowd thinned out after the train's arrival, the five men were encouraged to make a move. Kimball, it seemed, was not a man to let a grudge simmer for too long. With a small army at his back, he liked to take immediate action.

Longarm took a silver dollar out of his pocket and handed it out to the driver. "Take this. There's a carriage following me. Go down the next side street you come to and keep a steady pace. I'll be getting out first chance I get. Don't slow down. Keep right on going, back to the station. Do you understand?"

The man shouted back that he did.

Longarm hung on as his carriage wheeled suddenly down a side street a few moments later. Looking out the window, he saw that the carriage was still following. Then Longarm's carriage turned onto another street. The pursuing hack was out of sight around the corner. Longarm opened the carriage door and jumped out. The canvas gladstone was so heavy he almost lost his balance, but he kept on his feet and darted into a tobacco shop, almost tipping over the massive wooden Indian standing in the doorway.

Looking out around the Indian, he saw the hack racing after his carriage, the horses straining mightily to keep up with five men to haul. As soon as the hack had left the side street, Longarm walked back to the main thoroughfare and hailed another hack.

As he climbed wearily into the carriage, he had an ominous feeling in the pit of his stomach. And his stomach, over the years, had never been wrong.

Chapter 2

As Longarm rode down Salt Lake City's Main Street, he was impressed, in spite of himself. The street was a broad one, as were all the streets, it seemed. They were all squared nicely and construction was going on at a brisk pace. Through the open window of his carriage he could see the arched Tabernacle roof, looming impressively above the other buildings. Beside it, he caught a glimpse of another building under construction. It was of a much more massive design and was obviously the beginning of a great cathedral or temple. About the building site he saw massive blocks of granite and atop the slowly rising structure he glimpsed the gaunt outlines of four giant cranes, their taut guy wires gleaming in the late afternoon sun.

Everywhere he looked Longarm noted a grim, purposeful activity with little or none of the careless buffoonery encountered in the usual, swiftly growing settlements of the West. Nevertheless, the clean lines of the buildings and residences with their invariable white picket fences and neat gates, the spacious avenues, the somber but well-tailored dress of the men and women, had a curiously unsettling effect on Longarm. He became slightly depressed and lost some of the enthusiasm he usually carried with him into a new assignment. It was almost as if he had stumbled East by mistake. The impressive orderliness of the city fell over him like a pall and he reminded himself that Mormons did not use alcohol, coffee, tea, or any other stimulants. No wonder so many of them were hung up on multiple wives. What else was there to do? As his carriage pulled up in front of the hotel, Longarm got out with a grim resolve. He would accomplish this business as swiftly and as adroitly as he possibly could, then retreat to wilder, more congenial lands.

He paid the driver, entered the Wayfarer, and approached the desk, a massive affair standing along the far wall of the impressive, thickly carpeted lobby. Potted plants were everywhere and the cuspidors gleamed like loot from some pharaoh's tomb. Nicely dressed men and women promenaded about the lobby casually. Under the pillars and along the walls, the richly upholstered chairs and couches held many portly gentlemen reading newspapers and illustrated weeklies. Longarm winced when he saw the liveried bellboys. His allowance for tipping was minuscule and these fancy young lads were used to exorbitant sums simply for giving an old boy the right time. Longarm decided he would carry his gladstone himself and find his way up the stairs to his room without any help.

"Yes, sir?" the desk clerk inquired, his large, disdainful eyes noting Longarm's rough attire. "What can I do for you?"

"A room."

"Single occupancy, sir?"

"If you see anyone else with me, don't believe it."

The fellow sniffed with his long, bony nose at Longarm's flippancy and handed him a pen with which to sign the register. Longarm signed it, the clerk read it, and at once lost his air of superiority.

"Ah, Mr. Long. I have a communication for you."

The clerk reached back to a letter file, flipped through the envelopes, and handed a letter to Longarm addressed simply, *Custis Long, U.S. Marshal.* Tearing it open, Longarm was reminded once more that his coming to this city was getting to be a very poorly kept secret. The short note read:

Mr. Long:

> *At seven this evening you will find in the lobby of your hotel a gentleman in a dark bowler hat, wearing a red carnation in his lapel. When he sees you, he will leave. Follow him. He will take you to us.*

Daniel

Longarm grinned slyly at the cloak-and-dagger effect of the note—and he sincerely hoped that the fellow sent to meet him would be wearing considerably more than a dark bowler hat and a red carnation. He slid the note back into the envelope and looked at the clerk.

"You have a room for me?"

The clerk dropped his key onto the desk. "Number thirty-four, sir. Third floor." His palm slapped down on the bell and two bellboys started for him hungrily.

Longarm lifted his bag and waved them off, ignoring the sudden disdain that leaped into their eyes. *Cheapskate* was what they were calling him, he knew, but in such a grand and fancy establishment, a full-course meal could run as much as a dollar, and he shuddered to think what his room was going to cost. Already he could see himself arguing with a clerk over every single item on his expense voucher when he got back to Denver. He shook his head at the indignity of it and exploded inside. He told himself with a quick, iron resolve that he would have himself a hot bath and the best meal the hotel could put before him, and to hell with those prissy little pencil pushers!

Fired with this burst of independence, Longarm turned at the foot of the broad, carpeted stairs and beckoned to one of the bellboys. Taking out a cheroot, he lit it and followed the uniformed minion up the grand stairway.

At seven that evening the lobby was filled to overflowing with gentlemen in dark bowler hats. Fortunately, only one had a red carnation in his lapel. Longarm followed the man out of the lobby and into a carriage that took Longarm to a broad avenue to the east of Main Street, and slowed up at last in front of a substantial residence set back behind a high stone wall, faced with stucco. Through the gate they rode, and when the carriage pulled up, Longarm's silent companion with the red carnation hopped out and helped Longarm down.

When he rang the bell and was ushered in ahead of Longarm, it soon became apparent that the man with the carnation was Wells Daniel's butler. A tall, well-tanned, and healthy-looking man in his fifties met him with his right hand outstretched.

"Mr. Long, is it?" the fellow asked, shaking Longarm's hand firmly.

Longarm nodded.

"I'm Wells Daniel. Come in here, Mr. Long. We're all anxiously waiting for you. We've heard much about your abilities and we are sure you're just the man for this unfortunate business."

As he talked, Daniel escorted Longarm into a large, high-ceilinged room with shelves of books lining the walls. High, many-paned windows faced out into the night. Much of the furniture was of leather and highly polished. The carpeting was so thick that neither man made a sound as they walked in. Sitting around a long mahogany table were three men. They rose as Longarm entered, and as Daniel introduced each man, he smiled courteously and shook Longarm's hand. Each handclasp was strong, and Longarm got the immediate impression that he was in the presence of men accustomed to giving orders in this highly organized, impressively efficient community of Saints.

Indicating a chair to his right, Wells Daniel said, "Sit down, Mr. Long. I trust your journey was an uneventful one."

"Call me Longarm, if you want," he told the man. Then he took out a cheroot and lit it. No one raised an eyebrow. "I did happen to meet one of your Avenging Angels on the train. Seems he wanted to collect a longstanding tithe."

The man introduced to Longarm as Burns Meeker leaned forward. He was a fat fellow with small eyes and a very red, beefy face. "Go on, Longarm. I think this might be important."

"He was eager to collect the tithe in the form of a young lady riding on the train."

"And you," Burns Meeker said, smiling slightly, "talked him out of it."

Longarm nodded.

"Do you know who this man might be?" another of the men asked. This was Job Welling, a tough-looking, broad-shouldered gent who looked like he belonged at the head of a gang of roustabouts, not in this gentleman's castle. "This might be one of the fellows we're after."

"His name was Jason Kimball."

Job's eyebrows arched up a notch, then he leaned back in his seat and looked at Burns Meeker. With a slight smile he addressed Wells Daniel. "Looks like your man might have found the scent already." He seemed pleased.

"I need more to go on," said Longarm. "I am hoping you fellows can give me some much-needed information. First of all, why haven't you sent your own law officers after the people who kidnapped this girl?"

"That's simple," said Wells Daniel. "Our sheriff, Amos Barker, is the brother of a man we feel is a member of this group of fanatics who have taken the girl. His name is Karl Barker."

Burns Meeker smiled at Longarm. "He's a good friend of Jason Kimball, I hear."

"What's the girl's name?" Longarm asked.

"Emilie Boggs," said the other man, the only one who had not yet spoken. "My daughter, and I want her back, Longarm. Untouched."

This was Quincy Boggs, a lean, angular fellow with mild blue eyes that seemed perpetually wide open since his brows were practically invisible, so light was his hair.

"I'll do what I can," said Longarm. "How long has she been gone now?"

"At ten tonight," Boggs said, "it will be three days."

The man's voice quavered, but did not break or crack. Boggs was evidently under great stress and Longarm could feel the iron control the man was exercising over his emotions. As a result, Longarm felt their intensity with even greater clarity. He would like very much to bring this man's daughter back to him. Untouched, as he said. But it was a long shot at best.

"The other reason we cannot rely on our own authorities, Longarm," continued Wells Daniel, "is that these fanatics are sincere. Lorenzo Wolverton, their leader, has had a revelation, it seems. He feels that Emilie Boggs was revealed to him in a vision, that she is destined to be his Celestial Bride—come hell or high water."

"What he means," interrupted Job Welling, "is that we dare not move on these men openly. All we need to do to make their cause respectable is to turn them into martyrs."

"What is their cause?" Longarm asked.

"Polygamy," snorted Boggs. "Celestial Wives. A return to the old ways of Joseph Smith—and Brigham Young."

"Brigham Young hasn't been dead that long," Longarm reminded them.

"No," snapped Boggs. "And more's the pity."

"That remark is uncalled for," snapped Burns Meeker, turning to Boggs, his tiny eyes narrowed. "But I can certainly understand your distress. Unfortunately, it is this kind of talk—this attitude of yours that you have made no effort to conceal over the years—that might well have brought on your present troubles."

"I am quite well aware of that," said Boggs. Boggs glanced across the table at Longarm. "The leader of these . . . fanatics is an ally of Mordecai Lee, one of Young's relatives and reportedly a leader of that rabble who perpetrated the Mountain Meadow Massacre. I have made no secret of my contempt for those men and their actions."

"There you go," said Meeker, thrusting his massive head toward Boggs, "admitting to a gentile that there was such a thing!"

"Easy, gents," Longarm said. "Let's just simmer down and eat this apple one bite at a time. I ain't interested in that massacre, or any hurt feelings in discussing what might have happened. All I want to know is where is this feller, Lorenzo Wolverton. Seems to me that's the long and the short of it. Once I know that, I can simply go there and get that girl back for Mr. Boggs, here." He glanced at the man. "Though I sure ain't going to guarantee she'll be untouched."

"Mr. Longarm," said Job Welling, his wide blue eyes regarding Longarm coldly, "these men might be fanatics in a sense, but they will not force Miss Boggs to their will."

"I see. They'll convince her. Is that it?"

"Precisely," said Welling, glancing over at Boggs, as if daring him to contradict him. The man had failed completely to catch the irony in Longarm's statement.

Boggs, however, just shook his head at the man's lack of understanding and looked over at Longarm. "We don't *know* where their settlement is, Mr. Long. We know only that they are in the area somewhere. One of their number you met earlier today on the train—Jason Kimball. We've called on you to find them and bring back my daughter, with a minimum of fuss and without creating any martyrs to their cause."

"In addition, Longarm," said Wells Daniel, smiling slightly, "we cannot—after this meeting—offer you any public support. Too many of our conservative colleagues would be infuriated to learn that we had gone to the federal government for aid in this matter."

"In other words, after this meeting you are cutting me loose. I'm on my own."

"Yes," said Meeker, his small eyes fixed almost malevolently on Longarm. "I for one will deny that I ever saw you."

Longarm nodded wearily. "By the way," he said, "who the hell are you, anyway? What's your position in this town?"

"A fair question," said Wells Daniel. "I am a member of the Council of Twelve Apostles; the rest of the gentlemen here are members of the First Council of Seventy."

Longarm smiled. "That don't mean a whole hell of a lot to me. What I meant was, have any of you jaspers got any political heft I could count on in a pinch?"

"Longarm," Wells Daniel said, a slight, amused smile on his face, "political power and the power of the Mormon church are well-nigh inseparable in Salt Lake City. But as we said before, you cannot look to us in the future. We cannot allow ourselves to become involved openly in dealing with Wolverton and the rest of his Avenging Angels."

"You have daughters of your own. Is that it?"

Job Welling spoke up. "Daughters and wives and sons, not to mention our own lives."

Longarm stood up and looked around the table at the four men. "You ain't told me a hell of a lot, that's for sure. Somewhere out there is a band of Avenging Angels with a young girl. You want her back with as little fuss as possible." He glanced at Boggs. "Untouched."

"I want her back," said Boggs, "and I'm not so all-fired particular how much fur flies or how many petty factions are disturbed
by it."

"We all know how you feel, Quincy," said Wells Daniel, "and
Mr. Long knows how we feel."

"Then let me out of here and I'll get to work," Longarm said.

"Of course," said Wells Daniel, as he got up from his chair.
With a gracious smile, he escorted Longarm from the room.

At the door, as they waited for his carriage to be brought
around, Wells Daniel said, "I more or less side with Boggs in this
matter. Get the girl. If heads must roll, so be it. But get the girl.
This outrage must not go unpunished, no matter how sincere the
perpetrators."

"But I'm not to count on any of you fine fellows if I get myself
caught between a rock and a hard place."

The carriage drew up in front of the steps.

"That's right, Longarm. That's the way it has to be."

Longarm nodded. "And if I do manage to bring the girl back,
what do I do with her?"

"Bring her here. I'll contact Boggs."

Longarm touched the brim of his hat and left Wells Daniel
standing in the open doorway. As the carriage drove off, Longarm did not look back.

"Ah, Mr. Long," caroled the desk clerk, "your sister arrived an
hour ago and I sent her up to your room. I hope you don't mind.
She was so . . . distraught when she discovered she had missed
your train this afternoon."

Longarm swallowed the surprise he felt at this announcement,
nodded to the clerk as he took his key from him, then hurried
across the lobby and up the stairs. As he started down the hallway
to his room, a piratical character, who smelled faintly of sheep
dip and whom he recognized at once as Jason Kimball, stepped
out of a doorway and thrust the barrel of a revolver into the small
of Longarm's back.

"Keep right on going to your room, Mr. Custis Long, Deputy
U.S. Marshal."

"No need to be formal," Longarm drawled. "You can call me
Longarm."

Jason responded by thrusting the barrel of his revolver still
deeper into Longarm's back. When Longarm got to his door, he
paused and reached into his jacket pocket for his key.

Mistaking the reason for this move, Jason Kimball swore savagely and brought the barrel of his sixgun down on the top of Longarm's head. As Longarm fell, barely conscious, to the floor of the narrow hallway, his key dropped out of his hand. Realizing his mistake, Kimball picked up the key, unlocked the door, and pushed it open. Sitting up groggily on the floor, Longarm at first did not know what to make of the sudden explosion that erupted from his room.

He saw Kimball stagger back and then fire twice into the room. Another shot from inside the room caught the man in the face, pieces of which went slamming into the wall behind him. The gunfire had thundered monstrously in the hallway, and as Longarm pulled himself to his feet, doors were being flung open on both sides of his room. He ignored the astonished faces that peered out at him and reached out to catch the falling Jason Kimball. The man turned dumbly to him, then collapsed forward onto his knees, his bloody face burying itself in Longarm's pants. Longarm stepped back, allowing the felow to collapse forward onto the carpet, ignored the two men hurrying down the hall toward him, and looked into his room.

The light that filtered in through the open doorway was little help, beyond revealing the dim form lying on his bed. Fumbling for a match, he entered and lit the lantern on his dresser. Turning to the bed, he saw the body of Rosalie Bond. A pearl-handled over-and-under Remington .41 was still clutched in her lifeless hand. Where her slim waist should have been, there was only a bloody tangle of dress and shattered flesh. A rapidly spreading stain was growing under her body.

A florid-faced man, his eyes wide with excitement, was standing in the doorway. "What have you done, you fiend!" he demanded.

Another one crowded into the doorway beside him, this one taller and seemingly just as belligerent. When he saw Rosalie Bond, he swore and looked at the other fellow. "You saw this?"

The red-faced fellow nodded enthusiastically. With an indignant stab of his forefinger, he indicated Longarm. "That man there! He caught these two together!"

The other's eyes lit up. "Aha!" He turned to someone in the hall behind him. "Get the hotel manager! Get the sheriff! We'll hold this fellow here! Hurry!"

As footsteps pounded down the hall toward the stairs, Longarm reached over and took the Remington from Rosalie's hand. He hadn't realized how dedicated she had been to the task of paying

back those who had worked so effectively to bring her brother to
justice. A consummate actress, she had convinced him that she
was only a frightened little girl on her way home to St. Louis
when he left her. *Such a foolish girl,* he thought. *Such a waste.
But thank you, Rosalie. You just might have saved my life.*

He got up from the bed and looked down at the girl for a moment, then examined the Remington. It was a definite improvement over the pepperbox. With a single shake of his head, he
dropped the weapon onto the coverlet and turned to face the two
men still trembling with indignation in the doorway.

"Get out of my way," he told them quietly, aware of a splitting
headache all of a sudden.

"Sir!" cried the florid one, "you must stay right there until the
sheriff comes. You will have to answer to him for this night's das-
tardly work!"

If Longarm had been in the proper frame of mind, he would
have smiled. The fellow sounded like a character in a Ned Buntline story. He reached under the bed for his gladstone, lifted it,
and pressed it gently, but firmly against the two men. When he
felt them begin to ease back, he heaved. They were sent flying out
of the doorway and went down on their backs in a tangle of arms
and legs.

He stepped over them, shouldered his way through the crush
of spectators, and hurried down the hallway. He used the main
stairway to the second floor, then took the back stairs to the street
level. He came out in an alley behind the hotel. Moving off in the
darkness, he headed west. This would take him to the other side
of the railroad tracks. The driver of the carriage that had brought
him back from Wells Daniel's place had told him that this was
where the Utah House and a few other such establishments were
allowed to flourish.

Ma Randle hurried to greet him. "Mr. Long!" she cried. "How
nice to see you again so soon." She caught sight of the large stain
on his pants—and then noted the gladstone in his hand. "Are
you—are you planning on moving in?"

Longarm looked quickly around. He was standing in the lobby
of a very elegant house. Gaslight cast a soft, pulsing glow that was
reflected in the many gold-framed mirrors that covered the walls.
The bar was farther in, and the dark green of gaming tables glowed
in the soft light. The click of rolling dice came to him clearly.

Liquor, gambling, and sex in the land of the Mormons. Who would have believed it? Longarm looked at Ma Randle.

"I'd like to talk to Annie," he told her.

"Annie?" She smiled in sympathy. "She's occupied, I'm afraid. The gentleman has requested her for the entire evening." She indicated the gaming tables. "She's in there now with her escort. Gambling excites him, it seems."

Longarm nodded. "I'll wait, then."

She frowned. "Will none of my other girls do?"

Longarm felt unduly conspicuous standing there. "Could we go someplace private?" he suggested to the madam. "Someplace where we could palaver without me looking like some country bumpkin inquiring about the price of a girl?"

She laughed, her dark eyes gleaming with pleasure at the way he put it. "Of course, Mr. Long. Step into my office."

She led him into a suite of rooms off the lobby. The first room he entered was obviously her office. The furniture was almost stark in its simplicity, leather for the most part, curtains without frills at the windows, and a large desk dominating one wall. As he entered, he glimpsed through an open doorway a bedroom containing what appeared to be a very large canopied bed, its coverlet fashioned of gleaming red silk. Garish but exciting.

Ma Randle turned in front of her desk and leaned back against it to face him. Longarm put down his gladstone, took off his Stetson, and sank wearily into a comfortable arm chair. "I'll be honest with you, Miss Randle," he said. "I'm riding the owlhoot trail. There's a good chance the sheriff is looking for me right now. But that's a long story. What I need from Annie is information concerning that jasper who tried to take her away with him on the train."

"Jason Kimball?"

"That's right. He seemed to know her and she appeared to know quite a bit about him."

"Why are you interested in him, Mr. Long?"

"Call me Longarm," he said, smiling. "It's not him I'm interested in now. It's his friends."

"But you want his whereabouts for a start?"

"Well, I'm afraid I already know where he is now."

"Oh?"

"He's on his way to the city morgue. Either that or he's still lying on the carpet outside my hotel room."

"You . . . shot him?"

As she asked this, she pushed herself away from the desk, her dark eyes widening in alarm.

"No, I didn't. But like I said, that's a long story. Right now I'd just like to talk to Annie for a few minutes. I need to know where Kimball and his friends would be hanging out."

"Why do you need to know this? They are very dangerous people. No one dares get mixed up with the Avenging Angels— and that's who you are talking about. And you have *killed* one of them?" Her voice was hushed with the enormity of what she was asking.

"I told you. I didn't kill him."

"Just because he was interested in taking Annie away! How gallant, but how foolish!"

Longarm looked at her for a moment, wondering if she was perhaps playing with him. When he realized she was serious, he was impressed. These Avenging Angels had everyone buffaloed, it seemed.

"If you want," she said, "I'll help you get out of Salt Lake City. But it will cost you."

He looked at her. She was wearing her hair up in a fashionable pile on her head and her slender body was sheathed in a dark maroon, low-cut satin gown. A single pearl glowed softly as it hung from its pendant just above the slight cleft of her small breasts. That was all the jewelry she wore, but her eyes, again, seemed more than a match for any jewelry fashioned by man.

"Thank you for offering to help me, Miss Randle. But I'm not leaving until I speak with Annie."

"What makes you think Annie is the only one who can tell you about these people?"

"You know someone else who can?"

"How do you think it is possible for me to operate this . . . establishment in Salt Lake City, Longarm?"

He shrugged. "I imagine the usual methods, Miss Randle. A payoff here, a favor there."

She smiled coldly. "You may call me Felicia. I hate 'Ma Randle' almost as much as *Miss* Randle." Her smile faded away entirely. "At sixteen I was invited by my sister to join in a Celestial Marriage with her husband. She was working very hard, you see, and not only that, she was lonely. The Sealing Ceremony was very impressive. And then . . ." She shrugged and looked away.

"As soon as I could, I fled that man—and all his chattering, imbecile wives. Of course I was excommunicated and warned never to go to the gentiles with my story. And the Avenging Angels left me one alternative—this place. They were the ones who gave me the money to open the Utah House."

"You're in their pay, then."

"I hate them. Also, Longarm, I fear them. No one can escape their fury. They ride with God on their right hand and the devil on their left. They are black-hearted fiends who show no mercy and kill with impunity." She shuddered. "What poor little Annie could tell you about them would barely fill a thimble, I'm afraid."

"But you are working for them."

"I am one of their soundest investments. It is as simple as that. But I hate them, Longarm. If I could, I would stop them. But nothing can stop them. Nothing."

"You said you thought you could help me."

"If I knew what you were after, I might be able to help you."

"Why would you want to?"

She smiled. "I hate them—and I like you. The men who come here—the men who must pay for the company of a woman—are not appealing to me. Men of your caliber, it seems, do not often frequent the Utah House. It is one of the unfortunate aspects of my profession that few would imagine. I daresay you are surprised."

Longarm shrugged. "It makes a kind of sense, at that."

"Then, if you'll help me, I'll help you."

"You know where the Avenging Angels might have their settlement?"

"There are many such settlements throughout the territory, Longarm," she replied, "but I assume it is the one headed by Lorenzo Wolverton, the one to which Jason Kimball belonged, that you are interested in."

He was impressed with what she must know as soon as she mentioned Wolverton. He nodded. "That's right."

"Of course I can only make a shrewd guess as to where it is. But it seems to me a most likely location. And it is near here."

"Where?"

She smiled, took his hand, and led him gently toward her bedroom. "You must earn what help I can give you," she told him, her eyes lighting mischievously. "And I warn you, if you are not all that my fevered imagination tells me you are, I will most probably not be able to remember a thing about Lorenzo Wolverton and his loyal followers." She smiled disarmingly at him. "Not a single blessed thing."

She paused in the doorway to her bedroom and let him go in ahead of her.

"Make yourself comfortable," she told him. "There's a pitcher of water on the commode next to the bowl and a bottle of whiskey on the dresser. I'll be right back. I must leave someone in charge, you see."

She turned and disappeared quickly through the door of her office.

It was a shame, but he did not trust her. Which meant he would simply have to play this one by ear—or some other portion of his anatomy. Longarm knew that the usual practice in sporting houses was to keep your boots on. He felt, however, that something other than the usual was called for under these circumstances. He tugged off his boots, stepped out of his pants, and pulled off his longjohns and vest and jacket. He hung his gunbelt on the bedpost at the foot of the bed where Felicia would be sure to see it.

Placing a chair at the head of the bed, he carefully folded his vest over the back of it, allowing the watch chain to hang in full view. If Felicia had a question about it, he was certain he would be able to come up with something light and humorous. Then he pulled his Colt from his rig and proceeded to empty its chambers into the side pocket of his coat.

Certain he had taken care of any surprises from that quarter, Longarm padded over to the washbowl on the commode, poured water into it, and added a healthy measure of whiskey. He cleaned himself thoroughly—a whorehouse ritual he considered perfectly civilized. Then with only his shirt on to cover his lean nakedness, he sat on the edge of the bed to wait, a bemused smile on his face.

He wished the chief could see what he was willing to go through for the government.

Felicia returned, flushed and eager. She moved swiftly through her office, turning down lamps as she went. Closing the bedroom door, she turned down the single lantern on her dresser and faced him, an appreciative smile on her face as Longarm stood up. She undid her hair and let it cascade down over her shoulders. Then she reached back and unclasped her gown. It shimmered in the soft glow of the lamp and fell to her feet. In a twinkling, her petticoat followed. Then she turned her back to Longarm. He stepped close, aware of the intoxicating perfume of her long, dark tresses, and with fumbling fingers managed to help her unlace her French corset. By the time he had finished with it, he was aware that she had already stepped gracefully out of her lace-trimmed drawers and added them to the growing pile at her feet. At last came her chemise, and she stood naked before him. Only her stockings remained, but she left these on, and Longarm was not about to bring the matter up.

"I warn you," she said softly, stepping toward him, "you had better be good."

She reached out and unbuttoned his shirt. As she pulled it off to reveal his complete nakedness, she started to say something.

Longarm placed a finger over her mouth. "Talk with your body, Felicia," he said.

She smiled, touched his face lightly, then traced a soft line down his cheeks, down his heavily corded, deeply tanned neck to the tightly coiled hair of his chest. She kissed his shoulder and he felt the moist heat of her tongue sliding along the slope of his shoulders to the strong cords of his neck. And then she began nibbling delightfully on his ear lobes. All the while her fingers had been working their magic on his back and thighs. Now they began to caress him, gently at first, then more vigorously. She pulled her lips from his ears then and kissed him hard, her tongue darting, her rich dark hair spilling over his shoulders.

A flame of hot desire lanced upward from his groin and he felt his pulse quickening. He pulled away from her teasing tongue and laughed aloud. Reaching down, he took her by her slim waist, lifted her off the floor, and heaved her gently backward onto the bed. She uttered a tiny cry of surprise at the ease with which he had lifted her. And then he dropped beside her on the bed, his powerful fingers thrusting between her thighs, finding her moistness.

It was her turn to laugh now, a deep, husky sound that sent shivers down his back. She moved to him hungrily, eagerly. He shifted and was on her. Her hand reached down and guided him home. He began thrusting while she started rotating her hips with a frantic, delicious abandon. Yet as he drove into her, her violent writhing almost dislodged him.

He grabbed her hips firmly, slowing slightly the wild movements of the woman under him until at last she flung her head back and raked her nails down his back. In that instant they came as one, Longarm still driving, feeling himself explode within her,

her entire body shuddering, wrenching in ecstatic reaction. Once more, and then again, she climaxed until at last she went limp beneath him.

But she kept her arms about him. "You kept it in!" she cried, her eyes filled with the sweet pleasure of it. "How ever did you manage?"

"You do go on some at that, Felicia. I've heard of some women a mite too quiet under a man. I reckon you've got the opposite problem."

"Again!" she breathed. "Please, again!"

He tried to protest. This, after all, had been a very long day. But her foreplay was inspired and soon he found himself more than ready.

"Let me get on top," she requested eagerly. "It will be easier for you!"

Without waiting for his response, she climbed on top of him and soon Longarm found himself hard put to keep up with her; but she kept driving, down upon him until at last she uttered a long, low moan and began to shudder. He climaxed then as well, and suddenly she leaned forward, her mouth found his shoulder, and her teeth dug into his flesh. He felt for a moment as if he'd been flung into a gunnysack with a wildcat, but at last—after a final orgasm—she collapsed, exhausted, onto him.

She laughed huskily, her face resting on his hard chest, her hair spilling over his face and neck. "How was that?" she whispered, her voice low, warm.

"That was fine, Felicia."

She lifted her head abruptly from his chest. He saw sudden concern in her eyes. "Longarm, there's something I must tell you—"

Before she could say anything further, Longarm saw the dark shape looming over them and the gleam of a sixgun.

"Get off him, Felicia!" The voice was harsh, masculine.

Longarm grabbed both of Felicia's arms above the elbows and flung her upward toward the shadowy figure. Her tumbling body caught the man in the chest, and as the fellow stumbled backward, Longarm reached for his vest. His fingers caught at the gold chain. He pulled the derringer from the pocket, then rolled back across the bed.

By this time the intruder was back on his feet, a tall man with his hat still on, a badge pinned to his vest gleaming in the lamp's glow. Felicia had sent for the sheriff, it seemed.

"Get out, Longarm!" she called to him. "Save yourself!"

This was Amos Barker, the man he had been told was a brother to one of the Avenging Angels he was after. Barker turned as Felicia called out, gun in hand, tracking Longarm's rolling, twisting progress across the silken coverlet of the huge bed. He fired quickly and the round buried itself in a pillow. The air was suddenly alive with tiny feathers. As Barker brought his revolver around for a second shot, Longarm dropped to his knees on the floor, steadied his right hand, aimed, and fired. The slug planted a neat black hole in the center of the sheriff's forehead.

The man looked startled as he backed slowly toward the dresser, his gun hand swinging down. He began to slide down the front of the dresser, twitching convulsively. Once, twice, three times the gun in his hand discharged, filling the bedroom with its thick, acrid smoke.

Barker's first shot caused a low cry from Felicia. The second shot silenced her. By the time the third round had been pumped into the woman's body, Longarm was at her side. He pulled her to one side as the sheriff slipped sideways and crashed heavily to the floor. Longarm cradled Felicia's head in his arms. In the dim, smoky light, he saw her dark eyes flicker open.

"I'm hit, Longarm. Am I going to die?"

A quick examination of her wounds did not encourage Longarm. He said, "You'll be all right. But you promised to help me. Remember?"

She smiled dreamily. "It was so nice, Longarm. I never should have sent for Barker. I tried . . . to warn you."

He nodded. "Never mind that, Felicia. You had to keep on the right side of them, so you sent for Barker. I understand that. It's all right. But now tell me. Where is that settlement?"

Someone began pounding on the door to Felicia's office and Longarm heard voices shouting through the door.

"You're not angry with me, Longarm?" Felicia asked with genuine concern.

"Of course not," Longarm reassured her. "Just tell me. Please, Felicia."

"They're living in the badlands . . . west of the Salt Lake Desert. Follow the tracks after you leave the last water tower." She closed her eyes and leaned back. "Hills, badlands," she murmured. "Beautiful valley. In the middle of the badlands . . . Little Zion . . ."

A boot began kicking, against the door. Longarm started to get up, but Felicia's hand reached up and grabbed his arm.

"Stay!" she cried. "I'm cold . . . so cold!"

Taking a deep breath, he went down on one knee beside her again and continued to cradle her head. Suddenly her grip on him relaxed and her arm dropped lifelessly to the floor. He lowered her head gently to the carpet.

He got quickly to his feet and yelled into the office, "Hold your horses! I'm coming!"

The pounding on the door ceased abruptly.

"This is Sheriff Barker!" Longarm yelled. "You damage that door and I'll have you pay for it! Get back away from there!"

An immediate argument started up on the other side of the door, but it seemed to him that the voices quieted as the crowd moved back from the door.

Longarm dressed quickly as the tumult on the other side of the door slowly built to its former intensity. At last, snatching up his gladstone, he strode quickly through the office to the door and flung it open. At sight of him, they recoiled. He moved swiftly into their midst, using his gladstone as a buffer.

"Damn it!" he cried. "Can't a man get any peace and quiet anywhere in this town? You woke up Ma!"

This astonished most of them, confused the rest. They stood back and watched his tall form stride angrily to the door before one of the girls broke from the crowd and darted into the office. Pulling open the door and stepping out into the night, Longarm hurried down the steps of the Utah House, disappearing into the darkness, heading for the railroad tracks.

He was leaving a trail of dead bodies in his wake, and he could not count on help from the men who were behind his mission to this place—except for one of them. Quincy Boggs. It was his daughter Longarm was after, and there was no doubt in his mind that Boggs would give him all the assistance he needed, especially now that Longarm had a line on where the settlement was.

The tracks, gleaming in the moonlight, appeared just ahead of him. Hurrying across them in the darkness, he glanced to the west, his eyes following the gleaming rails of the Central Pacific. Somewhere out there in the darkness lay the vast salt wasteland known as the Great Salt Lake Desert—and just beyond that, in a desolate place of rocky hills and cliffs Felicia had called the badlands, a bunch of Mormon fanatics had built themselves a community.

He shook his head as he headed for the hack stand on the other side of the train station. Those Avenging Angels were sure as hell going to make it tough for a lone deputy U.S. marshal to take back one of their women. And this night's frustrations were liable to make them plumb out of sorts. They were probably getting their welcome mat all brushed and ready for him right now.

Chapter 3

"My God, Mr. Long!" Quincy Boggs exclaimed. He pulled Longarm quickly inside and closed the door.

Turning to the buxom housekeeper who had refused to let Longarm cross the threshold at that time of night, he comforted her with a generous pat on the shoulder. "That's all right, Molly. I know this gentleman."

Molly had crossed her fleshy arms over her wide bosom in obvious disapproval. Now her gimlet eyes noted the front of Longarm's jacket and pants, as if to say that until such a mess was explained to her satisfaction she would remain opposed to Longarm's presence in the house. Longarm saw the glance and smiled at the woman.

"May as well come out and say it, ma'am. I had a terrible accident. I was hoping some kind lady like yourself could maybe clean my jacket and pants."

The woman unfolded her arms and looked with sudden uncertainty at Boggs. He smiled at her.

"Yes, Molly," he said, "perhaps tomorrow you could see to that for Mr. Long. I am sure he would appreciate it."

"I sure would, ma'am," said Longarm.

"Is this man staying, Mr. Boggs?"

Boggs glanced at Longarm. Longarm nodded.

"Yes he is, Molly. Make ready the third floor guest room, the one facing front."

She pulled herself up to her full five-feet-five, took one last look at the disreputable outcast she had met at the door, then lumbered off, shaking the floor slightly with each footfall.

Boggs looked at Longarm, his lean face creased in a smile. "She's very protective," he explained. "We have three daughters, and with my wife gone she has become as wary as a mother grizzly—for all of us."

Longarm took off his hat and lifted his gladstone. "Where can I stow this for now? I'm getting tired of lugging it around."

"Leave it right there and come with me into the library. You have no idea how glad I am to see you! In heaven's name, man, what have you been up to since last we met?"

Longarm glanced at him. "You mean that business at the hotel?"

"Precisely!" Boggs pushed open the double door leading to the library and stepped aside to let Longarm move past him. "A woman and one of the Avenging Angels were found dead in your hotel room—and you were reported to have fled the scene."

"That about covers it, for now," Longarm agreed, starting for one of the upholstered chairs. "I'll fill you in about the rest of it later."

"The *rest* of it?"

"Daddy! Who's this?"

Both men turned to face the open doorway. Two young ladies were standing in it; each one was dressed in a long, white, frilly nightgown, their luxurious, straw-colored hair combed out so that it fell beyond their shoulders, all the way to their narrow waists. They were at least eighteen; one of them was closer to twenty. It was this one who was the more forward of the two, her eyes staring boldly and appreciatively at Longarm as she pressed into the library with her sister at her heels.

Boggs laughed. "I might have known. Nothing goes on in this house without these two on hand to approve—or disapprove!" The man was obviously delighted with his daughters. Longarm got the impression that this had once been a happy house, filled with the laughter of young girls. It was no wonder Boggs was so upset at losing one of them in such a cruel fashion, and so outspoken in his condemnation of the Avenging Angels.

Boggs looked back at Longarm with a smile. "Mr. Long, may I present Marilyn and Audrey, Emilie's sisters. The shy one in back is Audrey. This outspoken nymph is Marilyn." Boggs turned to his daughters. "Girls, this is Deputy U.S. Marshal Custis Long. He has come to bring your sister back to us."

Marilyn—who had wide blue eyes and a sprinkling of freckles on her milk-white cheeks—reached out at once and took Longarm's hand boldly. "Oh, Mr. Long. Please do bring Emilie back to us!"

"Yes!" cried the other, rushing up and taking Longarm's other hand in hers. He felt her warm eagerness as she pressed his hand in her excitement. "Please, do! We have all been perfectly wretched at the thought of Emilie in the hands of those terrible people!"

"Emilie is a match for any man!" Marilyn explained proudly, with an angry toss of her head. "But that's just it. She won't submit easily."

"Let's hope she won't have to," said their father, taking both of their hands and leading them from the room. "Now you must leave us alone. Mr. Long and I have much to discuss. You'll be able to see him again at breakfast. Now scoot upstairs to your bedroom!"

"Oh, is he staying?" Audrey cried, delighted.

"Just for the night. Now, scoot along, or I'll sic Molly on you."

Laughing, the two girls bolted through the doorway and Longarm could hear them talking excitedly and giggling irrepressibly all the way up the stairs.

Boggs closed the library door and turned to Longarm, an indulgent smile on his face. "You see why we want Emilie back, Mr. Long? You see how close we all are—how much we . . . love each other."

"You can call me Longarm," Longarm said, dropping back into the upholstered chair. "And yes, I reckon I do understand. You've got quite a handsome flock there."

"There's much of their mother in all of them," Boggs said musingly, as he sat down across from Longarm. "It is as if in losing Helen, my wife, I had been given a little bit of her in each one."

Longarm recognized real emotion when he rode onto it and he had learned a long time ago not to try to tie those kinds of feelings down with words, but this man Boggs seemed to handle the problem without any difficulty—and he left Longarm with a deep sense of what he was feeling. Longarm hadn't been very certain until now—but he guessed he could trust this man for sure. Hell, he didn't really have much choice in the matter.

"Now," said Boggs, "what in tarnation happened at that hotel, anyway?"

Longarm told him as briefly as possible—that a woman out to get him had been waiting in his room for him. When Jason Kimball appeared in the doorway, the fireworks began.

"I knew I couldn't explain it—and from what you gents told me about the local sheriff, I realized I would have quite a time untangling myself. So I took off."

"And?"

Longarm's account of what happened at the Utah House left Boggs shaking his head in disbelief.

"How do you account for the sheriff showing up like that?"

"He's in with the Avenging Angels and the Randle woman sent for him as soon as I entered her place. She knew, I guess, that they were after me and wanted to chalk up some points for her side, looks like."

"How did she know?"

"Jason and his boys saw me talking to her after I got off the train. When they lost me, they went to her. They must have filled her ear some, 'cause just as soon as she could leave me, she sent for Barker."

"Barker dead?" Boggs shook his head in wonder. "For this business, that's no loss, I am afraid, but he was a fine and diligent peace officer."

"You mind my asking something?" Longarm said.

"Go right ahead."

"I can see why you couldn't call on Barker, but what about the Utah Territorial Police?"

Boggs shook his head. "Shot through with Avenging Angels or their sympathizers. Many of them are still wanted for the Mountain Meadow Massacre."

Longarm nodded.

"You must not misunderstand me, Longarm. I am a devout Mormon. Our Prophet, Joseph Smith, was a divinely inspired man. His vision of a modern Zion here in the West has been realized. A new social order is abuilding—and we are in the midst of that great business this very moment! It is God's work we are doing and I, for one, am proud to be a part of this momentous task."

Longarm had heard preachers before, most of them spouting fire and brimstone and tearing at their hair all the while, but Boggs did not strike him as that type. He spoke with feeling and enthusiasm, but kept the fire in his eyes banked. Longarm nodded to the man, not so much to encourage him as to let him know he was still in the same room with him.

Boggs smiled. "Sometimes I let my enthusiasm carry me away, I'm afraid. But what I want you to understand, Longarm, is that I hold to the basic tenets of our faith with great firmness and conviction. It is only the foolish notion that a man should have as many wives as he pleases that I find impossible to accept."

"Imagine it could run into quite an expense at that," the deputy observed.

Boggs smiled. "Of course. In more ways than one. Did you know that there are many Mormons, building even now in the West, who do not hold to this nefarious doctrine? Did you know that the Prophet's wife herself, Emma, flew into a rage when her husband showed her the paper enunciating this doctrine? She flung the paper into the fire, as a matter of fact."

"Didn't do her much good, huh?"

Boggs smiled. "No, it didn't." Boggs looked at Longarm with a pleased light in his eye. "It does me good to talk to a gentile like you, Longarm. Gives me needed perspective."

"That so? Glad to hear it."

"At any rate, we must get rid of this doctrine if we are to join the federal government as an equal state. We have lost out already because of this foolish practice. Until we wipe it out entirely, I see no hope of our being accepted into the Union." He shook his head sadly and leaned back in his chair.

Boggs appeared to have run out of steam, but Longarm was not sure and waited in case there was still some in the boiler. He didn't mind sitting in the chair and waiting. He could use a little rest. He had been run ragged this day, and was beginning to feel a mite weary. The room was quiet and comfortable and the many books in the shelves that lined the walls looked as if they had been read. Some books were out on tables and a few were put back onto the shelves upside down. It appeared to him that this room was used quite often—and he could almost imagine the three daughters curled up on chairs and sofas, poring over the books, deep in study one moment, laughingly reading aloud to each other the next.

"Well, Longarm, what are your plans now?"

Longarm looked back to Boggs. "I will need help tomorrow in getting a horse. I intend to ride out to Fort Douglas. I reckon I won't have any trouble requisitioning a couple of army mules. I can load them onto a Central Pacific freight car, then ride as far as that last water stop. From there, I'll be looking for signs, but I'll get Emilie with as little fuss as possible and bring her back on one of the mules. How's that?"

"You make it sound very simple."

"It won't be, and that's a fact. But that's the general plan. You keep repeating that to yourself and you won't get riled up and fidgety waiting for word. 'Course, I know it won't be easy."

"It's dangerous, isn't it?"

"I could get my head blown off. They tried twice already. Leastways, that's what I figure that Kimball fellow had in mind when he escorted me to my room."

"Poor Emilie," the man said, shaking his head. "This whole thing—it's madness."

"You think that fellow Meeker was driving the right spike when he said he blamed your loose talk for what happened to your daughter?"

"I am afraid he was. This is their challenge to all of us who dare to suggest that we call them to account for their barbarities, that we rid ourselves of the doctrine of polygamy. Don't you see? If Emilie submits, if she becomes one of them . . ."

Boggs shook his head in sudden anguish.

Longarm got to his feet. "I reckon I could use some shut-eye along about now, and you appear a bit worn through yourself. If you'll see to a carriage tomorrow that could take me to a livery, I'll be on my way to Fort Douglas first thing in the morning."

"I'll see to that myself. My carriage will take you to a livery on the outskirts of the city." The man got up. "I expect there will be considerable annoyance and perhaps even a little panic at the events of this night, Longarm. You've certainly managed to stir things up." He shook his head. "But maybe that's just what this city needs."

"I wasn't trying to shake up the city," Longarm said, starting for the door. "Just trying to keep my scalp on straight."

Not in a long, long time had a bed felt as good as this one did to Longarm. The city was quiet, the moonlight just beginning to flood in through the large window, the sheets starched and clean. He stretched luxuriously and turned his face away from the moonlit window panes.

He heard a soft giggle, which was immediately stifled.

"Hush!" whispered a voice that Longarm immediately recognized as Marilyn's.

And then two kittenish bodies landed on the bed. Before Longarm could figure out what was happening, the bedclothes were ripped unceremoniously back. In the moonlight, his long flanks and the dark thatch of his pubic hair became startlingly visible.

"Ohhh, look!"

Marilyn and Audrey, both as naked as plucked chickens but considerably more enticing, crowded against him. He turned to face Marilyn, but Audrey was happy to take second best and snuggle up to Longarm's backside, both arms around his chest as she hugged him with all her might.

"He's so big!" Marilyn exclaimed. "Oh, glory! There's so much of him!"

"Keep it quiet!" managed Longarm in a hushed whisper. He didn't know whether to groan in despair or whoop in excitement. He had had busy days before, but this one was getting plain ridiculous. *No fear,* he thought foolishly. *There ain't no way that little fellow is going to get up for* this one.

"Poor little thing," Marilyn murmured, as her fingers traced a hot path up his inner thighs.

Longarm tried to pull back, but the sister on his back just squeezed tighter and sank her teeth into the back of his neck. It was amazing, but this seemed to do the trick. He felt himself growing and moved his loins slightly in what should have been an attempt to pull away—but wasn't.

Now, look here, old son, he warned himself, *how would you explain this if Boggs came in right now—or that old squaw, Molly!*

And then it was too late for such worries as Marilyn's mouth found his. She kissed him with delirious abandon and pulled him over onto her. He felt her legs open for him, her fingers guiding him in. In a moment, with Audrey on his back riding him like a bronc, he was probing deep with measured thrusts, thinking, *The hell with it, tomorrow is going to be a long day, the beginning of a long, hot search . . .*

The blazing sun reflected off the hard-packed earth of the parade ground, and Longarm was forced to squint through the glare as he rode up to the headquarters building that served Fort Douglas. It had been a short ride from Salt Lake City, but already Longarm was beginning to feel the oppressive weight of the sun. The headquarters was a long, low barracks that looked to be wilting visibly from the heat. Longarm glanced at the flag on the pole. It hung lifelessly, giving him the distinct impression that if he looked a mite closer, he'd see the flag was singed around the edges.

Dismounting, he dropped his reins over the hitch rail and feeling slightly guilty about leaving the horse standing in that sun, he walked into the building and presented his papers to the sergeant. A moment later he was ushered into the C.O.'s office and introduced to a Captain Meriwether. He was a lean, dusty individual with a clean-shaven face, alert green eyes, and neatly combed hair the color of bleached mustard. He stood up to shake Longarm's hand, then indicated the chair by his desk with a quick, decisive motion of his hand.

"What can I do for you, Marshal Long?"

"Call me Longarm, Captain."

The man smiled. The smile was properly distant. His head inclined slightly in acknowledgment of Longarm's request. "All right—Longarm. But what is it I can do for you?"

"I need two mules."

"Mules?" The captain's eyes narrowed in merriment at the request. "You going prospecting for the government?"

"Not exactly."

"We have fine, blooded stock in our remuda, Longarm. Finest horseflesh I've seen since coming out here."

"Where you from, Captain?"

The man leaned back in his chair, his hands resting lightly on the armrests. He was obviously pleased to contemplate his origins. "Connecticut, Longarm. Lovely, rolling, fertile land."

"Do much riding as a young 'un?"

"Grew up in the saddle, Longarm." He smiled proudly. "It didn't hurt my progress at the Point one bit. That's why I say I know horses. I do. And you're welcome to our best."

"How long have you been out here, Captain?"

He frowned. "A few weeks. A dry, arid, desolate country by my reckoning. And dealing with these Mormons is going to be quite a challenge." He spoke of the Mormons with more than a touch of disdain.

"Not all Mormons are alike," Longarm said softly.

"Perhaps, Marshal," Meriwether said abruptly, "but to the business at hand. We have fine horses if you care to requisition them. Do you still want mules?"

Longarm wasn't anxious to educate this young shavetail from the Point, but what the hell. The man was courteous enough, and meant well, as far as Longarm could see. Maybe it wouldn't do any great harm to try. Longarm cleared his throat carefully.

"Yes, Captain, I do. Like you just said, this here is arid country and right now that sun out there is coming down mighty hard— like a hot fist. And your fine, blooded stock would have one devil of a time standing up to those conditions for any length of time, especially where I'm heading. I reckon it's right the mule was the only animal Noah didn't take into the ark, and like they say, it ain't got any pride of ancestry nor hope of progeny; but a mule is reaching his full get-up-and-go about when a horse is starting to run downhill. Mules can be ornery just like some people we all know, but they can do as much work as a horse on one-third less food, they're subject to fewer diseases, and their tough hide and short hair make them a damn sight more able to shake off saddle sores."

Meriwether smiled. "That's quite a recommendation, Longarm. A very long speech, indeed."

"Sometimes I do run on, and that's a fact," Longarm replied.

Meriwether laughed easily. "No harm done, Longarm. Of course you realize how expensive an army mule is. One hundred and fifty a mule, as a matter of fact."

Longarm winced. "That should tell you something, Captain."

"I must admit I was surprised at how prized this obstinate beast is in this country."

"It's the country that makes the conditions, Captain. It's too big to fight. You got to figure out how to go along, mostly, or it'll just swat you like a fly. The mule helps you to go along."

Meriwether smiled. "I dare say General Crook would agree with you."

"How's that, Captain?"

"The general rides to battle on a mule, Longarm. And I understand he prefers them to horses for packing—can get as much as three hundred and twenty pounds on a single mule." The captain rose to his feet. "Excuse me, Longarm. I'll send an orderly to see to your mules. Meanwhile, I would be honored if you would join me in a small libation. I like a man who talks plain. It's a relief, as a matter of fact."

Longarm thanked the man and leaned back in his chair as the captain left the room. He would have preferred to pick out the mules himself, but he didn't see how he could refuse the captain's hospitality.

And that long speech, along with the ride, *had* left him a mite dry.

Longarm ducked his head slightly as the engine's smokestack showered him with soot. Looking up a moment later, he watched the Central Pacific train move off due west. He had had a little difficulty detraining the somewhat skittish mules from the freight car, but they were standing quietly behind him now, ears flicking, and like himself, it seemed they were somewhat oppressed by the blistering heat.

It was late in the afternoon and Longarm had no intention of leaving the meager shade provided by the water tower. He had plenty of time. He would move out at night. He looked around at the gleaming white tablecloth that stretched as flat as a rule in all directions. He had availed himself of Captain Meriwether's maps of the Great Salt Lake Desert, as it was called, and what the maps revealed to him had sobered him somewhat.

A desolate expanse of close to four thousand square miles, it was about a hundred miles wide at its narrowest. The north and south edges of the desert were simply too far away to think about. Behind Longarm to the east were the irrigated farms of the Mormons and beyond them, still farther east, the Wasatch Range. Ahead of him, due west, was the Goshute and Toana fault-block complex, a low mass of hills and mountains that loomed ahead of him in the shimmering haze. They looked close enough to reach after a quick gallop, but Longarm knew they were at least thirty miles away. Somewhere among those spurs of rock that thrust out into the desert he would find the settlement. It would need water and that meant a well. The well's windmill would be the finger beckoning him to the settlement. That was the way his hopes were going, anyway.

Longarm let his back slide down the wooden support of the water tower until he was sitting on the ground. He pulled his hat down farther to cut some of the glare and settled down to wait for the blessed, cooling darkness.

Longarm had ridden parallel to the tracks for close to twenty miles before he tacked northwest toward a great misshapen shoulder of rock that loomed out of the starlit night. A spur of the fault toward which he was heading, it extended far enough out onto the flats to be the hills Felicia had mentioned.

As the tracks disappeared in the darkness behind him, he noticed the sudden glow in the sky over his right shoulder and glanced back. The edge of something vast and very red loomed above the horizon. Turning back around he saw a long, golden band suddenly appear along the top of the fault. As he watched, the band grew. The flaming globe of the sun was poking its eye out of the east, pouring a rosy brightness over the desert.

At once a cool wind sprang up. Crows, wheeling out of the west, tumbled toward him, cawing frantically. Abruptly they coiled up into the clear air and vanished back the way they had come. Dust devils—only it wasn't dust, it was salt—began dancing toward Longarm from the east. He pulled his bandanna up over his mouth and nostrils and put on the goggles he had purchased for this purpose.

Before the full blast of the sun struck him, Longarm reached the shore of the ancient lake bed and let his mule pick its way across the shale and then into a narrow canyon. The going was rough; the ground was a shattered, broken mess of shale and detritus, but he kept the mule going, the animal behind tugging unhappily on its lead. Slowly they rose into the barren hills, Longarm's optimism fading fast until he found the first faint traces of a wagon's track. Keeping after it, he saw it become a dimly etched roadway that vanished entirely for long stretches.

The immense sun was soon overhead, the wind-whipped sand finding its way into his eyes and nostrils despite his precautions. His tongue reached out to moisten his cracked lips and came away with the tang of salt on it. The sun hung overhead now, the bright white light glancing off the canyon walls and the humped rocks with a withering intensity.

At noon he pulled himself wearily out of his saddle in the shade of a narrow canyon. He had not slept since yesterday. He had ridden through the night and this forenoon. Though he hated to give in to his fatigue, he realized he would have to sleep here in this canyon at least until nightfall, and then keep going somehow through the night. Crows overhead and the snorting anxiety of his two mules as they neared the canyon had alerted him to the presence of water, and as soon as he had unsaddled the mules, they made for the tiny stream, as Longarm followed patiently. He pushed aside the undergrowth, mindful of rattlers, and slaked his thirst, using his hands held together as a cup. The water was ice-cold, almost like a tonic. Sitting down, his back leaning against a portion of the canyon wall, he rubbed his wet hands over his face, washing off some of the grit. His eyes smarted. He took off the goggles and washed them in the cold water.

He turned then to selecting a spot for his dry camp. He was at the moment crouched in a tiny jungle of hard-nosed growth: pepperwood, a scrubby little wavy-leafed oak, Apache plume, blackbrush, and, most spectacular, the coral-colored globemallow, its bright presence mottling the canyon floor, with only patches of wild buckwheat to break its dominance. He glanced up at the walls of the canyon looming above him and realized he would not have to endure the direct rays of the sun for the remainder of the day if he stayed right where he was. He decided that his present spot was as good a place as any to camp.

He got up and hobbled the mules, satisfied they would not go far from the stream. They began foraging almost at once. He returned to the stream then and poked through the underbrush with the barrel of his rifle, looking for snakes. He found a nest of gopher snakes, scattered them, and continued his search. His fatigue told him he was silly to continue looking for rattlers, but he persisted doggedly for some time before giving up and starting to go back for his gear.

He froze in his tracks.

Only a couple of inches to the rear of his heels, a small rattler was coiled. There was no mistaking the wedgelike head, the tip of the segmented tail peeping out of the coils. It was, Longarm knew, not a diamondback, but a smaller species Longarm had heard called the horny rattler—a reference to the small, hornlike knobs above each eye. Longarm watched the snake tensely. It was a small, dusty-looking serpent and dangerous enough. Its bite might not kill, but would sure as hell put a damper on Longarm's enthusiasm for this mission.

The heat of midday, Longarm realized, had made the snake sluggish, but not comatose. With one quick stride Longarm left the snake behind, then turned and poked at its head with the tip of his rifle barrel. He could not risk a shot. At this time of day and among these rocks, the report would carry for miles, alerting any settlement in the area. As the muzzle of the rifle neared the serpent, the snake lifted its head from its coils, eyes brightening, narrow black tongue flickering as it tested the air.

Longarm poked at the head. The head wove back, then struck. Longarm heard the click of the rattler's fangs against steel. The wet gleam of its venom was visible suddenly on the barrel. The snake reared, anxious to fight. But Longarm simply poked the rifle at it again, driving it back, herding it away from the stream. Giving up at last, its head aloft—the slit-eyed, weaving head shaped like an infernal ace of spades—tail whirring, the rattler retreated sideways before Longarm's prodding rifle barrel. Across a barren slope of rock it slithered with amazing speed and snapped like a rubber band out of sight under a sandstone slab.

Longarm returned to the stream, redoubled his investigation of the area he had chosen for his camp, found no more snakes, and unrolled his soogan. As the fierce eye of the sun slipped slowly down the western sky, the shadows in the canyon darkened, cooling the place substantially. Longarm, too hot and weary for preparing food, pillowed his head on his arm, enclosed the butt of his Colt in his right hand, and slept.

The sound of low, whispering voices—one of them rising to a querulous whine—and then the sharp report of a slap awakened Longarm. In a split second he was sitting up alert, his Colt in front of him, the barrel pointing into the pitch-darkness from which the sounds had come. Listening, he heard the soft, muffled sound of someone—a girl—crying. A man's hoarse whisper, rough and uncompromising, came to him also. The two of them were with the mules and as Longarm slowly rolled back the soogan and rose to his feet, he heard the soft clop of their hooves as they were being ridden out of the canyon.

He strode from the screen of bushes that flanked the stream and saw the two of them desperately urging on the mules. He ran after them. They heard his footfalls and the one behind—the man—turned in his saddle, then bent low over the mule and began kicking his heels into the animal's flanks. With an unhappy snort the mule quickened his pace, moving alongside the other. The girl was making no effort to hurry, however, and on the narrow trail her mule was able to slow the other one considerably.

"Damn you, girl!" Longarm heard the older man cry.

Ten feet behind them by this time, Longarm told them to hold up or he would shoot. He kept his voice low and as menacing as possible. He had no sense that these two were dangerous, just a mite foolish and maybe a little greedy. More important was where the hell they had popped from. He was evidently nearer the settlement than he had realized.

The fellow twisted around in the darkness to face Longarm, who saw the glint of a rifle barrel. The barrel was long, foolishly long, but that did not lessen its power to intimidate and Longarm swung his Colt against the side of the barrel. The clash of steel in the canyon echoed sharply. With an oath the fellow let go the rifle and ducked back around on his saddle. Reaching out, Longarm grabbed the rider's coat and pulled up, digging in his heels. Gasping, the fellow was dragged from the saddle. Stepping back and panting heavily, Longarm let him land on his back. He came down heavily, his vivid cursing silenced immediately. In the dark the man lay still, a large, ungainly package of meat and clothing, his big, floppy hat a black smudge over the spot where his head should be. Searching carefully in the darkness, Longarm retrieved the man's rifle. It looked like an early Hawken.

The girl had pulled up, dragged the mule around, and ridden back to where the man still lay unconscious on the ground. As Longarm returned with the rifle, she said to him, "Did you kill him?"

The cold matter-of-factness of the query chilled Longarm. Without replying, he knelt beside the man and rested the back of his hand against the man's neck. The blood was still pounding through the carotid artery. He looked up at the mounted girl.

"No," he said, "I didn't."

"Damn," the girl said softly.

"Maybe you'd better get off that mule and give me a picture of all this. And go slow. I just woke up."

"You wake up fast, sure enough."

She dismounted. "It wasn't my idea to steal these mules," she told him. "We seen you climbing up here and waited until dark. The damn fool rode his own horses into the ground a ways back." She paused and looked down at the still figure. "He never could do nothing right."

"That so? Who is he?"

"Ezekiel Bannister. A fool."

"I've been getting the idea pretty strong now—like old meat caught in the sun—that you don't hardly like the man. So what are you doing with him?"

"It ain't none of my doing. He came after me and took me away from Little Zion. Kidnapped me, he did, and when they catch up with him—" He felt her eyes on him in the darkness. "You ain't one of them, are you?" Her voice seemed to catch hopefully.

"An Avenging Angel? Nope. Not hardly. You mentioned Little Zion. Would that be a Mormon settlement hereabouts?"

"It would."

"And Zeke here took you away from there?"

"That's what the damn fool did all right. I was working in the fields this morning and he dragged me away when I went for water. I didn't get no chance to holler out or nothing. I just hope Elder Smithson understands I didn't go willing."

"And who might Elder Smithson be?"

"My husband," she said with unmistakable defiance.

The man on the ground stirred, lifted his shoulders, and groaned softly. His hat tumbled from his head and he turned a pale, bearded face with wide, angry eyes upon Longarm. "Damn you," he managed hoarsely. "I could have killed you and taken the mules. But I let you be."

"Next time, Zeke, you'll know better," Longarm said. He reached out. Zeke took his hand, and Longarm pulled him upright.

The man stood unsteadily, saw his hat on the ground, and

reached for it. He was still so groggy that he almost went down again. He struggled upright, however, clapped the sad hat down onto his head, and looked at Longarm.

"I was just aiming to rescue my Sarah from them heathen devils, is all. A man ought to be proud of doing something as needful as that. The Lord ought to look down and bless his progress."

"The Lord looked down," said Sarah contemptuously, "and he seen what you was doing and he stopped you. Twice."

Longarm looked at them without comment. The two of them were in the same traces, but they sure as hell weren't pulling in the same direction, and that was a fact. But they had the information he needed, and for that he was grateful.

"You two come on over to my camp here. We'll light a fire to get rid of this desert chill and maybe we can settle things like civilized people."

"Maybe," grumbled Sarah.

"I'm willing," said Zeke, rubbing the back of his shoulder. He was still a bit groggy from the fall and was probably anxious for time to pull himself together before he tried anything.

Longarm led the way back to his camp by the stream, lugging the rifle and noting its heft. The Hawken was a fine firearm and it seemed a shame that this fellow was going to lose it. But Longarm didn't see how he could give it back to the man.

Zeke told Sarah to hunt up some firewood and the girl responded with eagerness. The night chill was causing her to shake miserably, Longarm noted. Zeke stomped his boots unhappily and let Longarm light the campfire. Then they sat cross-legged around it.

"Keep the fire low," Zeke growled unhappily. "Them devils is out there a-hunting me now, I reckon." He grinned wolfishly at Longarm. "I got one of their women, I did. Right out from under their noses."

"We're pretty well hidden in this canyon," replied Longarm. "Now let's have your story. Who are you two, and what might you be doing skulking around stealing mules at this time of night, way the hell out here in the middle of nowhere?"

Zeke cleared his throat and glanced across the fire at Sarah. "Sarah's my bride-to-be and she was forced into one of them Celestial Marriages three weeks ago. They took her from me and I aim to take her back."

Sarah spoke up then. "I ain't his intended," she snapped. "That's his idea, not mine."

"But Sarah," Zeke protested, "you laid with me! We done made love three times in the barn and once out back of your pap's house during harvest time. And you told me then how you felt. How warm and good!"

"I always do feel good after," she retorted. "What you want me to say? That I hated it and didn't like it nohow?"

"But I thought—"

"I know what you thought. I shoulda knowed better than to lay with you, but a woman's got her itchin's just like a man and you was always hanging around slobberin' after me like a big, sad puppy dog and I took pity on you. That's the foolish truth of it and now I am getting my punishment for doing you a good turn."

"A good *turn?*"

She sighed, unwilling to continue the idiotic conversation, and Longarm did not blame her. In the flickering campfire her face grew alternately clear and dim, but what he glimpsed of her features was enough to set him to wondering at the lunacy of most adult-appearing men. He thought then of something Mark Twain had written pretty recently about Mormons. Back in Denver, old Wilson had read it aloud to Longarm. Mark Twain had visited Salt Lake City and seen how homely most of the women were. He submitted that anyone marrying one of them was doing an act of Christian charity, while the poor son of a bitch who marries sixty of them has done an act so sublime that the nations of the world should take off their hats to such a man and worship in dumb silence. That was putting it pretty mean, Longarm figured, but it wasn't too far off the mark. There was a cold severity in most of the women he had seen about the city that saddened him without his really knowing why he felt the way he did. And this young woman across from him at the moment seemed just as cold and practical, just as pinched and severe as all the rest of them. The poor fool that had gone after her was a pure and silly romantic for sure, but the woman's cold and humorless way of looking at things seemed almost as bad. There was no softness, no gentleness in her at all.

Zeke looked across the fire at Longarm, his eyes wide and hurt, looking for all the world like a dog that has just been smartly kicked by its master. "I reckon I got Sarah all wrong," he said.

"Yes," Sarah sniffed. "You sure enough did. And now you got me in terrible trouble. I just hope when Elder Smithson catches up with you, he will let me explain that this purely wasn't my idea." She looked at Zeke hard, then. "And don't you dare tell him about us!"

"I'd be ashamed to," said the hushed suitor, pulling away from the mean fury in her gaunt face.

Sarah looked back at Longarm, her face triumphant. "And Elder Smithson *will* catch up to us. He's after me now, I'm sure. He liked me the best of his wives. I could tell that right away." She threw her shoulders back proudly. "Them others was all worn out and always clucking like a yard of hens, scratching and quarreling all the time until it like to made the elder cry. I told him he should take a switch to them."

"You want to go back to Little Zion?" Longarm asked.

She nodded eagerly.

"I'll take you back," he said. "You just show me where it is." He looked at Zeke. "I guess you just might be better off without your intended. You'd make tracks faster, and that's a fact."

Zeke glanced with disillusioned eyes at Sarah. "You just don't love me, do you, Sarah? You don't want to marry me."

"No I don't," the woman snapped.

The man looked back at Longarm. "You let me have my Hawken and I'll be on my way."

"What makes you think I'd trust you with a firearm? You tried to shoot me with it not so long ago."

"No I didn't," the man said wearily. "It ain't even loaded."

Longarm reached over and picked up the rifle. Zeke was right. He had gone after his beloved with an unloaded weapon.

"I got the balls and powder in my pouch," Zeke explained. "I just ain't had time to load it."

Longarm considered for a short moment, then hefted the rifle at the man. "Take it and make tracks," he said. "And don't look back."

The man got to his feet and looked unhappily down at Sarah. She did not even bother to return his look. She was, Longarm could see, infinitely weary of the man and his need for her. "So long, Sarah," he said, his voice constricted, as if he still couldn't believe she would prefer living in a harem to living with him. "I hope you'll be real happy at that place."

"I will," she snapped. "I was till you come along. Now git, afore the elder catches up with you and fixes you good. Next time, leave well enough alone." She flung a quick look up at him then. "Just because a woman lays with you, don't think it means anything grand or wonderful. She's more'n likely just scratchin' an itch. Jest like you."

The fellow nodded dumbly, backed out of the circle of firelight, then turned and hurried away through the darkness. As his steps faded, Longarm looked across the fire at Sarah.

"How far is Little Zion?"

"Felt like a hundred miles the way that man was dragging me along after the horses gave out." She shrugged miserably in the night chill and tried to move herself closer to the warmth of the fire. "If we could get to a high place, I could maybe point us in the right direction."

"How long would it take us?"

She shrugged. "The rest of the night and most of the day, I guess."

"We have two mules, don't forget."

She brightened. "That's right. We won't be walking."

Longarm looked up at the night sky. The moon was out of sight beyond the canyon wall, but it was full and bright. "We'll start now if you're willing."

She looked at him shrewdly. "What are you up to, mister? You ain't a Mormon, are you?"

"No, I'm not."

"You just prospecting out here in all these rocks?"

"Maybe."

"You expecting some reward if you bring me back?"

"Maybe."

She shrugged. Obviously, all she cared about was returning to the settlement. Longarm stood up. With a weary sigh, Sarah stood up also and leaned over the fire for one last taste of its warmth. In the bright light of the campfire, her gaunt appearance and grim lines caused Longarm to wonder again at the devotion the foolish Ezekiel Bannister felt for this woman. That must have been some ride in the hay she had given him.

With Sarah riding beside him, they crested a ridge before noon the next day and caught sight of a dim figure far below struggling closer to the edge of the Great Salt Lake Desert. It was Zeke. From the ridge Longarm could see far beyond Zeke out across the pale expanse of featureless desert to the dim line of the Central Pacific's tracks on the horizon. If Zeke could reach them, he could maybe flag down a train. He would never make it otherwise without a mount and in this heat—already blistering so early in the morning—he would have a difficult enough time just getting to the tracks.

Two lesser ridges loomed between Zeke and Longarm, the

terrain formidable, the distance at least four miles. Only because of the shimmering heat that raised such hell with distances could Longarm be sure that the lone figure so far below was Zeke. What clinched it was the long rifle he was carrying.

"See him now?" Longarm asked.

"Yes, I see him."

"He's going to have a hard time making it back."

"That ain't my concern."

Longarm looked back at Zeke—and saw at once that he had already lost his chance to make it. A small crowd of riders broke out of a canyon and strung out in a line as they galloped toward him. Longarm saw Zeke pull up and turn. He began to run then, but it was hopeless. He got just beyond a low finger of a rock and was getting down on one knee, probably to load and prime his Hawken, when Longarm saw him topple forward. He was still on his knees when the other shots caught him in the chest, sending him backward onto the sand.

Only then did the sounds of the shots reach Longarm. The echoes were feeble and lasted only a short while, and then the land was still—as still as the body lying on the sand before the riders. All of them were dressed in black and only one of them dismounted to inspect the dead man. It did not take him long, and he retreated to his horse, carrying Zeke's Hawken. At once the riders wheeled away and galloped back into the canyon and out of sight, leaving Zeke's body for the vultures.

Longarm looked at Sarah. "I guess the Elder Smithson found Zeke."

There was a thin smile on Sarah's face, a grim, cold gleam in her eyes. She was satisfied that Zeke had been killed without blabbing anything about her to any of the Avenging Angels. She took pleasure, too, Longarm figured, in the neat, quick way that her people had rid her of a tiresome nuisance. Longarm found himself just a mite uncomfortable with the woman's total lack of feeling or understanding of what Zeke Bannister had felt for her.

"We could fire a shot," she suggested hopefully. "Let them know I'm here, safe with you."

It was pretty clear to Longarm what would happen then. Those riders would make short work of him. They would never let him near Little Zion—not alive, anyway.

"They're well out of sight now," he told her. "And there's no telling how far they might be by this time. I'd just as soon keep going."

"All right," she said, looking at him curiously, "but could we stop in a little while? I need to rest up some. I've been going all night."

"As soon as we find a place with some water," he promised her.

The spot he found was cool enough, tucked well in under an overhanging rock shelf with a small pool fed by trickles of icy water oozing from cracks in the canyon wall. He checked the ground around the water hole for snakes before helping her down from the mule. He wasn't sure, but he had the odd sense that she clung to him a little longer than was necessary.

"I have to tend to some of my needs," she told him, straightening her dress. She looked uncomfortable and Longarm realized how very difficult it must have been for her to ride astride with all the clothes—not to mention the corset—she had on. "You ain't told me your name yet, mister. Don't you think we should be introduced proper?"

"Name's Long, ma'am."

"You can call me Sarah," she told him. She turned then and vanished in among the rocks.

He was about to yell after her to watch out for snakes, but didn't think it proper when she was in that kind of a hurry.

Longarm tended to the mules, lifting off their saddles and watering them. Then he hobbled them and made a dry camp under the rock overhang where it was coolest. He took care of a few things he had to tend to and then filled the canteens. By this time, Sarah was back.

She slumped down close beside him. Quite close. Longarm was not able to move away from her without it seeming obvious, so he stayed put and handed her a canteen. She took it and swallowed the water down greedily, wasting a lot of it out of the sides of her mouth. She handed him back the canteen, then wiped her mouth with the back of her forearm. She looked at him. The water—or something—put a sparkle into her eyes.

"I told you," she said. "I knew Elder Smithson would send riders after me." She looked at Longarm then, her eyes alight with sudden warmth. "You better make sure no harm comes to me. I guess I'm your safe passage through these hills. So you be good to me."

He looked at her, astonished. She was wearing a long gray skirt, a gray bodice with a soiled lace frill on it about the neck and wrists, and a severe black bonnet. Her somewhat scrawny neck was encrusted with week-old dirt, her hair tied into a bun and securely out of sight under the bonnet. There was very little that was attractive about her. And if she meant what he could hardly believe she meant, he did not know whether to jump up and run or just sit there and die.

"You can just rest easy, ma'am," he told her uncertainly. "You're safe with me. I won't hurt you none. You got my word on that."

She caught the uncertainty in his voice and frowned, a little bit like a schoolmarm who just got the wrong answer to a cipher problem. His mistake now, Longarm realized, was in making her spell out what it was she wanted.

Sarah leaned her head on his shoulder. "That's not what I meant," she said, her voice a little breathless—a little desperate, perhaps.

She'd got the itch, Longarm realized in a panic. He decided he would just have to run. He got up quickly, excusing himself clumsily, and hurried over to one of the mules.

Sarah was after him in an instant. "You don't find me attractive. Is that it?" she demanded, her pinched face white, her cold eyes laced with fury.

"Now I wouldn't say that, ma'am," Longarm protested, trying to sound as if he meant it. He turned his full attention to the mule then, patting his neck and pretending to examine one of his eyes.

But Sarah was seething by this time. "Oh, I know you men!" she cried bitterly. "You like only the pretty ones—always the pretty ones. The rest of us ain't supposed to have no feelings. But you try one of us in bed sometime, and you'll see! It don't take a pretty face to pleasure a man—not in the dark, not in a bed!"

"Ma'am, I do think this conversation has gotten a mite out of hand. I wouldn't want to shock you by continuing on with it."

"You're mocking me!"

Longarm sighed. "I suppose what you said is true at that, ma'am. Men do like a woman with pretty ankles and bright eyes. Ain't no harm in that, is there?"

"I suppose not," she snapped, "if *you're* the one with them pretty ankles."

"It's the way of the world, ma'am," he said, trying to mollify her.

"Well, it shouldn't be," she retorted. "And with us Mormons, that ain't the way it is. With us, it ain't how pretty a woman is. It's how good she is in the house and how she fits in with the other wives and how well she pleases her husband after a long day that matters." She paused and shook her head once for emphasis. "And with so many of us to a man, why, there ain't no chance for him to go off looking for a pretty face. He don't have the time. He don't have the energy!" She spoke this last with malicious triumph.

"And I guess maybe," Longarm suggested quietly, "you get some help with all that housework and them farming chores."

"Yes! That's right," she agreed, warming now to her topic. "Oh, I watched how my ma had to struggle with a patch of nothing under that big Nebraska sky, how it wore her down to a nubbin—and all for nothing. She never even bought a new dress in all the years I knowed her. And she was so lonely!" She shook her head. "At least this way we got help. We ain't lonely at all. And that fool Zeke Bannister wanted to take me away to some miserable shack in the middle of nowhere, so *I* could wear myself to a nubbin for *him!* Just like my poor ma!"

"He just didn't understand," offered Longarm, careful not to arouse her again. "He loved you and didn't think much beyond that."

"No man does," she snapped. "Fools! Every one of them!" She glanced up at him then. "It ain't nice what happened to Zeke, and I wish it hadn't, I suppose. But I purely didn't need him buttin' in like that and ruining things for me with the elders. That was a stupid thing he done, coming after me like that."

She frowned thoughtfully and looked away from Longarm. She was run down now, Longarm saw, and maybe letting herself feel at last what had happened to Zeke Bannister. He said nothing further to her and returned to the campsite.

She followed him back, a sullen, unhappy look in her eyes, and sat down opposite him. He handed her the canteen again. She took it and drank deeply. He did not watch her this time. When she handed the canteen back to him, he screwed the cap back on and then waited a decent interval before suggesting it was time for them to get moving again and went to saddle the mules.

When he helped her up onto her saddle this time, he noted that there was a cold, distant look in her eyes. Her hands did not linger on his as she took the reins he passed up to her.

A few hours later they were climbing a ridge she had promised would be a good spot from which to get further bearings. Longarm concentrated on the trail and tried to forget the heat. It had been powerful and unrelenting, yet Sarah had not uttered a word of complaint. She was a formidable woman indeed. It was not a charitable thought, he knew, but he kept wondering if maybe those Avenging Angels hadn't done Zeke Bannister a favor.

"There!" Sarah called out, pointing.

It was close to dusk, and as far as Longarm could tell, the irregular pinnacle of rock Sarah was pointing to was just one more chimneylike projection among the dozens that reached up out of the barren, lifeless wilderness of rock on all sides of them.

"That rock over there," she said firmly. "We're nearly to Little Zion!"

Longarm lagged back as Sarah urged her mule on ahead of him.

Soon she found a trail that took them over a short rise and then along a rocky ledge, beyond which they came to a well-traveled trail that led into a narrow canyon. Longarm followed Sarah into the canyon. After a while he heard the sound of water rushing headlong. Rounding a bend in the canyon, they came upon a prodigious gush of water splashing down out of a great rent in the canyon wall. From a large pool beneath it a steady stream of water poured along the sloping floor of the canyon. So broad was this stream that in spots it filled the canyon completely as it rushed along, at times reaching the bellies of his mules.

At last, as they splashed along through the swift water, the canyon walls parted, the stream was caught in earthen banks, and Longarm found himself riding into a broad and surprisingly fertile valley. Everywhere he looked he saw green, lush fields gleaming in the hot sun and flanked by the inevitable Mormon irrigation ditches. The stream rushing from the canyon was tamed at once by a series of dams, from each of which a complex network of irrigation ditches reached out. It was an impressive accomplishment. Obviously the founders of Little Zion knew what they were doing. In the middle of desolate badlands they had fashioned an Eden.

In the distance, well beyond the fields, Longarm could see a large cluster of weathered buildings with a windmill tower rearing skyward from their midst. In her eagerness, Sarah had ridden ahead. She turned and looked back at him, hauling in her reins.

"Well," she called back to him, "this is Little Zion. You better let me explain how come you're here. We been watched now for some time now, I'm thinking."

Longarm nodded and glanced back at the canyon walls. A

lone figure was standing on the rim of the canyon, his body clearly silhouetted against the still-bright evening sky. He was carrying a rifle. Longarm looked farther along the rocky barrier that enclosed the valley and saw another man, this one crouched with binoculars before his eyes. Then from the canyon they had just left came the unmistakable clatter of shod hooves on stone as a company of riders followed after them through the canyon.

Longarm had expected this.

He turned back around in his saddle and urged his mule on toward Sarah. "I would be much obliged," he told her, "if you would impress upon your people how helpful I have been."

As he caught up with her, she surveyed him coldly. "I'll tell them only what I know; that you were in the barrens alone and that when Zeke tried to steal your mules, you stopped him. And that you were curious to learn where Little Zion was, so I brought you here. Why you were so curious, I ain't got no idea. But I figure you'll be telling our people soon enough." She smiled without warmth at him.

"Perhaps I would like to join your thriving community."

"You said you weren't no Mormon."

"Well, just maybe you and your friends might be able to convince me what a fine religion it is, after all." He smiled at her gently. "A poor sinner such as myself could sure use a good set of directions on his way to paradise."

"You're mocking us! I can tell. But we Saints are preparing ourselves for a life everlasting! We'll be like gods in the hereafter. And here we're building for the resurrection and the coming Millennium! So you gentiles go on and mock us! That won't stop us none!" As she spoke, her face became lit with a holy zeal; a fire gleamed in her eyes. She pointed suddenly to the fields around them. "See that! Like the prophecies told us—we're making the desert bloom! You just go ahead and laugh at that!"

"All right, Sarah," Longarm said carefully. "Just lead the way."

As they rode along a broad roadway flanking the fields, Longarm noted the number of women laboring diligently in them. The women worked stooped over, cultivating with short hoes what appeared to be rows of corn. The closer he and Sarah rode, the more curious the women became. Soon they halted their labor to peer cautiously out at them from under the beaks of their bonnets.

When Sarah was close enough, a few of the women hailed her in greeting. Sarah smiled and waved back at them, obviously glad to be with her people once again.

After about a mile, Longarm looked behind him. Again he
was not surprised. Six riders, grim and unhurried, were pacing
them a half-mile to the rear, content to let Sarah lead Longarm
into their parlor. They were, Longarm was certain, the same riders Sarah and he had watched cut down without ceremony the
luckless Ezekiel Bannister.

Chapter 4

Lorenzo Wolverton was the last elder to enter the room.

Longarm, sitting in a wooden chair before the long table with his wrists bound behind him, watched the man enter and then make his way deliberately to the table and sit down facing Longarm. The six other elders had grown absolutely silent the moment Wolverton entered. Now they waited respectfully for him to begin the questioning. But Wolverton was in no great hurry to begin, it seemed.

He was the tallest of the elders, and the oldest, apparently. His full head of hair was a clean, scrubbed white that fairly shone. He had no mustache, but wore a long beard that extended halfway down his chest. It was as immaculately white as his hair. The eyes that studied Longarm from under full, snowy eyebrows were a cold, icy green, the mouth above the patriarchal beard a grim, unforgiving line. His cheeks, however, were pink and unlined, giving his appearance an unsettling combination of purity and wrathfulness.

As Longarm took the measure of Wolverton, the thought occurred to him that for once he might have outsmarted himself. Riding boldly in like this and announcing his purpose in coming to Little Zion might have caught them off guard for the moment, but Lorenzo Wolverton looked like someone who could eat the apple one bite at a time—and Longarm right along with it.

"I have your credentials here, Mr. Long," Wolverton said, his voice powerful and deep without straining for that effect. "You were not lying. You are a deputy U.S. marshal, a minion of the federal government. And you have come here without apology to take from us one of our sisters—a young lady soon to join me in Celestial Marriage."

"That's right."

The man's eyes gleamed now with a powerful ferocity as he contemplated Longarm. "Already you have killed the brother of Elder Barker sitting beside me, and Jason Kimball, one of our people." He paused to let that ominous intelligence sink in. "I do not see how you could have expected to walk in here like this and escape with Emilie Boggs, unscathed." He smiled grimly. "You must have more imagination than that."

"Jason Kimball was killed by a young lady who mistook him

for me. The sheriff tried to kill me without waiting for a trial. I
shot him in self-defense. Emilie Boggs did not choose to join you
in marriage, Wolverton, and my guess is that she has still not volunteered for that honor."

The elders on both sides of Wolverton stirred angrily at this
assertion. A few bent their heads in angry conversation. Wolverton quieted them with a single withering glance, then looked
back at Longarm, a flinty smile on his face. "Go on, Mr. Long.
Speak out. Tell us more."

"I figure you're not butchers and kidnappers here, that you really do want to build a community that will last—and I also figure
you're too sensible to think you can do it with stolen women. Now
you let me take Emilie Boggs back to her family and it might turn
out to be the smartest move the founders of Little Zion ever made."

Wolverton leaned forward, a slight smile on his face. "You do
not understand us at all, Mr. Long."

"You can call me Longarm."

"Longarm, then. You are a gentile, an atheist. You believe in
nothing except, perhaps, the gun at your side which we took from
you so easily. You believe in no miracles, no spiritual gifts. You do
not see the Millennium coming, your eyes are blind to revelations."

There was murmured assent to this indictment all down the
line as one after another of the elders nodded impassively. Longarm felt like a fish that had been left too long in the sun.

"We, on the other hand," continued Elder Wolverton, "have been
blessed. The scales have been removed from our eyes. We await the
Resurrection with confidence, the Millennium with certainty!"

Again there was a general murmur of agreement and a nodding of heads. Elder Wolverton had his congregation with him,
all right.

"Emilie Boggs was revealed to me in a revelation! Her person
appeared before me and in her eyes I read complete acceptance
of the truth! It lives within her now, but she does not yet acknowledge it. The false doctrines of her father, of all the other be-
nighted backsliders that surround him and that are poisoning the
well of our Prophet's church have temporarily blinded her. But
soon she will see as clearly as we do. Soon, of her own free will,
she will join us in bringing the Millennium to pass!"

Longarm was surprised the elders didn't leap to their feet
shouting hosannas. He had never heard, a more eloquent defense
of taking a woman against her will. But Longarm was not ready
to laugh aloud at the man. He was evidently entirely sincere—as

were the rest of the elders. Difficult though it was to believe, they saw nothing wrong in kidnapping Emilie Boggs.

"Think, Longarm," Wolverton intoned, his eyes lit with fervor, "what a salutory experience it will be for that apostate Boggs to learn that his beloved daughter has returned to the teachings of our Prophet—has accepted with glad heart the revelations that sustained us through cruel persecutions and exile—revelations that enabled us to outlast and defeat the despised gentile!"

Longarm leaned back in his chair. This kidnapping of Emilie, then, was as much a political move as it was a desire for the young woman to share his bed. The old fox was going to have it both ways, and Longarm found he had to respect revelations that could work things out as neatly as that.

The elder rose to his feet. The others hastily stood up also.

"Your education is incomplete, Longarm. One might almost believe that Angel Moroni has sent you for this purpose." He smiled, enjoying himself hugely. "You will be put to work for Little Zion. You will haul water. You will bend your back under the hot sun. You will see how hard work and devotion to a cause can transform barren earth to fruitfulness. And we will see what you have to say then. Perhaps when Emilie Boggs joins me I will send you back to her father with the joyful news!"

He turned and strode from the room, the others following after. Longarm tried to get a good look at them, but they all looked so much alike with their straggly long gray mustaches he knew he would have difficulty distinguishing one from another if he met them outside.

As soon as the door closed after them, the two Angels standing behind him came forward and hauled Longarm roughly to his feet. Longarm turned on them angrily to protest. He shouldn't have. He was struck viciously on the crown of the head with the barrel of a sixgun and sent plunging into darkness.

Longarm found himself sitting up in a small, lightless room, his hands tied painfully behind him. Someone was poking a spoonful of hot soup at him. He winced painfully. His head was pounding mercilessly. Opening his eyes a painful slit, he tried to focus on the features of the woman who was feeding him. His eyes widened suddenly.

"Annie Dawkins! What in tarnation are you doing here?"

"Shh! Eat this and I'll tell you. You've been unconscious for most of the day!"

"What day is this?"

"Wednesday."

The day after his confrontation with the elders. Longarm looked up at the one tiny window. It was not large enough for him to get even one shoulder through, and was barred. Very little light was filtering in through it. "What time is it?"

"Past suppertime. I volunteered to feed you."

"Thanks." He opened his mouth and she shoved a spoonful of food into it. It tasted like a combination of beef and greens. It wasn't seasoned and tasted flat. But he was famished and grateful for the nourishment. His wrists were bound so tightly behind him that he no longer had any feeling in his hands.

"You didn't tell me what you are doing here," he told her when he finished chewing.

"Soon's that devil Jason saw me with Ma Randle, he just came after me that same night. Ma couldn't do a thing to stop him. He told me then that he was going after you later."

"You haven't seen him since, have you?"

"No I haven't." She poked another spoonful at him.

"And you won't. He's dead, Annie."

She nodded. "That's what I heard. Two of his other wives came to visit with me and they told me he wasn't coming back to Little Zion."

"To *visit* with you, Annie?"

"There's a place for them like me that don't really want to marry up with these Angels. They keep us there till we get desperate enough to go through with it. There's been a couple of men in to see me since I heard about Jason. They been sweet-talking me in hopes I'd join up with them. Even their own wives have been in to see me. They need help with the work." She shook her head at the thought as she fed Longarm. "I guess I can sure understand that, Mr. Long. These woman really have to work out here. I never saw the likes of it."

Longarm swallowed her last spoonful. Already he felt much stronger. "You're not weakening, are you, Annie?"

"Nope," she said firmly, sitting back and putting the dish and spoon beside her on the beaten-earth floor. He was aware suddenly of a foul-smelling chamber pot waiting for him in the corner and realized just how badly he needed to make use of it.

"Annie, could you please untie my hands?"

"I don't dare to, Mr. Long. They told me if I did, I'd really get it."

"Just loosen the knots, then. I won't make a break or anything for a long time and if anyone comes in after you leave, they'll see I'm still bound. But it'll give me a chance, Annie."

She didn't think about it for long. "All right, Mr. Long."

He turned around so that his back was to her and in a moment she had loosened the rawhide significantly. He turned back around and rested against the wall, letting the blood circulate into his hands. Pins and needles swept into both of them along with the flow of blood. He began to rub them briskly together, as much as their still-bound condition allowed.

"Thank you, Annie. And call me Longarm, if you want."

"All right."

"Annie, I'm looking for Emilie Boggs. Are they holding her nearby?"

Annie nodded. "Only she's not with us and the others. They don't even let her out to work in the fields."

"I've come for her, Annie."

She nodded. "I know. All of us know." She grinned, "You didn't make any secret of it when you rode in with that Sarah Smithson. What'd you think of her, Longarm?" She smiled knowingly. "Ain't she a caution?"

"And a very hard woman, Annie."

Annie nodded in eager agreement. "We call her hatchet-face." She became thoughtful. "Longarm?"

"Yes?"

"Will . . . you take me out of here, too?"

"I'd like to, Annie. But it's Emilie I'm after."

"But I could help."

"You help me get Emilie and I'll come back for you, Annie. That's a promise."

She brightened for a moment, then went gloomy again. "But that'll take so long! I hate it here, Longarm! These men coming to see me are getting to look mighty good."

Longarm smiled at Annie. "Just think of those sunny fields out there, Annie. They stretch quite a ways."

She nodded unhappily. "You'll be working them soon, I hear," she said. "They was talking about that last night. All the women are waiting on you. They want to see how you take it." She smiled. "But I guess you got other plans."

"Will you help me get to Emilie?"

She nodded. "I reckon I will, Longarm. She's in a building

like mine, near here. It's the smallest one, and it's fenced in so she can walk outside during the day. I'll tell her you're here and see if I can get you the key to the lock on her door."

"Can you do that?"

She nodded quickly. "I bring her meals most every day, and I know where they keep the keys."

"They've taken my Colt and Winchester," he told her.

"I know where they might be. In the building next door. The arsenal, they call it. But I couldn't get into that room. I just saw the door open yesterday when one of the Avenging Angels was leaving. He just rode in with a bunch of his fellows on some mean errand, from the look of it. There sure were a lot of guns in there, anyway."

"Just get me the keys to Emilie's place, then."

Abruptly the door was flung open and someone was standing in the doorway. Not much light came in past the figure, since it was well into twilight by this time. Longarm looked up at the fellow, but could barely make out any of the features of his face.

"Let's go, whore!" the man replied. "You been in here long enough!"

Annie winced at his greeting, snatched up the spoon and dish, and scrambled to her feet. Without a further word to Longarm, she ducked past the fellow. He watched her go, then looked closely at Longarm, considered a moment, then entered the hut.

"I just better check to see if you're still trussed," he said, grabbing Longarm by the hair and pulling him away from the wall. As Longarm sprawled past him, he was careful to allow him a quick view of his bound wrists before rolling over painfully onto his side.

"Untie me, will you?" he complained. "I can't even use that pot over there, trussed up like this!"

"That's too bad," the fellow said.

In an excess of good feeling, he kicked Longarm in the side and sent him rolling in the general direction of the slop jar. Well-satisfied that Longarm was still securely bound, he turned and left the place. Listening carefully, Longarm heard him lock the beam in place across the door.

He sat up, his side throbbing miserably, worked his wrists loose, and then, in a kind of half-stagger, made it to the pot.

It was close to midnight by Longarm's reckoning when he heard the padlock rattle outside his door. He moved back against the wall, stuck his hands behind his back, and waited. The door swung wide and a small, chunky figure stole in, closing the door firmly behind him. With the door shut, the inside of the hut was as dark as an Apache's heart; it was only the light from the moon that enabled Longarm to tell that his visitor was a male.

He felt the man looming over him in the darkness and told himself that if this fellow started lashing out with his foot, he'd take him apart right then. He had not yet heard anything from Annie and was unwilling to make a move this early since he was not certain she had yet had time to get to Emilie. So he kept his back against the wall and waited.

The looming shadow stirred, then shifted abruptly and appeared to sit down before Longarm on the dirt floor. "You're awake, ain't you, Longarm?" the fellow said.

"That I am. You know me, do you?"

"I know what you're called. We all do. And I know why you're here. It's Emilie Boggs, isn't it?"

"Yes, it is."

He took a deep breath. "Forget her! Damn it! There's more important business for you to do here! You've got to bring in Mordecai Lee!"

"Who the hell is he?" Longarm asked, but he remembered the name. He was one of the Mormon survivors of the Mountain Meadow Massacre, still at large.

"You know who he is. He was one of the leaders of the Massacre. You're after him, ain't you?"

"I told you. I'm here to return Emilie Boggs to her family."

The man did not reply for a long moment. "You must bring in Lee. He's wanted. That this man should still walk free is an abomination. I saw what he did. I was *there!*"

"Then you're just as guilty as he is."

"But I have repented. Every day since, I have gone down on my knees and begged forgiveness, but I know I am unclean. I know that for me there waits no celestial kingdom. I will go with the unclean liars, the adulterers, the murderers. My deliverance can come only after the Second Resurrection. I accept this willingly! But that fool Mordecai Lee denies his guilt. He lives amongst us and is high in our councils! Little Zion cannot prosper under such a curse! Jesus will not listen to our prayers with this man at our side. You must take him from us—rid us of this abomination!"

"How many of you believe this?"

"None. I admit it, I am the only one who sees this. But I have had a revelation. I see fire and destruction visited upon us all. And it is this one who brings it upon us."

"You were there, you say—at Mountain Meadow?"

"Yes. Yes, it was terrible. It was worse than that." His voice grew immediately low, somber, as if suddenly he was witnessing the scene once again in all its horror: "The men and the women and the children gathered around me as I entered their fortifications. They believed our promises and hailed me as their deliverer from the Indians. Their guns, I noticed at once, were mostly Kentucky rifles of the muzzle-loading style. Their ammunition was about gone. I do not think there were twenty loads left in their whole camp. If they had had more ammunition, I am sure they would never have surrendered to us, or believed our promises of safe passage . . . I hurried the women and children to the right, on by our troops. When the men left their fortifications, they cheered our soldiers. They believed we were acting honestly." The man stopped talking then, and Longarm was reluctant to start him up again. The picture forming in his mind was not a pleasant one.

"Higbee then gave the orders," the fellow said, his voice barely audible now. "He told his men to form in single file, to take their places, just as they had been instructed earlier—to the right of the settlers. It was my job to kill the sick and the wounded who were in the wagons. McMurdy and Knight were with me in this. We had been told not to shoot until we heard our troops firing on the men who had just marched out. McMurdy had a rifle. I drew my pistol. When we heard the firing ahead of us, we knew it was our turn. McMurdy raised his rifle to his shoulder. He began to pray: *O Lord, my God, receive their spirits, it is for Thy kingdom that I do this.*"

Longarm heard what sounded like a sob break from the man before him, but he kept his silence and waited.

"Then," continued the man, his voice now so low that Longarm had to strain to hear him, "McMurdy shot a man who was lying with his head on another man's breast. The ball, I am sure, killed both men. I went to the wagon. I had yet to perform my part in this. I cocked my pistol. Somehow—I can't remember to this day how it happened—the gun went off prematurely. I shot McMurdy across the thigh, my pistol ball cutting his buckskin pants. McMurdy turned to me and said, 'Brother, keep cool. You are excited. You came near killing me. Keep cool, I tell you. There is no reason for being excited.'" Then the man repeated this in a kind of sing-song. "No need to be excited . . . no need to be excited."

He gave a deep, shuddering sigh, seemed to straighten in the darkness, and went on, "Knight shot a man with his rifle, shot him in the head. Then he brained a boy who was about fourteen years old. The boy had come running up to our wagons, and Knight struck him on the head with the butt of his gun and crushed his skull. Soon we were busy. The Indians came up then to help us. One of them from Cedar City—we knew him only as Joe—caught a man by the hair and raised his head up and looked into his face. I saw the man shut his eyes a second before Joe shot him in the head. At last, when it was all over, and I reached where the dead men lay, Major Higbee told me proudly that the boys had acted admirably, that they took good aim and that all the damned gentiles but two or three fell at the first fire . . ."

The fellow stifled a sob. It seemed to Longarm that the man had bowed his face into his hands. When he spoke next, his words were muffled: "*At the first fire! All but two or three!* And then Lee came riding up! He was excited and called it a victory! He cheered us all for a job well-done!"

The man was silent for a long while. Longarm sat without moving, astonished and deeply disturbed by this eyewitness account of a tragedy he had heard about only in brief, disjointed accounts. In fact, there were many authorities, Longarm realized, who denied that such a thing had ever happened.

At last Longarm said, "I am not here to bring in Lee—or you, for that matter. I am sorry. Why can't you just walk out of here and tell your story to the federal authorities? Why don't you take Lee with you when you go?"

"I am a coward. I could not leave my family now. I have three wives, eleven children. I am trapped."

"I am sorry for you," Longarm said.

He heard as well as felt the man get slowly to his feet in the darkness. "You have not come for Lee, truly?"

"You heard me right."

"Your proposal that we let you take Emilie back has stirred discussion in our councils. I do not think we can convince Elder Wolverton to relinquish his prize, no matter how politic it might be to do so. He has his revelations. I have mine. But I will speak for your proposal as strongly as I can, though I see no hope for it. I am sorry, Longarm. If the vote goes against you, you will die here."

For a moment Longarm debated the wisdom of leaping upon the fellow and making his break. But he reminded himself that this was not the way he had planned it. He held himself in check and watched as the fellow stepped back out through the door. He heard the man shut the padlock and walk off into the night.

The night air was cold, and Longarm shivered. But it was not the chill from the night breeze that disturbed him; it was the chill that remained in the hut with him as he recalled the Mountain Meadow Massacre and heard once again the words of that tormented elder as he retold his tale of horror.

Longarm was dozing fitfully a few hours later when he heard someone at the window. He scrambled to his feet and went to it. He heard Annie calling to him softly.

"I'm here," he answered through the dirt-encrusted window pane.

"I've unlocked the door. I slipped the key to Emilie's hut under it! Now remember! You said you would come back for me!"

"I will!"

As Annie moved off, Longarm hurried across the dirt floor, picked up the key, and pushed open the door. The moon was not as full as it had been the previous night, but it shone brightly enough in a clear, star-crowded sky. He saw the small, fenced-in house where Annie had told him Emilie was being held.

He reached into his crotch and took from it his derringer. Earlier, during the ride with Sarah while the woman was off among the rocks attending to her needs, he had fastened the small weapon to the inside of his thigh with the gold chain. At the time he had known he must find a better-than-usual hiding place for it. He had realized, once he had made the decision to use the woman as a guide to the settlement, that short of killing Sarah, there was no way he could keep her from informing her people, once she reached Little Zion, that he was skulking about in the area with two army mules. And since that left him no real chance for surprise, he had decided on the brazen approach—and the concealed derringer.

But now Annie's presence in Little Zion gave him a valuable edge. He hoped his breakout could be accomplished without gunplay. So far, it seemed, his gamble had paid off. He had little doubt that his apparent stupidity in riding in so openly was the reason they had not guarded him more closely.

That thought cautioned him. Holding his derringer in readiness, he looked quickly around. Not a soul was abroad. The night was as still as death. From what Annie had told him, he guessed the hut next door served as this warlike community's armory. He darted across the narrow yard to the door of the hut and tried it. It was not locked. He pulled it open. Someone was sleeping on a cot next to the far wall. Above him were racks containing rifles of all descriptions. Pegs along another wall held enough gunbelts to outfit a small army. A lantern on a table next to the cot was flickering low, its chimney blackened. Longarm stepped into the small hut and closed the door. In the dim light, he saw the fellow on the cot stir restlessly.

Longarm crossed the room swiftly, and holding his derringer under the man's nose, shook him awake. The fellow came alert the moment he looked into the muzzle of the derringer, all the fight draining out of him.

"Don't shoot," he managed.

"Get up and turn around," Longarm ordered him.

The fellow scrambled to his feet and turned his back to Longarm. Holding the barrel of the derringer between his teeth, Longarm tied the man's wrists behind him with the same rawhide they had used on him. He pulled a heavy Colt from one of the holsters on the wall and rapped the Mormon's head under the base of the skull, not too hard. The man's knees gave out and he collapsed in a heap onto the floor.

Longarm lifted the man and dumped him back onto his cot, his face to the wall. He found a ratty blanket at the foot of the cot and covered the man from his shoulders down. Anyone looking in would think the man was asleep. Longarm searched through the room and found his Colt and rig lying on a table with his hat. It had been knocked off when he had protested their arrest of him.

He strapped on his rig and checked out the Colt. They had not bothered to empty it, and he still had on his person the shells he kept in his coat pocket. Next, he lifted down a Winchester like the one that had been in the boot on his mule, clapped his hat on, and slipped out of the building.

The moon was bright enough that the shadows cast by the buildings were quite dark. Longarm darted from one shadow to another until he reached Emilie's prison. He unlocked the door and a slight figure materialized out of the gloom within and flung herself into his arms.

"Are you Mr. Longarm?"

"And you'd be Emilie."

"Yes!"

"Your father sent me—like Annie must have told you. You ready to go?"

"Of course!"

He took her gently by the wrist and pulled her from the one-room hut. "Keep down," he told her as they ran across the moonlit yard toward the shadow of the windmill tower.

Once they had reached it, he pulled her down beside him. The road leading back to the canyon was a broad ribbon of moonlight less than a hundred yards from them. Longarm pointed it out to her.

"Wait for me on the other side of that road," he told her, "behind that clump of rocks. I've got to get the mules and maybe provide a little diversion. That large barn over there—is that the stables?"

She nodded.

"All right. Get going now and keep down behind those rocks. Don't you pay any mind to what happens. You just stay there. I'll come for you."

Holding her skirts well above her ankles, she ran swiftly across the yard toward the road. As soon as she had vanished safely in among the rocks, Longarm headed for the horse barn. Once inside, he began his search for the army mules. When he could not find them, he concluded they had been appropriated by one of the elders, and selected two powerful roans instead.

He saddled them swiftly with saddles he found resting on the partitions between the stalls. Aware of how important a large supply of water would be, he collected a total of six canteens from three other saddles, strung them together with rawhide, and slung three over each of the saddle horns. He had worked as efficiently as he was able in the darkness and was reaching for a lantern hung from a nail when he heard voices and the sound of men walking past the stalls toward him.

He turned as two men materialized out of the gloom.

"That you, Alf?" one of them asked.

"Where the hell you going with them horses?" the other drawled.

"Going for a ride," Longarm replied, as he pulled the Colt from his holster and leveled it at the two men. There was enough light for both men to catch the gleam of Longarm's gun barrel.

"Jesus!" the first one said. "It's that damn fool deputy U.S. marshal!"

"Yes," Longarm replied, "and he's got a Colt centered on your belly button. Just stand easy." Both men were too astonished to say much. Longarm frisked them swiftly. Neither one of them was carrying sidearms.

Longarm stepped back. "Get on past me to the rear of the barn. You're going to be a great help in a minute or two."

"Help? What do you mean? We ain't going to help you!"

"You'll see." Longarm waggled the barrel at them and they moved past him.

He herded them into the feed room and placed a beam against the door. They would be able to dislodge it, but it would give them a battle. Then Longarm went back to the lantern, lifted it down from the wall, and lit it. He turned the wick up all the way, then tossed the lantern up into the loft. He heard the chimney shatter against a beam. As smoke began to coil down out of the loft, he hustled from the barn, leading the two horses.

The men inside the feed room began shouting. Longarm swung into his saddle and galloped across the compound toward the roadway. "Fire!" he yelled, shooting twice into the night. "The barn's on fire! Save the horses!"

Reaching the rocks, he pulled to a sliding halt in front of them and waited as Emilie raced out and tried to swing into the saddle. But she was too firmly corsetted and could not ride astride. As dark figures began racing from the buildings toward the barn, Longarm dismounted and told Emilie to get out of her corset. She was aghast, but pulled off her dress, then her petticoat. She turned her back to him and he ripped at the lacings on her corset and yanked it brutally off her. She gasped, then laughed nervously as she climbed back into her dress, leaving the petticoat and corset on the ground. In a moment she was astride her horse and the two were galloping down the road away from the rising clamor behind them.

Glancing back as they reached the fields, Longarm saw the roof of the barn just catching fire. The flames were leaping skyward, making the yard and the buildings surrounding it as bright as day.

"The poor horses!" cried Emilie.

"I left two men inside. They'll take care of the horses, I reckon." Even as he glanced back he saw the horses crowding frantically out of the barn, the two men driving the animals before them. Others were rushing into the barn for the remaining horses, and a bucket brigade was forming swiftly. Longarm could hear the frantic shouting as men issued orders and others tried to prevent the spooked horses from stampeding out of the compound.

As a diversion, his fire was working perfectly. But he did not know how much time it would buy, and he would much rather have found the mules. Over the terrain they had yet to negotiate, those two army mules would have been more than sufficient. The two horses they were riding seemed hardy enough and were the best he had been able to find in the barn, but they would have to be babied if they were to go the distance.

Even then, it would be shaving it a mite too close for comfort.

Through the night they rode, Longarm having filled all six canteens when they rode through the canyon. Emilie explained the fountain gushing from the wall of the canyon as the work of Elder Wolverton. A revelation had told him that a source of unlimited water—enough to transform a small stream into a broad river—could be obtained at that spot after he had seen a small trickle oozing through a crack in the canyon's wall. Dynamite had done the rest. It was this proof of the infallibility of his revelations that had given Wolverton the leadership of Little Zion.

Daybreak found them riding into a narrow draw. Again Longarm used the presence overhead of birds to tell him whether a stream could be found within it, and again he was right. The two of them pulled up wearily and dismounted. Longarm hobbled the horses after letting them drink their fill at the stream, and then they set up their camp in the shade of a small clump of juniper.

"We'll have to keep going," Longarm told Emilie. "But the horses need this rest, and so do we, I reckon."

"I certainly do, Mr. Longarm," she replied.

"Just call me Longarm, Emilie."

She nodded and he looked her over. She reminded him of her sisters as well as her father. She had his long, patrician features and her eyes had the same appealing wide-eyed quality. Her hair was light. Done tightly into a bun under the bonnet she was wearing, errant strands of it had come loose during the ride and now poked out from under the beak. The skin over her cheekbones was taut and smooth, her mouth firm, her chin strong.

She felt his eyes on her and began to do what she could to smooth her appearance. The dress was a mess and he remembered she no longer wore her corset or petticoat under it. It didn't seem to matter much. She was still as slim as a sapling.

"Sorry we had to get rid of your corset like that," he told her, smiling slightly.

"Oh, please, Longarm. To get out of there, I would gladly have emulated Lady Godiva, I assure you."

"No need for that, Emilie. You'd get a terrible burn in this country."

She laughed appreciatively. "Anyway, it is no chore to ride without that tiresome corset. I do think we wear them too tightly nowadays. I'm never comfortable, really, unless I'm in my night-clothes." She blushed suddenly, aware of what she was saying.

He grinned at her. "Guess I can understand that," he said. "I sure wouldn't want to go around tied up inside one of those things."

She frowned. "Are we safe now, Longarm?"

"Far from it, I'm afraid. We've got a ways to go yet, and most of it in daylight."

Longarm looked over at the horses. They had held up well enough, so far. But he was sure they would begin to wilt under the fierce heat this land generated. He decided he would let them set their own pace as long as their pursuers—and he was certain they were now closing fast—were not on their tails visually. His plan was to reach the desert around nightfall and then make a run for it through the night. If they could reach the water tower by day-break, he was sure he could hold off his pursuers until a Central Pacific train arrived. The approach of a train would, by itself, in-sure that the Avenging Angels would have to pull back. A train-load of witnesses was the last thing Wolverton and his Saints would want.

He looked back at Emilie. In the first light of day she looked incredibly fresh, her eyes glowing with the excitement of their es-cape. Longarm did not want to see that look fade or that excite-ment turn to despair. In that instant he realized that it no longer mattered that he was here because the federal government sent him. He wanted to see Emilie Boggs leave this place because it was what she wanted. And that was all that mattered.

"Let's go," he said softly. "We've got a long ride. For now, let's just let the horses find their own pace. We can't push them. Not yet, anyways."

"I understand, Longarm."

And as he got to his feet and started for the horses, he knew that she did, indeed, understand.

Time was a searing sun boring first into their eyes, then drilling holes in the tops of their heads. They rode slowly, saving the horses, through the same broken land he and Sarah had covered two days before—a rocky, scrambling, treacherous place, with the skeletons

of dead junipers gleaming in the sun. The earth was cut by winding, sheer-walled draws, deceptive and deadly as pitfalls. Flat-
topped buttes propped up the sky on all sides of them. Carved by
the wind and sand, rocky projections loomed menacingly over
them as they rode by, resembling hunchbacked gargoyles, misshapen monsters frozen in the terrible glare of the sun.

Buzzards circled overhead, hopefully, it seemed. He tried not
to notice their shadows as the buzzards passed between them and
the sun, but they did have a way of making Longarm nervous.
There were times when the buzzards seemed to know more than a
man did. He hoped this wasn't one of those times.

They rode on, heads down, the sun beating mercilessly upon
them. The air itself seemed to sear Longarm's cheeks. Only it
was not the air; it was wind-borne sand. By midafternoon a hot
wind had come up. His eyes became scorched and grainy. He
looked over at Emilie. She was trying to ride beside him, but kept
falling back. The freshness was gone from her face, her eyes were
slits. He had given her his bandanna and she wore it now, tied
about the lower portion of her face, but her nose looked raw, and
he wished he still had the goggles he had worn when crossing the
Salt Lake Desert.

He looked back to the trail before him, what there was of it.
Only occasionally could he see dim signs of wagon tracks, but
they were persistent and he never failed to find new tracks as long
as he kept going. When he thought of what those Mormons back
there had gone through to stock and supply their earthly paradise
in the beginning, he felt a grudging respect for their tenacity.

"Longarm!"

He swung about in his saddle. The roan she was riding had
halted, shuddering from neck to flank, head down and trembling.
White ropes of lather dripped from his mouth. He hadn't realized
how far gone her horse was.

Longarm pulled up. "We'd better rest them," he said, "but I
was hoping for some shade, some grass, and some water."

Emilie dismounted. The horse seemed to appreciate that and
straightened somewhat. Longarm dismounted, emptied some water from his canteen into his hat, and held it under the roan's
mouth. The horse emptied the hat in a twinkling and then almost
knocked his hat from his hands in his eagerness for more.

"Just hold it a mite," Longarm told Emilie's horse. "I got to
tend to your partner over here."

When he had taken care of his own mount, Longarm led both

horses into the shade of a rock outcropping, loosened their cinches, and lifted off their saddles. The horses seemed to heave enormous sighs of relief. Then he and Emilie sat down with their backs against a rock. Though its face was now in the shade, it was still quite warm from the sun's rays it had absorbed earlier.

"Do you think we'll make it?" Emilie asked. Her eyes no longer held that excitement they had exhibited before.

"If we find water soon, and if—" Then he looked at her and realized he was singing the wrong tune for this time of day. He laughed. "I reckon it won't do us any good to cross our bridges before we come to them. We'll make it. And that is a promise."

She took a deep breath and leaned her head back against the rock. "I believe you, Longarm. But even if we don't, I want you to know that even this is better than waiting in that terrible hut for that Elder Wolverton to visit me."

"He didn't hurt you, did he?"

"If you mean did he touch me, force himself on me—no, he didn't do that. But he *imposed* himself on me. He harangued me mercilessly, read endlessly to me from the Book of Mormon. And then—when all that was to no avail—he got on his knees before me and pleaded with me, begged me to—" She stopped herself suddenly, unwilling to go on, but quite obviously as appalled by the memory of it as she had been at the time it happened. "I am sorry," she said. "I suppose I should not have revealed that to you. It must be very distressing for you to contemplate the indignities I suffered at their hands."

"It is."

She looked at him and frowned. "I suppose I should have had pity on the man. He seemed in such dire need of me—of the love he craved from me. But I would be his fourth wife—and I am so certain that he must have told every single one of them the same thing." She shook her head in sudden perplexity. "How can a man that old, with that many wives to ease him, still be so needful of a woman?"

"Begging your pardon, Emilie, but I wouldn't want to shock you."

"I want to know, Longarm. It puzzles me deeply. Elder Wolverton seemed in great distress."

"Well, now," Longarm began hesitantly, "seems to me a lot of his problem might be a craving for variety, so as to keep his juices up, if you know what I mean. I guess some old folks just don't like to think they really are old. And like I heard tell once or twice, there ain't nothing that makes a man young again quicker than a young girl, if you'll pardon the expression, so to speak."

She laughed. "You are *so* circumspect, Longarm! It's really quite charming! But honestly, you know, you are not talking to a nun. I am a healthy, intelligent woman who knows a great deal about life—and appreciates every bit of it!"

"That's right sensible, Emilie."

"Yes," she said firmly. "It is. And that's why that old man . . . disgusts me so, may the good Lord forgive me for my lack of charity."

"I reckon He will, Emilie. He's let people go for lots worse, I hear."

She laughed at that and leaned her head impulsively on his shoulder. He liked very much the gentle feel of it and would have preferred to stay in that position until hell froze over—or at least until the sun went down—but he knew they had to keep going.

Gently, he straightened himself. She lifted her head from his shoulder and looked at him.

"Must we go so soon?" she asked.

Longarm nodded. "We've got to keep ahead of our friends, Emilie. They can afford to change mounts and press us hard. They've even got two army mules of mine to really make it tough on us."

He pushed himself erect, reached down, and helped Emilie up. She insisted on helping him saddle the horses, and in the sweltering heat he was grateful for her aid.

They mounted up and rode on for about an hour before Longarm's horse snorted and stomped.

"Smells water," Longarm said, turning back to the girl. "Must be just ahead."

Pure relief flooded the girl's face.

They rode around a bend in the trail they were following and saw the red mud bank of a water hole fed by a thin trickle of water lacing down the polished side of a rock face. They dismounted, filled their canteens, and watered the horses, then mounted up and rode on, the horses now moving at a shambling lope. The rock forms moving past them shimmered in heat waves like coals in a stove. The hot wind blew drifting streamers of dust at them. Longarm kept his head down, his eyes narrowed, but he could not keep the grit out of them. They stung powerfully. Red sand was piled in ribbed dunes against the bleached bones of downed junipers.

Misshapen hulks of rock rose up out of the earth, their surfaces pitted, potholed. The horses stumbled going around them, their shod hooves sliding whenever they tried to cross them. It was tedious going and the horses, Longarm now began to realize, were not going to make it to sundown. And yet they had to keep going.

Surprisingly, it was his horse that went first. Without warning, the horse shuddered and pulled up, head hanging. Wind wheezed from its exhausted lungs on a curiously high note, and the animal crumpled under him. Longarm swung free and landed on his feet beside the horse as it crashed heavily to the ground. The horse lifted its head, then fell back.

As Emilie hurriedly dismounted and stood beside him, he told her, "Best thing I can do is pull off the bridle and loosen the cinch. If he gets his feet under him again, he'll be free of the saddle, anyway."

She nodded, her eyes filled with compassion for the suffering animal.

When he had finished seeing to the horse, he instructed Emilie to sit behind the cantle on her mount while he rode in the saddle. They started up again with her cheek resting against his back, both arms snug around his waist. Despite the discomfort both of them felt because of the heat, Longarm felt surprisingly gentled by this arrangement.

Not long after, the impact of the sun's rays lessened as the buttes now continually passed between them and the lowering sun. Soon Longarm found that the trail they were following had descended to the level of the Salt Lake Desert. The dark, highly polished rock formations shouldering out of the ground were lower, less pocked from the wind and sand. Glancing down at these boulders as he rode past them, he was reminded that he was traveling over what had once been the beach of a vast inland sea. He could almost imagine the restless waters rushing between and over these rocks, smoothing them out, polishing them, while gulls and sea birds of another age rested upon them.

Within sight of the desert, Longarm pulled up. Off to his right, less than half a mile away, he saw a few small buzzards wheeling about a vaguely familiar rock formation. What little was left of Zeke Bannister was providing some nourishment still for the younger buzzards. It was a reminder of what would be waiting for him if he did not succeed in outdistancing his pursuers, and it made him somberly thoughtful on the loss of his mules, especially when he considered the condition of the horse under them at the moment.

He urged the horse into the shadow of some rocks and dismounted, Emilie slipping off the horse first to give him room to swing his leg over the cantle. She smiled wearily up at him as he began to loosen the cinch.

"Is it much farther? I was in a wagon when they brought me to Little Zion. Seems to me I remember a long journey over very flat ground. From the taste of salt in the air, I assumed it was the Great Salt Lake Desert."

Lifting off the saddle, Longarm nodded. "You were right, Emilie—and it's waiting out there for us now. We still got a ways to go."

She peered then at what she could see of the vast salt expanse that extended unbroken as far as the horizon. She appeared to shudder.

"Don't worry," he told her. "If those men after us don't force me, we'll wait until dark before venturing out onto it. There's a water tower on the Central Pacific tracks. We'll make for that."

"How far is it?"

"About thirty miles, I reckon."

"Do you think this horse can carry us that far?"

He looked at her for a long moment, then decided he would lie. "If we don't push him and give him all the rest he needs now. And maybe we can take turns riding him."

That seemed to satisfy her.

He turned his attention back to the horse—and her question returned to him with renewed force. The horse was streaked with dried lather and both his eyes were inflamed from the windblown sand and were running. The saddle-slick on his back was close to becoming one enormous sore. They had rationed their water and he had at least two canteens still set aside for the horse. He asked Emilie for his bandanna, then poured some water into it and squeezed it out onto the horse's slobbering lips and tongue until there was no more moisture left in the bandanna. Then he repeated the process until the horse was able to accept tiny doles of water directly from the canteen. When the horse had finished what was left in the canteen, Longarm hobbled him and let him find what grazing he could on the sparsely covered ground in among the rocks. On tottering legs the horse followed his nose.

By this time Longarm noticed how chilly it had grown. The suddenness of it warned him and he looked back the way he had come, to the west, and saw the long black curtain of a cloud that had drawn itself over the sky, like the wing of some monstrous bird. At about the same time he heard the distant muttering of thunder. Flecks of lightning gleamed in the bowels of the cloud. It was moving with desperate speed and the wind had changed direction. As if it too were confused, it began stirring up wicked dust devils, swirling tiny grains of sand up into their faces. Emilie had been standing beside him when the wind sprang up. She looked at him in dismay. He reached out for her and she buried her face in his shirt. He held her close and moved as close to the rock face as he could, shielding her as best as he could from the sudden fury of the wind.

The chill that came with the storm was surprising in its intensity. Both of them had been wringing wet with sweat from their day's journey through the blistering sun. Now they both shivered from the cold as their wet bodies felt the descending chill. Thunder cracked overhead now. Longarm looked up. The cloud was almost directly overhead. White tendrils were reaching down. Just behind the leading edge of the cloud, he saw a dusty, hazy curtain being dragged along. Rain. Long, lashing tendrils of rain.

There was another crash of thunder and this time it was accompanied by a blinding bolt of lightning—and then another, and still another. The thunder came now in deafening detonations barely seconds apart with the lightning keeping the ground around them bathed in a wildly eerie, almost continuous blue glow. Longarm glimpsed the horse struggling against its hobbles, neck distended, eyes wide in terror, a couple of yards away. It was obviously whinnying frantically, but Longarm could hear nothing except the ceaseless crashing of the thunder.

Emilie cowered against him as both leaned into the rock face for support. And then the rain was upon them. They heard it crashing down upon the hard ground moments before it reached them, sounding like a great faucet had been turned on. At first the rain just stung, then it grew in intensity, causing Emilie to cry out in pain. He bent over her still more, taking as much of the brunt of the lashing rain as possible on his shoulders. He found it difficult to catch his breath, so heavy was the downpour. It was almost as if they were both under water. He heard Emilie gasping for air and pulled back from the rock face to give her a chance to breathe.

And then—almost as swiftly as it had begun—the rain slackened. Drenched completely, Longarm stepped away from the rock and looked around. The horse was some distance from them, but apparently none the worse for his scare. The rain still pounded down and in fact the water on the ground was up past his ankles, but the thunder and the lightning had swept on. A cloudburst, he muttered to himself, was a real fine way to describe these sudden, demented downpours.

Emilie was shivering, her teeth chattering. "Well," she said. "First I was too hot, now I'm too cold. Some country, this, Long-arm."

"I guess I'll just have to agree," he said, admiring her spunk. "I'll see if I can find anything dry in the saddle roll."

He knelt by the saddle and undid the bedroll. A worn soogan was still dry on the inside. He threw it over Emilie's shoulders and soon she was no longer shivering. Then he sat down on a rock while the muddy water swirled about his ankles and watched her. She leaned back against the rock face, the soogan wrapped closely about her, only her face and head sticking out. The water was almost over the tops of her high-heeled, high-button shoes.

"Will this slow them down, do you think?" she called through the heavy rain.

"It should. A cloudburst like this can make those narrow arroyos pretty dangerous. We're lucky it caught us down here."

"Lucky!" She laughed and pulled the soogan tighter about her neck.

In an hour or so the rainfall had become a drizzle that gave way to a shower. The thunder became only a barely audible mutter in the east, the lightning just occasional flashes in the distance that lit up the belly of the storm clouds as they moved on to Salt Lake City. And then the dying rays of the sun transformed the world for a few brief moments before night fell.

They saddled up and rode out onto the Great Salt Lake Desert.

Chapter 5

They were a couple of miles out, at least, when Emilie asked him, "Does it ever end? It just seems to go on forever!"

Her cheek was resting against Longarm's still-damp shirt. He had packed away behind the cantle his sopping jacket and vest. The moon had come up, flooding the desert with its pale, somewhat bluish light. Though Longarm was used to the sight by now, for Emilie it was evidently a brand-new experience.

"Didn't you get a chance to see any of this when they took you to Little Zion?"

He felt her lift her head from his back to speak more easily. "No. Two men sat beside me inside the wagon and wouldn't let me look out once. But I knew we were riding over the Salt Lake Desert. I could taste the salt in the air." He felt her moving her head as she looked all around. "Is that all it is—just table salt?"

"There's clay mixed with it, but not enough to kill the whiteness of it. The glare is fierce in bright sunlight. That's why it's better that we travel across it at night."

She nodded and rested her cheek against his back again, her arms tightening slightly around his waist. This action caused a slight protective urge to stir within him again. He didn't mind it all that much, but it reminded him that he would find it difficult if things went wrong to treat this as just another assignment.

And things could always go wrong; they had a habit of doing just that.

They were heading southeast by Longarm's reckoning and he had expected to catch sight of the Central Pacific's tracks before this. More than once they had had to skirt large puddles of water left by the storm. Riding through brine would raise hell with the horse's hooves, and as it was, the ground was damp enough as a result of the rain to have caused the horse to stumble more than once as its feet broke through the dry crust. All that Longarm felt he could hope for now was for the horse to last at least until they were within sight of the tracks.

Abruptly, Longarm pulled up. The horse obeyed the reins, slowly, woodenly. He felt it tottering slightly under them. Ahead of them was a large pool of water left by the cloudburst. Moonlight flecked its smooth surface. They would have to go around.

"I'd better get off again," Longarm told Emilie, "and lead this feller awhile."

Her muffled assent came to him and he felt her slide off the horse. He swung down and then held the horse while she mounted again. As soon as her feet were secure in the stirrups, he led the horse north, looking for an end to the sudden pond.

Twice within the next hour his boots broke through the salt crust into the water-softened mud beneath. Each time he was forced to use some of the precious water left in his canteen to wash off the brine. Otherwise, he knew, it would dry and soon eat through his boots. By the time he succeeded in skirting the water, he had traveled some distance due east, which meant they had not gotten much closer to the tracks. Cutting southeast again, he noticed how tardily the horse responded to his lead. He glanced back at the horse. His head was drooping. Long tendrils of foam hung from his mouth and striped his chest. He was trembling from withers to hocks.

"You'd better get off," Longarm told Emilie.

She swung off the animal just in time, as the horse went down onto his knees, then toppled sideways. Twice he struggled to regain his feet, his head and neck craning desperately. Then he gave up. Longarm was not surprised, and felt more than a touch of compassion for the horse. He had lasted a good deal longer than Longarm had expected he would, and his only concern now was that the animal not suffer unduly.

He loosened the cinch as he had with the other horse and took off his bridle. If he did manage somehow to get up, he just might make it back to the badlands and water. If he did, of course, and his condition told their pursuers what they wanted to know, that was just too bad. He could not see himself shooting the animal on the strength of that possibility alone. He reached over and pulled the Winchester out of the saddle boot.

Slinging the remaining two canteens over his shoulder, he turned to Emilie. "All we can do now is keep moving until we reach the railroad tracks."

Emilie just nodded as she took her place alongside Longarm. As she trudged beside him, she glanced back a couple of times at the horse. Soon he was lost in the luminous darkness, and then she kept her eyes forward, peering like Longarm into the moonlit, ghostly emptiness of the desert.

Dawn—then full daylight—found them walking across what seemed an ever-broadening expanse of blinding nothingness.

They were flies crossing an immense tablecloth. The sun was a fearsome spider whose shimmering web they were trying desperately to escape. A constant wind blew out of hell, driving fine salt granules into their faces, down their necks, into every exposed crack in their clothing.

Though they had been extremely careful in their use of the remaining canteens, they were unable to keep the salt out of them; and soon this water not only failed to slake their thirst, it increased it. Longarm suggested that they use what remained to cool their necks and wash the salt from their faces. Emilie accepted this without protest and kept on. He was amazed at her stamina. She was matching him stride for stride.

After a while she moved close to him and began talking in a low whisper. Since the only sound was the gentle slap of their feet on the salt surface, he could hear her without difficulty. He wanted to discourage her from wasting the energy that she expended in conversation. But she seemed to need to talk. It was as if she were afraid there would be no time for conversation if they waited much longer, and she felt a need to make a few things clear to him.

She insisted that she was as good a Mormon as Elder Wolverton, that she too had read and studied the Book of Mormon. She believed without question that Angel Moroni had appeared before the prophet Joseph Smith, and that he had died a martyr for all of them. Emilie's grandparents on her father's side had pushed handcarts from Iowa City all the way to Utah and had been among the first to settle in Salt Lake City.

"I can understand," Emilie said, "why plural marriages might have been needed in the beginning to help populate this empty land, but as father says, its usefulness is long since over. We can't expect to join the Union with this practice condoned. Besides, I don't like it—and I don't know many women my age who do."

"I met one who was all for it," Longarm commented dryly. "She was the one who led me to Little Zion."

That silenced Emilie for a while and she trudged along beside him without speaking for some time. At last she sighed. "I've been trying to think why I don't like it," she said to him. "Perhaps I *am* selfish, just as the elder told me I was. But it is something else, too."

"And what might that be?" he asked, squinting down at her through the glare.

"I want it to be like it was with my mother and father. There was no one else for either of them. They had no time for anyone else, and now that my mother is dead, she is still enough for my father. They loved each other very much, and we live by the warmth of that love still, my sisters and I. But how can such a love develop among three or four people? Or even five? How can there really be any closeness? It's just an . . . arrangement, a convenience."

"Not very romantic at that," Longarm commented, smiling despite the heat and the awesome dryness of his face.

"Besides," Emilie continued, her voice hoarse now, but straining with eagerness to express herself to Longarm, "I want to choose my own husband, not have someone choose him for me. I want to have *my* revelations." She smiled up at him then, a brave effort indeed, considering how blistered her pale face had become from the heat.

"Well now, I reckon you will have, sure enough."

"If we can just keep on walking. Is that right, Longarm?"

He placed his hand in the small of her back and gently supported her as she walked. She had begun to stumble. "That's right, Emilie. If we can just keep on picking them up and laying them down."

She said nothing for a long while, and then sighed wearily. "Oh, Longarm, where *are* those tracks?"

"Just ahead," he told her. And he meant it.

For some time he had been denying the evidence of his senses. His tortured eyes had seemed to be torturing his brain, feeding him evidence of something out there on the horizon when all the while it was only another mirage, another shimmering lie. But this time he was sure of what he was seeing. The tracks seemed suspended in midair, but there was no mistaking the telegraph poles and the gleaming wires strung between them. The distortion caused by the heat mirage caused the poles and even the lines to appear uncommonly outsized for long moments at a time. But the tracks remained, fading at times, then looming toward him—but remaining always, persisting.

"Yes!" Emilie cried. "I see them! I see them!"

They both pulled up then and took a deep breath. They still had a long way to go yet, though the distortion caused by the heat created the illusion that the tracks were much closer than they were. Nevertheless, they had something solid now toward which they could move.

"I tell you," Longarm confided in Emilie as he started up, "for a while there, I had the foolish notion I wasn't moving at all. My legs were going and I was leaving tracks, sure enough—but everything else was standing still and laughing at me."

Emilie laughed. "I know," she said. "That's just how I felt."

They walked on for what seemed another hour at least. The sun that had been searing the backs of their necks was sitting atop their heads. The glare had increased to such a level that they no longer tried to see through it to the tracks. It was when Emilie staggered for the third time and he reached out to steady her that he noticed something to the right of her.

"What's that?" he asked, peering into the glare.

She looked but did not reply, and he did not need her guess. He knew. It was just a crowd of moving dots for now, but soon enough he would see the individual riders. Longarm and Emilie stood there and waited for what seemed like an eternity, peering into the shimmering glare. At last the riders became separate images wavering in the heat. Abruptly, it seemed, they appeared enormously large, grotesquely misshapen as they loomed out of the trembling air. Longarm heard the jingle of their bits.

"Oh, Longarm!" Emilie cried. "It's them! They have caught us!"

"Get down," Longarm told her.

As Emilie dropped to the desert floor, Longarm pulled out his Colt and fired into the air. The reverberation from his single shot was stunning in its intensity. The sound of it rolled like a cannon shot over the gleaming desert.

The riders pulled up in a sudden confusion of horses and men. Longarm heard discussion, but could make little of it. He heard the unhappy whinnying of impatient horses. And then at last someone disengaged himself from the crowd of men and horses and started to walk toward them, the curtain of heat causing him almost to disappear at times.

For a long while he walked and then, suddenly, he was in full sight, as clear as an etching, a white handkerchief attached to the barrel of his rifle. As he walked closer, Longarm saw riders pulling away from the group, spreading out to encircle him. The fellow continued toward Longarm.

"It's Elder Wolverton!" Emilie cried.

"Stop right there!" Longarm called.

The elder pulled up obediently. "We've been following your trail for miles," he called. "Now we're between you and the tracks and in a moment you will be surrounded! Surely you must see the futility of your present position."

"It ain't futile as long as I got this Winchester and sixgun."

"There are more than two dozen men at my back, Longarm. You'll get some of us, but we'll surely get you."

Longarm could not deny the logic of Wolverton's assertion. With his rifle he could keep them well back, but they had rifles also. And in this blasted heat and glare, he could not be sure of distances. It would be like shooting smoke. They would have the same difficulty, but it would be madness to think he could out-shoot all those men now encircling him.

And in such an exchange the chance of Emilie taking a bullet would be alarmingly high. Longarm assumed that the reason the Avenging Angels hadn't already opened up on him as they had on Zeke Bannister was the presence of the elder's bride-to-be.

Still, Longarm liked to play poker, and a good poker player should know how to bluff. "I don't care about that!" he called back. "I'll be happy to take a few of you with me—if that's the only chance I've got! And you'll be first, Elder!"

"And what of Emilie? Do you want her shot in the exchange? Is this how you rescue her from us?"

"She doesn't want to go back and I don't blame her. You can solve this nicely, Elder Wolverton, by simply backing off. Let Emilie and me go!"

"She is to be my bride! I have seen it!"

"Well, she ain't seen it—and she won't. You'd best try and have another revelation, Elder."

"Emilie!" the elder cried. "Listen to me! It is written that you and I will wed! We are destined for each other! Stop this foolish-ness and come back with me. I will make you first among my wives! You will stand by my side as I sweep the apostates from our church!"

Emilie got to her feet. "Does that mean you will sweep my fa-ther from the church's councils?" Her anger was fierce.

"Your father will be one of us. He will be my father-in-law! You see, it will all be well if you will just come back with me."

Emilie looked with despair at Longarm. She was torn. He shook his head at her.

"Get back to your Eden, Wolverton," Longarm called, "and take your Avenging Angels with you. This is one Mormon girl you ain't going to buffalo."

"Stay out of this, Longarm!"

"I'm in, Wolverton. All the way."

"You are a fool!"

"Maybe. But at least I don't go having dreams about women I want and then go out and kidnap them—and call it revelation!"

"You are an apostate—a godless gentile and you do not understand. I forgive you, Longarm. But my patience is wearing thin!"

"Hell, Wolverton, mine's already run out." He lifted his rifle. "I've got a bead on you right now. You call off your so-called Angels and I'll let you walk back to your horse and ride out of here."

"Pull that trigger and you and Emilie die with me. My men have their orders. But you see, it will not come to pass that way. I have already seen how it will be, and nothing you can do, Longarm, can alter that revelation. You're bluffing, Longarm. But I am not!"

Longarm looked around him. The riders had circled them completely by that time, and there were indeed more than a couple of dozen. Elder Wolverton was not taking lightly this expedition to retrieve Emilie. "Well, hell," Longarm said, levering a cartridge into the firing chamber of his Winchester. "I might as well take you with us, then. I sure ain't going to let you talk this young woman here into going back to a fanatic like you!"

As he raised the rifle to his shoulder, Elder Wolverton raised his hand to stay Longarm's trigger finger.

"Now, just a minute, Longarm! Let me speak again to Emilie! This is her decision to make. It is, after all, her life we are bargaining for!"

Longarm let his rifle down a little and turned to Emilie. "You want to talk to him?"

She nodded.

"Talk, Wolverton! But you'd better make it good."

"Emilie, listen. This man, you, and I myself will soon be dead if you do not let good sense overcome your natural reluctance to wed a man my age! If you will not think of yourself or of me, think of him. He has come far to save you and is a brave man. I promise you I will not have him killed if you will step forward now and return with me."

"It is not your age! It is everything about you! I prefer to die here!"

"You prefer that he die as well?" Wolverton asked.

Emilie looked up at Longarm, her face revealing how torn she was at that moment.

"Damn you, Wolverton!" Longarm said, bringing up his rifle again.

"His freedom!" Wolverton cried. "I promise you, Emilie. He

will live! We will not kill him if you will return with me. My patience is nearing its end. I am not accustomed to begging. It is only because of what I know that I persevere in this matter. Think of that man standing beside you. Think of him if you will not think of yourself."

"I will go back!" she cried.

"No," Longarm said.

"It is all over, Longarm," Wolverton told him. "Put down that rifle. Be a gentleman. Stand aside. The woman has made her choice. She still has not accepted me and she may never do so. That will be her choice to make. But no matter, it is no longer your concern. Be sensible and stand aside."

"And if I do?"

"You have my word that no harm will come to you."

"Your word?"

"Do you imagine that I would break my word with Emilie on hand to witness such a deed? It is a foolish way, indeed, to impress the woman one wishes to join in Celestial Marriage. She has my word—as have you."

"You'll let me return to Salt Lake City?"

"I did not say that. I said I would not kill you. And I will not."

"What will you do?"

"I will leave you alone on this desert at some distance from the railroad tracks. You will, in short, have very little chance of making it to safety. But this way you will have a fighting chance. Otherwise, Longarm, I would not give much for your chances of surviving this adventure."

"No!" cried Emilie. "You can't just leave him out here to die! I won't go back with you!"

"Let *him* decide."

Longarm looked at Emilie. He smiled and spoke quietly to her. "You can still refuse him when you get back there. I'll take this chance. It's the best deal we can get, I'm thinking."

"You might die out here!"

"I won't die. And I promise you, Emilie, I'll come for you again. And this time I'll make it stick."

"That's a promise?"

He nodded.

She looked then at Wolverton. "All right," she said wearily. "I'm thirsty and very tired. Do you have a horse for me?"

Wolverton smiled at Longarm. "We have better than that. We

have two fine army mules you were kind enough to deliver to Little Zion personally."

Longarm's captors not only had his two mules, they also had a wagon filled with water barrels and a remuda of spare mounts. They took Longarm's Winchester, his Colt, and his derringer, the latter along with his watch and chain. Then he and Emilie were allowed to mount the mules. For the rest of that day they rode steadily due north into the heart of the Great Salt Lake Desert. By nightfall they had covered close to thirty miles.

They pulled up then and Longarm was told to dismount. As he got off the mule, he asked for a couple of canteens filled with clear water. He addressed his request to Wolverton and for a moment the man looked as if he was about to refuse it. Then he looked at Emilie. Her face was livid at his indecision.

"All right, Longarm," the elder said. "You may have your water. Fat lot of good it will do you."

At that Emilie slid down off her mule and ran to Longarm. "I'll stay with you," she cried. "Let me!" She flung both arms around him and hugged him fiercely, pressing her face into his chest.

He disengaged her gently and looked into her face. Tears were in her eyes. "You just go back with that old man and wait for me, hear?"

She nodded bravely, aware as he was just how far-fetched such a hope had to be. But Longarm understood. Sometimes a man needs a big fat lie to believe in. And both of them needed this lie in particular.

Impulsively, she reached up, pulled his face down, and kissed him on the lips. Then she turned and ran back to the mule. Longarm caught the face of the elder in that moment and saw it go raw with shock and jealousy. The old goat probably had all kinds of notions as to what had gone on between the two of them since leaving Little Zion, but there was no way to prevent him from thinking that. And protesting that it wasn't so would not help Emilie much.

A sweat-streaked rider urged his horse close and dropped two full canteens at Longarm's feet, then pulled his horse around and rode back to the wagon. Emilie climbed back up onto the mule. Longarm's mule was caught up by another rider and led to the wagon, where its reins were tied to the rear of it.

"Good-bye, Longarm," said the elder. "May this be a fore-
taste of the hell and damnation that will be your certain reward!"

He pulled his horse around and with a stroke of his, arm,
turned the rest of the riders about. Longarm watched them ride
off for a long while. It took almost forever, it seemed, for them to
grow smaller in the distance, and their presence on the flat expanse was a comfort of a kind. And then, with a suddenness that
startled him, the entire party was swallowed up by the horizon,
though occasionally the clean sound of a bit jingling, the squeak
of the wagon's axle, came sharply across the vast emptiness.

He looked about him. The westering sun was sitting on the
horizon, a monstrous, swollen red eye. The crimson light it shed
turned the desert floor and the sky overhead a salmon pink. A
cool breeze touched his face and neck. Slowly, he turned completely around, his eyes searching an incredibly flat horizon that
for the first time was not a maddeningly undulating, shimmering
mirage.

He paused a moment and squinted. There was something on
the horizon, almost due north of his present position. He waited
for it to disappear, to flicker. But it sat there solidly. He took a few
steps toward it in his eagerness to see it more clearly, but it made
little difference. Then he stood stock-still and concentrated on
picking out details.

At last he was fairly certain what it was he was looking at—
the roof of a building. It was incredible, but that was precisely
what it looked like to him. The sun was dropping rapidly now, but
its rays still enclosed the projection and for just an instant the
roof stood out clearly. Then the sun dipped out of sight and whatever it was vanished, winked out like a lamp being turned off.

Longarm went back for the canteens. He hefted them. They
were full. He opened one and took a tiny sip. The water was clean;
that much, at least, the elder had given him. He frowned and looked
once more in the direction where he had seen that roof. Could the
man have been more human than Longarm had thought? Had
some sense of decency convinced the elder to leave Longarm
within sight of help? There was no doubt that whatever it was
Longarm saw was one hell of a distance from where he was
standing at the moment, but if he was careful with his consumption of these two canteens, he just might make it. Had the elder
given him at least that much of a sporting chance?

There was, Longarm realized, only one way to find out. Slinging the two canteens over his shoulder, he set out due north, hoping that as the night fell, he did not begin to trace a vast circle. He would have to rely on the stars.

Longarm drove himself on through most of the night, but well before dawn he had collapsed to the moonlit floor of the desert, a stumbling, shambling wreck, curled into a ball to keep out the bone-deep chill, and fallen asleep. When the sun reappeared on the other side of the world and sent its fingers of light probing at him, Longarm stirred, feeling like some worm that had been caught on a vast boardwalk after a night's rain.

He pulled his canteens to him. One was nearly empty. He shook it unhappily and struggled to his feet. For a moment he experienced some difficulty in standing erect. It was as if the sun were pushing him back down. He realized his hat had fallen off. He bent over to get it and put the hat carefully back on his head. He felt a little giddy and drank what was left in the nearly empty canteen.

And almost threw it back up. The pain in his stomach was knifelike. He doubled over and fought to keep the water down. At last the gagging subsided. For the first time he realized how hungry he was, how dried out. He wiped the tears out of his eyes and tossed away the empty canteen. That left him with only one full canteen of water to make it to . . . where?

The night before, he had been heading for a rooftop he had glimpsed on the horizon. Looking around him now, his narrowed eyes saw nothing but shimmering heat waves and the reflections of the blue sky just below the horizon line. Water. Cool water. Of course it wasn't. There was nothing out there. Nothing.

Except death, in the form of a fiery hand that was waiting to squash him with one merciless swat.

How you do run on, he told himself sardonically. *Now just brace yourself and remember what you told that girl—and get after that there roof. It's out there somewhere. You saw it, and it's there. And where there's a roof, there's a settlement.*

Perhaps he was looking in the wrong direction. What *was* the right direction? The sun hung halfway up the sky, not quite at full blast yet. So that was the east. Turning carefully, Longarm looked back, squinting into the white glare. He saw how his tracks had been tracing a pronounced drift westward, instead of due north. He turned himself carefully, as if he were steering a stubborn mule, and began walking.

He found comfort while he walked in looking back every now

and then to see how straight a track he was leaving—and to assure himself that he was indeed covering ground, that this was not some nightmare in which no matter how far you walked, you found you were still in the same place. The passage of time was marked clearly by the steady climb of the sun until at last it was almost directly overhead. The glare caused the ground around him to fairly dance. He kept his eyes as narrow as possible in an effort to keep out the glare. But it was impossible. He walked for a while with his eyes closed, but he began stumbling and the white glare beat upon his closed lids like a fist.

He took a sadistic delight in not drinking any of the water in his remaining canteen. He told himself he would not take a sip until he was sure he was on the track of that settlement he had glimpsed. At last, as the sun began to slip down the western portion of the sky, he saw once again—and this time with much greater clarity—what appeared to be a portion of a shingled roof. It now seemed to hang there in front of him just above the horizon. He even imagined he could see light gleaming through chinks in the roof. He attributed that to mirage, however. He did not want the roof to be anything but solid.

He stopped then and slowly, dramatically unscrewed the cap of his canteen and carefully allowed a few drops of the water to fall upon his tongue. He swallowed this carefully, then allowed himself a small trickle. With a smile, he screwed the cap back on and continued his trek, his steps firmer, his shoulders back.

It was close to midafternoon before he reached the buildings. Well in advance of getting there, he realized he had been the target of a devilish humor, the butt of a malicious, possibly fatal joke. He would have reached the place a full half-day sooner, he realized, if he had not drifted almost due west during the night, for when he finally approached the place, he found himself coming at it from the west. But that didn't matter at all. It made no difference whether he came at it from the south or from the west.

There was nothing for him to reach, only a battered cluster of frame shacks with all the roofs but one fallen in, the walls leaning, the window frames out. He had been thinking about it during the last quarter-mile of his trek, trying to figure out what it could once have been, standing out here in the middle of the Great Salt Lake Desert, and he wondered if perhaps it was an old Pony Express station, one of those that had been abandoned back in the sixties when the telegraph lines had been put through to the coast.

The closer he got, the more certain he became, that this was indeed what he was approaching. He saw what was left of a Conestoga freight wagon behind one of the three frame buildings still standing, and through one of the open sides of a barn, he could see the horse stalls, a single wooden bucket hanging on a nail.

Hope stirred within him that this station had not had to have its water supplied by tank wagons, that this one had managed to dig a well and that the well might still be functioning. At last, stumbling into the station, he reached out and grabbed hold of a corner of the most solid building, and hung on. The shade provided by the building was blessed. He felt better at once and looked around, hoping for some sign of that well. He circled the station.

No structure was solid. No wall was straight or without its gaping holes. Sun-bleached timbers and warped planking leaned crazily one way or the other. The buildings were ghostly skeletons, through which he looked in vain for any signs of a well. At last he admitted the futility of such a hope. There was no well.

He slumped slowly to the ground, his back to a wall facing the Conestoga wagon, and listened to the aimless flapping of the wagon tarp as it beat against the ribs of the battered hulk. The freight wagon was buried up to its hubs in drifted salt dust, the flapping canvas half rotted away. As he looked at the wagon, the hope within him died. He had only the water left in his canteen. By leaving him within sight of this abandoned Pony Express station, Elder Wolverton had cunningly managed to see to it that all of Longarm's remaining energy would be expended in going the wrong way.

It galled Longarm to realize how effective the elder's strategy had been. And when he recalled his brave words to Emilie, he stirred fretfully, then slowly, judiciously, unscrewed the cap of his canteen and let the smallest possible amount trickle onto his swollen tongue. He would husband every drop. He would hang on as long as he could. He would not join the ghostly hulk rotting in front of him until the last possible moment. Somewhere he had heard that where there was life there was hope, and Longarm believed it.

He had been in worse scrapes than this, he told himself. Then he chuckled softly, dryly. If he had, he really couldn't remember when or where.

Night fell like a benediction. The flapping of the canvas ceased, finally. The stars gleamed brightly, swarming like dust across the heavens. He leaned his head back against the wooden wall and drank in the sight. After a moment he took another sip of his water and just managed to secure the canteen before he fell into an exhausted sleep.

It was the flapping of the canvas that woke him. The eastern sky was bright with the coming sun. He watched it for a moment, then pulled himself to his feet. Perhaps there was something in one of the buildings he could use to fashion a signal with. He thought then of a fire, smoke signals.

This thought gave him a fleeting hope, but even as he considered it, wandering hopelessly through the ravaged buildings, he knew it was a foolish plan. Who would see the smoke? And seeing it, who would care? And if anyone cared, how would they get out to where he was? How many could invest in army mules for the sole purpose of rescuing luckless deputy U.S. marshals who got themselves stranded in the middle of the Great Salt Lake Desert?

They would need a magic carpet, he told himself, his thoughts moving sluggishly, foolishly inside his addled head. Bending, he found an old, rusty toolbox. With nothing better to do, he managed to pry up its rusted lid. He found a hammer, two screwdrivers, a bent square, a plane with no razor in it, a couple of boxes of nails, and a small hand ripsaw.

He straightened and looked around him. If he wanted to, with all this loose lumber lying about, he could build himself an outhouse. If he had a shovel, that is, to dig the hole.

He did not like the joke. He kicked shut the toolbox and worked his way aimlessly out of the shed where he had found it. The shed had obviously served as a makeshift blacksmith shop when the station had been in operation. He found a coal shuttle, and under salt drifts, pieces of coal. If he got cold, he would be able to warm himself. Moving out of the shed, he investigated the two other buildings. He imagined that what had been the stable still smelled, however faintly, of horse manure, but the drifted salt, like ageless snow, covered everything.

The sun was higher when he returned to the freight wagon and inspected it. The canvas tarpaulin slapped at him a couple of times, catching him across the face and neck, aggravating his scorched and blistered skin. He tried to rip it down, but could not in his weakened state. The wind, blowing steadily toward the center of the desert, tugged on it relentlessly. He inspected the axles idly. Without a horse, it made no difference what the condition of the axles was. The rear axle, he found, was broken, the spring hanging from the wooden frame and almost completely buried in the salt dust. As the sun climbed higher, he crawled in under the wagon for the shade.

He was going to die, he thought finally, without fear or panic. It was just a cold, solid, uncompromising fact. Perhaps he would die under this wagon, with only the flapping tarp to protect him from the buzzards.

Only there were no buzzards this far out. They weren't as foolish as deputy U.S. marshals.

He closed his eyes and tried to ignore the dryness of his mouth, the ache in the pit of his stomach—and the damned flapping of that canvas. He opened his eyes. If only the blamed thing would flap with some kind of regularity, like a clock. But it would be still for a while, perfectly still, then it would start flapping rapidly, causing the entire wagon to shudder along with it. With a sigh, Longarm crawled out from under the wagon and found a spot inside one of the buildings. He doled out a small taste of water, rolled it luxuriously around in his mouth, then swallowed it. For a few moments he wondered if it wouldn't be a good idea to swallow the entire contents of the canteen and be done with it. What was the sense in prolonging matters?

But he didn't like himself when he started thinking like that and slowly, firmly screwed the cap back onto his canteen and placed it carefully down beside him. The heat was stifling in the building and large, irregular bands of sunlight traversed his body as he lay there—but at last he slept.

When he awoke, the sun had almost set—and the flapping tarp was silent. It was the absence of that constant flapping that had awakened him. And it had stopped because the hot wind had ceased to blow.

He reached for his canteen—and frowned suddenly.

Without touching the canteen he struggled to his feet, stepped over the rotting timbers and planks, and left the building to stare at the freight wagon—and the now limp tarpaulin.

Hell! Sails drive ships! Windmills pump water out of the ground. Maybe he couldn't build himself a magic carpet, but he sure as hell could build himself something a whole hell of a lot more sensible—a land yacht!

He laughed, and found he couldn't laugh. He didn't have enough moisture in his mouth. All he succeeded in doing was cracking his lips. He went back into the building for his canteen.

Sipping carefully on the neck of the canteen, letting the moisture seep into his mouth, he considered once again his brainstorm.

Did he have tools? Yes, he had tools. How many wheels would he need? He could get by with two, and those he had—plus an axle. And of course he had the sail—a stubborn tarpaulin that had been nagging him since the moment he arrived. Yes, if he had the strength left, he could build it.

He went looking for that toolbox. God damn it! Of course he had the strength to build it!

Chapter 6

Longarm worked by the light of the moon, preferring it without hesitation to the fierce impact of the sun. It made things difficult at times, however, since he had trouble making accurate measurements in the dim light and cut himself repeatedly whenever he wielded the saw. Though the saw he had found in the toolbox was next to worthless, it was a saw and it did cut, and with it he was able to cut through the wagon's struts, freeing the tarp.

After that, his biggest problem was digging out the wheels from the drifts of salt and sand and beneath that, the clay. He broke the handle of the hammer while using it to free the spring, but with the spring he was able to gain enough leverage to lift the bed of the wagon off the broken rear axle. The rusted spring was an awkward crowbar and its rusted, pitted surface cut into his hands. His blood turned the rust into a sticky mess that made it almost impossible for him to handle the spring. But he persisted, and when at last he had swung the bed of the wagon free of the rear axle, he was so weak he was trembling from exhaustion and decided to take a break.

He slumped down against a wall and studied his progress so far, contemplating what he had yet to accomplish.

As near as he could figure, one of his biggest problems would be the mast. He would have to get rid of the wagon's sides to lighten it and strip the bed as close to a triangle as he could get it. The front wheels of the wagon he could still use. For a rear caster he would have to contrive a springy pole of some kind. Without a rudder or the ability to tack, he would just be able to sail downwind, but downwind should take him to the Central Pacific tracks. Yessir. That tarp, rigged as a square sail, would sure carry him along. For braking he would just have to use both feet on the rims of the wheels as long as the soles on his boots held out. But he would worry about stopping after he got the damn thing to go.

That mast, now. How the hell was he going to fasten it to the floor of the platform? How was he going to anchor it? He would need guy wires to steady it and a spar from which to hang the tarp. And nails. He would need sturdy nails that could be driven. Those he had found so far had crumbled into red powder at the slightest handling, or snapped or bent double when struck. He was sure it was the incredibly corrosive effect of all this salt. And

that hammer bothered him. He needed it. He would have to con-
struct a new handle for it, first thing.

Longarm closed his eyes, letting the cool wind blow over his
brow. Thoughts of his eventual ride aboard his land yacht crowded
in upon him. His mouth was as dry as old tinder and he meant to
reach out for his canteen. But his arm was heavy, his will weak.
Longarm slept.

When he awoke he felt as light and insubstantial as the tinder-
dry boards flapping in the hot wind about him. The sun was well
above the eastern horizon, impaling him with its relentless eye.
Longarm struggled to his feet, as weak as a kitten. Any movement of his lips caused them to crack. He felt of his face. It was
blistered and painful to touch. Both of his hands were swollen
and raw from the night's work.

Steadying himself by reaching out and grabbing hold of the
wall, he looked through the glare at the freight wagon and tried to
regain the enthusiasm he had felt the night before. It was difficult.
All Longarm felt at the moment was an incredible weariness.
And thirst, a terrible, unslakable thirst.

He might as well be attempting to finish that Mormon temple
single-handedly.

Finding a shady spot in one of the buildings, he slumped down,
unscrewed the cap to his canteen, and took small, careful swallows.
He felt a little better after that and looked about him. He was in
the building that had served as the horse barn. Hanging on a nail
from the wall facing him was the wooden bucket he had spied
earlier. It was in surprisingly good shape and was a large bucket
with sloping sides. It looked reasonably tight and still well-
caulked.

The idea didn't come to him all at once—but it came, and that
was the important thing. He would knock a hole in the bottom of
the bucket, stick the mast through it, and nail the bucket to the
floor of the wagon. The bucket would serve as an anchor for the
mast, and strips of canvas could serve as guy lines.

He struggled to his feet and lifted down the bucket. As he examined it and felt its solidity, he regained some of his enthusiasm.
He took a deep breath and looked around him with eyes inflamed,
and realized that he had damned well better be enthusiastic about
this crazy idea of his. The alternative was to finish the canteen and
die here, with not even the buzzards caring enough to pick his
bones clean.

Slowly, doggedly, Longarm set to work. His first task was to find a piece of wood he could use as a new handle for his hammer. It was a maddening job. The handle had broken off inside the head and clearing it was almost impossible. He had to use the wagon spring to drive the new handle through the head opening. By noon, however, he had himself a new hammer and had found enough nails—from the roofs, mostly—to begin to fasten the mast onto the bed of the wagon.

First he knocked a slit in the bottom of the bucket through which he intended to slip the board he would use for the mast; then he nailed the bucket, top down, to the bed of the wagon. The board he selected for the mast was hanging loosely from one of the walls and was more than twelve feet long. He nailed a spar across it to hold the sail, narrowed the board somewhat with his wretched saw, then drove the board down through the slit in the bucket's bottom. He contrived it so that the tip of the board would wedge itself between the boards used as flooring for the wagon. Though the mast leaned slightly forward, it stood solidly, already tugging slightly in the hot wind—an encouraging sign.

It was well past noon by this time and Longarm clambered down off the wagon to look at his mast and take another sip of water. He did not like the light heft of the canteen as he lifted it to his lips and forced himself to take less water than he had counted on.

He wanted to rest, to lean back in the shade and contemplate what he had already accomplished, but he did not allow himself this luxury. From somewhere in his past came the words of an old prospector: The only way to get an impossible job done is to go at it like you never figured it was going to end—and don't expect it to now. Then one day you'll look up and find it finished. And you hadn't even noticed.

Deciding he would tear strips from pieces of the tarpaulin for guying the mast later, he headed resolutely for the wagon spring and picked it up, climbed back up onto the wagon, and began swinging the spring like a crowbar, knocking out the sides of the wagon. He was so weak by this time that he sometimes had to swing twice at the same spot to break through. He kept at it doggedly, however, and when he had cleared away the sides, he sank to the floor of the wagon, the rusty, bloody spring leaning across his shoulder, and contemplated what he had yet to do.

The back corners of the wagon, he realized, would create too much drag and would prevent him from moving straight before the wind. In addition to the rear caster he still had to fashion, he would have to cut back the rear width of the wagon bed. That meant sawing it, and failing that, simply knocking the boards off. He stood up shakily, and heaving the spring over the side, let himself gently down from the wagon and went in search of the saw.

He found it with no trouble and clambered weakly back up onto the bed of the wagon and began sawing. The saw bucked and caught and behaved like a wild thing infuriated with the use to which it was being put. With his tortured eyes shut most of the time, his face baking in the torrid rays of the westering sun, Longarm persisted and by sundown had hacked and sawn away the left side of the wagon. Remembering grimly those words of the prospector, he continued sawing—his hands bloodied, his wrists and the lower portions of both arms lacerated—until he had cut away the right portion of the wagon bed as well.

Flinging the saw from him, he jumped down from what was left of the wagon and turned to look at his handiwork. The moon was no longer as high or as bright as it had been during previous nights, and in the dim gloom Longarm could see only that he had managed somehow to hack and tear the wagon to pieces. The result of his day's labor gave him little hope. Only the mast, no longer as straight as when he had first set it into the bucket, gave him any cause for optimism. Still, what was left of the wagon bed did indeed resemble a kind of ragged triangle—and that, after all, was what he had intended.

So what's next? He asked the question of himself in a kind of raw fever, standing in the cool night and trembling slightly from head to toe. The hacked wagon and the leaning walls of the station appeared to be dancing slightly, while the night air seemed almost palpable with ghostly forms. He kept thinking he was not alone—that some malevolent force was just waiting to pounce on him from out of the vast, pale darkness that surrounded him. He twitched nervously whenever a slight wind caused a hanging board to creak or slam.

He knew he was alone. He knew he was imagining things. But it did him no good to reassure himself in this fashion. The way he figured it, his brain was drying out just like every other cell in his body.

So what's next, old son?

Tear strips from the tarp and use them to steady the mast. But be sure you leave some of the tarpaulin, since you've been thinking of it for your sail. Remember? Yes, I remember.

He realized he was talking to himself.

He shook his head in disbelief and walked over to the tarp where it was lying on the ground. Tearing the strips was not easy. The damned thing was a lot tougher than it looked. He stuck to the torn sections, and staggering about drunkenly, finally managed to rip free enough strips to use for the lines. He twisted the canvas strips to strengthen them and then tied them around the mast until he had four strips hanging from the mast, two on each side. Then he went looking for his hammer and the pile of nails he had gathered.

He got lost.

Chuckling to himself, he straightened up and looked back at the station and the crazy land yacht out in back of it. He knew the hammer and nails were not out here in the middle of the Great Salt Lake Desert, unless someone had sneaked in and taken them out here to confuse him. He pondered that notion for a while, then shrugged and shambled back to the station.

It was luck—sheer luck—when his disintegrating boots struck the hammer as he returned to the station. Feeling around on the ground, he found five nails. He clambered wearily up onto the deck and hammered the four strips to the floor, securely guying the mast.

He didn't want to fasten the tarpaulin to the yardarm. Not yet. He didn't want it hanging lifelessly while he worked on the tail skid. He had been considering for some time in the back of his mind what he should look for and had wondered if there might not be some old pitchforks, or at least some handles, buried under the drifts of salt in the stable building. Such a handle would provide just the right amount of spring.

He went inside and began kicking at the salt dust with his boots. He thought he felt something and dropped to his hands and knees and began digging with his hands. The salt ate into his torn hands and he pulled back, finally. He leaned against the wall of the stable, closed his eyes . . . and slept.

He awoke with the sun almost directly overhead. Every muscle and bone in his body was sore. He didn't dare move his lips. He felt like he was burning up, and when he looked at his hands, he saw they were shaking. He figured maybe he had the Saint Vitus' dance.

Well now, we'll see about that, old son.

Feeling like he was a hundred and sixty years old and being asked to run to California and back for his breakfast, Longarm struggled to his feet, tried to blink the blinding sunlight out of his eyes, and looked around, recalling dimly what he had been up to for the past two or three days. How many days had it been, at that?

Two? Three? A week?

He shook his head to rid himself of the nagging riddle and forced himself to remember what he had been doing when he fell asleep. That crazy sonofabitching land yacht. That's what he had been up to—and now all he needed was a nice, long, springy pole for a rear caster. Well now, nothing to that. Let's see now. No problem at all.

Longarm spied the canteen lying in a patch of brilliant sunlight. So bright was the glare off the canteen that he had to avert his eyes. He forgot about the land yacht, then, and stumbled for the canteen. Snatching it off the ground, he shook it, a sinking sense of disaster in the pit of his stomach. The canvas covering had long since rotted off it and the canteen had been sitting in the blazing sun—with its cap on the ground beside it.

Lifting it to his mouth, Longarm felt only a tiny trickle of warm moisture fall upon his tongue. He held it up a moment longer, waiting, but nothing more came out of the hot, empty canteen. He flung it from him. It bounced off the front wheels of the wagon and came to rest in the broiling salt dunes.

He slumped down in the shade of the wall he favored and stared listlessly before him. He knew he had to get up and told himself that soon he would. Not really certain how long he sat there, he found himself moving sluggishly at last, as the sun probed at his face from a different angle. He shook his head and looked up at the deck and the crooked mast.

What was it he had to do next? The answer came slowly. He had been looking for the handle of a pitchfork, or some other such implement that might have been left behind when the former occupants cleared out of this place. The night before, he had thought he felt something beneath his feet over there where the stable had been. He pulled himself erect and went back to the spot. He kicked at the ground with his feet. A small handle was protruding from the salt dust. He reached down and yanked it loose. The tines had all been broken off, but five feet of the handle remained.

It wouldn't be long enough unless he attached it to a board. He went looking for one, stumbling, shambling, forgetting at times what it was he needed. He found a board that would do nicely and then spent an interminable time looking for a hammer. After he had found the hammer, he realized dimly that he needed nails. That stumped him for a while until he remembered how he had gotten the other nails he had used before. He clambered up the side of a

building, and with the claw of his hammer, pulled from the boards
a few more nails that had escaped the salt and the moisture. He
must have lost more than he kept as they eased out of the dry wood,
but he paid no heed and it seemed for a while that he had been per-
forming this strange activity as long as he could remember. At last
he came down and counted the nails more than once, unable to remember clearly what he wanted to do with them.

At last, in a kind of daze, during which he had to remind
himself repeatedly what he was doing, he sawed off the broken
tines from the handle, then nailed the handle to the board he had
found, bending the nails around the handle to secure it. Then he
thought a long while, considering his next move. It was, he finally decided, necessary to lift the rear of the deck, using the
spring as a lever, so that he could attach the caster to the deck.
It took an interminable time for him to work the spring in under
the deck and prop it up, using one of the rear wheels. But he
couldn't keep it up. At one point he found himself lying on his
back on the salt crust, looking up at the bottom of the deck, the
spring lying across his midsection.

Finally he managed to fasten the board to the back of the deck
with a few minutes of hard hammering. He kicked the spring to
one side and the deck sagged down onto the caster. The caster
held, the end of the handle sinking only an inch or so into the hard
salt surface. The greatest amount of sag, however, was where the
handle was joined to the board. If it snapped, that would be the
place. But he realized it was no good thinking of that.

Now it was time for the sail. He had some difficulty locating it,
even though it was where it had been ever since he had removed it
from the wagon. When he found it, he grabbed the edge of it,
pulled it up onto the deck—and stood there looking at the spar,
feeling foolish, empty of direction. Something was wrong and he
didn't know what it was. And then he remembered. How in hell
was he supposed to attach the sail to the yard? He had no lines.

For a moment he sagged under the weight of the heavy, salt-
laden canvas and fought an impulse to throw the sail down and retreat into one of the buildings, to get away from the withering
heat. Instead, he found himself putting aside the sail and jumping
carefully down from the deck. He was looking for his saw. It was
at his feet when he left the wagon, but he went past it twice until
he realized what he was stepping over. Then he pondered a while
until he remembered what he had planned.

He returned to the sail, slashed holes in its four corners, then tossed away the saw. Reaching up, he hung the sail on the spar, sticking both ends of the yardarm out through the holes. Then he took off his shirt, tore it into strips, and tying them to the holes in the lower corners of the sail, fastened the makeshift lines to the deck with a few well-driven nails.

At once the sail bellied out with a soft *whump*. But almost at once, the sail lost its belly and flapped loosely on the spar. Longarm looked to the west. It was hard to believe, but the sun was going down. And the hot wind was dying with its setting.

Longarm jumped off the deck and shook his head in wonder. Time had no logic, it seemed. Only a little while ago it was high noon. He frowned and tried to trace back, tried to understand where all the hours had gone—and realized that time, like everything else, was out of kilter for him.

And there was no getting around it now. No matter how hard and how fast he had worked this afternoon, he would have to wait until the next day.

He stumbled into the shade of one of the buildings and as the sun set and the long blue shadows crept over the salt wasteland, he tried to quiet his racing thoughts, tried to settle himself down. He glanced down at his hands—and was astonished at what he saw. They had long since stopped bleeding. But only because they, too, no longer gave a damn. They were like the claws of a hawk—bony, ridged, and frozen into one position. They didn't sting any longer. They buzzed. He turned them slowly so that he could look into their palms. Long, hardened ridges crossed them.

It had been, he realized dimly, one hell of a time to learn the trade of a boatwright—and one hell of a place to learn it.

Longarm leaned back to wait for the next day—and was asleep almost at once.

It was the flapping of the square sail in the hot morning wind that aroused Longarm. He looked at the tugging sail and got to his feet. The wind was strong and the sail was holding the breeze beautifully. So what was wrong? Why wasn't it moving?

Longarm looked at the front wheels. They were deeply mired in the drifted salt sand. He would have to dig them out.

He used the spring to break the wheels loose from the salt drifts and the hard-packed clay underneath. Once the wheels were free, he got behind the wagon, lifted the caster, and pushed the wheels out of their ruts. As soon as he let the caster down upon the smooth crust of the desert, the contraption began to move slowly forward. Longarm stood where he was and watched it go, pleased in an odd, objective fashion that what he had been laboring at all this time really did have some sense to it after all. Was he finally about to take this magic wind vehicle and sweep across the desert?

Longarm felt giddy, light-headed. He knew he should feel elated at what he had done, but he was aware only of an immense fatigue, so that everything came to him through a kind of hazy screen. It was difficult for him to think logically, or to concentrate on what he had to do next. But he knew he should be pleased. That much got through to him.

And then he realized that his land yacht was moving not south, but southwest. He stumbled after it, lifted the rear caster, and swung the craft to the left so that it was pointing due south. He let down the drag and almost at once the craft began to pick up speed. For a moment he just stood there, watching it move faster with each passing second—until he realized that he would have to run like hell now to catch up with it.

As soon as he overtook it and stumbled, sprawling, onto the deck, the craft slowed to a crawl and for a moment Longarm thought it would stop altogether. Then, once again, it began to pick up speed.

Longarm pulled himself around the mast, and leaning his back against it, positioned himself on the leading edge of the vehicle. He reached out with both feet. As the soles of his boots came down on the rims of the wheels, the craft slowed almost to a halt. Longarm let up. The craft began to pick up speed almost immediately. The trick, he realized, was not to use too much pressure. He pulled his feet back and rested his head against the mast. Though a hot wind was pushing him across the desert, there was a stiffening breeze striking his face. He was aware, too, of the baking sun on his bare arms and torso.

He reached out with his feet every now and then to slow himself down, but the buffeting his feet took discouraged him. Besides, he thought, why did he want to slow down? He wanted only to get to that railroad track. Pulling his legs back, he turned sideways so that he was lying athwart the deck. Glancing behind, he saw the thin line, almost perfectly straight, that was left on the clean desert surface by the trailing caster.

It was working just beautifully—as slick as a tallow factory.

Soon, however, he found that he was beginning to drift westward. Rousing himself, he braked the wheels with his feet until he had straightened his course once again. He was happy to pull his boots off the wheel rims. The heat generated by them was beginning to cook the bottoms of his feet. He was surprised that his boots were lasting. He figured they would not last much longer.

What he reckoned to be an hour, and then another hour, passed. Twice more he had had to brake and steer the craft with his feet on the rims, and the sole of his right boot—or what was left of it—went tailing off behind him a second after he pulled his foot back. That left him with one foot for braking and steering, but he wasn't worrying. His elation at his coming deliverance as a result of his contraption had faded now to a sober awareness of what had to be done when he reached the tracks. There would be no protection from the sun except for his hat and his pants. Yet he still had to wait for a train, and how long that would take he had no idea; he was only roughly certain of the time of day and he had no handy rail schedule to consult.

It was conceivable that after reaching the tracks and even after staying alive long enough for a train to come by, it would be too late to do him any good, or too dark for the train's engineer to see him.

Hell, why should they stop anyway for some crazy, ragged, burnt-out codger waving hello to them as they clacked past? The thought didn't comfort him at all, but he could not deny a kind of sardonic amusement at his predicament.

"Who's that fool out there on the desert waving at the train, Marybelle?" some passenger might ask his wife. "He's going to get an awful sunburn!"

"He's probably drunk, Alfred," Marybelle would reply with a sniff. "Don't encourage him by waving back!"

Longarm would have chuckled aloud at this imaginary exchange, but his mouth was so dry he thought it would break if he tried to use it. Funny as the imaginary conversation was, it could happen. The train could charge right on past him if all he did was stand on the desert and wave.

No. He would have to do something more dramatic. But what?

And then he saw the tracks, shimmering on the southern horizon. By this time he was rushing over the dead, flat, hard surface of the desert as fast as a galloping bronc, perhaps even a little faster. Longarm began to think of ways of slowing down. He could not use his only remaining shod foot without tipping the damned thing, maybe throwing him out and breaking his fool neck.

The tracks were no longer just a wavering line on the horizon.

With gratifying and surprising speed, they were becoming solid, gleaming rails of steel, neatly placed atop the gravel roadbed. Longarm had now to think seriously of stopping. For a moment he thought of scrambling to his feet and perching on the deck above the wheels so that, on the moment of impact, he could jump. But that idea did not please him. He turned then to the sail. Since this was the source of his speed, all he would have to do was rip it down.

He turned to it, grabbed the mast and pulled himself upright. He was reaching up for the sail when he heard a loud crack, like a pistol shot, and the deck abruptly pitched downward, hurling him past the mast. He reached out and tried to grab it as he went past and then found himself spinning drunkenly on the hard surface of the Salt Lake Desert. He spun only a second, his momentum causing him to lose his balance, and the next thing he knew he was sprawling facedown across the hard-packed surface of the ground while the land yacht, slowing swiftly, began to describe a sharp turn to the left.

It never completed the turn as it crunched with surprising force into the gravel roadbed of the train. The deck shattered, the mast cracked forward, but one wheel continued up the steep embankment, skipped lightly over the rails, and disappeared beyond the tracks.

Longarm got slowly to his feet and inspected himself. He was a sight. His chest hung in ribbons of bright flesh, the salt that had been ground into the open lacerations beginning to sting already. He felt his chin. It, too, had lost some skin. But the palms of his hands, toughened now to the consistency of cement, showed little blood. He walked slowly the remaining distance to the tracks and inspected the shattered craft.

He saw at once what had caused him to be spilled from the deck. The caster had snapped at the point where the pitchfork handle had been joined to the board. Perhaps his standing up and moving his weight back onto it had been what triggered the break. Whatever, he was at his destination, and when he saw the wreckage, he knew how he was going to be able to bring the first train from the west to a halt.

It took Longarm the rest of that day to drag just four beams up from the desert floor and drop them over the eastbound tracks. Then, as darkness descended, he gathered a pile of the tinder-dry remnants of the deck alongside the tracks on the desert floor. Pieces of one very dry board he ground under his remaining boot until he had reduced the wood to a powder. Placing this with burning, shaking fingers under the pile of wood, he waited with his two remaining sulphur matches.

He sat down then, cross-legged, in front of the pile of wood and waited for the train to come. If this bonfire didn't stop the train, then maybe the beams from the wagon lying across the tracks would do the trick.

But the moment he sat down to wait with his two matches, a fatigue he had hidden from himself the moment he had started to run after the land yacht returned and smote him like a sledge-hammer. He found he could not keep his eyes open. He could not sit upright. He began to weave. In less than a minute after sitting down, he slipped sideways and sprawled facedown on the desert floor beside the pile of wood.

He must have slept at least four hours. When he stirred, he saw the train chugging toward him silently, the flames from its firebox il-luminating the belly of the black cloud of smoke pouring from its stack. It was still too far down the tracks for him to hear the sound of its passage or its whistle. He was fully awake in an instant, how-ever, and realized that he did not have much time to get the bonfire going. But he had dropped the matches. He began patting the ground frantically around him in the hope of finding them, but the train kept on coming and now he could hear its rapid puffing and the clack of the wheels singing over the rail joints.

He gave up looking for the matches and stood on his feet. It was surprising how light he felt, how rested he was. He began waving his arms. The train showed no sign of slowing down. At the speed it was going, it might not be stopped by the four beams. The cow-catcher might just fling them aside into the night. Long-arm scrambled up the embankment and started to race down the tracks toward the train, waving his arms. The headlamp impaled him with its beam. He heard the *whoosh* of sand dropping to the rails and the screech of flanged wheels grinding the sand into the rails. The train's whistle shattered the desert night. Closer and closer came the thundering engine, the sound of its screeching wheels tearing at Longarm's ears, its whistle pushing at him shrilly—until at the last moment he dove off the tracks, the train grinding to a halt well beyond him.

But a good five yards from the barricade he had erected.

Longarm rolled over and looked at the halted train. He tried to get to his feet, but couldn't seem to manage it. The six coaches were lit and he could see silhouetted heads peering out at him. He heard the freight door slide back and the sound of feet striking the ground as someone dropped from the freight car and scrambled down the embankment toward him. He could see a lantern swinging from the dark figure's hand.

Again he tried to get to his feet, but it was no use. He seemed to be watching the whole show from a box seat. A part of himself smiled at the idea.

And then a fellow wearing a conductor's hat was leaning over him. He lifted the lantern he was carrying to get a better view of Longarm's battered torso and face. Then he shook his head and spoke to Longarm.

"What happened to you, mister? You look like you got run over by a sawmill."

"Barricade . . . on the tracks . . ."

"We saw that. The engineer and the fireman are taking care of it now. Who are you, mister? What happened?"

"Name's Custis Long . . . Deputy U.S. Marshal. Take me to Salt Lake City . . . to Quincy Boggs."

"I don't know no Quincy Boggs. And how do I know you're a law officer?"

"Just get in touch with Boggs . . . Salt Lake City."

Longarm felt his senses leaving him, and he could see that the conductor was not really interested in helping Longarm, apart from getting him to Salt Lake City. Longarm summoned his last remaining ounce of strength.

"One hundred dollars . . . reward. Quincy Boggs! One hundred . . ."

The last thing Longarm saw that night was the look of pure, undiluted greed that animated the conductor's face. As Longarm slipped into unconsciousness, he heard the conductor call for help, and felt the man's arm around his shoulder.

Chapter 7

Longarm awoke in heaven—that is, with the distinct impression that he was being tended by two angels. When Marilyn saw his eyes flicker open, she brightened and pulled back excitedly.

"Audrey! He's awake!"

Audrey appeared and peeked over Marilyn's shoulder. "How do you feel, Mr. Long?"

"How do I look?" he grated hoarsely.

"Awful!"

"Simply awful!" cried Marilyn in happy agreement. "But we know how to fix that!" She turned to Audrey. "Tell father—and Molly!"

As Audrey fairly flew from the room with her news, Marilyn sat back down in the chair she had pulled up to his bedside, reached back to a basin, and pulled from it a dripping cloth. She wrung it slightly and then leaned close and dabbed soothingly at Longarm's face and mouth. "Thirsty?" she asked.

"Don't know what ever gave you a notion like that."

"Open your mouth a little wider and keep it open," she instructed.

He did as she told him, and Marilyn squeezed drops of water into his open mouth. After a while the drops became a trickle, and then she pulled back and proceeded to wipe his face.

"More," he croaked.

"Just a little at a time," she warned him.

"More, I said."

She smiled impishly. "For more than two days now we've been carefully dripping water into that mouth of yours, waiting for you to say just that." She leaned back and poured water out of a pitcher into a tall, clear glass. "Sit up—if you can," she instructed.

"Of course I can."

But as he leaned his weight on his arms and tried to push himself upright, he was astonished at how little progress he was able to achieve. Either he had grown very heavy or he had grown as weak as a tabby—and he knew at once which it was.

"I'll need some help," he confessed.

She took him by the shoulders and pulled him upright, then told him to scoot back so that he could lean against the headboard of his bed. He did as she commanded and felt somewhat proud of his accomplishment as he took the glass of water Marilyn handed him. He sipped at it slowly, as carefully as he had at the dregs that had remained in his canteen out on that damned salt desert.

He got a little carried away and had to go a trifle more slowly, but by concentrating furiously on each swallow, he had almost finished the glass when the door burst open and Boggs entered, with Molly and Audrey right behind.

Molly did not seem at all pleased, and Longarm noticed that she simply moved to one side of the bedroom doorway, and with her back to the wall, watched the proceedings. Boggs, however, was alive with pleasure and approached Longarm's bed with a wide, pleased smile on his face. "You're better!" he exclaimed. "I can see that at once! You have no idea how—dried out—you were when they brought you to me." He frowned at the thought. "Dried out and—in just terrible condition!"

"Did they do that to you?" Audrey wanted to know.

"The Avenging Angels?"

She nodded.

"Yes, I guess you could say they had a hand in it. My own foolishness was no help, either."

"Well," said Boggs, "tell us about it as soon as you can. But you need rest now—and nourishment." He turned about and addressed Molly. "Molly! That broth! Bring it at once!"

The woman did not acknowledge Boggs's instructions, but she sidled out the door in an instant.

Boggs smiled down at Longarm. "That woman has spent long hours tending you," he said. "All through the first night. She cut off your clothes and bathed you from head to foot. Your back and shoulders were baked to a turn, and you gave her quite an argument as she worked over you."

"I don't remember any of it."

"That's a blessing. You were unconscious most of the time. And delirious."

Longarm looked at the man. He knew how anxious the fellow was to learn of his daughter, and it pained Longarm to have to tell him what he must. "Let me finish this here glass of water," he said, "and I'll tell you about Emilie."

"Of course."

The three settled back as he swallowed the water. It was incredible how much better it made him feel. He handed the glass back to Marilyn.

"I found Emilie and we were free for a while—until they

caught up with us on the Great Salt Lake Desert. It was my fault. I had gone after her with mules, but when we left Little Zion, we were riding horses."

"We know all about that, Longarm. I mean the fact that you left Little Zion with Emilie and that they went after you and brought her back. But how did you find her? Was she well? How were her spirits?"

Longarm frowned. "They were fine. She's a brave, resourceful young lady. But what do you mean, you know what happened?"

Marilyn spoke up. "We've had visitors, Mr. Long."

Longarm looked to Boggs for an explanation.

The man shrugged. "You did quite a bit of damage when you visited their settlement, Longarm," he explained. "It angered Elder Wolverton and the others. They came here at once to remonstrate with us—to warn us never to send another federal officer after one of their women."

"They came *here?*"

"Yes."

"And they said *you* were dead," said Audrey.

"You broke away from them when they were taking you back to Little Zion," said Marilyn, "and got lost in the desert. They said there was no chance you would make it back to civilization. Not alive, anyway."

"And for a while," said Boggs, "it appeared they might be correct. You were more dead than alive when that fellow from the Central Pacific pounded on our door and demanded his reward."

Longarm took a deep breath. He remembered now. He had promised the conductor a hundred-dollar reward if he would take Longarm to this house. "About that money," Longarm began, "I am sure I—"

Boggs stopped him with a gesture. "I paid him on the spot—and gladly! You need not trouble yourself further about the matter. And I will hear no more about it. I am sure, however, that if you hadn't had the wit to wave pecuniary temptation before that grasping mortal, he would have left you where he found you."

At that moment Molly entered with a steaming bowl of soup on a tray. Longarm could smell the broth the moment she entered. He was, he realized immediately, famished. As she set it down on the table by the bed, Marilyn and Audrey both pulled back.

Boggs said, "Molly will help you get that down, Longarm. We'll talk later. Come along, girls."

"I don't need no help eating," Longarm protested. "I been doing it for some time now, and I learned how just fine. Just give me the spoon."

Boggs laughed softly and ushered the girls out of the room ahead of him. As the door closed behind them, Longarm glanced at Molly. Her gimlet eyes regarded him coldly. "I understand you cut all my clothes off, Molly."

She said not a word. A spoonful of broth was heading remorselessly for his mouth. He opened it just in time. It was scalding hot and he tried to protest, but another spoonful came at him with all the relentless inevitability of time's passing, and he gave up the battle and submitted to Molly's ministrations.

In his present condition he was no match for the woman anyway.

Longarm was standing in his longjohns three days later, inspecting the new outfit Boggs had bought him, wishing he knew of a way to get back his derringer and watch from those jaspers in Little Zion, when Marilyn stole swiftly into the room, paying no attention at all to his lack of formal attire.

"Now, Marilyn," he said, "I'm plumb wore out with all your hospitality—and besides, this ain't no time—"

She placed her hand gently against his mouth. "It's not that," she told him softly. "I only wish it were! We've got visitors. I saw them outside. Come to the window!"

It was early in the evening. Marilyn turned the lamp on the dresser off and joined Longarm at the window. They were in the third-floor guest room in front and could see down onto the wide street in front of the house. Two carriages had pulled up and there were riders—an escort, it appeared—in front and back. The riders seemed a grim lot, with dark wide-brimmed hats pulled low on their heads, their coats and jackets as somber and depressing as their hats. He felt a slight chill as he watched them. As the riders dismounted, Longarm thought he recognized one of the men getting out of the lead carriage. He did. It was Wells Daniel. Behind him came Burns Meeker and Job Welling.

One of the riders who had dismounted was waiting by the carriage for Meeker and Welling. He turned as the two men approached him and then the three walked toward the house, Wells Daniel in the lead. Longarm felt a sharp thrust of anger. The rider who had joined Meeker and Welling was Elder Wolverton.

"What's going on, Marilyn?" Longarm asked. "That's Elder Wolverton down there—the man who kidnapped Emilie."

"I know," Marilyn said. "Molly told us. They're coming for you, Longarm."

"Molly told you?"

Marilyn nodded miserably, looking away from the window. "She's one of them, Longarm. Everything we've said, everything we've done all these years, she's been reporting to them. In our own home. A spy! Father didn't want to believe it. She had cared for Mother in her last illness, and to us she's been . . . like a second mother. Yet all this time . . ."

Marilyn bowed her head and began to sob quietly. Longarm moved to her side and put his arms around her shoulders to comfort her. He led her over to the bed. She sat down on the edge of it and looked up at him, tears streaking paths down her face. "We used to be persecuted, Longarm. I remember Mother telling us about it. But now we're persecuting our own people! There are secret courts now. Secret places of execution! I've heard of good church members as outspoken as Father, but not as powerful, who have just disappeared! And none of us knows who is a member of the Avenging Angels, and who isn't."

She paused and looked toward the window. "And now . . . we find that Molly is one of them!" Marilyn looked back at Longarm. "Oh, Longarm, what's to become of us? I'm frightened. Do you think they'll take Audrey and me away like they took Emilie?"

Longarm began to button his shirt, trying to think of a response that would comfort Marilyn, when the door swung open without a warning knock. Marilyn got to her feet and the two of them turned to see who it was.

Molly swept into the room with another woman on her heels. "As I suspected," said Molly. "You two are shameless!"

To Longarm's astonishment the woman behind Molly was Sarah Smithson, Elder Smithson's latest wife. She recognized Longarm, of course, and there was a malignant gleam of triumph in her eyes as she saw Longarm standing beside Marilyn, his shirt still not completely buttoned. Sarah glanced swiftly at Molly.

"You were right, Molly," she said. "We did find them together!"

"Apostate!" hissed Molly at Marilyn. "He's a gentile! And you're no better than he is!"

Longarm saw Marilyn fall back as if Molly had struck her. He did not blame the girl. Molly seemed to have been storing up all this bile for quite a spell. Now it was just boiling over, taking the cork with it. And poor Marilyn was getting all the worst of it. Molly's words must have hit her like a mule's kick. Only it was probably even worse than that. Marilyn had come to love the old battle-ax, Longarm realized.

"Back off there, woman," said Longarm to Molly. "You got no call to go on like that. Do what you come in here to do, then get out."

It was Sarah Smithson who replied, a cold, thin smile on her face, "You are wanted downstairs, Mr. Longarm. You and the apostates infesting this dwelling. It is time now for all of you to meet your judges!"

Marilyn gasped and looked at Longarm. He reached out and put his arm on her shoulder. "We'll be down," Longarm said, "as soon as I finish dressing."

"We'll wait," said Sarah.

"Oh, no, you won't!" snapped Marilyn, straightening her shoulders in sudden anger and advancing on the two of them. "Both of you get out of this room! This is still my house! You're intruders! You especially, Molly! Now get out of this room this instant or I'll scratch your eyes out!"

Molly took Sarah by the arm and pulled her back through the door. "We'll be waiting for you both!" she said with grim finality. "And don't try to escape. There are guards at the foot of these stairs—and others surrounding the house." She pulled the door shut behind them.

Marilyn turned back to Longarm, then. Her fury vanished in the instant, and she collapsed, sobbing, in his arms.

Their trial was to be held in the library. As Marilyn and Longarm entered, Audrey ran to throw herself into Marilyn's arms. The two girls then joined their father, who was sitting in one of his leather chairs before the window. A grim-looking Avenging Angel stood behind him, the brim of his black hat pulled low, his arms folded across his chest. In the growing dimness Longarm could not make out the fellow's features, so well did the hat brim cover his face. Longarm saw only an implacable jaw, a straight, grim, undeviating line for a mouth, and eyes hidden in darkness. The other Avenging Angels stationed around the room, especially the two that had herded them silently into the library, were just as grim, just as expressionless. They were all cut from the same fearsome doctrinal cloth.

Longarm paused in front of the long table that had been pulled around to face the door. Behind the table were Elder Wolverton, another elder—a short, stocky fellow who was vaguely familiar—and

Meeker, Welling, and Wells Daniel. Wolverton held the center of
this imposing group, his pink, cherubic cheeks fairly shining in the
gloom, his eyes grimly alight. He stroked his snow-white beard and
spoke to Longarm.

"You have a charmed life, it seems, Mr. Long."

"I told you before, you can call me Longarm."

"Before we go any further," spoke up Wells Daniel, "I think
we should give Longarm this telegram."

The elder shrugged. "Give it to him, then. But I warn you,
Daniel! It will have no bearing on this trial. The judgment of this
court is well outside the jurisdiction of that accursed federal des-
potism. Whether he has a legal right to be here or not is unimpor-
tant."

Wells Daniel appeared to flinch visibly under the weight of
Wolverton's measured scorn, but he rose from his seat, nevertheless, and leaning over the library table, handed Longarm the telegram. "It's from your superior, I believe," he told Longarm.

Longarm took it. "I could read it better if someone would turn
up a few lamps. This place is as dark as a back room in hell."

Audrey and Marilyn darted swiftly but noiselessly about the
room, lighting lamps and turning them up. Marilyn placed a lamp
on the table. Wolverton immediately placed it on the far end, his
eyes holding a stern rebuke for the girl. She looked quickly, fear-
fully away from his angry eyes and retreated back to her father's
side.

Longarm held up the telegram and read it.

WASHINGTON RAISING HELL RETURN TO DENVER I AM
CALLING YOU OFF THE CASE RETURN TO DENVER YOU NO
LONGER HAVE AUTHORITY IN UTAH TERRITORY

VAIL

Longarm glanced at Wells Daniel. "Guess that cuts the rug out
from under me, all right. You fellows behind this?"

"We had no choice, Longarm," said Burns Meeker, his small
eyes weary, his round face no longer florid. "My brother . . . has
already disappeared."

Job Welling spoke up then, his voice frail, distraught. "My
daughter Marylou has left with them, Longarm. She insists it is
her wish." He shook his head. "But I cannot believe that."

"Oh, ye of little faith," said Wolverton, his voice laced with
contempt.

"They've put the screws to you, have they, Welling?" Longarm was sorry for the man.

"Longarm," said Boggs from his chair, "Elder Wolverton insists that Emilie has consented to join him in Celestial Marriage. He says she wants her sisters to join her."

Longarm looked back at Wolverton. His dander was up, and for a little while he considered quite calmly what his chances would be of surviving if he leaped across that table and strangled the old goat. Wolverton smiled at Longarm.

"Go ahead, Longarm. Try it. You will expedite matters beautifully."

"Can we get on with this?" said the other, smaller elder.

At once Longarm turned to look at him. In that instant he recognized the voice—and the man. This was the tormented elder who had visited him that night when he was a prisoner at Little Zion—the man who still lived the nightmare of the Mountain Meadow Massacre.

"Yes," said Wolverton. "You are right, Brother Smithson. We should get on with this." Wolverton looked at Longarm, then picked up some notes and began to read slowly, deliberately. The man needed glasses, but was too vain to wear them.

"Custis Long, you are hereby accused of willful destruction of property, of arson, and of the resultant homicide of one Linus Tarboot. How do you plead?"

"What was that about Linus Tarboot?"

"He was killed in the fire you set," said Wolverton. "Or do you deny you set fire to the stables in order to cover your flight with Emilie Boggs?"

"I don't deny it. I'm sorry about Linus Tarboot. I didn't think anyone but those two jaspers I locked in the feed room were in the barn at the time. And I saw them get out all right when I was riding off."

"Linus was the man you trussed and left in the arms and powder room. The fire spread to that structure, and before we could extinguish it, the building blew. We did not know until some time after that Linus had not escaped the flames. We assumed he was with the rest of the bucket brigade, trying to stem the fiery destruction you visited upon Little Zion. I did not know of the death of this man before I set out after you and Emilie Boggs. Had I known, I would not have dealt with you so leniently in the desert, I assure you."

"Your earlier defense of your shooting of Sheriff Barker and your explanation of the death of Jason Kimball we accepted," said Smithson. "But the death of Linus we cannot condone, no matter what the circumstances. He leaves four wives and sixteen children."

Longarm remembered leaving the man trussed on his cot, his face to the wall. He did not like to think of the man trapped like that in a burning building, and he had a powerful wish that what had happened to Linus had not happened. But he saw no way that he could have foreseen it. A burning ember must have carried to the roof of the small house, igniting it. With everyone either rushing around trying to corral the horses or busy carrying water to the fire, the flames could have spread from the roof with startling suddenness. Longarm moved uncomfortably under Smithson's gaze.

"I'm sure sorry about that fellow Linus. I never had anything against him, and he did just what I told him to do. I am sorry for his wives and his children, too. But I did not kill Linus deliberately, and if I could have stopped such a crazy piece of bad luck from falling on that man, I would have. But maybe you all, sitting there so righteous, ought to think on what I was doing in Little Zion to begin with. I was there because you had taken a young lady—without her permission—from her home at night, piled her into a wagon, then shut her up in a shack until she agreed to do what you wanted her to do. If anyone is guilty of Linus's death, it's you, Elder Wolverton."

Longarm stopped then to take a breath. He hadn't talked that long at one spell since the time he'd cussed out a bronc that had thrown him halfway down a mountain because he'd heard a rattler.

"I am not on trial here, Longarm," said Wolverton. "You are—as are those here in this room who sent you on your ill-advised mission to Little Zion."

"How do you plead?" asked Smithson. "Guilty or not guilty?"

"If you think I'm going to play along with you silly jaspers, you really are chewing on loco weed. This ain't a court of law. You fellows remind me of little kids out in back of the barn playing secret society and worrying yourself to death over secret passwords. You're *older* kids, that's for sure—and you've got the chance to play with real guns and real lives—but you're still kids living in a make-believe world all your own. I think you ought to pack up your silly game and go home to mama."

"Good for you, Longarm!" said Marilyn.

"Shut up, hussy!" cried Sarah Smithson.

Marilyn recoiled, but her father comforted her and said, his voice quivering with anger, "I agree with my daughter. This man Longarm speaks the bitter truth! You are all dangerous children playing a dangerous game with real lives at stake! Well said, Longarm!"

Elder Smithson looked at Elder Wolverton, as if to say he should be the one to answer this challenge to their authority.

Wolverton leaned forward, his eyes fixed on Longarm, a zealot's fury burning in them. "It does not matter what you think, Longarm! Or the rest of these misguided fools who sent for you. It is what we think that matters."

"Why bother asking me, then?"

"You are right," the man snapped. He looked at Smithson. Smithson nodded and looked back at Longarm.

"Deputy Long, we, the chosen elders of Little Zion, pronounce you guilty of homicide in the death of Linus Tarboot. You shall be taken from this place and executed before this night is out."

"Swift justice," intoned Wolverton. "And this time, Longarm, you won't be given any loopholes."

"See here," broke in Wells Daniel. "We have this telegram calling Longarm back to his office in Denver. There's no need for this drastic action. The man will soon be out of the territory—and that by order of his superior!"

"We will accept this verdict of his guilt," said Job Welling, hunching his huge shoulders forward angrily. "But we demand as his punishment that he be exiled from the Territory of Utah. Surely that would be sufficient. You can't summarily execute an officer of the federal government of the United States."

Wolverton glared at them. "The United States is a foreign power still. Its citizens are rabble, gentiles who have persecuted our forefathers and would destroy us now if they could. Be meek with them and they will take everything we have built, everything Brigham Young brought forth upon this wilderness—and which you tiny men would forfeit for the paltry prize of statehood!"

"There must be another reason," snapped Boggs from his chair. "I've heard that political tirade used before to further other equally absurd proposals."

"Yes there is," said Wolverton, "and I admit it freely. This man must die because he is an enemy of Little Zion—as are all of you—and because he knows where our settlement is. Once back in Denver, allied with federal agents of a like mind, there is no

doubt in my mind that this man will invade and ravage our settlement, as he has done already."

There was a gavel in front of Smithson. Smithson glanced at
Wolverton. Wolverton nodded curtly. Smithson took up the gavel
and brought it down smartly. It rang out like a pistol shot in the
crowded room.

"This court is adjourned," said Smithson. "The prisoner will
be taken from this place and executed. It is so ordered." Once
again the gavel came down.

Wolverton stood up and moved out from behind the table with
Smithson following up on his heels, and Daniel, Meeker, and Welling
right behind them. As Longarm started to look across the room at
Boggs to say something to the man, he was spun quickly around
by two Avenging Angels and prodded from the library.

Sarah and Molly were standing by the front door of the house,
smiling with great satisfaction as Longarm was led out past them
and down the walk to one of the waiting carriages. As Longarm
ducked his head and climbed into the lead carriage, he tried to figure out what it was that made those two women hate him so much.
Maybe he could understand why Molly felt the way she did, for
she could not help but notice how nicely Longarm had gotten
along with Marilyn. But Sarah he had rescued from Zeke Bannister and then taken back to Little Zion, without once laying an improper hand on her.

And then he remembered that conversation they had had about
pretty ankles and how he had narrowly escaped her amorous attentions. Her anger, he remembered, had been intense, bitter. He
thought he had pacified her and gotten her to thinking of poor
Zeke Bannister, but he saw now, as he settled back in the seat between two grim-visaged Avenging Angels, that Sarah Smithson
was still furious that he had been able to restrain himself so easily
where she was concerned.

This was why she must have egged her husband on to join
Wolverton in this business, and why she must have insisted on
coming along as well to witness Longarm's comeuppance. Longarm recalled a proverb: *Hell hath no fury* was how it began.

With the two Avenging Angels on each side of him and another
sitting opposite him in the enclosed carriage, Longarm was driven
off through Salt Lake City. The broad streets seemed to him to have
been mysteriously cleared of other carriages; they were surprisingly empty of traffic. It was not late in the evening, and yet the en-

tire city somehow appeared to have lost its population as the grim, cheerless caravan wound its way through the streets.

The building into which Longarm was led was some distance from the heart of the city on the other side of a set of railroad tracks. Longarm had felt them clearly under the wheels of his carriage. The building's walls smelled of coal oil and kerosene. As he was being led into a small room, he heard the chuffing of a steam engine on the other side of the outer wall. There were two wooden chairs and a table, a potbellied stove, a foul-smelling chamber pot, and no windows. He saw all this in the light of the smoking lantern placed on the table by the Avenging Angel who pushed him unceremoniously into the room.

The dark-clad fellow left him alone in the room, locking the door behind him. At once Longarm set about trying to find a weak spot in the cell. The walls, especially the door, were quite solid. He cleared his throat loudly and realized with some apprehension just how soundproof the Avenging Angels' detention cells were. The fact that there was no cot indicated that he was not expected to spend the night. This had a chilling effect on him, but he promised himself not to panic.

Someone approached the door. He heard the key in the lock and then the door was pulled open. Elder Smithson entered warily. He saw Longarm standing within a few feet of the door and waggled an enormous Colt Walker at him.

"Get back, Longarm," the elder said. "Back!"

Longarm moved back as far as the table. Smithson entered and pulled the door shut behind him. Someone outside in the corridor promptly locked it.

"We could sit at that table," Smithson suggested. "No need to stand around like adversaries waiting to strike."

"Ain't that what we are? Unless I'm here under false pretenses, you just came in to execute me—judging from the size of that cannon you're packing."

"Yes. I am your executioner. Because of my earlier indiscretion, my weakness in coming to see you in Little Zion."

"I didn't tell a soul, Smithson."

"I know."

"Then who did?"

"My wife Sarah—the woman you rescued from Zeke Bannister and brought back to Little Zion. She followed me that night and listened at the door. She confronted me, then went to Wolverton." There was no mistaking the touch of bitter irony in the elder's voice. Longarm did not pursue the matter. The man was obviously sorely troubled by his present assignment, and when Longarm considered what he had done for the elder by bringing back his third wife, he realized the man had one corking good reason for shooting Longarm with that Colt Walker.

"This execution is supposed to put you back in good standing. Is that it?" Longarm asked.

"*Rehabilitation* is what it is called," Smithson replied, a pained, ironic glint in his eye.

"That's one hell of a jawbreaker for something as basic as murder. The only difference between this and that Mountain Meadow Massacre, Smithson, is the highfalutin words you jaspers are attaching to it."

"Yes," the man said softly, "you are right. Murder is just what it is."

"Then let me go."

"I can't do that, Longarm."

"Why not?"

"This place is guarded heavily at the moment. Sarah is outside the door. She is to watch me—to see that I perform this business properly."

"But you don't want to kill me, do you, Smithson?"

"Yet I must." His voice lowered. "And, indeed, Longarm, one of us must not leave here alive."

"Smithson, you said before that you wanted to expose this fellow Lee. If you let me get out of here, I'll help you do just that. You can go to the courts, the newspapers."

Smithson shook his head sadly. "That's utterly impossible, Longarm."

"*Why* is it?"

"My children. They would be his hostages."

"You mean Lee would—?"

"Yes, he would, Longarm."

"I think you're exaggerating, Smithson. Your wives would sure as hell protest something fierce. And how could Wolverton stand by and let Lee do something like that? He'd lose any authority he had over Little Zion. The other elders would not stand for it."

Smithson smiled sadly at Longarm's assurances. "There is something you don't know, Longarm."

"What's that?"

"Lorenzo Wolverton *is* Mordecai Lee."

Longarm blinked, astonished.

"Now, you'd better let me take this one bite at a time, Smithson. You think you can explain that?"

"Lorenzo Wolverton—the *real* Lorenzo Wolverton—died after the Mountain Meadow Massacre. Lee and I knew this, but no one else, because Lorenzo was being taken care of by the same band of friendly Indians that fought the settlers with us at the Meadow. Just before Lee and I visited their village to check on Lorenzo's condition, Major Higbee received a letter from Brother Brigham forbidding any interference with the immigrant train. When Lee saw that Lorenzo had died while in the care of the Indians, he decided then to leave that area of Utah, carrying with him the name of Lorenzo Wolverton. We buried Wolverton with Mordecai Lee's name on the marker. In this way did Lee escape what he feared would be the wrath of Brigham Young."

"What good did that do? Hadn't Wolverton done as much mischief as Lee at the massacre?" Longarm asked with puzzlement.

"No. Wolverton had been wounded before that. He played no part in the massacre. But Lee had been prominent. It was he who directed the fire on most of the children."

"The children?"

"Ten of them—from ten to sixteen years of age."

Longarm sighed. "I reckon I get the picture, all right. Your children would only make it a few more."

"And my wives," Smithson said with a weary sigh. "Except for Sarah, of course, he would not go easy on them. Naturally, there would be a trial—to make matters look perfectly legitimate."

There was a sudden pounding on the door. "Hurry it up in there, Elder! We must be riding soon!" called a powerful voice through the heavy door.

Smithson turned to the door, his face grim, as if he had come to a sudden, irrevocable decision. "Open the door, Grimsby! I want the burial shroud!"

The door swung back and a hulking figure loomed in the doorway and caught Smithson's eye. The fellow seemed somewhat suspicious of Smithson, and looked with surprise at Longarm, evidently disappointed to see him appearing so healthy. "You say you want the shroud now?"

"You heard me. Bring it in here."

"Yes, Brother," the fellow said, and vanished back out through the open doorway. As Longarm looked back at Smithson, he saw that he had pulled the Colt Walker out of his belt and now rested it on the table in front of him, its muzzle pointing at Longarm's head. Longarm sat back in his chair and studied the man.

The lamp gave Longarm a much better look at Elder Smithson's features than he had been able to get either in the Boggses' library or when Longarm was a prisoner in Little Zion. The man was not very tall, but his chunky figure contained not an ounce of tallow. He was in his late forties, his facial whiskers a steel gray, his eyes now hard and resolute—with little in them to indicate the soul-deep torment he had spoken of when he had visited Longarm in his cell in Little Zion. But the anguish was still there, eating at him; Longarm could feel it.

The fellow whom Smithson had addressed as Grimsby returned carrying a soogan-like tarpaulin over his shoulder. He dropped it to the floor and moved back out the door.

"Thank you, Grimsby," said Smithson.

Grimsby had seen the big Colt in the elder's hand and seemed a lot happier as he pushed the door shut. Smithson waited until he heard the key turn in the lock before he looked back at Longarm, and leaned toward him.

"Listen to me, Longarm—carefully."

"I'm listening, Elder. There ain't nothing much else I can do, seems like."

The elder held up a hand to caution Longarm and leaned still closer. "You must keep your voice down," he whispered. "What I tell you must not be overheard. Is that clear?"

With a frown, Longarm nodded.

"You were right, of course," the elder told Longarm, his voice barely audible. "This is not an execution. It is murder. But I cannot kill anymore, Longarm—no matter how anxious Sarah is to see you dead." He paused to let that sink in, then continued. "That shroud on the floor is our trademark, Longarm. Wherever our night riders go, they carry one of these rolled neatly behind their saddles—a terrifying and melancholy reminder of our slide back into persecution. After I shoot you, I am to tuck you within that grisly sleeping bag and lace it up. From a nuisance and a threat you become a neat bundle slung over a rider's cantle, to be buried somewhere in our fair valley. It will be good to leave such horror behind. . . ."

As Smithson talked, Longarm began to get a handle on what the man intended. It was in the soft, regretful tone of his voice.

Smithson was readying himself to pass from this present torment into another . . .

Abruptly Smithson stood up and stepped away from the table, the Colt still clutched in his right hand. "I said I cannot kill anymore, Longarm. I meant that, except for one more time—an execution long overdue."

Longarm got to his feet. "No need to make that kind of sacrifice," he whispered urgently. "There's no need, I tell you. Just give me that Colt and we'll both shoot our way out of here."

The man smiled and shook his head. "No. Very gallant and brave, but foolish. This way I will be gone, but you will be alive to bring Wolverton down and destroy his nest of scorpions. Now listen carefully. When I pull this trigger, you must act swiftly. Put on my hat and jacket. Squeeze into the jacket as best you can, then place me in the shroud and lace it up. My wife and Grimsby will come for the shroud. Let Grimsby take it without a word. You and my wife, sitting at that table, must wait until he leaves with my body. After that it will be up to you. What you do with my ambitious new wife is also up to you." He smiled and his voice dropped still lower, so that Longarm could barely catch the irony in it. "I am sure she will be able to think of something."

He moved swiftly to the door and called loudly through it, "Sarah! Get Grimsby! *Now!*"

As barely audible footsteps ran down the corridor, Smithson removed his hat and jacket and threw them onto the table. Before Longarm could protest further, Smithson rested the muzzle of the Colt Walker upon his right temple. The man's hand tightened. Longarm looked quickly away as the ferocious detonation filled the tiny room.

Reaching out quickly, Longarm caught the falling body as the Colt clattered to the floor. Then he lowered the dead man gently but swiftly to the floor beside the shroud, picked up the Colt, and jammed it into his belt. After unrolling the bag, he lifted the dead man into it—trying not to look at the shattered skull, the colorless mask of a face. He stuffed his own hat and jacket into the shroud, then laced it up tightly. Stepping swiftly to the table, he slapped the elder's wide-brimmed hat onto his own head, pulled the brim down to obscure his face, and slipped into the jacket. It was a tight fit, but he managed and was sitting at the table with his head bowed in apparent anguish at the execution he had just performed. His back was to the door when Grimsby and Sarah Smithson hurried in.

Sarah moved to his side and placed a comforting hand on his shoulder. Longarm reached back and took her wrist firmly in his, then drew her with a steady, unrelenting force into the seat opposite him. When she caught sight of his face, she could see also the black muzzle of the Colt staring at her from out of his jacket. It froze the cry on her lips.

"You going to give me a hand, Elder?" Grimsby called. He had been tugging on the body and had only just managed to get it through the doorway.

"No," said Sarah, her voice trembling from the menace in Longarm's eyes. "Elder Smithson is too upset. You'll have to get someone else to help."

The man muttered something and then Longarm heard him call to someone else. In a few moments he was joined by another Avenging Angel. They lifted the body of Elder Smithson easily between them and were soon gone.

"I don't understand," Sarah said. "Did—did you kill him?"

"He killed his own self, ma'am. A brave and terrible thing it was, too. He said I was to take care of you as I saw fit."

She started to snatch her hand out of his grasp, but Longarm just squeezed it a bit tighter and drew her across the table toward him. Then he took the Colt out with his free hand and pointed the muzzle at her right eye, holding it less than an inch away. "If you are quiet, I will not harm you, ma'am. If you raise an outcry, your husband's sacrifice will be in vain, for then both of us will be on our way in one of those real convenient sleeping bags you people carry around. Is that clear?"

"Perfectly, Mr. Longarm."

"It's Mr. Long to you, ma'am," Longarm said.

"We—we don't have to be enemies, Mr. Long. I assure you, I can be very understanding to them that needs it." She reached out and held his shoulder gently.

"Smithson said you would be able to think of something. You really are a caution, Mrs. Smithson, but I'd sooner curl up with a sidewinder than the likes of you."

She was furious, and this time she did manage to pull free. She jumped back and slammed against the wall, sending the chair crashing to the floor. Longarm stood up, his Colt trained on her. "I will not stand for your insolence!" she hissed.

"Do you know what I'll tell Wolverton if you don't help me out of here? I'll tell him this whole thing was your idea, that you and me had ourselves an affair while we were journeying back to

Little Zion—and that this was why you wanted to come along with your husband. He knows, I am sure, how loyal and faithful a wife you have been to your husband."

"You're hateful!"

"I know that. Meanwhile, you go out of this place just a little bit ahead of me and tell Wolverton that I'm not up to that long ride tonight, that the two of us are going to stay the night in Salt Lake City. Do you think you can remember all that?"

"You are much taller than my husband," she said. "They'll all notice."

"Not if you go first and speak for me, then return to help me to one of the carriages. I'll be stooped over quite a bit. Killing a man does not come easy to men like Elder Smithson."

She hesitated.

"Do you really think you will have a chance to supplant Emilie Boggs in the heart of Elder Wolverton? You *are* ambitious, ma'am. But it takes more than that, don't it? Remember all that talking we did about pretty ankles? Things ain't really so different on the Mormon side, are they?"

"I'll help you," she snapped. "But only because I know what a treacherous and cold-blooded man you are! I am in fear of my life while in your presence!'

"That's real comforting to these ears, you have no idea. So lead the way now, and take it real careful."

Without another word, Sarah turned and preceded him out of the small room. As they started down the corridor, Longarm caught sight of two men hurrying toward them carrying lanterns.

"Is that you, Elder Smithson?" one of them called.

"It is!" replied Sarah. "Get back to your horses. We do not need your help. Elder Smithson is feeling much better now."

The two men turned and hurried ahead of them. A few moments later, Longarm paused at the door of the building while Sarah walked out into the night. He watched her approach the lead rider, who was already mounted up and waiting. His long white beard fairly glowed in the moonlight.

Elder Wolverton leaned down to catch Sarah's words. He nodded curtly when she had finished, and took up his reins, as Sarah turned about and walked back toward the building. Longarm moved out of the doorway. Wolverton waved to him and called, "Take a little holiday. You have done well! Remember! He was a gentile! No need to get nervous over that!"

Then he put his spurs to his horse and the crowd of horsemen headed out toward the desert, with the inevitable water wagon and a small remuda following close behind. Stooping a bit, Longarm waved to the disappearing riders, then stepped back into the doorway. Longarm saw Boggs step down out of one of the two waiting carriages and hurry across the moonlit ground toward him. As Boggs neared him, the other carriage turned about and was driven off in a sudden clatter of hoofs, a hectic series of whipcracks sounding above them. The carriage and its occupants, Longarm sensed, were in flight from an obscene and terrifying place.

Longarm waited for Boggs with a slight, grim smile on his face. When Sarah reached his side, he pulled her to him with an iron grasp that made her cry out slightly. "Well done, woman. Now continue to behave and you might get out of this better than you deserve."

He relaxed his grip on her arm slightly and stepped out of the doorway to meet Boggs. Boggs pulled up suddenly, staring uncomprehendingly at him, his face suddenly as pale as the moonlit ground at his feet.

"My God! Is it really you, Longarm?"

"It is, thanks to a very brave man—a Saint who'd had his fill of murder and other such villainy. He has left me a charge, and I intend to fulfill it, no matter what Washington or my superiors have to say in the matter. Are you with me?"

"Of course, Longarm. You are all the hope I have now!"

"Are you alone in that carriage?"

"There are two Avenging Angels—and Molly."

"What is this place?"

"It was built to serve as a warehouse for the cotton we were supposed to produce in this land, but you know to what use it has been put—as does every Mormon in the city. It has become a charnel house, an abomination that haunts every child's nightmare—and every adult's as well."

"Are there any guards?"

"This place needs no guards. Its reputation alone is enough to keep every living soul well away from here. You saw how empty our streets became when those riders escorted us to this place?"

"I noticed."

"What do you plan on doing now?" Boggs asked.

"Are Marilyn and Audrey safe?"

"For now, yes. They are at home."

"Stay here with Sarah Smithson, Boggs."

Longarm walked swiftly across the dark ground to the waiting carriage and pulled back the leather side curtains. The three waiting occupants froze into immobility when they saw the gaping muzzle of the Colt Walker in Longarm's hand.

"Out!" Longarm directed sharply.

One of the Avenging Angels acted on a foolish impulse and his hand dropped to his holster. Longarm brought the barrel of the Walker down with such force that the sound of the man's wrist bone shattering under the impact filled the interior of the carriage. With a cry, the fellow grabbed at his wrist. He was the first out; the other two followed hard on his heels.

Longarm disarmed the two men, told Molly she'd better not have any weapons hidden on her, then herded them all toward the building. When they reached the doorway, Longarm gave one of the weapons to Boggs and told the man he would be needed to help cover them. Boggs agreed as Longarm directed the three ahead of him down the long dark corridor toward the cell he had just quit.

When they reached it, he told them to walk on into it. The two men did as they were told, but Molly hesitated. An unsteady hand went up to her face, as if to push away a strand of loose hair.

"She has a small pistol in her bosom!" hissed Sarah into Longarm's ear.

At once Longarm leaped forward and was in time to grab Molly's wrist as she pulled the derringer free. The small pistol went off, sending its slug into the ceiling, the detonation surprisingly powerful. Wrenching the pistol from her hand, Longarm wagged the barrel of the Colt at her and the woman stepped into the small cell after the others, her eyes glancing with withering hatred at Sarah.

Longarm turned to Sarah.

"You, too, Sarah. Get in there with your friends."

Sarah's face went white. "In there? With them? But I just—" She looked into the cell. The lantern on the small table still burned and the light from it showed the three watching her, it seemed, with eyes gleaming malevolently. It was she, after all, who had just prevented Molly from killing Longarm. Sarah looked back at him. "Please! Not with them! I saved your life!"

"Get in there, Sarah!"

"Please!" she screamed in terror.

"Get in there, or I'll throw you in."

Weeping softly, Sarah Smithson walked into the room. Longarm kicked the door shut. He slid the bolt and snapped the lock. He did not have the key to the lock, but he had no intention of worrying about that. Let the four of them—betrayers all—eat each other alive like scorpions in a glass.

As Longarm and Boggs hurried down the dim corridor, they heard faint screams coming from within the tiny cell.

Outside the grim building, as they walked toward the carriage, Boggs said finally, "She did save your life, Longarm. Wasn't that a very cruel thing to do?"

"I saw the bulge in Molly's bosom, Boggs, and I told her she had better not have anything on her to see if I could make her give it up voluntarily. When she didn't, I just decided to wait and let her make the first move. I knew what she was up to the moment her hand went to her face."

He shuddered. "Still, that poor woman!"

"That 'poor woman,' Boggs, put her husband into such a bind that he blew his brains out less than an hour ago in that same blamed cell."

"Blew his brains—? You mean Elder Smithson shot himself? He's dead?"

"That body they slung over a horse was dead, Boggs—sure as shooting. Like I said a little while ago. He was a brave man who'd just about had his fill of this dirty business."

Boggs was silent as they got into the carriage. He took up the reins and looked at Longarm. "What now, Deputy?"

"A little more of your hospitality, Boggs, if you don't mind. And then tomorrow I'll go see about retrieving a pair of army mules."

"Army mules!"

"That's right. Thieves took 'em. Larceny, I call it. Do you know what good, healthy army mules are worth today, Boggs? Three hundred dollars a span, that's what. Leastways, that's what the good captain told me, so I aim to help him get his mules back."

"I don't understand, Longarm."

"I know you don't, and that's your protection. But after I leave tomorrow, I'd be much obliged if you'd send a telegram to Denver for me."

Boggs started up the carriage. "Of course, Longarm."

"I'll give you the address. You just say I'll be reporting back to

Denver as soon as I bring in some stolen army mules. And you can sign my name to it."

Longarm leaned back in the carriage while Boggs, shaking his head slightly in puzzlement, drove over the railroad tracks and turned his horses onto the broad, once again busy streets of Salt Lake City.

Chapter 8

Sergeant Dillon mopped his face with a red polka-dot handkerchief, then stuffed it into his right rear pocket. He was worried about the operation, but unwilling to speak of his misgivings openly. That's how Longarm figured it, anyway.

"What is it, Sergeant?"

"Sorry to bother you, sir, and I know the captain said you was to be in charge, but we ain't got to no wagon tracks yet, and it's pure misery trying to find our way in this here pitch-dark."

"Well, you just rest easy, Sergeant. I've been over this country twice already and I'll sing out when I smell those wagon tracks."

The sergeant was riding beside him at the moment, with the rest of the ten-man contingent strung out in a double line over the rocky terrain. They had crossed the Great Salt Lake Desert during the night, then camped during the day, and had been riding now for close to four hours. What was left of the moon hadn't been up for long. They were going in the right direction and the land held a vague familiarity that was enough for Longarm, but he could understand the sergeant's concern. All this for two army mules?

"Pardon me, Deputy, sir, but I'm still a little uncertain about them orders the captain gave me."

"Just call me Longarm, Sergeant. You're liable to get your tongue all twisted into a knot with that 'Deputy, sir' handle. Now just what is it you don't understand about Captain Meriwether's orders?"

"Mules, sir. Is that what we're after? All this for two mules?"

"Stolen government property, Sergeant. Let's not forget that."

"No, sir. I understand, sir. But dynamite?"

"If you'll just let us eat this apple one bite at a time, Sergeant, you'll get all those important questions answered proper. But right now, let's not have this troop straggling any. And tell them to quiet down. This ain't Indian country, but it might as well be."

"Yes, sir!" The man started to pull away.

"Just a minute, Sergeant. Send up that Corporal Toohey, will you?"

"The dynamite man?"

"That's the man, Sergeant."

"Yes, sir."

"Call me Longarm, Sergeant."

"Yes, sir."

Longarm shook his head and peered through the gloom. They were at least five hours away from Little Zion, but already the grotesque rock forms that reared out of the darkness seemed vaguely familiar as they loomed ominously over the trail. He expected the trail to begin to rise presently, bringing them onto a ridge. When and if it did that, he would know for sure that he was on course.

Like Boggs, Longarm did not believe that Emilie had finally consented to marry Wolverton. The old fox was just making do with moondust, and hoping more than thinking. But Longarm had tough going when it came to convincing Boggs not to panic. The man was all for selling his house and moving out of the territory, taking his daughters with him. The fact that Molly had been a spy all these years—for nine years, it turned out—had really shaken Boggs and Longarm could hardly blame him. Naturally, under the circumstances, all Boggs could think of was saving his remaining daughters from this arrogant band of night riders who had been so bold and so damned sure of themselves that they had ridden right into Salt Lake City, marched into his own home, and put a deputy U.S. marshal on trial.

Longarm had located the other members of the council as soon as he could. They, too, were equally uncertain, until Longarm pointed out to them that if they let these jaspers get away with what they had just done, they might as well do what Boggs was ready to do—hightail it like scared rabbits, or march their kin and their own daughters up to the nearest Avenging Angel and tell him to do his damnedest.

What they all had to realize was that if they didn't fight back, they left themselves no compromise. They would either have to get out or give up.

Longarm figured he'd set some bees loose in their bonnets. If he succeeded in bringing back Emilie and destroying that scorpion's nest as Smithson wanted, he hoped they'd be able to muster enough gumption to organize and encourage the other Mormons to take a hand in things and maybe take their land and their city back at the same time.

Of course it was only a hope. Nothing's as easy for most people, Longarm realized, as letting things drift without doing anything—until the bugs are out of the walls and crawling over the tables and

chairs. And by then, as likely as not, it's too late. Still, he had promised Emilie he would come back for her—and there was poor little
Annie Dawkins waiting for him, too.

So it didn't really matter what Boggs or his fellows told him or
how many telegrams he got from the chief—he was going back to
Little Zion for those two army mules. He chuckled, wondering how
he could explain all this to that sergeant, or if he should even try.

A trooper pulled up beside Longarm. Longarm glanced at him
and saw the corporal's stripes in the dim moonlight.

"You'd be Corporal Miles Toohey, I reckon."

"That's right, sir."

"Call me Longarm. Think you can do that?"

"Yes, sir—I mean, Longarm."

"Fine. What experience have you had with dynamite, Corporal?"

"Plenty, Longarm."

"How much is plenty? You talk like an Indian. Details,
Corporal. You work for the railroad?"

"No, Longarm. I'm not a Chinaman."

"Didn't figure to hurt your feelings with that question, Corporal. So out with it, if you don't mind. What's your experience
with that stuff?"

"I worked at the Sutro mine in Nevada in '74, when they
switched from nitro. Dynamite was a hell of a lot safer, and it did
a whale of a job blasting that tunnel."

Longarm had heard reports about the Nevada tunnel and how it
had been blown. His question concerning the railroad, though, had
been equally legitimate, no matter how pained the corporal was at
his question. The Chinese were not the only ones who learned to
blow tunnels for the railroad, though they seemed to like black
powder, not dynamite.

"You got what you need?" Longarm asked.

"I checked it out before we left Fort Douglas, Longarm. You
must have spent quite a lot for all that equipment."

Longarm smiled as he recalled the puzzlement on Boggs's face
when he told him he needed the dynamite to help him recover two
army mules. But Longarm was careful not to tell the man why he
wanted the dynamite, just as he had told none of them what he was
about, really. It was best for all concerned that they know only what
he told them—and that was precious little. Maybe he wouldn't
even tell Vail—not all of it, anyway.

"Yes, I did spend quite a bit, Corporal, and it wasn't even my money. So you be damn sure you take good care of it. I don't want it going off too soon—or too late. Right on time. You got that clear?"

"Yes, sir."

"Call me Longarm, Corporal, and go on back to that wagon. I want you to ride alongside it until we get to where we're going."

"Yes, Longarm."

Longarm waved to him, and the fellow pulled his mount around and waited for the column to move past him.

The trail, Longarm noted, was rising definitely now, heading for a high, rocky ridge that seemed to lift into the stars. He felt much better, suddenly. Though the sergeant didn't know it, they were traveling over that wagon road right now. Sometime before dawn they'd be close enough to get down off their horses and start searching the rocks surrounding Little Zion for Mormon lookouts.

The tall finger of rock that Sarah had pointed out to him the last time he had come this way still beckoned to him as it towered against the stars. Longarm led the troopers across the short rise and then along the precarious rocky ledge. In the darkness it was a nervous passage, but the weary troopers followed Longarm in good order. Longarm ignored the trail leading down into the canyon, cutting carefully up a steep slope, trashy with detritus, until they found a level stretch.

He turned in his saddle and motioned the men off their mounts as soon as he saw that the remuda and the wagon had joined them on the flat. The driver of the wagon was cursing, not very softly, as he brought his wagon to a halt. The remuda was a mite skittish, Longarm noted.

He swung off his mount and waited for Sergeant Dillon to approach. As the sergeant stopped before Longarm, he looked about nervously.

"What's this place, sir?" he asked. "We almost there?"

"We're getting warm, Sergeant, and that's a fact. Leave Corporal Toohey back with the wagon and the remuda. The rest of your men follow me."

The sergeant nodded and returned to the troopers. Longarm could hear the man issuing orders and called out to him softly to keep it down. From then on there was almost perfect silence as the sergeant issued his orders and the rest of the men moved up to join Longarm.

When the sergeant rejoined him, Longarm led the party due west over the rocky flat. It would be dawn in less than two hours, Longarm realized, which meant they would have to shake it. The night seemed to be getting blacker. At last Longarm noticed a great emptiness yawning at him just ahead.

He held up his hand. "Careful now!" he whispered.

They crept forward until they were on the lip of the escarpment. Below them, stretching into the night for a distance of at least five miles, was the valley—Little Zion. The men sucked in their breaths. Lying under the night sky, the valley was still breathtaking. The broad stream issuing from the canyon was visible. Coiling easily about the valley, punctuated by a series of four dams, it looked like a vast hair ribbon holding the valley together.

The fields, lush under the night sky, seemed to exhale a heady fragrance that hung in the air about them. It was an almost tangible presence. Longarm sighed. It would be a shame to bring all this to an end. And then he thought of the night riders, the fear, the furtive executions in the dark of night, the implacable dogma on which this lovely, fertile valley was built, and he felt regret no longer.

Pointing to the settlement in the distance, he said to the sergeant, "We'll circle this valley and meet above those buildings."

"Circle the valley?"

"That's right. This valley is well-guarded. There are sentries up here all along this rim. When I rode in a week or so ago, I saw them."

"You want us to take them?"

"Without firing a shot. Capture them, truss them up, and leave them. Think your men can do that, Sergeant?"

The troopers crowded around them had been listening. There was a low mutter of assent. Of course they could. A few grinned, their teeth flashing in the darkness, and they elbowed one another eagerly. Action was something they had given up on, stationed in that sweltering hotbox on the edge of the Great Salt Lake Desert.

"They'll do it," said the sergeant.

"Good. We'll split up then. You take half and circle south. I'll take the rest and go north. We'll meet above the settlement."

The sergeant nodded and quickly divided the men.

The low shack was barely visible on the horizon, its slanted roof cutting a straight line across the stars, the only straight edge in a nightmare of rock forms crowding upon them out of the predawn darkness.

Trooper Billy Perkins was at Longarm's elbow. Longarm turned to Billy. "Tell the others to hold up. Looks like we've got one ahead of us."

"I don't see nothing."

"That's all right, Billy. You just go and do what I say or I'll lay this barrel across your head."

The fellow vanished quickly back into the darkness. Longarm waited patiently, heard the low mutter of voices, and a moment later was joined by two other troopers, with Billy just behind them.

Longarm pointed without a word at the shack. The men peered closely, then nodded. "Spread out," Longarm said softly. "Circle the place. And remember what I said. No gunfire. Use your rifle butts if you have to."

They nodded and melted away in the darkness. Longarm, keeping low, moved swiftly forward and found himself on a rough path that led straight to the front of the shack. He left the path before he reached the shack, and circling around behind it, found a window and peered in. In the darkness he could see nothing for a while until at last he made out a sleeping form on a cot directly across from the window. There was another cot against the adjoining wall. It was empty.

With his Colt drawn but not cocked, Longarm circled around the shack, and found himself on the lip of the escarpment, staring at a thin man with a long, straggly beard, a slouch hat, and a Sharps rifle resting in the crotch of his pants as he leaned back against a smooth rock face. The man was snoring softly, his straggly whiskers moving with each exhalation.

As the three troopers scrambled silently over the rocks toward him, Longarm put up his hand to halt them, then turned back around, and leaning forward, slowly placed one hand around the long barrel. When he was certain he had a firm grip, he yanked.

"Hey! What in tar—!"

The muzzle of Longarm's Colt, held a few inches from the man's face, quieted him almost instantly.

"Get up," said Longarm softly, moving back. "And don't do anything sudden."

The fellow swallowed unhappily and did as he was told.

"Now lead the way back to the shack," Longarm directed. "And keep those hands up."

As the man started past him, Longarm spoke softly to Billy, who hurried ahead of Longarm, taking the two troopers with him. In a moment, as he followed behind the lanky Mormon, Longarm heard his men bursting into the shack. There were no shots and only a single, stifled cry.

He smiled. So far, this operation was proceeding as slick as silk.

Leaving both sentries securely bound in the shack with the door locked and barred, the three troopers, with Longarm in the lead, continued along the rim. Longarm had only three troopers with him because he had decided to leave one man with Toohey to guard the wagon and horses in case of a surprise strike by the Mormons. Since the sergeant had a greater distance to cover, Longarm sent five men with him. All in all, a force of eleven men to take this hotbed of Avenging Angels was cutting things a mite fine, but the way Longarm had it planned, the element of surprise was the key. And so far, they still had that on their side.

The next two pairs of sentries were not as easy to take as the first two had been. One sentry almost got off a shot before Billy Perkins lifted the back of his head with a rifle butt. His companion heard the scuffle and came running just in time to throw both hands into the air. The remaining two were just stirring about in their shack, making breakfast. When they heard Longarm's men approaching, they picked up their rifles, stepped out in front of their shack, and asked loudly if that was Burt something-or-other with the salt pork and what was he doing coming up that early. When Longarm appeared out of the darkness with his Colt trained on them, they were too surprised to offer resistance and were trussed up like the others and left in their locked shack.

In less than an hour Longarm and his party had reached a position above the settlement. It was still quite dark, but he could make out the individual houses and outbuildings clearly as he peered down from the rocks.

The settlement was laid out with great precision. Most of the homes and buildings were neatly spaced inside what appeared to be an almost perfect square. The windmill tower was at the very center, and south of this were three rows containing five homes each. Broad avenues ran between the three rows. Each home was spaced the same distance from the next, like checkers on a checkerboard, with even the outhouses spaced with tight precision at the right rear corner of each home. In the soft light filtering down from the stars, the privies looked just as neat and finely engineered as the homes.

Most of the sheds and barns and other outbuildings were north of the windmill tower. What had been the largest barn was now a blackened crater and next to it was another, smaller crater—the tiny hut that had served as their armory. The Avenging Angels were undoubtedly hurting for firearms as a result, Longarm realized. At the same time that he thought of this, he thought of that man he had trussed and left to burn on that cot. It was not something he would ever be able to think about without wincing slightly, he realized.

Next to the windmill were the fenced-in compounds that held Emilie and anyone else in violation of Little Zion's laws, and still farther to the west, well out of the square that made up the settlement, there was a large, almost baronial residence. This house was not built of wood, but of stone faced with stucco—and beside it there was another residence—a long, low building with curious gabled windows running down its length. At once Longarm was reminded of another such building that had been pointed out to him by the driver of the carriage who had returned him to the hotel from Wells Daniel's home—the residence of Brigham Young. There was no wooden eagle perched atop the main gate before this particular residence, but otherwise this structure was a perfect duplicate of the apartment building with its twenty gables that adjoined Brother Brigham's residence in Salt Lake City, the seraglio that housed his many wives.

There was no doubt in Longarm's mind who lived in this impressive residence. Or why Lorenzo Wolverton wanted so much to have Emilie Boggs move into that gabled residence.

Trooper Sim Johnson approached through the darkness. Longarm pulled back from the rocks and stood up. He had sent Johnson scouting for a trail of some kind leading down to Little Zion from this point. He knew there must be one, since he had seen a roadway leading in this direction from the stables when he had been led into his prison.

"What did you find, Johnson?"

"There's a trail, all right. It leads from the settlement up past here and over that ridge. It's pretty well-traveled, too, and heads north into the mountains."

"How much traffic could it carry, you reckon?"

"Not much heavy stuff, sir. It's pretty steep and rocky and narrow. No wagons carrying supplies and such could make it. Just horses, mostly."

"Thank you, Johnson."

The fellow nodded and moved back to where the others were

waiting. Longarm looked up at the sky. He was wishing Sergeant Dillon would hurry up and beginning to wonder if maybe he and his men had been stopped, when the sergeant and his four men materialized out of the gloom.

Dillon walked up to Longarm, a smile on his face. "We surprised them all. I guess they were so used to never having anything happen, they just couldn't believe it when it did. Like you told me, they're trussed up and locked away."

"Have any trouble?"

"One of them tried to run."

"You didn't shoot, did you? I didn't hear anything."

"One of the men caught up to him and tripped him with his rifle. The fellow went down so hard on the rocky ground that we had to carry him back to his lookout post."

"All right. Now listen. This is going to be the hard part. I'm going back to Corporal Toohey. While I'm gone, I want your men to build the makings of a fire on top of that rock up there. I've already scouted it. There's an easy way up. After you've done that, I want you to wait for me at the head of the trail Private Johnson has discovered. I should be back before dawn if I don't run into any trouble. Wait for me."

"Yes, Deputy, sir."

"It's Longarm, damn it! And that's an order, Sergeant."

The sergeant smiled. "Yes, sir, Longarm."

Longarm groaned and hurried back through the predawn darkness.

Corporal Toohey was not in sight, but Cal Brenner, the trooper Longarm had ordered to stay back with him, was asleep under the wagon. He slept with his mouth open. Longarm wished he had a scorpion handy that he could drop into the trooper's mouth. He was looking for something when he heard a twig snap behind him and whirled, his Colt appearing in his right hand in one quick, striking motion.

Corporal Toohey was standing just behind him with a stick of dynamite in his hand and a grin on his face.

"I was gonna drop this in," the corporal told Longarm. "That's a big mouth he's got."

Longarm smiled, turned back around, and nudged the trooper awake with the toe of his boot. Then he holstered his Colt and looked at Toohey.

"Did you look over that canyon wall like I told you?"

"I did that."

"And?"

"Let me get this straight, now. You want to blow the wall so that it closes off all the water coming through, and then you want to blow the other side of the canyon to block it off completely."

"You got it."

"Mr. Longarm—all this for a couple of *mules?*"

"*Army* mules, Corporal. *Army* mules."

"Yes, sir, Mr. Longarm."

"Let's get busy. Trooper Brenner can help us carry the stuff." Brenner nodded sleepily. "That's dynamite you'll be carrying, Trooper," Longarm informed him. "You better wake up a little or you'll be blown up a lot!"

The fellow hopped to it and Longarm left him to the corporal, went back to his horse, and rode down into the canyon. In a moment the two followed, Toohey carrying a spool of fuse, the corporal—wide awake now—carrying a couple of boxes of dynamite. Longarm got off his horse, accompanied Toohey to the face of the canyon wall, and looked up.

The jagged hole in the canyon wall from which the thick gout of water was spurting was not more than ten or fifteen feet above the canyon floor. They were standing upstream from the spot. As they stood watching, a fine spray fell over them.

"We better move back," Toohey said. "I don't want to get this fuse wet."

"This is Bickford Safety," Longarm said.

"I know. I've worked with it before. But this here batch is old stuff and the waterproofing tape is loose."

"It will work, won't it?"

Toohey looked at Longarm. "We'll know when it blows. But that ain't all our problem. The only good crack that'll go deep enough for me to use as a blowhole is about five feet over that crack where the water is pouring out. And if you'll look close, you'll see the canyon wall leans out some at that point. I'd need to be a fly to make it up there."

"You'll have to reach it from above, then."

"That's what I been thinking," Toohey said with a sigh. "You think you can lower me down that wall?"

"Sure, but we'd better do it fast. That sun's due up in an hour. What about the other side?"

"Let me do that now while I'm down here. That won't be no problem, not with that overhang. I'll tamp in the dynamite and leave the rattails hanging till later."

Longarm looked across the canyon at the wall Toohey was planning to blow. The water had cut well in under the canyon wall, so deeply, in fact, that it looked like a cave. Several great cracks in the wall were visible, despite the darkness. It would not take much to bring the whole wall crashing down. But Longarm wanted to cut off the water supply as well. It was the only way he could see to discourage more or less permanently this nest of night riders.

As Toohey and Brenner splashed across the canyon floor to the other side, Longarm went back to his horse and remounted. Before he rode out of the canyon, he took one more look at the face of the canyon wall above the spot where the water was coming from. In the darkness he could not see the overhang the corporal mentioned, nor could he see any cracks that could be used for blowholes, but the fellow seemed to know what he was doing, and he had been studying the problem since Longarm had left him here. The problem now was to find a good spot above the canyon from which to lower a man carrying dynamite and blasting caps down this face of rock.

He rode out of the canyon and back to the wagon and the waiting horses. He dismounted, took a rope with him to the canyon's edge, and looked over. It was difficult in the darkness to find reliable footing as he moved along the rim, but finally he came upon a spot that was almost directly over the break in the canyon wall. He looked around then and found a small juniper whose roots seemed pretty deeply spread, around which he could snub the rope.

In the darkness he could not make out the two men placing the dynamite charges below him in the canyon, so he moved back from the rim and began knotting the rope to make it easier for Toohey to make it down. He had almost finished the task when Toohey and a pale, shaken Trooper Brenner, hefting two boxes of dynamite, one on each shoulder, struggled toward him out of the gloom. The footing was precarious in the darkness and the private kept stumbling.

Longarm looked nervously at the fellow as the trooper neared him. "Careful, damn it! You're liable to start this party before any of us gets a chance to send out the invitations."

Brenner didn't laugh; he just set the boxes down very carefully, then collapsed on a rock and began mopping his brow.

Toohey looked over the rim and nodded, satisfied, then walked back to the boxes and began stuffing sticks of dynamite down his shirtfront. Next he gathered up a handful of copper blasting caps and stuck them into his shirt pocket. As he did so, he picked up the spool of fuse, and passing by Longarm on his way to the rim, said, "Got to be careful with these blasting caps. A friend of mine, a real Cousin Jack, got some of them mixed in his pipe tobacco. Fellow was awful careless."

Toohey tugged on the rope, checking to see how well Longarm had snubbed it, then, with his arm through the spool and a small hammer for tamping and a knife to cut the fuse stuck in his belt, he started down the rope.

"What happened to Cousin Jack?" the private wanted to know.

As Corporal Toohey's head disappeared below the rim of the canyon, he called back, "Oh, Cousin Jack ruined a perfectly good meerschaum and the end of his nose."

Then there was silence as Toohey climbed down the rope. Leaning over the edge, Longarm watched the man until he disappeared in the gloom of the canyon. After a short while the rope stopped tugging on the lip of the canyon and remained relatively still.

Longarm turned to Brenner. "Put them two boxes back in the wagon and hobble all the horses. Then get back here."

The fellow struggled off with the dynamite and Longarm turned back to the straining rope. It was still quiet as Toohey worked. Longarm glanced at the eastern sky. There was still no sign of the dawn, but he knew he had less than an hour to put this all together.

Then the rope began to smoke some as Toohey began his climb back up. Calling to Brenner to give him a hand, Longarm reached over the rim and began hauling Toohey up out of the canyon.

In a few moments Toohey was standing on the lip of the canyon, a broad grin on his face. "Mr. Longarm, sir, I found myself the biggest damn blowhole in the world. Then I stuffed in every stick I had with me and tamped it in real solid. When that blows, this whole damn mountain's gonna cave in."

"All right, Toohey. Now I got just one more question for you. How much time do I have after you light both them fuses?"

The man considered for a second or two. "About fifteen, twenty minutes. Give me less'n a half-hour on the outside, if—like you explained to me—you want this side of the canyon to go first."

"I do." Longarm turned to Brenner. "Take the hobbles off one of the horses," he told the trooper. As Brenner hurried away, Longarm turned back to Toohey. "After it blows, stay here with Brenner to guard the horses and the wagon."

"From who?"

"Mule-stealing Mormons."

Longarm's horse had a difficult time in the darkness. The terrain along the rim of the escarpment was no help, either. But Longarm made it back to Dillon and the rest of the troopers in half the time it had taken him to return on foot. Some of the troopers were asleep on the bare ground. Dillon himself looked worn, his red face still sweating, his eyes weary and filled with uncertainty. Like Toohey, he was probably asking himself how they could be going through something like this just to retrieve a couple of army mules.

"We've got a few minutes by my reckoning, so relax," Longarm told the Sergeant.

The man nodded unhappily and shivered in the cool night air. "Toohey get all that dynamite set to blow, Longarm?"

Longarm was pleased that the trooper had finally managed to call him as he preferred to be called. He smiled at the man. "Not all that dynamite, Dillon. Just enough to do the trick, I hope."

The fellow nodded.

Longarm looked at the eastern sky and decided he had better get things rolling. He cleared his throat. "Sergeant, take your men down this trail now. Break them up into pairs and spread them out in the shadows of them buildings on this side of the windmill tower."

"And then what? Go looking for them danged mules?"

"We'll get the mules later, Dillon. When that canyon blows, there's going to be one hell of a lot of confusion down there. Men'll be running from their houses, the women right after them. And while everyone's rushing around like chickens with their heads lopped off and the others are mounting up to go see what happened, I'll be freeing a young Miss from her prison. Now if I have any trouble doing that, I'll be looking for you fellows to give me a hand. You got that clear, Sergeant?"

The fellow took out his handkerchief, his eyes bugging slightly, and nodded.

"Okay, go on down there." Longarm looked at the other men waiting farther down the trail. "You men remember! Keep your asses down and your mouths shut until you hear that canyon blow."

Sergeant Dillon turned and motioned the men ahead of him down the trail. Longarm watched them go for a moment, then turned and hurried up the slope toward the bonfire makings waiting for him. He found the spot. There was plenty of tinder, and he wondered as he struck a sulphur match where they found it in this barren country.

In a matter of seconds the bleached wood had caught and the flames were as high as his waist. Longarm let the fire build still higher for a few more minutes, then kicked aside the burning wood and heaped dirt and sand on the flaming embers that remained. The fire was out almost as quickly as it had been ignited, but he had no doubt Toohey had seen the signal. He now had a little less than half an hour before the canyon went.

Longarm moved back down the slope, hoping he could make it to the settlement before it grew much lighter. Glancing to his left, he saw the eastern sky beginning to light up. From far below him came the crowing of a rooster, his clarion call echoing and reechoing about the rocks.

Good, thought Longarm. In such a natural amphitheater those two blasts would not go unnoticed.

As Longarm crouched down in the shadow of the settlement's small blacksmith shop, his broad shoulders still heaving from the exertion that had brought him down that trail so swiftly, he remembered Captain Meriwether's first reaction to Longarm's request for ten troopers to go with him after two army mules.

Meriwether shared completely Longarm's concern for Emilie Boggs and his contempt for the Avenging Angels. Since his recent transfer to the Utah Territory, he had been anxious to find out the truth about this rumored band of night riders. But how could he bring an arm of the U.S. military down on an apparently peaceful settlement of Mormons, especially considering the touchy relations between the U.S. War Department and the Mormons since the so-called Mormon War?

Longarm had agreed that this was a dilemma, then pointed out that the captain now had a perfect excuse to do something. As Longarm explained, if horse stealing was a major crime, then stealing U.S. Army mules—far more durable and valuable in this country—was a crime against the Union that no self-respecting commanding officer could allow to go unchallenged—not when there was a deputy U.S. marshal handy who was perfectly willing to take full responsibility.

Meriwether had thought on it a bit longer and then, with a smile, he had agreed to let Longarm lead ten of his troopers into the badlands . . .

Trooper Billy Perkins ducked around the blacksmith shop and

dropped to one knee beside Longarm. "It's daylight, Mr. Longarm, sir. Sergeant Dillon wants to know what happened to that diversion you was expecting."

"Tell him to—"

A deep, ground-shuddering growl filled the air, followed by a heavy *whump*. Immediately after that, another, even more violent shaking of the earth occurred, and this time the explosion rattled among the rocks that surrounded the settlement like a series of stupendous cannon shots. The detonations rolled and surged about the escarpment, appearing for a while to get louder with each echo. By the time the roar of the two explosions had faded away, the sound of men's and women's voices began filling the air with cries of alarm. Longarm heard doors slamming, the sound of running boots. A hastily constructed corral alongside the burnt-out barn was crowded with horses. All of them were milling nervously.

With Billy Perkins staying close beside him, Longarm rose to his feet and moved to the corner of the building to peer out at the settlement. The morning sun had not yet risen above the cliffs crowding Little Zion, but enough light from the sky was filtering down to give Longarm a good picture of the situation. In the distance, a dark plume of dust and smoke was rising into the rapidly lightening sky. As Longarm watched, the column, after reaching a great height, began to spread out, the dust and debris filling a larger and larger portion of the sky—while beneath it more smoke and dust continued to pump skyward.

Women and children were pointing to this towering pillar of smoke as they ran from their houses, and Longarm saw not a few of them falling to their knees in supplication. Men were crowding into the corral, lugging their saddles and rifles. Other men, already on horseback, were galloping down the road toward the site of the explosions, and at the same time Longarm could hear men calling out to others to get their weapons—that this must be some kind of an attack.

A very tall, bearded fellow in his twenties appeared suddenly around the other corner of the shop. He halted in the act of strapping on his gunbelt. As Longarm turned to face him and swing up his rifle, the fellow vanished back around the corner. Longarm could hear the man running to warn the others. Peering around the building, Longarm saw him covering the distance to the corral at a steady run. But as Longarm had hoped, no one in all this confusion was paying much attention to him. They were too busy cutting out their horses.

Longarm leaned his rifle against the building and took out his Colt. "Where are the others?" he asked Trooper Perkins.

Perkins pointed to a thick clump of junipers at the base of the cliff far over to Longarm's right, near the boundary of the settlement, and then to a small wagon shed close to the road. "Sergeant Dillon's in the shed with his men. Perkins and Sim and the rest of the men are behind them pines."

Longarm nodded. The men behind the junipers were closer to where Emilie was being kept. "Go on over to the pines," he told the private, "and tell the men to cover me. I'm heading for that small building over there, the one with the high wire fence around it. As soon as you see me coming back toward this shop, fall in with me."

Billy nodded and darted across the open space toward the pines, his uniform bright and shiny in the morning sun that was now breaking through the dissipating cloud of smoke. Longarm held his breath, waiting for someone to spot him. But not a cry was raised and in a moment he disappeared from sight.

Longarm moved out from behind the shed and walked swiftly toward the small, fenced-in prison where he hoped Emilie was still being held. There was a padlock on the gate. He shot it off. Someone running by looked at him curiously, but Longarm paid no attention. Pushing the gate open, he walked rapidly to the door and leaned his head against the panel.

"Emilie! You in there?"

"Yes! Who is it?" It sounded as if she were standing just on the other side of the door.

"Longarm! Step back. I'm going to shoot off the lock."

He fired at the lock. It flew apart, and Longarm pulled the door open.

Emilie was standing before him, a look of terror on her face. "But you are dead! Elder Wolverton brought your body back from Salt Lake City."

"Am I buried?"

"Yes!"

"Well, I wouldn't put much stock in what Elder Wolverton told you. Or ain't you got wise to that yet?"

She ran to him. He took her hand, pulled her from the house, and was almost to the fence when he heard shots coming from the road. Longarm looked in that direction and saw two Mormons staggering back away from a fusillade of bullets, trying to return fire from the wagon shed.

Sergeant Dillon and his men had been discovered.

At once, those men who were not already far down the road on their horses began to run toward the shed. There were perhaps seven or eight of them and most of them carried rifles.

Longarm pulled Emilie through the gate and together they ran toward the blacksmith shop. But as they neared it, the young fellow who had discovered Longarm earlier stepped out of the doorway with two companions, rifles in their hands. Longarm flung Emilie to the ground. Moving sideways and crouching low, he began firing at the young man standing in the doorway. Longarm's first shot caught him high in the chest and sent him crashing back against the fellow behind him. The other had his rifle already up and firing as Longarm continued to crab sideways. The ground exploded at his feet as he carefully returned the man's fire. His first shot at the Mormon took a portion of the doorjamb, the second one caught the man in the shoulder and spun him back into the shop.

By this time, Billy Perkins, Johnson, and three other troopers had raced up to join Longarm; their combined fire cut down the third man crouching in the doorway. But the fire had alerted the other Mormons, and as Longarm dragged Emilie to her feet and dashed with her the remaining distance to the blacksmith shop, he saw at least five men peeling back from the wagon shed and coming after them on the double.

And then they were inside the shop.

"Billy," Longarm said, "you wait until me and the others are clear of this shop, then take Miss Emilie up the trail to wait for us. You got that?"

"Yes, sir, Mr. Longarm."

"Remember," Longarm repeated. "Wait until we are well clear."

As Billy nodded, Longarm told the other troopers to follow him and darted out of the shop. Retrieving his rifle from the rear of the shop, he levered a fresh cartridge into the chamber, then led a charge across the compound toward the five oncoming Mormons. He stayed low, and levering rapidly, pumped out a rapid, murderous fire that destroyed the enthusiasm of the Mormons. Two dropped almost at once, another staggered.

Dragging their wounded, they ducked behind what was left of the barn. Longarm and his troopers crowded down beside the charred remains of the arsenal. The firing immediately diminished. Then Longarm saw Sergeant Dillon and his men coming at the Mormons from behind.

"Let's go," cried Longarm as he led his men toward the belea-

guered Mormons. A bullet cut down the trooper beside Longarm.
Longarm ducked to one side, and then he was in among the barn's
blackened timbers.

A crazed Mormon raised himself up out of one of the damaged
stalls, a large revolver in his hand. Longarm fired in one quick re-
flex, driving the fellow back through a railing. But he was not
dead. As Longarm tried to duck past him, he twisted, raised his
gun, and pointed it at Longarm. Longarm crabbed sideways, his
shoulder crashing through loose, charred slats, and fired point-
blank into the man's chest. The Mormon was flung back, lifeless,
and disappeared in a shower of ashes and soot.

It was every man for himself now. As Longarm looked quickly
around him, he caught sight of filthy, sooty creatures wrestling or
shooting it out point-blank in a nightmare of hanging beams and
blackened walls. He heard a cry of rage behind him and felt a
hand come down like a sledgehammer on his right shoulder. As
Longarm went down, he twisted and turned away, shielding his
head. A beam struck his forearm and glanced off. Longarm leaped
to his feet and met the ferocious charge of a man at least two feet
taller and a foot broader than he was.

The fellow drove him back into a stall, through the partition, and
then onto his back inside another. The fellow managed to get two
blood-slicked hands around his throat, but Longarm twisted over,
knocked the fellow's grip loose, and rolled over onto him in turn.
He was slugging away at the man's head and shoulders when he
realized that the battle was over. The man was lying there silently
beneath Longarm, both eyes wide open.

Longarm scrambled to his feet. Only then did he notice the
fire-blackened steel tines—two of them—poking up almost an
inch out of the man's chest. He had also been shot twice, Longarm noted, shaking his head in disbelief.

The fighting around him had subsided. Picking up his rifle and
the Colt he had dropped when he was surprised, he called out to
Sergeant Dillon.

"Out here!" the man called back.

Longarm stumbled out of the wreckage and found that all but
one of the troopers were unscathed. This one—Win Truit—had a
calf wound and was in great pain. Longarm didn't see any Mormons around.

"No prisoners, I see," said Longarm.

The sergeant shook his head. "None. But we ain't out of the
woods yet!" The man pointed down the road. "Look!"

A crowd of riders was racing back from the canyon with more than fire in their eyes, Longarm had no doubt.

"We better get ourselves into position," said the sergeant. "I figure behind that wagon shed, up the slope amongst those rocks, and behind that there windmill tower."

Longarm nodded. "Let's move it!"

As the troopers moved out with the sergeant to take up their positions, Longarm looked back at the blacksmith shop. He could not see Perkins nor Emilie, and he assumed that they had long since cleared out and were up the slope somewhere, waiting. Then he looked more closely and caught sight of an arm hanging out of the doorway—a uniformed arm.

He ran back across the compound and found Perkins lying on his back, his eyes open, his face gray with pain. "I got hit," he whispered, "Mr. Longarm, sir. In the back. I can't move. I can't feel nothing at all!"

Perkins was frightened, terribly frightened, his slightly freckled face pale, his light green eyes filled with mute terror at his condition. Longarm wanted to comfort him, but all he could think of at the moment was Emilie.

"You'll be all right, Perkins. What happened?"

"Riders. Three of them. They came from that big house out there. One of them had a beard—a long, white snowy one!"

"Go on, Perkins. What happened to the girl?"

"They charged the shop. I swear, they musta knowed we was holed up in here. I never got the chance to pull out like you told me. I shot one of them out of his saddle, but they kept coming. Then one of them sneaked up behind the shop and cut me down. They took the girl, Mr. Longarm, sir."

"Where?"

"Up the trail."

"The two of them?"

"That's right, but one was wounded bad. I winged him as he started up the trail."

"Which one did you hit? The one with the beard?"

"No. The other one. I didn't want to chance a shot at the other fellow with the beard. The girl was riding up front of him on the horse." Perkins closed his eyes for a moment. "I wanted to go after them," he continued a moment later, his voice growing fainter, "but that was when I lost the feeling in my legs. Now . . . it's just traveling all the way up my body, Mr. Longarm. Right up to my chest . . . !"

Longarm brushed the young man's hair back off his forehead. "You'll be all right, Perkins. Just you lie still."

The fellow nodded. "Leastways," he said, "it don't hurt no more." He closed his eyes.

Longarm glanced out of the doorway and was astounded at what he saw. Three houses were in flames. As he watched, one of a trio of women ran from each house, a firebrand in her hand. Two of the women had guns and were shooting at the windows of houses not aflame. A crowd of screaming, panicked women and children were fleeing the burning homes; and though Longarm could not be sure at this distance, he thought he recognized one of the women carrying a firebrand. Annie Dawkins.

Each woman carrying a torch disappeared into another home. Shots and screams came from these homes, and almost at once, smoke began pumping from the shattered windows. As the three left the now burning homes, Longarm saw that they had been joined by two other women. And soon others were joining them.

The women were burning their homes!

The sound of firing from the direction of the road caused Longarm to spin around. He saw Mormons falling from horses as they ran into Sergeant Dillon's ambush. His men were firing from well-concealed emplacements and they were making each shot count. Longarm looked back at Perkins.

"Perkins, I'm going now. But we'll be back for you."

Perkins's eyes remained closed. Longarm shook the trooper and felt the heavy immobility—the softness of the still body. Perkins was dead.

Longarm ducked out through the doorway and raced across the compound to join three troopers positioned at the base of the windmill tower. Sergeant Dillon had waited until the Mormons had ridden past the shed and were well into the compound before opening fire. By this time many of the Mormons had lost their mounts in the withering cross fire and were lying, some dead, others severely wounded, behind their downed horses. Those Mormons still capable of returning fire were doing it in a desultory, halfhearted fashion.

These were the Mormons, Longarm realized, who had ridden to inspect the rubble-filled canyon. Now they were being treated to the piercing lamentations of their wives and children as they watched their homes and all their possessions go up in flames. Surely they must now be ready, Longarm concluded, to admit the hopelessness of their cause.

Longarm called out to the troopers, "Hold your fire, men! Let's see if these jaspers want to stop this thing right here!"

The firing ceased. Longarm waited. Slowly, obviously with great reluctance, a mean-looking fellow, his scowl directed at Longarm, got to his feet from behind a downed horse. He kept his hands in the air and he was not wearing a sidearm. As soon as he was upright, two others got to their feet also. From behind a shed two more stepped out; their hands were in the air as well.

All that were left were five men. Longarm recognized the first man to surrender. It was Karl Barker, the brother of the sheriff Longarm had shot in the Utah House.

As the troopers left their emplacements and hurried over to frisk the men and pick up what weapons were lying about, Longarm left the cover of the windmill tower and walked up to Karl Barker.

The elder bristled as Longarm approached. He was half a foot taller than Longarm; his face was lean, with sharp, prominent cheekbones, his chin jutting, his eyes smoky and filled with a merciless fire. He was still vibrant with indignation and threw his shoulders back, like a skittish horse about to bolt, as Longarm came to a halt in front of him.

"You'd be Elder Barker, I take it," said Longarm.

"Damn you," the man growled. "Elder Wolverton said you were dead. We buried you last night."

"Alongside your other victims," commented Longarm. "That must be some graveyard, Barker—with not a marker in sight."

Barker's gaze did not waver, but the fellow seemed to lose a little of his iron defiance. "I don't care, Longarm. I am only sorry you were not buried there."

"Do you know who you *did* bury, Barker?"

"No."

"Elder Smithson."

Barker's eyebrows shot up in surprise.

"He was a true martyr, Barker. A martyr to his conscience—not like your brother or the other Avenging Angels lying around us now. I'll leave you to see to your wounded, and then you may do as you please. But I suggest you leave off riding at night and intimidating innocent Mormons, who have as much right to what they believe as you do. Or maybe that's too much for you to chew on at one time."

The man started to make a retort, but the ramrod posture he had been maintaining sagged slightly as he looked about him at the dead and wounded and heard the faint cries for help. The other men who had surrendered with him were looking to him for guidance. He started to turn to them, to issue orders—then paused and looked back at Longarm.

"What was it you used on the canyon?" he asked. "Nitroglycerin?"

"Dynamite. Forty percent straight dynamite—supplied by Job Welling, a Mormon you couldn't intimidate, Barker."

Barker shook his head sadly. "There's no canyon there anymore. The water has been cut to a trickle. I told Wolverton he was going too far, intimidating Boggs, Welling . . . the others."

"You didn't tell him loud enough."

"Where is he?" Barker's eyes lit slightly, as if he were hoping to hear that Elder Wolverton had been killed in the attack.

"He lit out with Emilie Boggs. He took the trail north."

The man seemed confused by this. "He . . . ran away? Left us?"

"That's right, Barker. But he won't get far, I promise you."

Barker's smoldering eyes fastened implacably on Longarm's face. "Get him," Barker said softly. "Kill the son of a bitch!"

Then Barker left Longarm, and with his remaining men began seeing to the dead and wounded. Women ran up to him to help, while others, sobbing and wailing, dropped beside sons or husbands still prostrate on the ground.

The sergeant stepped over to Longarm. "Two wounded," Dillon said, with some satisfaction. Then he frowned. "Where's Perkins?"

"He's dead, Sergeant. You'll find him over there in the blacksmith shop, with four dead Avenging Angels nearby."

The sergeant swallowed, his face suddenly sober. "I'll get a detail over there right away."

"Before you do, Sergeant, there's one thing you should see to at once."

"What's that?"

"The *mules*, Sergeant. The army mules! What in tarnation did you think we came this far for, anyway? Don't you remember?"

"Oh! Yes, sir, Mr. Longarm. At once! Right away! I'll get men on it at once!" The sergeant looked around at the desolate, body-strewn compound, and then beyond, at the still burning houses. Not one of them had escaped the flames. The air was dim with smoke. Obviously, the sergeant didn't know where to begin. This much confusion and desolation was a new experience for him.

"Try the stables near that large stone house outside the

compound, Sergeant. Try everywhere," Longarm told him. "I don't care how long it takes, Sergeant. Find those two army mules and bring them to me."

The sergeant nodded and hurried off toward his men, who were busy building a huge cache of weapons near what had become their headquarters, the wagon shed. Longarm turned about and started across the compound toward the small, single-story buildings that had been used for the detention of those the Avenging Angels considered their enemies—or their future brides.

Before he could get there, he saw about six women running from the burning houses with guns and the remnants of firebrands in their hands—toward the same buildings. They wasted no time in shooting off the locks and as Longarm approached, three very happy women poured out of the shabby, unpainted buildings.

Longarm caught sight of Annie then. He was right. She had been one of the leaders. She had a huge revolver in her hand, and she was hugging a fragile young thing who was weeping with relief to find herself free.

"Annie!" Longarm called.

Annie turned swiftly, and jumping to see over the heads of the other women, squealed with delight when she saw him. The huge revolver still clutched in one hand, her other hand pulling the young girl after her, Annie burst through the crowd and flung her arms around Longarm's neck.

"I knew when I heard those explosions that you'd come back!" Annie cried. "I knew it! They said you were dead and buried, but I knew you weren't!"

She hugged him more tightly about the neck, causing the butt of the Colt to dig into his back. Grinning, Longarm gently disengaged her arms from around his neck and then carefully took the revolver from her.

"Oh, don't worry about that, Longarm," she assured him. "It's empty."

"We'll see," he said, pointing it at the sky and squeezing the trigger.

A thunderous report erupted in their midst, freezing every laugh, stilling every cry of delight. Longarm was a little awed at the power the old Colt still packed. He examined it. It was a Colt Navy .36, still in fine shape. He checked the chambers. Now it was empty.

He handed it back to Annie. "Never say a gun is empty until you check it."

Annie took the gun back, shivering slightly.

"Who's this young lady with you, Annie?"

"She hasn't been here long," Annie said. "Her name is Mary-lou."

Longarm frowned and looked more closely at the girl. "Mary-lou Welling?" he asked.

"Yes," she said, nodding eagerly. "You know my father! Did he send you?"

"In a way," Longarm replied. "At least he supplied me with what I needed to wake this place up this morning."

"They told me if I didn't come with them, they would harm Daddy. I told him not to send anyone after me. But I'm so glad you came!"

Longarm admitted that he was glad, too. He told them that those women who wanted to could go back with Sergeant Dillon and his men. Many of them would have to saddle what horses were left in the corral and ride astride. It would be a long trip, but there was a wagon for water, and there would be plenty of fresh horses. "And when you get back to Salt Lake City," Longarm said, finishing up, "I hope you'll tell whoever has a mind to listen that the Avenging Angels have just had their wings scorched—so that means you people ought to stand up a little straighter now, the next time they come sneaking around. You think you two can remember that?"

"I certainly can," said Marylou stoutly, her tears gone completely now. "I'm going to tell everyone!"

"And I will, too," said Annie.

"We both will," said Marylou, "because Annie is coming to live with me!"

"Marylou!" Annie exclaimed. "You *know* what I told you . . . I mean . . ."

"Never *mind* that. I don't care." She smiled. "And if *you* don't tell anyone, I am sure *I* won't."

Annie looked at Longarm and smiled. "Well, maybe I'll give it a try."

Sergeant Dillon was approaching. There were two troopers behind him leading the two army mules. The troopers seemed enormously relieved and the sergeant just a bit troubled.

"This here what you wanted, Mr. Longarm?" Sergeant Dillon asked.

"Where did you find them?" Longarm asked as he approached the mules.

"In a stable in back of that big stone house."

"Did you notice anything a bit special about the long, low building next to the stone house, the one with the gabled windows?"

"The one that looked like a chicken house?"

"It looked a mite more substantial than that, Sergeant."

Dillon nodded. "It was. And I did notice. Seemed like there were some women in there. Some of them were pounding on the windows. But we got enough women about, so I left them in there—for their own safety."

"I see. Well, first chance you get, Sergeant, let them out. Then tell them I'll be bringing back their husband as soon as I can."

"Their *husband,* sir?"

"That's right, their husband. Will you do that?"

"Of course, Mr. Longarm."

Longarm had been inspecting the mules carefully all this while. The examination made him feel much better. "These are the mules I wanted, Sergeant. And they are in fine condition, just fine."

The sergeant cleared his throat, his face growing red. He reached for his polka-dot handkerchief.

"Something bothering you, Sergeant?"

"It's just . . . hard to believe, Mr. Longarm, sir. All this—" He mopped his brow, then waved his arm graphically about him. "All this destruction, these wounded men—just for a few mules. Even if they *are* army mules."

"You're right, Sergeant. There is a great deal more to it than that. And in an hour or so, soon's I get myself organized proper, I'll be riding off with these mules to finish what we started here. Meanwhile, I suggest you confiscate every weapon you can find." As he spoke, he took Annie's Colt from her and tossed it at the sergeant. "Add them to that pile your men started and burn it. Make a nice snappy bonfire, Sergeant."

"Are you sure we can do that, Mr. Longarm?" the man asked weakly.

"Of course, Sergeant. Those weapons are stolen army ordnance. No doubt about it."

The sergeant sighed and nodded.

"And Sergeant, you'll also have to see to it that these women get safely back to Salt Lake City. You are responsible for them now."

The sergeant looked around with astonishment at the circle of women that had slowly been forming around Annie and Longarm. There were at least nine women. Many of them wore skirts that

were singed, while their faces were smudged with soot as a result
of their recent fiery revolt. These were the women who had never
really wanted to become a part of this hidden settlement, and who,
like Annie, had only given in to the custom of multiple marriage
out of desperation after being brought here under duress. Once
they had seen their chance to strike back at their masters, they had
taken it—with a vengeance.

The sergeant looked back at Longarm. He didn't seem unhappy at what Longarm had told him. "Well, if they'll help me
with some of my wounded troopers."

"I'm sure they will, Sergeant. Just ask them."

As Longarm led the mules away, he saw an eager circle
of women closing tightly about a very flustered—but not at all
displeased—Sergeant Dillon.

Longarm smiled.

An hour or so later, as Longarm rode past the blacksmith shop
and thought of Trooper Billy Perkins and of the two-hour start
Lorenzo Wolverton had on him, he wasn't smiling at all.

The ride up the steep trail was a difficult one, but the mule
he was riding handled the climb with a fine, steady nimbleness.
Lorenzo Wolverton and the other rider with him were forking
horses, he reminded himself with some satisfaction; the elder
and Emilie were riding double and Perkins had wounded the
other rider. He would catch them.

As Longarm reached the crest finally, he looked down at the
ruin of Little Zion. A heavy pall of smoke still hung over the valley. In front of the wagon shed a tall bonfire was burning, pumping a fresh column of black smoke into the air. Longarm nodded
in satisfaction. He wasn't worried any longer about Annie and the
rest of the girls getting back all right. Sergeant Dillon could be
counted on to follow orders.

Now all Longarm had to do was concentrate on overtaking
Emilie Boggs and her two captors.

Chapter 9

Four hours or so later the trail leading from the settlement petered out as the badlands gave way finally to foothills and gentler, less wild terrain. Longarm still had no difficulty tracking the two horses, and he was a little relieved to be leaving the arid basin behind him for the higher plateau country. The air was already cooler, brighter.

Following Wolverton's tracks, he came to a small and narrow meadow. He pulled up and saw nothing moving on it and ran his mule across it into the timber. The tracks kept steadily on through a sparse stand of pine. It looked like first-growth stuff, massive at the butt and rising in a flawless line toward a canopy of top covering that made a solid umbrella against sunlight. It was cool as he rode, the pines sawing high above him, and very little underbrush to hide any tracks. At some angles he was able to look a hundred or two hundred yards in a single direction.

Wolverton and his companion's tracks were sharply etched in the spongy humus. It was almost as if Wolverton were beckoning him on, daring him to come and take Emilie away from him.

The land grew rougher again and the pines turned smaller and ravines began to come down toward him, but these were almost gentle ravines—a far cry from the rugged, wild draws he had left behind. Longarm found the tracks taking him onto the crest of first one ridge and then another. He dropped at last into a broad ravine clothed in good, thick ground cover that for a while gave him some difficulty in tracking. He crossed over it and rode to the next ridge.

The land was no longer tame, he noted. Rolling dunes of sand lifted across the trail and clay gulches cut sharp barriers before him that he could not jump. Here and there a pine tree stood as sentinel over the bleak hills before him, black and bulky and high. For an uncomfortable period Longarm lost sign and was relieved to find it again as he trailed up a shallow creek.

Dismounting, he found the tracks close to the water's edge. No moisture had yet crept into the prints. He stood and peered ahead of him in the direction the tracks were taking and saw they were heading into still higher, more rugged country. He let both mules drink for a few moments in the swift creek, filled his canteen, and mounted up.

The tracks now seemed to trace a line as straight as a telegraph wire to the mountain range he had noted earlier. Soon the tracks were cutting through a rocky defile, one side of it a cliff reaching straight up, gray and weathered and cracked. Longarm rode cautiously along, alert now to the possibility of ambush. Wolverton and his companion had simply done too little to cover their tracks.

Once through the defile, Longarm found himself approaching a rising wilderness of huge boulders that seemed to have been piled there by some furious giant long ago. Beyond the broken world in front of him the dark bulk of the mountains rose high into cold, clear sky: formidable ramparts that seemed flung up before him as a warning.

The sign was getting clearer, fresher. He was gaining on them. Longarm rode more cautiously as great, shouldering masses of rock and timber lifted on both sides of the trail. Then he caught the glint of a rifle barrel in the rocks to his right, high above him.

Swiftly he untied his lead from his trailing mule and at once the mule made no effort to keep up. Longarm suddenly spurred his mule, pushing it to a gallop. He held his breath, waiting for the shot to come, gambling that when it did it would prove the owner of that rifle a poor marksman. The shot came when Longarm had almost concluded that whoever it was had about given up the idea of ambush. It was a flat report that sent a flurry of echoes chasing after it.

Longarm grabbed his Winchester from his saddle boot and flung himself from the saddle. There was another shot. This time the bullet whined uncomfortably close and ricocheted off a boulder just behind him. It had not been a poor shot for that distance, Longarm realized. He slapped the rump of his mule and sent him trotting up the trail into some rocks, then dove to cover himself in a small stand of pine. Quickly, he unstrapped his spurs, pocketed them, then levered a cartridge into the chamber of his Winchester.

Another shot from above showered him with tiny shards of pine cones, and this time the *thunk* of the round as it buried itself in one of the pines was just too damned close. Wolverton or his wounded ally had a pretty good bead on him. But Longarm was remembering the vantage point where that glint had come from, and he knew that from his present position he could outflank it.

Keeping down, he ducked back across the trail and lost himself in a very thick growth of young timber, then angled quickly up the rockstrewn slope. From somewhere above there came another shot, but there was no sound of a bullet coming to rest anywhere around him. The rifleman was just shooting to keep up his courage. As Longarm approached the crest, there was another shot, followed by the sound of a slug whining off rocks far below. The fellow was still firing blind, hoping.

Racing along the crest of the ridge, Longarm leaped down to the flat surface of a huge boulder, then clambered swiftly up its slope until he was well above the narrow perch where he had first sighted the gleam of that rifle barrel. Dropping to his belly, he inched his way along the stone ledge until his head was just peering over the lip. Below him at a distance of perhaps a hundred feet, a single Mormon was crouched, his rifle resting on a shelf of rock in front of him. The man had an unobstructed view of the trail far below, yet the man—seemingly without aiming—was methodically squeezing off shots at nothing.

Longarm watched the fellow send two more rounds onto the trail, then decided to look around for Wolverton and Emilie. He slipped back down the rock, then followed a narrow ridge of a trail until he was still higher, high enough to see well beyond the trail below and the meadowland beyond it. But there was no sign of Wolverton and no horses—not even one for this fellow still peppering the trail like a mechanical toy someone had wound up and left.

Returning to the boulder, Longarm took careful aim—and fired. The rifle jumped from the Mormon's hands with a suddenness and violence that profoundly satisfied Longarm, who watched the shattered rifle clatter down the slope, then stood up.

"Stay where you are, mister," he called.

The fellow turned slowly toward him. He made no effort to draw the sixgun at his waist. He waved a feeble right arm and Longarm saw the long dark stain that extended from just under the arm all the way down past his waist. Even as Longarm watched, the fellow collapsed forward onto the rocks.

Longarm pushed himself back down the rock, got to his feet, and raced along the ridge until he was able to drop to a trail that wound onto that small overlook where the Mormon had positioned himself.

He found the man still slumped among the rocks. Longarm pulled him upright and examined his wound. The slug had entered his back just below his left shoulder blade and apparently ranged through the man's lungs to come to rest somewhere in the chest cavity. His face was pale, his breathing labored, a thin trickle of blood coming from one corner of his mouth. Tiny beads of perspiration stood out on his forehead and his straggly beard was damp. Private Billy Perkins had more than winged this man.

His eyes remained closed as Longarm examined him. They flickered open when Longarm let him down gently, his back resting against a rock. Coughing slightly, he looked up at Longarm, his eyes showing a kind of grudging respect.

"I told the elder it was you come back," he said softly. "I told him, but he insisted, said you was dead—said it was someone else leading that attack . . . wouldn't believe it was you . . . !"

"They left you?"

"The girl didn't want to—but *he* did. Had another one of his revelations, he did . . . son of a bitch! They were going to the northwest . . . then into Canada, set up another Little Zion, the girl at his side." He smiled bitterly. "The martyrdom of his followers would bring flocks of true Saints to his banner! He's mad—all of us were mad . . ." He began to cough then and each hack sent a shudder through Longarm. It sounded as if pieces of the Mormon's lungs were coming loose with each paroxysm.

"How far ahead of me are they?"

The man left off coughing with an exercise of iron will. "They each got a horse now, so they'll be making good time. But the man is riding his horses too hard. He thinks they are as mad as he is . . ." The man started to cough, then forced himself to quit. He looked back up at Longarm through watering eyes. "He left me for dead . . . but I crawled up here, Longarm, to wait for you—"

"That loyal, are you, still?"

"No . . . not loyal . . . wanted to warn you, tell you which way he went . . . ! Those shots to get you up here—" He smiled weakly. "Took you long enough."

"Tell me, then."

"Snake Creek Pass, northwest of here . . . got a cabin there . . ." He smiled bitterly. "Used it for supplies on our . . . missions to keep the faithful . . . faithful . . ."

He resumed coughing, the sound more harrowing now than before. Longarm knew then that all he could do was watch. This loyal lieutenant of Elder Wolverton had goaded himself into living just long enough to betray his former master and was now making his agonizing way through a very narrow passage into whatever heaven or hell awaited him. The man's coughing grew weaker with each paroxysm, his hands bracing him feebly as they clutched at a slab of rock before him. He began to lean over the rock now as blood came in fresh clots from his gasping mouth.

"Jesus," the man whispered in wonder. "Oh, my Jesus!"

He tried to push himself away from the rock and the sight of his blood, but succeeded only in falling away from the rock and collapsing to the ground beside it. Longarm reached down and tried to pull the man upright. The fellow's head swiveled toward him, his eyes wild with fear.

He started to cry out something—then went slack in Longarm's arms. It was almost as if the man's tormented spirit had flung itself past him at that moment as it quit this dying carcass of a sinner. Longarm let him fall back onto the narrow, rocky ground and stepped back.

He did not have time to bury the man. He glanced skyward and thought he saw a single buzzard coasting high up, well to the north. He looked back at the quiet body. He did not even know the man's name, he realized, and hadn't thought to ask him. Well then, he would leave him for the buzzards as so many other Saints had been left before him when the Avenging Angels had collected their tithes and settled their scores.

Longarm turned his back on the dead man and made his way carefully down the mountainside. The mule he had been riding had found a home in among the rocks where he had sent him. When he approached, the mule cleverly managed to present to Longarm only his hind end, his rear legs poised and ready. Realizing that the worst place from which to consider a mule is directly from behind anywhere within a radius of ten feet, Longarm pulled back and contemplated the back of the mule's head. His ears were pricked, alert for any comment Longarm might care to deliver. Longarm thought for a moment that the mule was smiling.

"All right, you four-footed son of Satan! I'll leave you for the Indians. Not a one would lower himself to ride you, but they'll sure as hell find time to boil you in their pots! The damn fools just love mule meat!"

He turned and hunted for the other mule. He was leading it behind him on his way through the canyon when he looked back and saw the other mule standing well out of the rocks, looking rather anxiously after him. Longarm pretended not to notice, and when he heard the animal cantering after him, he did not look back. The mule reached his side in a few moments and slowed to a walk.

"What's the matter?" said Longarm. "Don't you cotton to feeding the Indians hereabouts?"

The mule jerked his head up angrily, his cheeks quivering indignantly. Longarm reached over, grabbed the trailing reins, and mounted up. Dropping his rifle into the boot, he leaned over the neck of the mule and said. "I was just riling you a mite. No Indian in his right mind would eat anything as tough and ornery as you!"

The mule bucked slightly, then went back to his walk, and Longarm snubbed the lead from the other mule about the saddle horn and pointed the animal toward the high country and Snake Creek Pass.

Longarm knew this country in northwestern Utah Territory just well enough to realize that if Lorenzo Wolverton was allowed to go on through Snake Creek Pass and into Oregon, Longarm would have a long, long chase ahead of him. He clapped spurs to the mule and was pleased at its response as it began a smooth, ground-devouring lope.

Longarm came upon Snake Creek before sundown. He had decided against following the trail left by Wolverton and Emilie and had cut across very rough country, counting on the surefootedness and stamina of his mules in an effort to arrive at the pass before or not long after Wolverton. He had changed mounts twice in the process and was well pleased with the mules' performance. The mountains he had glimpsed earlier, that had seemed so ominous and dark, he now perceived as pine-clad and gently rolling, enormous hills. The creek was a wild, shallow torrent with great handsome boulders in its midst that rushed out of these hills, heading for a dusk-shrouded V in the distance—Snake Creek Pass.

Longarm followed the creek until he was within five miles of the pass; then he cut south to a higher benchland that roughly paralleled the creek, keeping in the timber as much as possible. It was dark when he reached the pass. Moving well up onto the benchland through the pines, he found the hills scarred with great white outcroppings of rock, some of them extending straight up and disappearing into the gloom of the young night, an effective barrier that forced him to ride farther into the pass.

He kept the wall of rock to his left as he rode, using it as a guide in the darkness under the pines that crowded close to the mountain wall. The rich pine humus underfoot effectively muffled the sound of his passage, but soon the encroaching shoulder of the mountain began to force him back down through the timber toward Snake Creek. It was not long before he came upon a well-worn game trail overlooking the stream. He followed the trail until the moon crept out from behind the shouldering hills and hung directly overhead.

He pulled off the trail then, and kept in the timber for a while longer until he was through the pass. At once the character of the land changed as he broke out onto a vast meadow that dropped by imperceptible degrees to a dark timberland far below, stretching like a vast carpet into the night.

Where was the cabin?

Feeling too exposed out on the meadow, Longarm cut back into the timber he had just left, and then dismounted. He was weary, having ridden most of the day and now well into the night. He hunkered down, his back to a pine, considering whether or not he should camp for the night. He didn't want to do that. He needed to corner the elder in this pass before Wolverton went on through, or he might never find the man, or Emilie. One look at that carpet of forest extending westward to the Sierras and the Pacific beyond had shown him that.

He was taking out a cheroot when he came alert. He stood up and put away the cheroot. Raising his head like something wild, he sniffed at the night air that swept down from the north. It carried with it the strong scent of pine and cedar—and wood smoke. It was not a campfire. The concentration was too great for that. In his mind's eye, Longarm could almost see the freshly cut wood being fed into a Franklin stove, the sheet iron stovepipe shuddering as it belched the heavy, pungent wood smoke into the night.

The cabin was across the creek on the north slope of the pass, more than likely.

Longarm mounted up and rode toward the creek, keeping in the timber all the way. It was not easy finding a ford in the moonlight, but at last he cut across the creek and up a steep embankment that gave way to a high meadow. At the far end, against a background of towering pines, he caught a glint of lamplight. As he rode toward it, the light winked out periodically. The cabin was set among trees.

If he had ridden by during daylight, he considered ironically, he might well have missed the cabin. From the game trail on the other side of the creek he would not have seen the meadow.

He rode east across the high meadow; the damp night air was pungent with the scent of sage and bearberry. Finally he reached the timber. He dismounted and followed the timberline on foot until he was close enough to see clearly the cabin window he had glimpsed from a mile below. He tied the mules to a sapling and moved closer to the cabin until he was almost within the window's bright rectangle of light that flooded the woodland crowding close upon the cabin. The building was set well back in the trees, in keeping with its purpose, Longarm realized.

Circling the cabin, Longarm found his progress blocked by the beams of a large corral leading from a low pole barn. There were only two horses in the corral, both trembling with exhaustion in the moonlight and with streaks of lather still drying on their flanks, their noses buried in a grain trough. They were too exhausted and too hungry to spook at his appearance and he kept moving, circling the barn and returning to the cabin. It was built of rough pine logs, the chinks filled with clay. The roof was shingled and the north end of the building consisted mostly of a fireplace and chimney. Longarm had been mistaken. The wood smoke had been pumping out of a fireplace, not a Franklin stove.

From all the signs, Wolverton and Emilie had recently arrived at the cabin. The fire was probably the result of Emilie's demand that Wolverton rid the cabin of its chill. It was just a guess, of course, but Longarm could imagine Emilie doing everything she could to forestall the eager Wolverton.

By this time Emilie must have concluded that all hope of deliverance was futile.

Once he had circled the cabin, he pulled up, considering. There were only two entrances, front and rear. He went back around to the woodpile and selected three hefty pieces, then returned to the front of the cabin.

Facing the door, he placed two of the pieces of wood on the ground beside him, kept one in his left hand, drew his Colt, shifted the Colt to his left hand and the wood to his right, then heaved the wood up onto the shingled surface of the roof. It struck with a loud thump, then rolled end over end down the roof, slid sideways, and then dropped off the roof into the high grass.

At once the lantern inside the cabin was turned low and blown out.

Longarm waited. He thought he heard the sound of a table being overturned, or a chair, and the sound of heavy-booted footsteps approaching the door. He waited, but the door was not flung open. Of course. That would be too foolish a move for a man like Wolverton. Longarm bent, picked up another piece of neatly split cordwood, and flung it at the door. It hit with a resounding thump.

He could imagine Wolverton standing by the door, his hand on the latch, trying to fathom what it was for sure. Perhaps it was a bear. This was not the usual way one man called another out. Longarm reached down for the last piece of wood and hurled it onto the far end of the roof. It struck smartly, rolled up a few feet, then tumbled backward until it dropped off the roof.

That was too much for Wolverton. He flung open the door and rushed out, turning at once to the roof. There was a rifle in his hand and he raised it to his shoulder as he faced that end of the roof where the last piece of wood had landed.

"Emilie!" Longarm called. "Get out the back door! Hurry!"

Wolverton flung himself around, firing as he did so. The slug sang past Longarm's cheek. Wolverton levered and fired a second time as Longarm crabbed sideways, returning the elder's fire. As a pine came between him and Wolverton, Longarm heard the rear door slamming, and realized that Emilie was out of the cabin and hightailing it into the woods.

There was no chance now that Wolverton would be able to use Emilie as a shield, or force Longarm to deal by threatening her. It was just between Lorenzo Wolverton and Longarm now.

From behind the pine, Longarm called out to Wolverton. "Put down that rifle, Elder! You ain't going nowhere with that! The girl's gone! And your latest revelation ain't worth a bucket of warm spit."

"You are dead, Longarm! I do not need to listen to a dead man!"

Wolverton fired. The slug buried itself in the pine. Longarm fired back; it was his third shot. The round whined off one of the cabin's logs. Wolverton had been crouching. Now he stood up, and levering rapidly, loosed a deadly fusillade at the crouching Longarm.

"You can't kill me, Longarm! Just as I can't kill you! Perhaps we are both immortal!" The man's voice cracked in near-hysteria.

As the bullets whined past Longarm, he managed to get off another shot. Abruptly Wolverton turned and darted around the corner of the cabin. Swearing, Longarm scrambled to his feet and raced after the man. He stayed low as he rounded the corner of the cabin and it was a good thing he did. Wolverton was waiting in the darkness. Wielding his rifle like a club, he swung on Longarm. The rifle butt knocked off Longarm's hat, but that was the only damage as Longarm's shoulder rammed the elder amidships. Both men went down. Longarm's head struck the cabin wall, momentarily stunning him.

He managed to hang on to his Colt, however, and fired at

Wolverton as he rolled away from the cabin. Wolverton pulled back as he scrambled to his feet and pumped a round at Longarm. The bullet buried itself in the ground at Longarm's right temple as he squeezed off another shot at the figure towering over him in the darkness.

The slug must have caught him. Wolverton appeared to stagger back against the cabin. Still upright, however, Wolverton chambered another round and managed to get off another shot at Longarm. But this one went wild. Longarm aimed carefully and squeezed the trigger.

The hammer came down on an empty chamber.

Leaning against the cabin, Wolverton laughed—a low, sinister laugh that told Longarm his quarry had slipped over the edge into madness—if, indeed, the man had ever really been sane.

"Now we'll see who's mortal," whispered Wolverton as he pumped another cartridge into his Winchester's chamber.

"How many times have you tried to kill me, Wolverton?" Longarm asked, hoping for time now to gather himself so that he could charge the elder before he fired. "Twice? Three times? You even buried me once, didn't you!"

Wolverton gasped. Longarm saw the rifle barrel, gleaming dully in the darkness, begin to waver.

"You said the Angel Moroni sent me. He *did*, Elder! To punish you! To bring you to perdition! Look about you now in this darkness, Elder. See those faces! They are the faces of those children you slaughtered long ago. Do you really think the Angel Moroni will forgive you that deed? Have you repented that crime? Have you gone to your knees before him?"

"Stop!" cried the elder. "Stop! For the love of God, Longarm! You cannot know these things!"

Longarm flung himself upward at Wolverton. Knocking the rifle from the man's hands, he grabbed him by his shirtfront and flung him to one side, sending him crashing into a tree. The fellow slumped to the ground without a word. Longarm snatched up the rifle and walked over to the elder.

The man's head was hanging loosely forward. Longarm looked down at him. "Can you get up, Elder?"

The man was weeping softly.

Longarm went down on one knee beside the elder, using the man's rifle for support. He looked into the man's face. The fellow looked at him. "The faces . . . the faces . . ." Wolverton whispered, his eyes wide with horror. "The young faces—all around me in the darkness . . ." He looked closely at Longarm. "You . . . see them, too!"

"Can you get up, Elder?"

From the darkness beside Longarm, Emilie, looking wan and ghostly in a long, torn dress, stepped closer. "Is he dead, Longarm? Did you kill him?"

"I don't know, Emilie. Help me to get him inside."

The old man offered no resistance at all as they pulled him to his feet and gently led him into the cabin. Emilie lit the lantern and turned it up as Longarm guided Wolverton to a small cot against the wall. The wood in the fireplace was still burning, but the fire needed more fuel: Emilie went after it as the elder, his eyes closed, lay on his back on the cot and let Longarm examine him.

The single round that had struck Wolverton had caught him just below the right shoulder; it must have done considerable internal damage before coming out just below his shoulder blade, but it was by no means a fatal wound. Had the man possessed the will, he could easily have fired upon Longarm when he came up with an empty gun.

The elder opened his eyes as Emilie reentered the room, her arms piled high with firewood. As she knelt in front of the fireplace to feed the wood to the fire, Wolverton said, "But she was in my revelation." He grabbed Longarm's vest with long, powerful fingers and pulled Longarm closer. "Does she know of them, too?"

"Them?"

"The children . . . ! And the others . . . ! All around. In every dark place, they wait. And now they wait for me—*there,* too!"

He released Longarm's vest, closed his eyes, and turned his head to the wall. Longarm waited to see if he would speak again, then got to his feet and went over to Emilie. She was standing before the fireplace, her still fearful eyes on the elder.

"How is he?" she asked. "Will he—?"

"Die? I don't think so. His wound is not fatal. But we'll have to get him some help or it might be—back to what's left of Little Zion. I did promise his wives I would bring him back to them."

She left Longarm's side, walked over to the cot, and looked down at the old man. "He looks so . . . shrunken now," she said. "And just a little while ago . . ." She shuddered, as if she still expected the elder to rise in a fury before her, his wild eyes fixed upon her.

Suddenly Emilie bent closer. "Longarm . . . !"

He knew from the tone of her voice what she had discovered. He was at her side in an instant. She turned and bowed her head on his shoulder. He held her gently and looked past her at the elder. Yes. Longarm had seen enough of it lately to recognize death when he came upon it. The curiously shrunken, alabaster features of the old man spoke only of mortality now.

Weeping softly, Emilie looked up into his face. "But you said he wasn't wounded that bad."

"I was thinking only of bullets, Emilie. He had other wounds."

She looked at him. "Those things you said to him out there. I heard you. What did you mean?"

"It's a long story, Emilie. It had to do with that Mountain Meadow Massacre. He was there—a part of it."

"Oh?" She frowned and pulled away. "I've heard about that."

"Elder Smithson told me about it. Wolverton's real name was Mordecai Lee. Like Smithson, he had been running from that business ever since."

"Running? Elder Wolverton?"

Longarm nodded. "We all got different ways of running from things, I reckon."

She turned slowly then and looked down at the sunken face, the long, shriveled figure. "He was such a terrifying man. He had these visions. He told me about them. He frightened me, Longarm."

"I guess maybe they frightened him more."

Longarm led her away from the cot.

"Why don't you take that lantern into the next room and wait while I go to the barn for his bedroll," Longarm suggested. "Did he leave it with his saddle?"

She nodded, picked up the lantern, and took it with her into the other room. The only light left in the room came from the flames flickering in the fireplace. The dancing light gave a rosy hue to the dead man's features and imparted a hectic life to his quiet limbs.

Longarm turned quickly and left the cabin to get the bedroll for Elder Wolverton's last sleep.

Chapter 10

It was well on toward dusk of the following day when Longarm and Emilie reached Little Zion. The body of Elder Wolverton was slung over one of the mules; Longarm and Emilie were riding the horses. As they reached the bottom of the steep trail that led down from the rocks to the valley, Emilie looked at Longarm, her eyes wide with astonishment.

"You told me what had happened, Longarm," she said, "But it's even worse than you said!"

Longarm could only agree with her. All but one of the houses had been razed to the ground, which—added to the destruction Longarm himself had caused when he set fire to the barn—gave the entire settlement the look of a place that has just lost a war. Sherman's March to the Sea could not have appeared more devastating than this.

A small knot of somber men was standing in front of the wagon shed. Sergeant Dillon and his men were nowhere in sight. As the knot of men broke up and started toward them, Longarm saw that what he had thought at first were rifle barrels were instead long-handled spades. He saw then the neat mounds of raw earth spaced evenly about the compound and realized how busy these men must have been this day.

Elder Barker was in the lead as the men approached. His face hardened when he saw Longarm, but there was a question in his eyes. Then he caught sight of the soogan slung over the back of the lead mule, and a grim, barely noticeable smile lit his features.

Longarm pulled his horse to a halt as Barker walked up to him. With a brisk nod of his head, he indicated the soogan. "You got him?"

"Guess you could say that."

Barker looked at Emilie then. "You all right, woman?"

"Yes," she said. "I am. Now."

That seemed to satisfy him. He looked back to Longarm. "We still got some digging to do and as long as there's light, we'll tend to it. If I were you, I wouldn't stay here past dark. We ain't got any firearms left us—but we'll find something."

Longarm nodded. "Obliged for the warning."

"Just didn't want you tempting us." His grim smile lit his face for a moment. "Old habits die hard."

Longarm urged his horse on, leaving the elder leaning wearily on the handle of his shovel.

The yard between the stone house and the wives' quarters was crowded with women all busy cleaning and cooking with four very large kettles hanging over open fires. The women were coming and going from the impressive mansion with a familiarity that told Longarm it no longer served as the citadel of a tyrant. As he and Emilie rode into their midst, they all turned to face him silently, their work ceasing on the instant.

"I said I'd bring back Elder Wolverton," Longarm announced. He indicated the body slung over the mule. "There he is. His wives and the rest of his kin can have him now."

"Why?" a woman called sharply, angrily.

"To bury him," Longarm told her. "I reckon you'd be wanting to give him a decent burial. You his wife?"

"One of them," she snapped.

Longarm looked quickly around. He could sense the antagonism, but it did not seem to be directed at him or Emilie.

One of the women stepped closer to Emilie's horse and looked up at her. "You got away from him, did you?"

"Yes," Emilie said, her face coloring.

"You were lucky," the woman replied. She looked up at Longarm approvingly. "Very lucky."

Longarm took a deep breath. "If you don't want his body," he said, "I'll bring him over there to those men to bury."

"No," a woman said, walking slowly toward the mule over which Wolverton's body was slung. "We want him."

Longarm watched as the women—acting in concert now—approached the mule. Suddenly one of the women broke from the tightening circle, rushed at the body, and began beating on it. Her sisters pulled her back, as others—their fingers flying—untied the burden and pulled it off the mule's back. The excited crowd of women caused the mule to buck some, but Longarm paid no heed as he turned his face away so that he would not see the vicious abandon with which the women vented their fury on what was left of the man who had been their lord and master.

"Let's get out of here," Longarm said to Emilie.

"Yes, please!"

As they approached the trail a moment later, Emilie called to him, "You knew that would happen, didn't you?"

"I had a notion."

"Why? Why did you bring his body back to them?"

Longarm shrugged. "I just thought they might like to get that off their chest. Maybe they'll feel better now. He had ridden off with you and left them, you know—locked in those quarters he'd built to keep them."

She shuddered. "It was awful!"

"Yes it was." He looked at her. "Remember what Barker told us. If we're as wise as we should be, we'll take that warning of his to heart, I'm thinking."

"Can we get far before dark?"

"Far enough. And this time we've plenty of transportation. Two army mules, and no one on our tails."

She brightened considerably as Longarm led the way back up the trail. It was dark when they both took their last look at the valley and headed for the badlands and the Great Salt Lake Desert beyond.

Longarm chuckled again as he puffed on his cheroot and read the telegram a second time.

WASHINGTON RAISING HELL FORGET MULES STAY ON THE
CASE FORGET MULES

                                                                    VAIL

Longarm folded the telegram and put it into his vest pocket alongside his new derringer. A bright new gold chain connected it with the recently purchased Ingersoll, courtesy of a very grateful Quincy Boggs.

"As I was saying," said Boggs, looking around him happily at his three daughters, "we've got back our backbones, thanks to you. Never again will any of us allow a band of night riders to tell us what we believe. We are Mormons and proud of it. But we can differ among ourselves without intimidating those who believe differently than we do. That's in the United States Constitution, Longarm, and as soon as we join the Union, there will be no more doubt about it."

"Oh, Daddy," said Audrey. "All you've been doing lately is making speeches."

"I know," the man said, glowing. "As a leader of the reform movement that brought in Deputy U.S. Marshal Custis Long, I find that I am asked to speak everywhere—with devastating effect, I am sure."

Longarm laughed. "I am sure."

"But as I was saying, I was very improper and read that telegram. As soon as I did, I decided to act. Together with the rest of the council, we took direct action on that infamous detention center in our midst. You remember the place, I am sure, Longarm."

"Took action?"

"We freed those you had imprisoned, Longarm. One of the women was in very bad condition, the widow of that man who shot himself. We let them go, Longarm, with the provision that they leave Utah. Two of our council members paid for their tickets and sent them on their way. I need not tell you how glad I was to see Molly go."

"And then?"

"We gave the Salt Lake City Fire Department a chance to show how they can control a fire once it gets under way. It was quite a successful demonstration. I am sure we can find something more constructive to erect on that abandoned site."

"Daddy," Marilyn said, "we'll be late!"

The man grabbed at his pocket watch and noted the time. "Oh, dear! So we will be, if we don't hurry—and I don't want to miss Eddie Foy. He came through before, and I was unable to see him." He stood up. "Are you sure you won't join us, Longarm? The Salt Lake Theater is the finest theater west of Saint Louis!"

"Oh, Father," said Emilie, shaking her head. "You're an incorrigible booster, really. I am sure there are theaters just as large in Denver." She smiled at Longarm. "Isn't that true, Longarm?"

"I won't get no prizes contradicting your father. Fact is, I'm never in Denver long enough to go to any of them places. But I hear Eddie Foy is a very funny man."

Boggs looked at Emilie. "Are you sure you won't come with us, Emilie?"

"Oh, Father!" said Marilyn. "You can't have us all go off and leave poor Mr. Longarm all alone in this big house!"

"And besides," said Emilie with a laugh, "I'm exhausted. Longarm and I have ridden over half of Utah in the past weeks. A quiet evening at home is something I have been dreaming of for a long, long time."

"Of course, of course," said Boggs. "Forgive me. Come, girls!"

With Marilyn on one arm and Audrey on the other, the man fairly flew out of the living room. Longarm heard the girls' laughter on the front steps, then listened as they hurried down the long walk. After a few moments all was silent, and Emilie looked quizzically at Longarm.

"Would you like another grape, Longarm? You seemed to favor them at the dinner table."

"They are a luxury after such a long, hot ride."

There was a bowl on the table. Emilie took a bunch from the bowl, got to her feet, and approached Longarm's armchair. Perching on one of the arms, she smiled and held up a grape for him. Longarm obliged by leaning his head back.

"Open up," she said.

"Make me."

She did by tickling the corners of his mouth with a finger. As he smiled, she dropped the grape in. He chewed on it.

"Delicious," he admitted. "I sure could have used a bunch of them when I was fixin' that wind wagon, or whatever you call it."

"I'm sure. Longarm?"

"Yes?" He opened his mouth for another grape. She dropped it in.

"Do you know what I've been doing for the past two weeks—even longer, in fact?"

He smiled at her. "Keeping out of Wolverton's clutches."

"Yes, Longarm." She dropped another grape into his mouth, and then took one herself. "That's exactly what I was doing. And do you know what I felt when I saw them leave you in the middle of the desert like that?"

"No, Emilie, I don't."

"Well, you can imagine," she told him, suddenly serious. "Despair. I was certain I would never see you again. But you had promised to come for me, and I clung to that through all that followed."

"I'm glad I didn't disappoint you, Emilie."

She smiled and dropped another grape into his mouth. "And you won't disappoint me now, will you, Longarm?"

She took another grape for herself. She had been leaning closer all during this conversation, and Longarm was aware of tiny beads of sweat standing out on his forehead—and of other side effects, as well.

"In short, Longarm," she said, dropping a very large, juicy grape into his mouth, "I have been saying no for the longest time and dreaming of you. I don't want to say no any longer and I don't want just to *dream* about you, either." She swallowed a grape and smiled with delight. "Do you understand what I am telling you, Longarm?"

"I've been concentrating real careful, Emilie," he told her, smiling. "But it seems to me I heard you tell your father you was hoping for a quiet evening at home."

She dropped an especially succulent grape into his mouth. "Afterward, Longarm," she told him, leaning forward and lightly brushing his forehead with her lips. "Afterward."

She slipped off the arm of his chair. "I have a hundred little things to tend to, Longarm. Why don't you finish that cheroot you just lit. Then, if you want the rest of these grapes, well . . ." She smiled, and left him smoldering in the chair.

He was astonished at how long it took him to finish the cheroot, but at last he dropped its remains into the cuspidor by the door, left the room, and hurried up the stairs.

Her bedroom was dark, and as he entered, he found her by the maddening smell of her. They embraced, and he felt her cloud of hair fall about his neck and shoulders. She was wearing nothing, he realized, under the long silk nightgown. Her fingers found his lips and she dropped into his mouth a large, most succulent grape. He laughed delightedly as its sweet moisture filled his mouth.

"This," she whispered huskily, "is my thank you, Longarm—for keeping your promise, for not disappointing me."

He kissed her on the lips, then on her sweet, graceful neck, and told her that she was more than welcome, and that she should now consider the debt paid and let him concentrate on this more delightful mission, because he sure as hell did not want to disappoint her this time, either.

She laughed and drew him to her bed, determined, he could tell, that neither one of them should be disappointed this evening.

NOVEL 4

Longarm
and the
Wendigo

Chapter 1

It was a glorious morning in Denver and Longarm felt like hell. The tall deputy squinted as he left the musty brown darkness of the Union Station to get punched in the eye by a bright morning sun in a cloudless sky of cobalt blue. A sharp breeze blew from the snow-topped Front Range, behind him to the west, as he walked stiffly east toward the Civic Center. The mile-high air was clear and scented with summer snow and green mountain meadows. Longarm wondered if he was going to make it to Larimer Street before he threw up.

At the corner of Seventeenth and Larimer he found the all-night greasy spoon he'd aimed for and went in to settle his guts. He wasn't hungry, but ordered chili and beer as medication.

The beanery was nearly empty at this hour, but Longarm recognized a uniformed member of the Denver Police Department seated at another stool down the counter and nodded. He'd only nodded to be neighborly, but the copper slid his own stein and bowl over next to Longarm's and said, "'Morning, Uncle Sam. You look like somebody drug you through the keyhole backward! You spend the night drinking, whoring, or both?"

"Worse. I just came up out of Santa Fe on a night train that had square wheels and no seats worth mention. Rode shotgun on a gold shipment bound for the mint, here in Denver. Spent the night hunkered on a box in the mail car, drinking the worst coffee I've tasted since I was in the army. I suspicion they use the same glue in Post Office coffee as they put on the back of their stamps."

He took a huge gob of chili, washed it down with a gulp of beer, and added, "Jesus, you can't hardly get real chili this far north of Texas. Pass me some of that red pepper to the lee of your elbow, will you?"

The copper handed him the pepper shaker and opined, "Oh, I dunno, the cook here makes a fair bowl of chili, for a white man."

Then he watched with a worried frown, as Longarm proceeded to cover his beans with powdered fire. To the policeman, Longarm was sort of interesting to study on. The Denver P.D. was sincerely glad the deputy marshal was a lawman rather than on the other side; arresting anything that big and mean was an awesome thought to contemplate.

The deputy U.S. marshal was civilly dressed in a threadbare

business suit of tobacco tweed, but a bit wild and wooly around the edges. His brown flat-topped Stetson had a couple of large-caliber holes in it and the craggy face under the brim was weathered as brown as an Indian's. The big jaw masticating chili under the John L. Sullivan mustache needed a shave, and though he wore a shoestring tie under the collar of his townsman's shirt, he somehow managed to wear it like a cowhand's bandanna. They said he packed a derringer in addition to the double-action .44 in that cross-draw rig he wore under the frock coat. They said he had a bowie in one of the low-heeled army boots he stood taller than most men in. But the big deputy was one of those rare men who didn't look like he *needed* weapons. When he was in one of his morose moods, like this morning, Longarm looked able to knock a lesser man down with a hard stare from his gunmetal eyes.

The copper asked, "You aim to *eat* that shit with all that pepper in it, or are you aiming to blow yourself up?"

Longarm chewed thoughtfully and decided, "That's better. Chili's no good unless it makes a man's forehead break out in a little sweat. I can still taste that damned Post Office coffee, but I reckon I'll live, after all."

"You must have a cast iron stomach. You, ah, wouldn't want to let your friendly neighborhood police in on it, would you, Longarm?"

"In on what? You want me to fix your chili right for you?"

"Come on. They never detailed a deputy with your seniority to ride with the Post Office dicks. Somebody important robbing the mails these days?"

Longarm took a heroic gulp of beer and swallowed before he belched, with a relieved sigh, and replied, "Jesus, that felt good. As to who's been robbing the midnight trains between here and Santa Fe, I don't know anymore than yourself about it. I just do what the pissants up at the Federal Building tell me."

"I hear since the Lincoln County War's run down there's about eighty out-of-work gunslicks searching for gainful employment. You reckon any might be headed for my beat?"

Longarm studied for a moment before he shook his head and said, "Doubt it. Denver's getting too civilized for old-fashioned owlhoots like we used to see over at the stockyards. Your new gun regulations sort of cramp their style. To tell you the truth, I sort of dozed off once we were north of Pueblo. Colorado's getting downright overcivilized of late, what with streetlamps, gun laws, and such."

"By gum, I run a cowboy in for a shooting just two nights ago, over on Thirteenth and Walnut!"

"There you go. That's over on the other side of Cherry Creek where the poor folks live. 'Fess up. You ain't had a real Saturday night in the main part of town this year, have you?"

"The hell we hasn't'! I'll bet Denver's still as tough a town as any! I disremember you saying you heard any shooting in Santa Fe! I'll bet the hands riding into Denver of a Saturday night are just as mean as any you met down New Mexico way!"

"No bet. Santa Fe's got sissy as hell since the new governor said folks can't shoot each other any more in Lincoln County. Hell, I was in Dodge last month and you know what they got? They got uniformed police and honest-to-God streetlamps in Dodge now! Things keep up this way and we'll likely both be out of a job!"

Leaving the policeman nursing his injured civic pride, Longarm paid the silent, surly Greek behind the counter for his breakfast and resumed his walk to work, feeling almost human. He knew he rated the day off for having spent the night on duty, but these new regulations about paperwork meant he had to report in before he could go home to his furnished digs for some shut-eye.

The Federal Building sat at the foot of Capitol Hill. Longarm went in and climbed to the second floor, where he found a door marked *UNITED STATES MARSHAL, FIRST DISTRICT COURT OF COLORADO.*

He entered, nodded to the pallid clerk pecking at his newfangled typewriting machine, and made his way to an inner door, where he let himself in without knocking.

His superior, Chief U.S. Marshal Vail, glared up with a start from behind his big mahogany desk and snapped, "Damn it, Longarm! I've told you I expect folks to *knock* before they come busting in on me!"

Longarm grinned and was about to sass the plump, pink man behind the desk. Then he saw Vail's visitor, seated in an overstuffed leather armchair near the banjo clock on the wall and tipped the brim of his hat instead, saying, "Your servant, ma'am!"

The woman in the visitor's chair was dressed severely in black, with a sort of silly little hat perched atop her coal-black hair. She was about twenty-five and pretty. She wasn't quite a white woman. Maybe a Mexican lady, dressed American.

Marshal Vail said, "I'm glad to see you on time for a change, Longarm. Allow me to present you to Princess Gloria Two-Women of the Blackfoot Nation."

Longarm managed another smiling nod before the girl cut in with a severe but no less pretty frown to say, "I am no such thing, Marshal Vail. Forgive me for correcting you, but, John Smith and Pocahontas notwithstanding, there is no such thing as an Indian princess."

Vail shrugged and asked, "Aren't you the daughter of Real Bear, the chief of the Blackfoot, ma'am?"

"My father was war chief of the Turtle Clan. My mother was Gloria Witherspoon, a captive white woman. There are no hereditary titles among my father's people, and even if there were, no woman could inherit the rank of war chief."

Vail looked annoyed but managed a wan smile as he nodded and asked, "Just what is your title, then, ma'am?"

"I'm a half-breed. On rare occasions, I'm called *Miss*."

Longarm ignored the bitterness in her almond eyes as he leaned against the back of another chair and suggested, "I don't reckon your family tree is what you've come to Uncle Sam about, is it, Miss Two-Women?"

Vail cut in before she could answer, saying, "I've got the lady's complaint down, Longarm. It's your next job."

Longarm didn't think it was the time to point out that he rated the day off. He knew it wouldn't do any good and the odd little bitter-eyed woman interested him. So he nodded and waited for Vail to fill him in.

The marshal said, "This lady's daddy sent her to see us, Longarm. A bad Indian's gone back to the blanket. I got his wanted papers here somewhere . . . anyway, I want you to run up to the Blackfoot reservation in Montana Territory and—"

"Ain't you assigning me to a job for the B.I.A., Chief?"

The girl said, "The man my father is worried about isn't a problem for the Bureau of Indian Affairs, sir. They don't know he's alive. My father reported him to the Indian agent at Fort Banyon. They told him they'd file a report on the matter, but of course we know they won't. Like myself, Johnny Hunts Alone is nonexistent."

Longarm asked, "You mean he's . . ."

"A half-breed. You don't have to be so delicate. Half-breed's one of the nicer things I'm used to being called."

Vail found the "wanted" flyer he'd been rummaging for and said, "He may not exist to the B.I.A., but Justice wants him bad. Matter of fact, we don't have him down as an Indian, half or whatever. We've got him as one John Hunter, age thirty-six, no description save white, male, medium height and build. When he ain't hiding out on reservations, he robs trains, banks, and such. We got four counts of first degree on him in addition to the state and federal wants for armed robbery."

Longarm pursed his lips and mused, "I remember seeing the wanted flyers, now. Funny, I had him pictured in my head as just another old, uh . . ."

"White man," Gloria Two-Women cut in, stone-faced. Both men waited as she continued, "Like myself, Johnny Hunts Alone is a Blackfoot breed. In his case, his *mother* was the Indian. They say his father was a Mountain Man who, uh, married a squaw for a trapping season. She gave him his half-name of Johnny, hoping, one would presume, his father might come back some day."

Longarm asked, "Was he raised Indian, then?"

"To the extent that I was, I suppose. I've never met him. They say he ran away to look for his white father years ago."

Vail explained, "The way I understand it, this Johnny Hunts Alone, John Hunter, or whatever, can pass himself off as white or Indian. He sort of raised himself in trail towns, hobo jungles, and such till he took to robbing folks instead of punching cows. The reason he's been getting away with it for years is that we could never find his hideout. According to this little lady's daddy, the jasper's up at the Blackfoot reservation right now. Miss Gloria, here, will introduce you to her daddy and the chief'll point the owlhoot out to you. Seems like a simple enough mission to me."

Longarm sighed and said, "Yeah, it always does. You mind if I ask a few questions? Just the result of my suspicious nature."

Without waiting for permission, he stared soberly at the girl and asked, "How come your Blackfoot relations are so suddenly helpful to Uncle Sam, Miss Two-Women? Meaning no disrespect, the Blackfoot have a reputation for truculence. Wasn't your tribe sort of cheering from the sidelines when Custer took that wrong turn on the Little Big Horn a few summers back?"

"Like the Cheyenne and Arapaho, the Blackfoot were allied with the Dakota Confederacy, if that's what you mean. Since you're so interested in the history of my father's people, you probably know the survivors have been penned like sheep in one small corner of Montana."

"I read about it. Did this Johnny Hunts Alone take part in the Great Sioux Uprising of '76?"

"Of course not. Do you think my father would inform on a fellow warrior?"

"There you go. So why *is* your daddy so anxious for us to arrest one of his people?"

"Honestly, don't you know anything about Indians? The renegade is *not* a Blackfoot to my father and others like him. Johnny Hunts Alone ran away before he was ever initiated into any of the warrior lodges. When our people were fighting for their lives against the Seventh Cavalry, he was off someplace robbing banks."

"So your dad and the other chiefs don't owe him much, huh?"

"Not only that, but the man's a known thief and a troublemaker. Thanks partly to my mother, Real Bear speaks English and can read and write, so perhaps he's more aware than the others of what a wanted fugitive on our reservation could mean to us."

"What's that, ma'am?"

"Trouble, of course. Our tribe is ... well, frankly, licked. Most of us are resigned to making the best of a bad situation. But there are hotheads among my father's people who'd like another try at the old ways. Some of the Dream Singers have been having visions, and meetings have been held in the warrior lodges of which I don't feel free to tell you the details. My father is one of the more progressive chiefs. He's trying to cooperate with the B.I.A. He's trying to lead his people into the future; he's man enough to face it. An outlaw hiding among the young men, boasting of how many whites he's killed—"

"That makes sense, ma'am. As you were talking just now, it came to me I'd heard your daddy's name before. Real Bear was one of them who voted with Red Cloud against the big uprising. Though, the way I hear tell, he did his share of fighting once his folks declared war. You mind if I ask you some *personal* questions, ma'am?"

Vail cut in to point at the clock above Gloria's head as he snapped, "She might not mind, but I do, dang it! You folks have a train to catch, Longarm! You can jaw about the details along the way. Right now I want you to get cracking. I'll expect you back here about this time next week, with Johnny Hunts Alone, John Hunter, or whomsoever, dead or alive!"

It wasn't until he'd escorted Gloria Two-Women aboard the northbound Burlington that Longarm gave serious consideration to her race. Under most circumstances, he wouldn't have given it much thought, for she was a pretty little thing and his mind was on the job ahead.

As the conductor nodded down at the railroad pass they were traveling on, Longarm asked, "What time are we due in Billings? I make it about twelve hours before we have to change trains, don't you?"

"We'll be getting into Billings around ten this evening, Marshal. Uh . . . you mind if I have a word with you in private?"

Longarm glanced at the girl seated across from him, gazing stone-faced out the window at the passing confusion of the Denver yards, and got to his feet to follow the conductor with a puzzled frown. The older man led him a few seats down, out of the girl's earshot, before he asked in a low whisper, "Is that a lady of color you're traveling with, Marshal?"

"You're wrong on both counts. I'm only a deputy marshal and she's half white. What's your problem, friend?"

"Look, it ain't *my* problem. Some of the other passengers has, uh, sort of been talking about the two of you."

"Do tell? Well, I'm a peaceable man. Long as they don't talk about us where we can *hear* it, it don't mean all that much, does it?"

"Look, I was wondering if the gal might not be more comfortable up front in the baggage car."

Longarm smiled wolfishly, and took the front of the trainman's coat in one big fist as he purred, "She ain't a *gal*, friend. Anything in skirts traveling with *me* as her escort is a *lady*, till *I* say she's something else. You got that?"

"Loud and clear, Marshal. This ain't *my* notion!"

"All right. Whose notion might it be, then?"

"Look, I don't want no trouble, mister!"

"Old son, you've already got your trouble. You just point out who the big mouth belongs to and then maybe *you'd* best go up and ride in that baggage car!"

"I'm just doing my job. Forget I mentioned it."

"I'd like to, but I got a twelve-hour ride ahead of me and I don't aim to spend it fretting about my future. I'm going to ask you one more time, polite. Then I'm likely to start by busting your arm."

"Hey, take it easy. I don't care who rides this durned old train. It's them two cowhands up near the front of the car. I heard 'em say some things 'bout niggers and such and thought I'd best head things off."

Longarm didn't turn his head to look at the two young men he'd already marked down as possible annoyances. He'd spotted them boarding the train. They looked to be drovers and one was packing a Patterson .44 and a bellyful of something stronger than beer.

Longarm let go of the conductor's lapel and said, "You go up to the next car. I'll take care of it."

"I got tickets to punch."

"All right. Go on *back* to the next car."

The conductor started to protest further. Then he saw the look in Longarm's cold blue gray eyes, gulped, and did as he was told.

As Longarm sauntered back the way he'd come, Gloria looked up at him with a bemused expression. He nodded and said, "We'll be picking up speed in a mile or so. You want a drink of water?"

"No thanks. What was that all about?"

"We were talking about the timetable. Excuse me, ma'am. I'll be back directly."

He walked toward the front of the car, shifting on the balls of his feet as the car swayed under his boots. One of the two men in trail clothing looked up and whispered something to the heavier man at his side. The tougher-looking of the two narrowed his eyes thoughtfully but didn't say anything until Longarm stopped right above them, letting the tail of his coat swing open to expose the polished walnut grips of his own Colt, and said, "You boys had best be getting off before we leave the yards. Might hurt a man to jump off a train doing more'n fifteen miles an hour or so."

The one who had whispered asked, "What are you talking about? We're on our way to Billings, mister."

"No you ain't. Not on this train. You see, I don't want you to be upset about riding with colored folks, and since I aim to stay aboard all the way to Billings, we'd best make some adjustments to your delicate natures."

The heavyset one with the gun looked thoughtfully at the weapon hanging above Longarm's left hip and licked his lips before he said, "Look, nobody said *you* was colored, mister."

"Is that a fact? Well, it's likely the poor light in here; I'm pure Ethiopian. You want to make something out of it?"

"Hey, come on, you're as white as we'uns. *You* wasn't the one we was jawing 'bout to that fool conductor!"

His companion added, "You just wait till we gits that troublemaker alone, mister. He had no call to repeat a gent's observings."

"Boys, this train's gathering speed while we're discussing

your departure. You two aim to jump like sensible gents or do I have to throw you off unfriendly-like?"

"Come on, you can't put us off no train! We got us tickets to Billings!"

"Use 'em on the next train north, then. I'll tell you what I'm fixing to do. I'm fixing to count to ten. Then I'm going to draw."

"Mister, you must be loco, drunk, or both!"

"One!"

"Look here, we don't want to hurt nobody, but—"

"Two!"

"Now you're getting us *riled*, mister!"

"Three!"

"Well, damn it, Fats, *you* got the durned old gun!"

"Four!"

The heavyset one went for his Patterson.

He didn't make it. Longarm's five-inch muzzle, its front sight filed off for such events, was out and covering him before Fats had a serious hold on his own grips. The drover snatched his hand from his sidearm as if it had stung his palm as he gasped, "I give! I give! Don't do it, mister!"

"You did say something about disembarking, didn't you, gents?"

"Look, you've made us crawfish. Can't we leave it at that?"

"Nope. You made me draw, so now you're getting off, one way or the other. Let's go, boys."

After a moment's hesitation, Fats shrugged and said, "Let's go, Curley. No sense arguing with a crazy man when he's got the drop on us."

His younger sidekick protested, "I can't believe this! I thought you was tough, Fats!"

But he, too, slid out of the seat and followed as Longarm frog-marched the two of them out to the vestibule between the cars. Fats looked down at the blurring road ballast and protested, "Hey, it's goin' too fast!"

"All the more reason to jump while there's still time. It'll be going faster, directly."

"You got a name, mister?"

"Yep. My handle's Custis Long. You aim to look me up sometime, Fats?"

"Just don't be in Billings when we gits there, mister. We got us *friends* in Billings!"

Then he jumped, rolling ass over teakettle as he hit the dirt at twenty-odd miles an hour. Longarm saw that he wasn't hurt, and as the younger one tried to protest some more, he ended the discussion by shoving him, screaming, from the platform.

Longarm holstered his gun with a dry smile and went back to where he'd left Gloria. The petite breed's face was blank but her eyes glistened as she said, "You didn't have to do that to impress me. You've already called me 'ma'am.'"

Longarm sat down on the seat across from her, placed his battered Stetson on the green plush beside him, and said, "Didn't do it for you. Did it for myself."

"You mean they offended your sense of gallantry?"

"Nope. Just made common sense. They got on drunk and ugly and we have a good twelve hours' ride ahead. Had I given 'em time to work themselves up all afternoon, I'd likely have had a killing matter on my hands by sundown. This way, nobody got hurt."

"One of them might dispute you on that point. I was watching out the window. The fall tore his shirt half off and left him sort of bloody."

"Any man who don't know how to fall has no call wearing cowboy boots."

"What am I supposed to do now, call you my Prince Charming and swoon at your feet?"

"Nope. I'd rather talk about the lay of the land where we're headed. You said your daddy, Real Bear, is the only one who can point out this Johnny Hunts Alone to me. How come? I mean, don't the other Indians know a stranger when they see one?"

"Of course, but you see, it's a new reservation, just set up since our tribes were rounded up by the army in '78. Stray bands are still being herded in. Aside from Blackfoot, we have Blood and Piegan and even a few Arapaho gathered from all over the north plains. My father doesn't know many of the people living with his people now, but he did recognize Johnny Hunts Alone when the man passed him near the trading post last week."

"The owlhoot recognize your dad?"

"Real Bear didn't think so. My father knew him over fifteen years ago and they've both changed a lot since, of course. It wasn't until my father got to my house that he remembered just who that familiar face belonged to!"

"In other words, we're traveling a far piece on the quick glance and maybes of one old Indian who might just be wrong!"

"When you meet Real Bear, you'll know better. He doesn't forget much. Aren't you going to ask about our house?"

"Your house? Is there something interesting about it, ma'am?"

"Most white people, when they hear me mention my house, seem a bit surprised. I'm supposed to wear buckskins, too."

"Well, I ain't most people. I've been on a few reservations in my time. What have you got up there, one of them government-built villages of frame lumber that could use a coat of paint and a bigger stove?"

"I see you *have* seen a few reservations. Ours is a shambles. The young white couple the B.I.A. sent out from the East doubtless mean well, but . . . you'd have to be an Indian to understand."

Longarm fished a cheroot from his vest and when she nodded her silent permission, thumbnailed a match and lit up, pondering her words. He knew the miserable fix most tribes were in these days, caught between conflicting policies of the army, the Indian agency, and loudmouthed Washington politicos who'd never been west of the Big Muddy. He took a drag of smoke, let it trickle out through his nostrils, and asked, "What's this other trouble you mentioned about the young men wanting another go at the Seventh Cav?"

"The boys too young to have fought in '76 aren't the real problem. Left to themselves they'd just talk a lot, like white boys planning to run off and be pirates. But some of the older men are finding civilization more than they can adjust to. You know about the Ghost Dancers?"

"Heard rumors. Paiute medicine man called Wovoka has been preachin' a new religion over on the other side of the Rockies, hasn't he?"

"Yes. Wovoka's notions seem crazy to our Dream Singers, but the movement's gaining ground and even some of our people are starting to make offerings to the Wendigo. You'd have to be a Blackfoot to know how crazy *that* is!"

"No I wouldn't. The Wendigo is your Dad's folks' name for the devil, ain't it?"

"My, you *have* been on some reservations! What else do you know about our religion?"

"Not much. Never even got the Good Book that *I* was brought up on all that straight in my head. Blackfoot, Arapaho, Cheyenne, and other Algonquin-speaking tribes pray to a Great Spirit called Manitou and call the devil 'Wendigo,' right? I remember somethin' about owls being bad luck and turtles being good luck, but like I said, I've never studied all that much on anyone's notions about the spirit world."

"Owl is the totem of death. Turtle is the creator of new life from the Waters of Yesteryear. I suppose you regard it all as silly superstition."

"Can't say one way or another. I wasn't there. It might have took seven days or Turtle might have done it. Doubtless sometime we'll know more about it. Right now I've got enough on my plate just keeping track of the here and now of it all."

"Does that make you an atheist or an agnostic?"

Longarm bristled slightly. The last person to call him an atheist had been a renegade Mormon night rider who had left him to die in the Great Salt Lake Desert. He had had plenty of time to ponder on the godless behavior of those who accused others of godlessness. "Makes me a deputy U.S. marshal with a job to do. You were saying something about devil worship up where we're headed, Miss Gloria."

She shrugged and replied, "I don't think you could put it that way. People making offerings to the Wendigo aren't Satanists; they're simply frightened Indians. You see, it's all too obvious that Manitou, the Great Spirit, has turned his back on them. The Wendigo, or Evil One, seems to rule the earth these days, and so—"

"Is he supposed to be like *our* devil, with horns and such, or is he a big, mean Indian cuss?"

"Like Manitou, the Wendigo's invisible. You might say he's a great evil force who makes bad things happen."

"I see. And some of your folks are praying to him while others are taking up Wovoka's notions about the ghosts of dead Indians coming back from the Happy Hunting Ground for another go-round with our side. I don't hold much with missionaries, since those I've seen ain't been all that good at it, but right now it seems you could use some up on the Blackfoot reservation."

"We have a posse of diverse missionaries on or near the reservation. My father would like to run all Dream Singers off, Indian as well as white. I hope your arrest of Johnny Hunts Alone will calm things down enough for him to cope with."

Longarm nodded and consulted his Ingersoll pocket watch, noting that they had a long way to ride yet. The girl watched him silently for a time before she murmured, "You're not as dumb as you pretend to be."

Longarm smiled. "Pretending such things sometimes gives a man an advantage. Speaking of which, you've got a pretty good head on your own shoulders. I can see you've been educated."

"I graduated from Wellesley. Does that surprise you?"

"Why should it? You had to go to school someplace to talk so uppity. I know those big Eastern colleges give scholarships to bright reservation kids. It'd surprise me more if you'd said you'd learned to read from watching smoke signals."

"You are unusual, for a white man. By now, most of your kind I've met would have demanded my whole history."

"Likely. Most folks are more curious than polite."

"You really don't care one way or the other, do you?"

"I likely know as much about you as I need to."

"You don't know anything about me! Nobody knows anything about me!"

Longarm took a drag on his cheroot and said, "Let's see, now. You're wearing widow's weeds, but you're likely not a widow. You're wearing a wedding band, but you ain't married. You were born in an Indian camp, but you've been raised white and only lately come back to your daddy's side of the family. You've got a big old chip on your pretty shoulder, too, but I ain't about to knock it off, so why don't you quit fencing about with me?"

Gloria Two-Women stared openmouthed at him for a time before she blurted, "Somebody gave you a full report on me and you've been the one doing the fencing. Who was it, that damned agent's wife?"

"Nobody's told me one word about you since we met, save yourself. You knew I was a lawman. Don't you reckon folks in my line are supposed to work things out for themselves, ma'am?"

Before she could answer, the candy butcher came through with his tray of sweets, fruits, sandwiches, and bottled beer. Longarm stopped the boy and asked the girl what she'd like, adding, "We won't stop for a proper meal this side of Cheyenne, ma'am."

Gloria ordered a ham on rye sandwich, a beer, and an orange for later and the deputy ordered the same, except for the fruit. When the candy butcher had left them to wait on another passenger, she insisted, "All right, how did you do that?"

"Do what? Size you up? I'm paid to size folks up, Miss Gloria. You said your mama was a white lady, and since you're about twenty-odd, I could see she must have been taken captive during that Blackfoot rising near South Pass in the 'fifties. When the army put 'em down that time, most white captives were released, so I figured you likely went back East with your ma when you were, oh, about seven or eight. You may talk some Blackfoot and you've got Indian features, but you wear that dress like a white woman. You walk white, too. Those high-buttoned shoes don't fret your toes like they would a lady's who grew up in moccasins. You sure weren't riding with the Blackfoot when they came out against Terry in '76, so I'd say you looked your daddy up after he and the others settled down civilized on the reservation just a while back. Here, I'll open that beer for you with my jackknife. It's got a bottle opener and all sorts of notions."

He opened their drinks carefully, aiming the warm beer bottles at the aisle as he uncapped them. Then he handed her one and sat back to say, "I was born in West-by-God-Virginia and came West after the War. I fought at Shiloh . . ." Longarm's voice trailed off.

"You were doing fine. What made you stop?" Gloria asked.

"Reckon both our tales get a mite hurtful, later on. We're both full grown, now, and some of the getting here might best be forgot."

"You know about my mother deserting me once she was among her own people, then? How could you know that? How could anyone know so much from mere appearances? Is that orphanage written on my breast in scarlet letters, after all?"

"No. I never met your mama, but I know the world, and how it treats a white gal who's ridden out of an Indian camp with a half-breed child. You ought to try to forgive her, Miss Gloria. She was likely not much older than you are right now, and her own kin likely pressured her some."

"My mother had a white husband waiting for her. I wonder if she ever told him about me. Oh, well, they treated us all right at the foundling home and I did win a college scholarship on my own." She sipped her beer and added in a bitter voice, "Not that it did much good, once I tried to make my way in the white man's world. I was nearly nine when the soldiers recaptured us, so I remembered my father's language and could identify with that side of my family. You were right about my reading about the new reservation and running back to the blanket, but how did you figure out my widow's weeds?"

"Generally, when folks are wearing mourning, they mention someone who's dead. On the other hand, one of the first things I noticed was that chip on your shoulder and your hankering to be treated with respect. I'll allow some folks who should know better can talk ugly to any lady with your sort of features, but widow's weeds and a wedding band gives a gal a certain edge in being treated like a lady."

"It didn't stop those two cowboys you put off the train."

"They were drovers, not cowhands, ma'am. And neither had much sense. Most old boys think twice before they start up with a lady wearing a wedding band, widow's weeds or no. They were likely drunker than most you've met. So 'fess up, that's the reason for the mournful getup, ain't it?"

She laughed, spilling some of her beer, and answered, "You should run away with a circus! You'd make more as a mind reader than a lawman!" Then she sobered and added, "You're wrong about the ring, though. I am married, sort of."

He didn't rise to the bait. She'd tell him in her own good time what she meant by "sort of" married. From the smoke signals he'd been reading in her eyes, she couldn't be married all that much.

Chapter 2

They had to lay over in Billings for a grotesquely routed train that promised to take them close enough to the Blackfoot reservation. Gloria said they'd be able to hire a buckboard for the last few miles, and Longarm's saddle, Winchester, and other possibles were riding with him to where he could commandeer a government mount from the army. The local train connecting up with the line north wasn't leaving Billings before morning and they got in a little after nine-thirty. They spent an hour over steak and potatoes before Longarm had to deal with the delicate matter of hotel accommodations.

It wasn't checking in with a woman he was worried about. He had enough cash to pay for separate rooms. But even in the dim light of a gaslit town, Gloria's Indian features drew stares, and some of them weren't friendly. Billings was only a few miles from the old battleground of Little Big Horn and the local whites had long memories as well as buried kinfolk in the vicinity. As they entered the lobby of the Silver Dollar Hotel, he murmured, "Should anyone ask, remember you're a Spanish lady from Sonora."

"I'll do no such thing!" she murmured, adding, "I'm a Blackfoot and proud of it!'

"Maybe, but I've got to do the fighting, so I reckon you'd best just hush and let me do the talking, hear?"

He strode over to the hotel desk and flashed his federal badge at the night clerk. "We need two rooms. I'll take one with a bath."

The clerk nodded impassively and shoved the registration book toward the deputy. "I can fix you up with adjoining rooms, bath between. This lady, uh, your missus?"

"Of course not. What would I want with two rooms if we were married up? Do I look like a sissy?"

The clerk laughed as Longarm registered for them both, signing Gloria in as "Miss Witherspoon."

Unfortunately, the girl glanced over his shoulder to protest, "That's not my name, damn it!"

A couple of sleepy-looking gents lounging among the potted ferns of the lobby sat up to stare with greater interest as Longarm sighed and said, "Now, Miss Gloria, let's not make a fuss about it. You said your mama's name was Witherspoon, and—"

"I am Gloria Two-Women. My mother abandoned me and I'll not bear her name, even for a night."

The clerk raised an eyebrow. Longarm quickly touched the side of his forehead and confided, "She's a federal witness I'm taking up to Fort Benson. She's a mite, uh, confused."

"She says her name is 'two women,' Deputy."

"There you go. I told you how it was. She's only one woman at a time as anyone here can plainly see."

One of the lobby loafers got slowly to his feet as he said, "I can plainly see she's *Indian*, too! What are you, mister, a squaw man?"

"Paying for two rooms, friend, I don't reckon it's your concern. I am also a deputy U.S. marshal and you are stepping on the tail of my coat, so why don't you go back yonder and warm your seat some more?"

"I rode with Terry in '76 and I don't give two hoots and a holler who you work for, mister. You got no call to bring Indians in here!"

Longarm saw two others rising, now, and the desk clerk was muttering unfriendly things about the town marshal. He took Gloria's elbow in his free left hand, nodded, and said, "We'll be on our way, then, gents."

He half-dragged the girl outside, as behind them the lobby rang with jeering laughter. He started up the boardwalk with her, chewing his unlit cheroot, too steamed to say much.

She marveled, "You just let them run us out like we were trash!"

"Nope, it was your hankering to see a fight that got us run out. If you aim to sleep this night, you'd best stuff a sock in that pretty mouth of yours next place we try!"

"Why didn't you stand up to them back there? I thought you were a man!"

"Was, last time I looked. I likely could have whupped the whole lobby, if it had made a lick of sense. But I was looking for a couple of rooms, not another Little Big Horn."

"Oh, you know you could have backed them down!"

"Maybe, but then what? You like to sleep in hotels angry folks are throwing rocks at all night, Miss Gloria? Suppose I *had* bullied us a brace of rooms? Then suppose those browned-off vets had gone looking for some help? I'm supposed to be a *peace* officer, not the biggest boo in Billings. We'll try a block up the street and maybe this time you'll have more sense."

"I can't believe it. You were so brave when those men were annoying us on the train."

"Yeah, I can see I made a mistake back there. You like to see white men humiliated, don't you?"

"I just have to stand up for my rights, damn it."

"What rights? They were going to give us two rooms and a bath, weren't they? Where does it say in the Constitution you have a right to be a pain in the neck?"

"I'm not ashamed of being what I am."

"Like hell you ain't. Look, I know the sort of sass you've had to take off white folks in your time. You want to put feathers in your hair and do something about it, it ain't my nevermind, but let's eat the apple a bite at a time, huh? Your daddy sent you to fetch a deputy U.S. marshal to bail him and his folks out of a fix. Suppose you let me get there peaceably before you start another uprising!"

"I don't have to put up with insults, just because of my race."

"Yes, you do. No matter what your race is, somebody don't figure to like it. I was chased from hell to breakfast by Apache last summer, just for being white. When we get where we're going, you'll likely see me catching a few dark looks from your daddy's folks, too. The thing is, there's enough trouble in this world for all of us, even when we don't go looking for it. I see a hotel sign up ahead. This time, damn it, I'll thank you to be that Mexican lady I told you about!"

"*They* take a lot off your kind, too."

"That's true. If we were checking into a hotel in Texas, I'd say you were a Blackfoot. Hereabouts, they ain't mad at Mexicans."

He escorted her into a smaller, shabbier hotel and this time there was no incident at the desk. There was no adjoining bathroom to their two small rooms upstairs, either, but Longarm didn't comment. There were chamber pots under the beds and he supposed it might be a good lesson for the young woman.

He let her into her own room and handed her the key, with a warning about opening to anyone but himself, then gave her a terse good-night nod. He went to his own room, and before lighting the lamp, stared down into the street for a time. He'd been watching in the glass windows to see if they'd been followed from the other hotel, but it seemed as if his crawfish act had satisfied the local Indian fighters.

He locked the door and sat on the edge of the brass bedstead, tearing up a newspaper he'd found on the dressing table. He crumpled the shreds of newspaper and threw them on the threadbare rug between the bed and the locked door before he hung his gun rig on a bedpost, put his watch and derringer under a pillow, and got undressed.

Nude in the darkness, he scratched his chest morosely as he thought of the bath he'd missed. He needed a shave, too, and there were soot and fly ash in his hair from the long train ride north. Well, he'd just have to bear with it for now. Damn that fool squaw!

As he was sliding under the covers there came a soft rap on his door. Longarm got up, drew the .44 from its holster, and went over to the door, standing to one side as he asked, "Yeah?"

"It's me, Gloria. Are you still awake?"

"Yep, but I'm naked. What can I do for you, ma'am?"

"I want to apologize for the way I acted down the street."

"Forget it. We're both worn out from all that riding, smoke, dust, and such. You get some shut-eye and I'll see you in the morning."

"Can I come in for a moment? I'm too keyed up to sleep."

He went over to the bed and slipped on his pants before going back to open the door. The girl was wearing a white shift and was barefoot. Her tawny skin seemed darker against the white cotton in the dim light and her hair smelled like wilted tea roses. He shut the door and locked it behind her as she stepped on a paper ball and exclaimed, "Good heavens! What's all this paper doing on the floor?"

"Old Border Mex trick. Keeps folks from pussyfooting in on you while you're snoring."

"Do things like that happen often, in your line of work?"

"Not often. *Once* would be too often, though. I don't have a chair in here for you. You can sit on the bed and I'll sort of stand here while you tell me what's on your mind."

She went to the bed, slipped the shift off over her head, and sat down, stark naked, before she said, "I want to sleep with you."

Longarm blinked but managed not to gasp his surprise as he waited a breath to steady his voice. "Just like that?"

"What's the matter? Don't you want to sleep with me?"

"Well, hell, sure! But I sort of figured—"

"I know what you've been figuring, all day. Most men would have made their move by now. This time tomorrow, we'll be on the reservation where it'll be a federal offense for you to trifle with me. I knew this was the one night you'd have to try and, damn it, you just move too *slow*, Longarm!"

Grinning, he unbuttoned his pants, let them fall around his ankles, and stepped out of them. She lay back as he loomed over her, wrapping arms and legs around him as he sank into her tawny body with both feet braced firmly on the rug. She thrust her body to meet his own hungry thrusts and her open mouth was a warm pit of savage desire as she sucked his tongue almost to the point of pain.

He let himself go without attempts at finesse or mutual orgasm, the first time. Then, having made her acquaintance, he moved them both to the center of the bed and got down to serious lovemaking, murmuring, "Still think I move too slow?"

"Let me get on top. I like to take charge."

"I noticed." He grinned, rolling off to let her have her way. And have her way she did. Every time Longarm tried to respond with movements of his own, she'd kiss him and whisper, "Just float with me, darling. Mama knows what she's doing. I'll take good care of baby. You'll see!"

Longarm knew better than to argue with a lady, so he lay there, spread-eagled and as puzzled as he was delighted by the lovemaking of this strange, dark little woman.

It was too good to last forever; she'd literally wrung him out like a lemon and as she took his limp flesh between her moist lips he sighed, "You've got to let it rest up a mite, honey. I don't reckon I could get it up again with a block and tackle right now!"

She laughed and threw herself down beside him, resting a head on his shoulder as she fondled him and purred, "We'll see about that. Did you—?"

Longarm silenced her with a finger on her lips. "Don't say nothing. I've just been looking up through a knothole in the bottom of heaven and I want to hear the angels sing some more."

"Am I as good as a white girl?"

"That's a fool thing to say. You're at least as good as *any* kind of gal, white, red, or even blue. I disremember doing it with a blue gal, but I doubt she'd teach me anything you left out."

"You're sure I satisfied you completely, darling?"

"You've got your hand on how satisfied I am. If I was more satisfied I'd be dead."

"Then why did he leave me, the brute?"

Longarm nodded in sudden understanding as he sighed and said, "Likely crazy, if you ever done him like that. Who are we talking about, the brave you're 'sort of' married up with?"

"My husband's a white man, the son of a bitch!"

"Oh. I was wondering what we were trying to prove just now. When did this lunatic run off on you, Gloria?"

"About a year ago. He was a soldier at the fort. He said—he said he loved me."

"Yeah, most men do, when they marry up with someone. What happened to him? He get transferred out?"

"Of course. There's not much you don't know about Indian matters, is there? My father warned me it would happen, but I thought Roger meant it. You know what my father tried to tell me?"

"Sure I do. The new army regulations say no soldier can trifle with a reservation gal unless his intentions are honorable. Your Roger had to marry you or leave you be, and seeing you're so pretty . . ."

"Roger said he considered me a white girl! He said he'd take me with him when he left the fort. He said he'd told his folks about us and that they'd be proud to have me back East. He said . . . he said . . . God damn it, you know what he said. You men all say the same things when you mean to do a woman wrong!"

"Well, he likely meant it at the time, honey. I know what it's been like for you, but—"

"You know nothing, white man! You don't know what it's like to grow up wishing you were white, or even black, for God's sake, if only you could belong *somewhere*!"

"You seem to be accepted by your tribe, Gloria."

"A lot you know! Why do you think they call me Two-Women? If my father hadn't been a chief—"

"Now just back up and study what you're saying, honey. Your father *is* a chief."

"Perhaps, but if he'd been just another brave—"

"If? If? Hell, if the dog hadn't stopped to pee he'd have caught the rabbit. Everything in life's an 'if,' and we have to make do with the ifs the Good Lord gives us. Try 'if' another way and your mama never would have been taken by Blackfoot. Or you could have been born dead, or a boy, or some other Indian kid named Mary. You know what you're doing, honey? You're picking a fight with 'if' instead of living with all you got!"

"That's easy for you to say. But if you'd been born a breed . . ."

"Well, I wasn't born a breed. Or the Prince of Wales, either. I was born on a hard-scrabble farm to folks too poor to spit. I'd have settled for being a Hindu maharaja with elephants and dancing gals to play with, and my complexion could be damned. So don't go cussing me for being white. It wasn't my idea and it ain't been all that easy."

"What would you have done if you'd been born an Indian, or colored?"

"Can't say. It never happened. I'd likely be another jasper, but I'd likely have managed to make do with what I was. Those ifs don't give us much choice."

"You'd have made a terrible Indian. You think too West Virginian."

"Likely you're right. Seems to me your own head's screwed on funny, though. If you don't like the name Two-Women, how come you almost got me shot by insisting on it over at that other hotel this evening?"

"It's my name, the only name I have."

"What's wrong with your mother's name, Witherspoon?"

"Those people rejected me. My father's people accepted me, however grudgingly, as at least a half-person." She shuddered as she added, "Not that I don't have to put up with sly remarks on the reservation. Some of the older squaws got quite a laugh when my soldier boy deserted me as the cast-off squaw he must have considered me."

"Gloria, I suspicion you fret too much over things. Your daddy must think highly of you or he'd never have sent you on a mission for his tribe."

She fondled him, almost painfully, as she asked, "How am I as a lover? Am I really the best you've ever had?"

Longarm was only half-lying as he nodded and ran a hand over her moist flesh, assuring her, "I don't like to brag, but I've been with some nice gals in my time and, yes, you are purely the best I've ever got next to."

"Do you think you'll always remember me as the best lay you ever had?"

"I'll have to. Anything better would kill me, but what's this about remembering? We're just getting started."

"No. After this night, you'll never be able to touch me again."

"I won't? Well, sure, we'll have to be careful once we're up near the reservation and all, but—"

"Never," she insisted, adding, "You can do it all you want tonight, if you're man enough, but one night of love is all I give. To anyone. I suppose you think I owe you an explanation?"

He said, "No. I suspicioned it was too good for you to be really enjoying it. I heard about an actress back East who plays the same trick. She's had men dueling over her, blowing out their own fool brains and beating on her door at all hours with flowers, books, and candy."

The beautiful breed's voice was downright nasty as she asked cruelly, "Are you suggesting you'll be different, Mr. Longarm?"

"Oh, I'll want you. I'll likely remember this night as long as I live and some night, alone on the trail, I'll do some hard wishing, most likely. But I don't reckon I'll play your game."

"Pooh, you don't even understand my reasons."

"Sure I do. You're a pretty little thing all eaten up inside with hate for us menfolks. One fool man betrayed your love and now you reckon you can get back at us all by turning the tables. You're playing love 'em and leave 'em 'cause you got loved and left. Your revenge is to drag us poor old boys into bed and pleasure us crazy, leaving us with nothing but the memory of the best lay any man could ever dream of, and no way to ever get it again. I'll allow it's mean as hell, but it ain't original."

She sat up suddenly to snap, "I suppose, now, you're going to try and say you lied before? I suppose you're going to pretend it won't bother you never to have me again?"

Longarm thought before he answered. He knew, now, that much of what he'd just enjoyed had been an act of curious cruelty.

He decided the hell with it. Real women were complicated enough and it wasn't as if the supply was likely to run out.

She insisted, "Well, am I? Am I not the greatest lay you've ever had, or ever will have?"

He feigned a mournful sigh and said, "Yeah, I know when I'm whipped. If you don't let me call on you this weekend, I'll likely wind up jerking off under your window. Can't we make an exception, just this once?"

Her voice was triumphant as she chortled, "No. I swear by Manitou you'll never sleep with me again. Two-Women has spoken!"

He rolled over as if to fall asleep. He figured it was the least a man could do, considering.

After a time, bored with her game, Gloria got softly out of bed and tiptoed back to her own room, the victor of her own grotesque game of revenge. Longarm got up and locked the door, muttering, "Thank God. I was afraid I'd never get any sleep tonight!"

Chapter 3

Longarm could see there was trouble long before he and Gloria reached the cluster of frame buildings in the rented buckboard he was driving. A huge crowd of Indians stood around the reservation agency across from the log trading post the center had grown up around.

It was midafternoon as they arrived and the sun floated above the purple Rockies far to the west. The Blackfoot reservation occupied an expanse of rolling short-grass prairie fifty miles across, but the tracks of the Iron Horse crossed the reservation and they'd been able to get off and rent the buckboard at another town just over the horizon to the east.

Gloria sat primly at his side, less friendly than ever, having not quite managed to claim him as her latest victim the night before. Longarm had been too gallant to make the obvious remark about black widow spiders when he found her dressed and coldly formal at dawn.

An Indian ran over as Longarm reined in near the edge of the crowd, and shouted something to Gloria in the high, nasal dialect of her tribe. The girl blanched and gasped, "Oh, God, no!"

Then, before Longarm could ask her what was up, she was out of her seat and running through the crowd, who gave way with expressions of compassion for the pretty little breed.

Longarm shouted to anyone who'd listen, "What's going on? Anyone here speak English?"

A short moon-faced man in faded denims and a very tall black hat came over to say, "I am Yellow Leggings. When I was young I killed a soldier and took his horse with me to Canada. Heya! That was a good fight we had at Greasy Grass! Were you there?"

"No, I'm still wearing my hair. What's all the fuss about?"

"I was a Dog Soldier. Now I am only a reservation policeman and they do not pay me on time. Wendigo has struck again. This time He-Who-Walks-the-Night-Winds took Real Bear. The people are very frightened."

Longarm nodded, sweeping his gunmetal gaze over the silent, unblinking faces crowded around him. He turned back to Yellow Leggings. "Where'd it happen?"

"In his house. The almost-girl you rode in with lives there,

too. I think it was a good thing she was not home last night. The
Wendigo would have torn her apart, too."

"Which house was his?"

"That one, north of the agency. The agent and some of the Indian police are in there now. I didn't want to go inside. I am not
afraid of man or beast, but I don't like to be near spirit happen-
ings. I told them I would stay out here and keep order."

"Can you get somebody to tie this mule to a post, Yellow Leggings? I'd better see what's going on."

"Go, then. I will see to your wagon and the things in back. I
never steal in peacetime."

Longarm jumped down with a nod of thanks to the older Indian and elbowed his way through the crowd. Somewhere ahead
of him, a woman screamed shrilly in mindless grief.

He went to the indicated cabin of unpainted lumber, and finding the door open, went inside.

Gloria was being comforted on a couch by a thin, blond white
woman and an older, fatter squaw. Gloria was still screaming, her
face buried in her hands. Longarm saw that there was another
room and went to the entrance as a harassed-looking young white
man came out, blinking in surprise to see another white. Longarm said, "I'm Deputy U.S. Marshal Custis Long. You must be
the Blackfoot agent?"

"I am, and you have come to the right place, lawman. I hope
you have a strong stomach."

Longarm followed the man into the bedroom, where two Indian police in those same tall hats stood over what looked at first
like a badly butchered side of beef on the bed.

Longarm suppressed a wave of nausea as he recognized the
form on the blood-soaked mattress as that of a man. From the
blood on the walls and ceiling it looked as if he might have been
skinned alive.

The agent said, "His name was Real Bear. You'll have to take
my word for it, he was an Indian."

"He was the man I came up here to see. How long ago did it
happen?"

"Nobody knows. They found him like this about an hour ago.
We were supposed to hold a meeting this afternoon and I sent one
of my police over to fetch him. Now you know as much as I do."

"Not quite. You say he didn't turn up for a meeting. What was
the meeting about?"

"Just the usual stuff. Complaints about the government rations being late, as usual. Some trouble about stolen livestock. Nothing that can't wait, now."

"One of your Indians said something about *another* Wendigo killing. Has anything like this happened before?"

"Not here at the center. Some of the old folks have been jawing about spirits out on the prairie, but I don't seem to be missing anybody. To tell you the truth, I didn't take it too seriously. I'm shorthanded here, and I've been having trouble with the damned army again, and—"

"I know people in the B.I.A. Anybody think to look for sign?"

One of the Indian policemen looked up to say, "No sign. No footprint. Nobody see Wendigo come. Nobody see Wendigo go. We find only . . . this."

Longarm touched a finger to a blood spatter on the wall and said, "Dry. Must have been done last night in the dark."

The agent snorted and said, "Tell me something I haven't figured out an hour ago! Of course he was killed at night! Who in hell's going to walk out of here covered with blood and carrying a man's skin, in broad daylight?"

Then, before Longarm could answer, the agent suddenly ran to the window, leaned out, and threw up.

Neither Longarm nor the Indian police said anything as he recovered, turned wanly from the window, and said, "Sorry. Thought I got it all the first time. I, uh, never saw a thing like this before."

Longarm's voice was gentle as he said, "It ain't a thing you see every day. Maybe we'd best go outside to talk about it."

"I have a duty to investigate," the young man said.

"Sure you do. So have I. But this'll keep. If these other peace officers can't find sign to read in here, the two of us ain't likely to. I see our next best bet as some solid jawboning on the whys and wherefores."

"Well, we'd best take the chiefs daughter over to our place and put something strong in her. Right now I could use a drink myself!"

"Let's go, then. Which one of these peace officers is the ranking lawman, hereabouts?"

Both Indians and the agent looked surprised. Then the agent nodded at the taller of the two and said, "I guess Rain Crow, here, has the most seniority."

Longarm nodded at the Blackfoot and said, "Glad to know you, Rain Crow. You can call me Longarm. I reckon you'd best come along while we put some twos and twos together."

Rain Crow asked, "You want me to come with you, in the agency?"

"You're a lawman, ain't you?" Longarm shot a quizzical glance at the agent, who quickly nodded and said, "Of course. I'm assigning you to help the marshal, Rain Crow. He'll need a guide around the reservation and help with his horses and—"

"I'll get a *boy* from you to wrangle for us," Longarm cut in, adding, "I'm going to need *men* like Rain Crow as my deputies."

To his credit, the young agent caught on and nodded as the Indian followed them out of the blood-spattered bedroom.

Out in the other room, they found the couch empty. The agent nodded again and said, "Good. I see Nan and old Deer Foot managed to get poor Gloria out of this god-awful place. We'll likely find 'em in our kitchen."

"Nan would be your wife, Mr. . . . ?"

"Durler. Calvin Durler. My wife, Nan, and I have been out here about a year. I'm afraid we're still pretty green."

"You talk like a farming man, Calvin. I was born in West Virginia, myself."

"I'm afraid we're from farther east. Our home was in Maryland."

"Tidewater Maryland or the Cumberland?"

"Cumberland, by God. I'm not *that* much of a dude!"

"There you go. I suspicioned you had hair on your chest, Calvin."

The youth laughed and said, "I'm still ashamed of throwing up like a baby, but I thank you for the neighborly way you took it."

"Hell, you never threw up on *me*, Calvin. Maybe if more folks got sick to their stomachs when folks they knew got killed, we'd live in a more peaceable world."

The three men went outside and elbowed their way through the upset, questioning Indians to the larger agency residence. Calvin Durler led his guests to the side door and they went in to find Nan Durler brewing coffee in her sparsely furnished, whitewashed kitchen. Her husband asked, "Where's Gloria?" and the blond woman replied, "In the bedroom. I made her lie down. Deer Foot's with her."

"Deer Foot's our housemaid," offered Durler to Longarm, who'd figured as much.

The agent took a brandy snifter from a sideboard and poured two glasses, holding one out to Longarm. The deputy held it out to the Indian, saying, "Where's mine, Calvin?"

The agent and his wife exchanged glances. Then Durler said, "I didn't make up the regulation, Longarm, but it's against the law to give an Indian a drink."

"Yeah, I heard," said Longarm, placing the glass, untasted, on the sideboard.

The Indian said, "I know what is in your heart, but it is all right. I will not be offended if you white men drink without me."

"You may not be, but I would," said Longarm. "When my deputies can't drink, I can't drink. Maybe we'd best all have some coffee."

Durler nodded eagerly and said, "That's just what I need, a hot cup of coffee. I'll pour it, Nan."

But Nan Durler, who'd been watching and sizing up the play, shook her head and said, "The three of you gents sit down. It's my place to pour for guests."

With the niceties out of the way for the moment, Longarm faced the other white man and his new Indian sidekick across the plank table and said, "All right, I'm a man with an open mind, but I can't buy a spook dropping down out of the sky to skin folks alive. So what we have is a human killer as well as his victim."

He saw the hesitation in the Indian's eyes and asked, "You got another notion, Rain Crow?"

"I don't know. The Dream Singers say Wendigo walks the night because our people have turned from the old ways. I know you think this is foolish, but—"

"Hold on. Foolish is a strong word, Rain Crow. I ain't one to sass my elders. Some of the old folks, red or white, just might know things I don't. I'll go along with evil spirits, if I cut an evil spirit's trail, I have to say, though, most of the men I've seen killed have been killed by other men, up to now. Chief Real Bear sent word to us about a rogue Blackfoot breed named Johnny Hunts Alone. Does that name mean anything to either of you gents?"

Durler looked blank and shook his head. Rain Crow frowned and said, "I have heard the name. The old ones say his white father rode with us long ago, in the Shining Times of the beaver trade."

"Real Bear reported that he'd come back to the reservation. You're a reservation peace officer, so you likely know a lot of folks hereabouts."

"I know many people, many. But this man you speak of is a half-breed."

Longarm nodded. "Yep, somewhere in his midthirties. What's

his being a breed have to do with it? You have breeds living among you, don't you?"

"Of course, but not many, and they are known to everyone. Real Bear's daughter in the other room is half white. There is the Collins family and the Blood woman called Cat Eyes. Then there is Burning Nose and—"

"In other words, breeds are rare enough for everyone on the reservation to take note, or likely gossip some about 'em?"

The Indian smiled. "The old women like to tell dirty stories and everyone knows how breeds come into the world. Yes, if there was a half-white Blackfoot called Johnny, I would have heard about him."

"You think Real Bear was lying, then?"

"No. He was a good person. If he said this man was among us, it must be so. Yet it is not so. I don't have an answer for this."

"Try it another way. Could a breed be passing himself off as a full-blooded Blackfoot?"

"This is more possible than that Real Bear lied, but he would have to look like a full-blood and he would have to act like a full-blood. You know how it is with breeds."

"No, Rain Crow, I don't know any such thing. You don't like breeds, do you?"

The Indian looked uncomfortable. Longarm said, "They have the same troubles on our side of the fence, Rain Crow. Most white folks suspicion breeds of all sorts of things."

"You think they're bad people, too?"

"No, I think they've got a hard row to hoe. Whites don't trust 'em because they're part Indian. Indians likely wonder if they can fully trust a man who is half white. I reckon a breed gets looked at sort of closer than the rest of us. Though, when you think on it, the best chief the Comanche ever had was a breed named Quanna Parker and the worst renegade who ever scalped a white man was a lily-white bastard named Simon Girty. So I'd say breeds are likely no better or worse than most folks, but I'll go along with you on Johnny Hunts Alone having a hard time passing himself off as a full-blood. Not just because he's a breed, but because he was raised mostly white. He'd have to be clever as old Coyote to pass muster here on the reservation."

"Heya! You have heard the tales of Coyote?"

"Sure. You ain't the first Indian lawman I've worked with. Let's study more on where this jasper might be hiding. You know the layout, Rain Crow. Where would you be if you were a white-raised Blackfoot?"

"The reservation is very big. It has five towns and much open range. How do you know he didn't leave when Real Bear recognized him?"

"Come on, Rain Crow, you ain't going to play cigar store Indian on me, are you?" Longarm prodded gently.

The young Blackfoot looked away and said, "You don't think Wendigo killed Real Bear. You think he was killed by a real person."

"There you go. And Real Bear was a good man with a good heart, so if he was killed by a real person—"

"Heya! The only one who'd want him dead would be someone who was afraid he'd been recognized! Someone who didn't want Real Bear to tell on him!"

"Now you're talking like a lawman, old son. So do you reckon we should look for spooks, or—"

"I will start asking the old ones about the Shining Days when the man called Johnny Hunts Alone lived among us," said Rain Crow, getting to his feet and leaving without ceremony.

As soon as the policeman was gone, Longarm grinned at the agent and his wife and said, "I'd purely like some of that brandy now."

Durler laughed and poured each of the three of them a shot, saying, "You sure have a way with Indians. I swear to God, I haven't been able to get much cooperation from any of my charges."

"I noticed. Maybe you could start by *talking* to them."

Durler protested, "Nan and I have been doing our best to make friends with our charges and—"

"That's the second time you've called them your *charges*," Longarm cut in. "Before the army whipped 'em down and fenced 'em in, they thought of themselves as *men*."

"I see how you played on Rain Crow's pride, Longarm, but I've got responsibilities here, and damn it, they act like children around most white men."

"Sure they do. That's probably because every time they *haven't* acted like children, lately, somebody's shot at them! You take away my gun and smack me alongside the head every time I try to think for myself and I'll act childish, too. But I wasn't sent up here to tell you how to do your job for the B.I.A. I ain't buttering up your, uh, charges, to *steal* your job, neither. You see, I ain't about to track down a renegade hidden out amidst all these folks unless I get some of 'em on my side."

"You think you can talk the Blackfoot into turning the renegade in?"

"Well, *one* Indian did it. Now that I'm here, it'll only take one more."

"In other words," Durler said, "you think some of the Indians are hiding him from us?"

"He has to be hiding somewhere. What *else* are the Blackfoot hiding from you?"

"Hiding from me? I don't know. What would they be keeping from me?"

Longarm shrugged and said, "A reservation's like a jail in some ways. There're always things the cooped-up folks don't want the warden, or the Indian agent, to know. If Real Bear was working for our side, Johnny Hunts Alone would be on the other."

Durler nodded and said, "You mean the troublemakers might be hiding him from you. If only we knew who the troublemakers were."

Longarm's eyebrows rose a notch, then he frowned and asked, "Don't you know which Indians are bucking you, Cal?"

"Not really. All of them seem a little sullen and none of 'em come right out and say they aim to scalp me. I think some of 'em might be drinking when I ain't looking."

"I smelled firewater when a couple passed me to windward, but you always have drinking on a reservation. It's as natural as small boys smoking corn silk behind the henhouse. How about Dream Singing? Gloria Two-Women made mention of some Ghost Dancing her daddy was worried about."

Durler laughed and shook his head, saying, "Oh, I'm not worried about that crazy new religion of Wovoka and his raggedy Paiutes. We got a notice about it from headquarters. The army says it's not serious."

Longarm looked disgusted and said, "Army didn't think much of Red Cloud's brag over in the Black Hills, either. 'Fess up, Cal. Do you *know* if there are any Ghost Dancers on this reservation?"

Durler shot a sheepish glance at his wife, who seemed very interested in her fingernails at the moment. Then, seeing she wasn't going to help or hinder, he sighed and said, "Damnation, Longarm, I've got over fifteen thousand sections of damn near empty prairie to cover!"

"I know. How much of it have you ever really looked at?"

"Not one hell of a lot, as you likely suspicion. But it ain't as if I haven't been trying to do my job! I've got six villages, a model farm, and more damn paperwork than ten Philadelphia lawyers could handle! I'm putting in a sixteen-hour day and I'm still swamped, as Nan can tell you!"

His wife looked up to nod grimly as she muttered, "He's up past midnight, every night, with those infernal books of his!"

Longarm looked away, uncomfortable with the message he thought he might be reading in Nan's upset eyes. To steer the conversation away from a topic he thought might be getting under both their skins, he said, "I know you've a lot of corn to shuck, Cal. How are you getting on with the other white folks?"

"What white folks? We're up to our necks in Blackfoot. They hate us for being white and the whites in town and over at the army post hate us for feeding the rascals. The only white who ever comes out here is the sutler who owns the trading post across the way. He comes when the spirit moves him, which ain't often. I'm supposed to issue cash to my Indians, but Washington's slow in sending it and the sutler doesn't give credit."

"I know the type. He likely has an uncle in Washington, too. It's all cash and carry? No swapping for furs and hides or—? Never mind, that was a fool question, wasn't it?"

Durler smiled thinly, glad to be able to pontificate on something he knew better than his visitor. He said, "Yeah, the Shining Times are gone and so are most of the buffalo. The Indians still hunt a mite. Not enough game left for trading the old ways. We give each Indian family a small cash allowance and the trading post sells 'em the most expensive salt and matches this side of the Mississippi. Like you said, somebody likely has an uncle."

"That council meeting Real Bear never made it to was something about missing livestock, wasn't it?" the marshal asked.

"Some of the Indians complained of white cow thieves. Don't know if it's true or not. Along with the demonstration farm, which grows mostly weeds, we have a reservation herd, which sort of melts away as you look at it each sunup. It's a toss-up who's worse as a farmer—a Blackfoot or a cowboy. I know for a fact some of 'em have run steers for private barbecues. There are a lot of hard feelings between us and the local whites, so it wouldn't surprise me all that much if a few government cows wind up wearing a white man's brand."

"Surprise me more if they left you alone. What reservation brand have you registered with the territorial government?"

Durler said, "Oh, most of 'em are delivered with *U.S.* stamped on their hides. I haven't been able to teach my Indian herders all that much about branding, and as to a registered brand, well . . ."

"Good night!" Longarm exclaimed. "And you've still got one cow left! You sure live in the midst of Christian neighbors, Calvin!"

"Look, I'm an Indian agent, not a cowhand. I *thought* I was a farmer, before I tried to grow stuff in this prairie sod. They told me the Indians would help us, but—"

Longarm shoved himself away from the table and got to his feet, saying, "I've got to get over to the fort and borrow a horse from the remount sergeant. I'll be back before sundown and we can jaw some more. You got an icehouse or something we can store the body in?"

"Store it? Ain't I supposed to *bury* Real Bear?"

"Sure, after I get a sawbones to look him over and tell me what he died from."

"Come on, we know how he died! He was skinned alive."

"Maybe. I'd like an M.D. to give me an educated guess as to bullets, poisons, and such, though. He'll keep a day or so in this dry, thin air, so you put him in a shady spot with maybe some chopped ice in the box with him. I'll show you how when I get back. I want to make it over to the fort and back by daylight."

He tipped his hat to Nan and ducked out the side door as the agent followed him toward the buckboard. The crowd of Indians was still in place, standing sullenly silent and not appearing to notice either white man as they crossed the village street. Longarm found a young boy seated on the trading post steps with the reins of his rented mule in hand. He gave the kid a nickel and a smile for his trouble. The kid put the coin in his britches and went away without saying thanks or looking back. Longarm couldn't tell whether they were all pissed at him, the agent, or white folks in general.

It occurred to Longarm that unless he found the killer of Real Bear pretty quickly, things were likely to get ugly hereabouts.

Fort Banyon was little more than an outpost, manned by an over-aged second lieutenant and a skeleton platoon of dragoons. A cluster of log buildings surrounded a parade ground of bare earth and was surrounded in turn by a rail fence, broken in places. Everything from the tattered flag drooping from the flagstaff of lodgepole pine to the threadbare uniforms of the men lounging on the orderly room steps told Longarm there hadn't been a general inspection for some time and that morale was low, even for a frontier garrison.

He wasn't challenged as he drove through the open gateway and across the parade to the orderly room. The C.O., a dumpy man with a florid face and an unbuttoned officer's blouse, came out on the porch to stare at him morosely as Longarm hitched the mule to a rail. As the deputy walked over to the steps the officer asked, "Did you bring mail from town?"

"No sir. I'm a deputy U.S. marshal, not the mailman. I need a mount. I generally ride a gelding at least fifteen hands high. Got my own saddle and bridle."

"What are you talking about, mister? This is an army post! We don't sell horses!"

"Aw, hell, Lieutenant, this argument I keep getting from you fellows is as tedious as shitting on an ant pile. I know you're supposed to give me an argument and we both know that in the end, I'll get the horse. So what say we agree it's a hell of a note how the Justice Department imposes on the army and I'll be on my way."

Before the officer could reply, his first sergeant came out to join him. The C.O. said, "Lawman. Says he wants a horse."

The sergeant shook his head at Longarm and said, "We're short on mounts, mister. We're here to keep an eye on them Blackfoot, not to be a remount station."

"Yeah, I noticed how scared you are of Indians. Your pickets damn near shot me as I came in. You look like an old soldier, Sarge. Do we have to go through all this bullshit? You know damn well I'm riding out of here on one of Uncle Sam's ponies, and if you keep me here much longer I aim to make you feed me supper, too!"

"You've got requisition papers, I guess?" the sergeant said.

"Sarge, I've got carte blanche. I'm covering first degree murder. Federal. So give me something to sign and I'll be on my way."

The two army men exchanged glances. Then the lieutenant shook his head and said, "Nope. I'm shorthanded on men and mounts. Maybe you can borrow a pony over at the reservation agency. They're federal, too."

"Yeah, and my legs drag when I ride Indian ponies. I ride with a McClellan saddle and too much gear for one of those skinny critters I've seen over yonder. Maybe if Custer hadn't shot all those Indian ponies they'd *have* one fifteen hands high, but he did, and they don't."

"You don't like our army, mister?" the lieutenant bristled.

"Why, boys, I like it more than I can tell you. Hell, if I was *mad* at you, I'd likely try and give you a hard time."

"You feel up to giving a platoon of dragoons a hard time, mister?"

"You mean *whup* all thirty-odd of you? Not hardly, Lieutenant. I'm a friendly cuss. So why don't you lend me a mount and I'll tell you what; I'll just forget about a few old reportables next time I wire the government."

"Reportables? You must be drunk, lawman! You got no power to report doodly shit about *army* matters!"

"Well, I ain't connected up with the Inspector General's office, though, now that you mention it, I do have some drinking pals in Denver who work for the I.G. All us lawmen sort of exchange information."

He looked around thoughtfully before adding innocently, "But you're likely right. I don't figure the I.G. would be interested in little things like no guards posted or a few busted fences or that flag nailed up there night and day without proper hoisting lines. Tell me something, Lieutenant. How *do* you hold proper flag ceremonies twice a day, the way you've got it sort of up there for keeps?"

The officer scowled and started to bluster. Then he shrugged and told the sergeant, "Give the blackmailing son of a bitch a horse."

"Does the lieutenant want him, ah, well-mounted?"

"By all means, Sergeant. He's a fellow federal officer," the C.O. said sweetly.

Longarm followed the first sergeant down the barracks line to the corrals as some of the enlisted men who'd heard the exchange followed. Longarm sighed wearily. He'd been through this same hazing so many times, he knew the routine better than most soldiers did.

They got to the remuda corral, where a civilian in buckskins perched atop a corral rail, jawing with a uniformed stable hand. The first sergeant introduced the civilian as a scout named Jason, then winked at the horse wrangler and said, "Cut old Rocket out for this nice deputy, will you?"

The stable hand grinned and took a throw rope from the gatepost as Longarm said, "I'll trot back and fetch my saddle."

"Don't you aim to watch us pick your pony, mister?"

"No, I know you'll do right by me. By the time you get that bronc roped and steadied, I'll have time to fetch my saddle, walk to town, get a drink, and walk back."

He knew he was only half jesting, so he strolled back up the line to the buckboard, removing his Winchester and possibles from the saddle in the wagon bed with slow deliberation. He knew that while they might even try to kill him, they wouldn't steal his gear, so he left it in the buckboard.

As he turned with the McClellan braced on one hip, he saw that the civilian scout, Jason, had followed him part of the way up the company street. Jason was almost as tall as Longarm and a bit older. There were a few gray hairs among the greasy thatch on his head and in his spade-shaped beard, and his suntanned face was creased with friendly laugh wrinkles. Jason fell in at Longarm's side as they walked back to the corral, saying, "They treated me the same way when I was first posted here, mister. I ain't generally a tattletale, but I reckon they've gone overboard with old Rocket!"

"Bad bronc, huh?"

"No. Rocket's a killer. I can see you know which end of the horse the bit goes in, but if I was you I'd pass on Rocket. It's not like it is a shameful thing to do. There ain't a man in this outfit who is ashamed when it comes to old Rocket."

"I thank you for the warning, Jason. If I live, you can call me Longarm."

"Where do I send your possibles after the fool horse throws you and stomps on your head?"

Longarm didn't answer. He saw that the soldiers had roped and blindfolded a big gray gelding and led him into an empty corral next to the remuda. As the others held Rocket, Longarm threw his saddle over the broad back and cinched it, asking, "Ain't most of these grays assigned to army bands?"

The stable boss grinned and said, "Yeah, old Rocket was a mite, uh, spirited for parades. So they sent him out here to fight Indians. You ain't scared of spirited horses, are you, lawman?"

"Let's get it over with," said Longarm, getting the bridle on over the blindfold after punching Rocket in the nose to make him open his mouth for the bit.

He put a foot in the stirrup and hoisted himself up into the saddle, ready for anything. But nothing happened. The big gray stood as placid as a plowhorse while Longarm settled in the saddle and got a firm grip on the reins. He muttered, "One of that kind, huh?" Then, in a louder tone, he said, "All right, yank the blinds and give me room."

The soldiers scattered as the stable boss pulled the bandanna blindfold out from under the bridle and joined his messmates on the surrounding rails. The big gray blinked at the sunlight, took two steps backward toward the center of the corral, and tried to jump over the late-afternoon sun, as someone shouted, "Hot damn!"

Longarm yanked hard on the reins to force the gray's head down and to one side as they came down. The Spanish bit he'd rigged his bridle with had been purchased with such emergencies in mind, and while he customarily rode with a gentle hand on the reins, he could hurt a horse with the bit if he had to, and right now he had to.

Rocket didn't like it much. He was used to army bits as well as having his own way. With his head held down almost against Longarm's left stirrup, he had to buck in a tight circle; any good rider can stay aboard a bucking horse as long as it bucks in a repeated pattern. Some of the soldiers might not have known this, so they were impressed as the big lawman rode easily, swaying in tune with the mindless anger of the killer bronc.

Then Rocket saw he wasn't getting anywhere bucking in a circle, so he danced sideways and threw his full weight against the corral rails. He had intended his rider's right leg to take most of the shock, but Longarm saw it coming, kicked free of the right stirrup, and got his leg up in time. The big gray followed up his knee-breaking attempt with a sideways crabbing, the purpose of which was to throw Longarm before he could get his leg back down in place. Longarm expected that, too, so it didn't work.

The big gray fought to raise his head, trying to get the cruel bit between his teeth. Then, when he saw that the enemy tormenting him had the bit well-set, he decided, as long as his muzzle was down by the man's left foot, that he might as well bite it off.

Longarm snatched his toe back as the big yellow teeth snapped at it, then he kicked the gray's muzzle, hard. Rocket tried a couple more times before he gave up on that one, his nostrils running blood.

They circled the corral a few more times, spinning like a top, but the gray was tiring, and like any bully, Rocket didn't like to get hurt; Longarm was the meanest critter he'd ever been ridden by.

"You got him, mister!" someone shouted. "Just stay on a few more minutes and that old bastard will be your asshole buddy!"

Longarm shouted, "I don't want to marry up with him, I want to *work* with him!"

He steadied the gray as he stopped bucking, rode him once around the corral at a weary trot, and reined in by the rails, climbing quickly off and perching by the boss wrangler, maintaining his hold on the reins. Rocket saw an opportunity and pulled suddenly back to unseat him, but Longarm leaned back and gave the Spanish bit a vicious yank, drawing more blood. After that, Rocket stood very still indeed as Longarm said, "That was sure interesting. Now, I'd like to pick out a gelding fifteen hands high and if you give me another bronc I'll *kill* the son of a bitch. Then I'll come for *you*, personal."

"You made your point when you stayed aboard old Rocket, mister. We was just having a little friendly fun. I'll issue you Betsy. She's a good steady mare."

"No you won't. I said I'd pick a gelding. I reckon I earned it, don't you?"

The wrangler noted the chilly look in Longarm's eyes and nodded soberly. "Yep, I'd say it's time to quit while I'm ahead."

Chapter 4

Longarm got back to the Indian agency near sundown, riding a tall chestnut and leading the mule and buckboard.

Calvin Durler came out to help as he unhitched and unsaddled in the agency corral. Durler said, "Nan's got a room fixed up for you and we have Real Bear in the root cellar, wrapped in a wagon tarp. Nan didn't like it much, but what the hell, we haven't harvested enough to mention, so the cellar's mostly empty and I put her preserves on the other side."

Longarm nodded. "I'll run the body into town come sunup. The army post has no surgeon but they tell me there's a county coroner in Switchback. You do have a telegraph line here, don't you?"

"No. We're supposed to, but they never installed it. I use the one at the federal land office in town on government business. The land agent's sort of mad about it, too. Who'd you aim to wire?"

"My office. They figured I'd just come here, arrest the jasper Chief Real Bear pointed out, and be on my way back by now. I don't reckon they'll think Johnny Hunts Alone got the drop on me if I don't get in touch tonight. You're sure I won't be crowding you folks?"

"Hell, we're delighted to have white folks to talk to. Nan and me don't go to town much. The locals seem to blame us for past misdeeds of the Blackfoot, and maybe some Comanche, too! We've got us some champion Indian haters in this territory!"

"Well, Montana was all Indian land up till a few short years ago, so the locals are mostly the same people who drove the Indians back into this one corner to start with. How's Gloria Two-Women taking her daddy's murder, now? Did you get her calmed down enough for me to talk to yet?"

Durler shook his head exasperatedly. "Oh, she's jumped the reservation again. Says her name now is Wither-something-or-other."

Longarm arched an eyebrow. "Do tell? When did all this happen?"

"While you were over getting this horse. Gloria said a lot of crazy things, then she sort of took herself in hand and went over to her house to pack her duds. Deer Foot helped, but it's a funny thing—Gloria won't speak Blackfoot anymore. She says with her daddy dead she's not an Indian anymore. How do you figure that?"

Longarm shrugged. "Likely makes as much sense for her to try to make it as a white woman, after all. If I'd been here, I'd have suggested she try living in Oklahoma, where breeds have an easier time than most places. Maybe she knew that, though. She didn't say where she was going, huh?"

"Nope. Just rode to Switchback to catch a train. They could probably tell you at the station where she took it to, if you really want to question her about what happened."

"Hardly seems worth it," Longarm sighed. "She was with me when her daddy was killed, so we know she didn't do it. I, uh, got to know her pretty well on the train ride up from Denver, so I don't reckon she left anything out I could use. Real Bear never pointed out the renegade to her, so even if she was here, she couldn't identify the jasper for us. Is Rain Crow back with anything, yet?"

"He was by here an hour ago. He hasn't found out much we didn't know already. He did say the old ones don't think a man did it. They say the Wendigo punished Real Bear for turning his back on the old ways and accepting a breed as his daughter." Durler shook his head wearily and added, "It's as well Gloria lit out. She was a proud little thing and some of the talk about her is right ugly."

Longarm studied a crow flying past and tried to appear disinterested as he asked, "Oh? What sort of gossip are the old squaws spreading about the gal?"

Durler shrugged and said, "The usual back-fence bullshit about any gal who lives alone, if she's pretty. She lived right next door, so Nan and I can tell you she was proper. They say she was married to a white man once. It was before we got here, so I can't say what went wrong. As far as I know, she was a perfect lady."

"I'll remember her as perfect, too," said Longarm, shifting his weight to meet the younger man's eyes again as he changed the subject. "I noticed you've got corn in the feed troughs. You been shipping it all this way with all this free grass around?"

"I grew the corn on my so-called model farm. The soil hereabouts is piss-poor or I'd have grown a real crop."

Longarm laughed and said, "You must be one hell of a farmer, Cal. If you'd asked me if you could grow corn on this reservation I'd have said it was impossible!"

Durler stared morosely down at the tawny stubble all around and said, "It damn near was. Like I said, it's poor soil and the Indians shirked such honest toil as I assigned 'em."

Longarm knew it wasn't his job, but he couldn't keep his mouth shut about such an obvious greenhorn notion. He said, "There's nothing wrong with the soil, Cal. It's the crop that was all wrong. You're a mile above sea level and damn near in Canada. About the only farm crop you can grow up here is barley. Corn's a lowland crop. Needs at least twenty inches of rain a year to survive."

"Yeah, I noticed our fields were a mite dry. I had Indians haul water to the corn. They didn't cotton to it much, but I knew Indians ate corn, so . . ."

"Cal," Longarm cut in, "it ain't my call to tell you how to run your spread, but there's Indians and there's Indians. Your Blackfoot lived on wild game, roots, and such, before the army showed them the error of their ways. It's no wonder they've been shirking. No offense intended, but you ain't showing them how to farm the high plains. You're showing them how to make the same mistakes every other nester who's been dusted out has made, over and over."

Durler's jaw had a stubborn set to it as he snapped, "I'll admit I don't know this country, damn it, out what am I to do? My job is to make smallholders instead of hunters out of the Blackfoot. They gave me the job because I was a fair farmer, back East!"

"I don't doubt it, Cal. There are abandoned homesteads all over the prairie left by men who came out West with the skills they learned in other parts. You just can't farm out here the way you do back East."

"Will you show me how, then?"

"I don't aim to be here all that long. For openers I'd say to drill in some rye and barley next time. Then I'd get some of the old-timers to advise me about the climate, soil, and such."

"None of the nesters will talk to me, damn it!" the agent said sourly.

"I didn't mean *white* old-timers. These Indians were here long before it got so civilized. I know they're not keen on farming and you'll have as much to show them as they have to show you, but you'll do better *talking* to them than *lecturing* them. You get my drift?"

"Hell, only a handful speak English."

"I know. It would make your job a lot easier if you and Nan learned Blackfoot."

"Good God! We'd never be able to in a million years! I don't know one word of Blackfoot!"

"Sure you do. They speak Algonquin, which is about the easiest Indian language there is for a white man to pick up. Damn near every Indian word we already know is Algonquin."

"I tell you, I don't know word one!"

"How about squaw, papoose, moccasin, tomahawk, or skunk, or possum?"

"Those are Algonquin words?"

"So are tom-tom, powwow, wampum, and succotash. I'll bet you know what every one of those words means, don't you?"

"Sure. I reckon they must have been the first Indian words the white folks learned when they got off the boat."

"There you go. You're halfway to learning the lingo already. You don't have to learn to speak it perfectly, but they'll respect you for trying. My Spanish is awful, but most Mexicans brighten up when I give 'em a chance to laugh at me, rather than the other way around. A little gal in a border town once even helped me learn a bunch of new words." Longarm smiled. "The lessons were purely enjoyable."

The agent chuckled. "I'll see if we can get Deer Foot to teach us some Blackfoot. Meanwhile, supper should be almost ready."

They went inside and found Nan Durler as good as her husband's word. The fare was simple, but well-cooked, and like most country folk, the three of them ate silently. It was something they didn't think about; witty dinner conversation is a city notion.

Nan had made a peach cobbler for dessert and insisted on Longarm's having two helpings before she'd let him step out onto the porch for an after-dinner smoke. He'd expected his host, at least, to join him. But he found himself alone on the steps, puffing a cheroot as he watched the stars come out over the distant Rockies.

It was peaceful outside, now. The Indians had drifted off home after jawing about the murder of their chief all afternoon. Somewhere in the night a medicine drum was beating softly, probably to keep the Wendigo away. Longarm judged the drum to be a good two miles distant, so he decided Rain Crow could tell him, later, what the fuss was all about.

He was halfway through his smoke when Nan Durler came out to join him. She said, "Calvin's at his books again. Sometimes he spends half the night on those fool papers for the B.I.A."

Longarm nodded without answering as the blonde sat beside him on the steps. After a while she shuddered and said, "They're at that old drum again. Sometimes they beat it half the night. I don't know if I hate it more when the Indians are whooping it up or when they're quiet. Back home we had crickets and fireflies this time of year."

"Night noises are different on the prairie. I sort of like the way the coyotes sing, some nights."

"It wakes me up. It's no wonder the Blackfoot think the Wendigo walks at midnight out here. Some of the things I hear from my window are spooky as anything."

"Well," Longarm observed, "you're pretty high up for rattlers, hereabouts. I can't think of much else that can worry folks at night."

"The other night, I heard the strangest screaming. Calvin said it was a critter, but it sounded like a baby crying."

"Thin, high-pitched hollerings? Sort of *wheeeeee wheeeee wheeeee*?"

"Yes! It was awful. Do you know what it might have been?"

"No 'might' about it, ma'am. It was a jackrabbit."

He didn't add that jackrabbits screamed like that as they were being eaten alive by a silent coyote. He didn't think that part would comfort her.

She shuddered again and said, "I guess it could have been 'most any old thing. Sounded like it was getting skinned alive . . . oh, dear . . ."

"I'll be hauling the body into town, come morning, ma'am. I could wrap him in a tarp and leave him out in the buckboard overnight if it frets you to have him in your root cellar."

Nan grimaced and said, "Leave him be, but let's not dwell on it. I'm going to have to take at least two of the powders the doctor gave me if I'm to sleep a wink tonight."

Longarm asked cautiously, "Oh? You take sleeping powders often, ma'am?"

Her voice was bitter as she said, "Just about every night. My husband seems more interested in his books than in sleeping and I get so . . . so *lonely* when the wind starts to keen out on the prairie!"

"Most folks get used to the prairie after a time, ma'am."

"Most folks have neighbors, too. The Indians look through us, and you know we're outcasts to the other whites around here, don't you?"

Longarm shrugged and said, "Well, who wants to butter up to the grudge-holding kind, ma'am? There are likely others over in town who aren't so narrow-minded."

"I doubt it. You should see the looks they give us when we ride in from the reservation! You'd think the Indian Wars were still going on!"

Longarm noticed that she'd somehow moved closer to him and decided she was probably too upset to have realized it. He shifted away a little and said, "The Blackfoot were hostile Indians and it hasn't been all that long, ma'am. Some folks are sore about the Civil War and *those* memories are almost old enough to vote. You've got to remember some of your neighbors, red and white, were swapping lead not five years ago this night."

She moved closer, as if uneasy at the gathering dusk and asked, "Have you fought Indians, Longarm?"

He saw that there wasn't much room left for his rump, so he stayed put as he answered, "Yep. You name the tribe and I've likely traded a few shots with 'em."

"But you don't seem to hate Indians at all."

He tried to ignore the warmth of her thigh against his as he looked away and suggested, "I've been lucky about Indians. They never tried to do more than lift my hair. I mean, they never killed a woman or kid of mine. I was over at Spirit Lake just after the Sioux first rose under Little Crow and it was mighty ugly, but none of the dead white folks were my kin. I've left some squaws keening over their own dead in my time, so I can afford to forgive and forget. But it was right ugly out here until recently. The soldiers and other whites have done some terrible things, too, and not every Indian is the noble savage some have written about. Ugly feeds on ugly, and like I said, it wasn't all that long ago. We have to give both sides a mite more time to get used to having one another as neighbors."

Nan's hand was suddenly on Longarm's knee as she said, "You think Calvin is a fool, don't you?"

"I never said such a thing, ma'am!"

"You didn't have to. I've seen the mockery in your eyes. To you he's just a green kid, isn't he?"

Longarm got to his feet, not knowing how else to get her hand off his knee, as he said, "Getting sort of chilly, ain't it?"

She remained seated, looking up at him oddly as she asked, "Are you afraid to answer me?"

Longarm shook his head and said, "I thought I had, ma'am. You asked did I think your man was a fool and I said he wasn't one. He's younger than me and has a few things to learn. But he'll do."

"For you, maybe. Where are you going? It's early yet, and I'll never get any sleep this night."

"I'd be proud to sit out here and jaw some more," he said as tactfully as he could, "but I've got to get some shut-eye, and like I said, there's a chill in the air."

"I noticed," she said, looking suddenly away.

He saw that she didn't intend to go inside, so he said good night and left her sitting there, nursing whatever was eating at her. He noticed that she didn't answer, either. She surely seemed a moody little gal.

He went to his room and locked himself in from force of habit before sitting on the bed to pull off his boots. He frowned at the door for a time, then he said, "You're getting a dirty mind, old son. You just leave that damned door locked, hear? Her man is just down the hall, and damn it, a gent has to draw the line some damned where!"

The town of Switchback, as its name indicated, was a railroad community where the trains added a second engine to negotiate a sudden scarp in the high plains before going over the mountains to the west.

Longarm left the dead Indian with the county coroner and walked across the rutted street to the land office, where he found a federal official named Chadwick in charge. Chadwick was about forty and looked like a superannuated buffalo hunter, except for his broadcloth suit. Longarm told the land agent his reasons for calling and Chadwick led him back to a lean-to shack behind his office, where he kept the telegraph setup.

A writing desk stood under a long shelf of wet cell batteries. A sending and receiving set shared the green desk blotter with paper pads and some leather-bound code books. Chadwick asked if Longarm knew how to send, and seeing that the lawman needed no further help, left him to his own devices.

Longarm got on the key, patched himself through to Denver Federal, and sent a terse message:

CHIEF REAL BEAR MURDERED STOP STILL LOOKING FOR
FUGITIVE STOP INVESTIGATING BOTH CASES STOP SIGNED
LONG DEPUTY U S MARSHAL DENVER

Then he left without waiting for a reply. If he gave Marshal Vail a chance to contact him, he'd probably be saddled with all sorts of foolish questions and instructions.

He accepted a cigar from the land agent, and as they shared a smoke, filled his fellow federal man in on what had happened. Chadwick shook his head and said, "I heard the medicine men are jawing about evil spirits again. You don't think it means more Indian trouble, do you?"

"Don't know what it means. While I'm here, I'd best ask you some questions about the situation. You have many cattle spreads hereabouts?"

"Of course. That's what I'm doing here in Switchback. Since the rails came through and Captain Goodnight brought the long-horns north, Montana's turned to cattle country. Ain't that a bitch? Five, six years ago this was all buffalo and redskins!"

"I noticed the electric lamp over the railroad yards. Anyone wanting to claim more land would come to you, wouldn't they?"

"Sure. Most of the good stuff's been filed on, though. I guess you want to know how many offers I've gotten on the reservation, right?"

"I admire a man who thinks on his feet."

"Knew what you suspicioned the minute you told me about the dead Indian. But you're barking up the wrong tree. I've had requests to extend the open range west into the reservation, but everyone knows by now that my hands are tied. Land and B.I.A. are both under the Department of the Interior, but I can't file claims on Indian-held land and neither can anyone else."

"So there'd be no money in it for white folks hereabouts to trifle with the Blackfoot. How about revenge?"

"You mean some white man killing Indians just for the hell of it, like Liver-Eating Johnson? Maybe, if he was sort of crazy. This Indian you brought in was killed right on the reservation, right?"

"Next door to the agency."

"There you go. You show me a white man who can creep to the center of a reservation, kill a chief, and creep back out without leaving sign, and I'll show you a white man who can out-Indian an Indian! I was out here when the Blackfoot were still in business killing folks, and while I don't like 'em all that much, I'll give 'em the edge on skulking. You know what I suspicion? I suspicion that old Indian was killed by one of his own! I don't know a white man in the territory who could have pulled it off the way you say it happened."

"I'd say you've got a point," Longarm agreed. "Most Indian killers pick 'em off along the edges of the reservation. I've got a warrant on a breed named Hunter or Hunts Alone. Any of the spreads hereabouts hire a breed hand, lately?"

"A breed, working on a Montana spread? Hell, they'd hire a nigger first. Not as if they have. I've never seen a nigger cowhand, have you?"

"Yep. First man ever killed in Dodge City was a colored hand called Tex. Someone shot him the first day of the first drive up from Texas and they've been shooting ever since. I'll take your word for it that most Montana hands are white, though. How about the railroad or some other outfit?"

"You mean here in Switchback? I know just about every man in town, at least on sight. I don't miss much, either, and I don't like Indians. If there was a half-breed working in Switchback, even swamping out saloons, I'd have seen him, maybe five minutes before I ran him out of town. I could tell you *stories*, Longarm!"

"I've heard 'em. Found some fellows after Apache worked 'em over, too. We don't have a good description of Johnny Hunts Alone, though. He could take after his pa's side of the family. No telling how white he might look."

"Didn't you say Chief Real Bear said he was on the reservation?"

"Yeah," Longarm said. "I see what you mean. He couldn't look *too* white, unless some of the others have fibbed about not noticing."

"He's got to look nigh pure white or pure Indian, then, whether he's hiding out with them or us. You can't have him both ways."

"You're right. I thank you for the smoke. I'd best get over and see what the doc can tell me."

Longarm left the land office and went back to the coroner's. Inside, he found Real Bear even more messed up than when he'd been found. The coroner seemed cheerful, considering, as he looked up from the god-awful mess in his zinc-lined autopsy tray and said, "They fractured his skull before they started taking him apart. He was struck from behind with a blunt instrument and most likely never knew what hit him."

"That's some comfort. You can't tell what the weapon was, huh?"

"If I could I'd have said so. You mind if I keep his skull? Save for being stove in a little, it's a beaut."

"I told his kin I'd bring him back for a proper funeral, Doc. Are you a headhunter? I took you for a Presbyterian."

"I'm writing a paper for the Smithsonian on hereditary bone structure. The Mountain Men spent more time screwing squaws than trapping beaver and some of the skull formations out here are getting interesting as hell."

"Going to bury him head and all anyway. But while we're on the subject, Doc, I've got papers on a Blackfoot breed who may be passing as anything. Is there anything I should be watching for?"

"You mean like the mark of Cain? It would depend on both parents. I've met pure-blooded Indians pale enough to worry about sunburn and some Scotch-Irish as white as you or me who have those same high cheekbones and hooked noses. I'd say if your man's part Algonquinoid he might be a bit hatchet-faced for a white, but his complexion could go either way. If you could get your suspect to take down his pants, a lot of Indians have a dark sort of birthmark on their tailbone."

Longarm grinned as he thought of a pretty little squaw he'd had with the lights on and doggie style, but he shook his head and said, "That doesn't seem a decent request, even from a lawman to a suspect. Could you sort of put him back together for me, Doc? I'd like to carry him home in a neater bundle."

"Come back in about an hour. You figure they'll leave the body in one of those tree houses, or was he a Christian?"

"The Indian agency doesn't let 'em bury folks in the sky anymore. I know what you're thinking, Doc, but forget it. This one's gone for good."

He said he'd be back directly and stepped outside, glad to inhale some fresh air after the medicinal smell of the coroner's lab.

He headed back to where he'd left the buckboard, wondering what his next move ought to be, and suddenly grinned as he spied a wooden Indian standing in front of a cigar store next to a saloon. He muttered, "We were just talking about you!" and changed course to pick up some more smokes.

The unplanned move saved Longarm's life, but only by an inch.

Something buzzed across the back of his neck, followed by the report of a high-powered rifle, and he wasted no time wondering if it had been an angry hornet. He loped for cover at a long-legged run without looking back as another bullet ticked the tail of his coat, and then he dove headfirst through the front window of the saloon, sliding across a table on his belly in a confusion of broken glass, scattered chips, and cards, as the men whose poker game he'd broken up flew backward from the table in all directions, swearing in surprise.

Longarm landed on his shoulder, rolled, and came to his feet with his gun in his hand and facing the shattered window as he shouted, "Hold it! I'm purely sorry about how I came in, but I come in peace!"

A gambling man kneeling in a corner with a drawn derringer got up, saying, "We heard the shots outside, stranger. How'd you get so popular?"

Longarm moved to the other window and looked out, gun in hand. It came as no great surprise to him that the street and boardwalks were devoid of life or movement. Everyone within sound of the shots had taken cover.

The bartender joined Longarm at the window. He had a barrel stave in one hand but his voice was reasonable as he said, "Before you bust *this* window, friend, who's paying for the one you just come through so sudden?"

Longarm kept his eyes on the buildings across the way as he took out his wallet with his free hand and flashed his badge, saying, "Uncle Sam is paying for the glass and a round of drinks for everyone. Get back out of the light, though. That jasper was firing an express rifle!"

The gambling man with the derringer laughed and said, "Hell, nobody shoots folks I'm drinking with! You want me to see if I can circle in on the son of a bitch for you, Marshal?"

"It's a kind thought, friend, but I imagine he's pulled up stakes, and I don't want gunplay with all those shops across the way likely filled with folks. I guess it's safe for us to have that drink now."

"Any idea who tried to bushwhack you, Marshal?"

"I'm only a deputy, and I've got lots of folks gunning for me. Getting shot at comes with the job."

He turned from the window to see the dozen-odd men in the saloon lining up along the bar as the bartender poured a long row of drinks. Longarm bellied up to an empty place and called for a shot of Maryland rye as he holstered his .44 and took out a voucher pad. When the barkeep brought his drink, he tossed it back in one throw, grimaced slightly, and explained, "I'm saying I busted fifty dollars worth of window in the line of duty. I can't write off the booze, of course, but figuring a nickel a shot—"

"Hey, that window came all the way from Saint Louis, mister."

"That's why I'm saying it was worth fifty instead of the twenty-odd you paid for it. Don't shit me and I won't shit you.

I'm an expert on busted windows and I owe a certain obligation to the taxpayers."

"How 'bout seventy five and I'll throw in another round of drinks?"

"Nope. I didn't hurt anybody and I ain't charging for the interesting diversion added to a dull afternoon, so I figure the boys rate one drink on me for such inconvenience as picking up cards and chips off the floor. If you want to argue about the damages, you are free to sue Uncle Sam for more. And now, having done my Christian duty. I'll be saying adios."

Without waiting for a reply, Longarm moved over to the swinging doors, risked a peep out front, and stepped out on the plank walk. Nobody shot at him, so he shrugged and went next door to the cigar store he'd been headed for in the first place.

As he stepped inside the richly scented darkness of the little shop, a female voice snapped, "Freeze right there, you son of a bitch!"

Longarm froze, staring soberly down the barrel of an S&W .45 in the right hand of a big blonde wearing the cotton shirt and batwing chaps of a working cowhand. Her face was sort of pretty under the beat-up Stetson she wore cavalry style, dead center and tipped forward.

Longarm said, "Your servant, ma'am. I'd tip my hat, if you didn't have the drop on me."

"What in thunder's going on out there?" the woman asked.

"I'm a deputy U.S. marshal and somebody just took a couple of shots at me. Now you know as much as myself."

The store owner's bald head appeared above the edge of the low counter he'd been hiding behind and he said, "I sure wish you'd put that gun away, Miss Sally."

The big blonde hesitated, then shrugged and lowered the muzzle of her revolver. Longarm noticed she hadn't put it back in the holster riding above her ample hips, so he kept his hands away from his own sides as he put them on the counter and said, "I came in here for some nickel cheroots. Do I save money buying 'em by the boxful?"

"You want some nice scented cheroots I just got in? They smell sort of lavender when you light up."

"Not hardly. I only want to smoke, not smell pretty."

The girl called Sally laughed and said, "He's been trying to sell them sissy cigars for months. You got a name, Marshal? They call me Roping Sally."

"*Deputy* marshal, ma'am. My name is Custis Long. They call me Longarm."

"I can see why. Custis is a sissy name."

"I know. My mama was a gal, Miss Sally."

"Hell, I don't hold with that 'Miss Sally' shit. My friends treat me like I was one of the boys."

The storekeeper explained, "Roping Sally owns the Lazy W. Her cows are scared of her, too."

Roping Sally laughed, finally got around to holstering her gun, and said, "My poor sweet cows are waiting to join up with the Blackfoot, too. So give me my plug and I'll be on my own way, damn it."

Longarm raised an eyebrow and asked, "Are you the owner Calvin Durler's been buying beef from, out at the Indian agency?"

"I'm one of 'em. Got a herd of twenty waiting over in the railroad corral right now. Letting 'em sort of rest and drink their fill before my boys and me herd 'em over to the reservation."

Longarm smiled sardonically and said, "The government pays by weight instead of by the head, huh?"

Her face was innocent, but her voice was mischief-merry as she nodded and replied, "Yep. That's why I'm watering and feeding 'em fit to bust before I run 'em over in the cooler afternoon. As long as that dude's paying by the pound, I may as well sell him plenty of water and cowshit with the beef. Damned Indians lose 'em before it's time to slaughter, anyway."

He nodded. "So I heard. It's no federal matter, I suppose, but watered stock is one thing and cow thieving is another. Don't reckon you have any ideas on who's been running off some of the reservation herd, huh?"

"It ain't me. Sometimes I suspicion the Indians just lose cows down a prairie-dog hole. Agent out there's supposed to be making cowhands out of 'em but he don't know his ass from his elbow. He keeps buying beef and they keep getting lost, strayed, or stolen. Makes it a good market for the rest of us, though it does take forever to get paid."

"Well, you don't sell your best stock to Uncle Sam, do you?"

"Hell, do I look stupid? Prime beef goes east to Chicago for the top price and cash on the barrelhead. I don't sell them poor redskins really *dangerous* sick cows, though. Just such runts and cripples as might not make it alive to Chicago's yards. I *shoot* critters with anthrax, consumption, and such. Some folks say I have too soft a heart to be in the cattle business, but it wouldn't be right to feed folks tainted beef."

"I can see you're a decent Christian woman—no offense intended. I have a dead Indian over at the coroner I'll be carrying back to the reservation in a little while. I'd be pleasured to ride out with you."

Roping Sally shook her head and said, "You'd best go on ahead, unless you like to ride right slow. I drive beef at a gentle pace. We'll likely mosey in about sundown."

"No use running weight off twenty head, huh? I knew a trail boss one time who used to haul a tank wagon along and water his stock a mile outside of Dodge."

Roping Sally laughed and took a healthy bite from the cut plug the storekeeper had handed her. She said, "I know all the tricks of the trade, but I fight fair. I figured you for a gent who knew his way around a cow. You rope dally or tie-down?"

"Tie-down. I value my fingers too much to mess with that fancy Mexican dally roping."

"Tie-down's too rough on the critters. I'm a dally roper, myself."

"You must be good. I notice you've got ten fingers."

" 'Course I'm good. That's why they call me Roping Sally. If you're out there when we ride in this evening, I'll show off a mite with my border reata. The Indian kids get a kick out of watching me, too."

Her boast gave Longarm an idea, but he didn't mention it. He said, "I'm staying at the agency, so we'll meet around sundown, Roping Sally."

Then he finished buying his smokes and went to see if the dead Indian was put back together yet.

Chapter 5

The funeral of Real Bear took about fifteen minutes, Christian time, and maybe twelve hours, Indian time. Longarm didn't hang around to see the Indian ceremony. Calvin Durler read a short service over the open grave in the little burial plot a mile from the agency and Nan Durler threw a clod of earth and a handful of wildflowers on the pine planks of the chief's coffin.

Then, as the three whites moved back, a Dream Singer called Stars Were Falling moved to the head of the grave with a rattle and started chanting as some kneeling squaws with shawled heads began to wail like coyotes.

Longarm and his host and hostess went back to the buckboard. Calvin drove back to the agency house with Nan at his side and Longarm sitting in the wagon bed, his boots dangling over the tail gate.

He'd told Cal the cattle were coming, so, after dropping Nan off at the house, the two men saddled up and rode in the other direction to the fenced-in quarter-section in which the reservation herd was supposed to be kept.

Calvin Durler sat his bay mare morosely as he tallied the small herd in the big pasture, muttering, "Damn. I'm supposed to have thirty-seven head. I only make it thirty-six. I'm missing one. I'm missing the damned kid who's supposed to be watching, too."

Longarm swept his eyes over the nibbled stubble of buffalo grass and said, "I see a break in the fence, over to the left of your windmill and watering tank. What are you missing?"

"I just told you. A cow," Durler said impatiently.

"They're all cows, damn it. Are you short a calf, a heifer, a steer, or what?"

"Hell, Longarm, I just count 'em. I don't know 'em personal."

"Yeah, you're overgrazing too. Takes more than five acres a head of this short grass to graze longhorn. You're treating them like a dairy herd instead of range cows."

"Look, it's the only way I know. How would you do it if you were me?"

"You've got a water tank to keep them from straying more than a few miles. I'd get rid of that foolish barbed wire and let 'em at the grass all about."

"Then how would we catch 'em when it comes time to slaughter?"

"Round 'em up, of course. Don't you have *any* Indians who know how to drive critters in off the range?"

"I can't get 'em to watch the fool cows while they're fenced, and to tell the truth, I don't know much more than they do about working these spooky cattle."

"I see some that ain't branded, too. You do need help and that's a fact."

Before Calvin could defend himself, Longarm squinted off to the east and said, "I see twenty—no, twenty-one head coming out to join you."

Durler looked across the quarter-section and nodded, saying, "That's Roping Sally and two of her hands with the new stock I ordered. Wait till you meet her. She is purely something."

"We met in town this afternoon. Sure sits a horse nice and— Boy, look at that, will you? The herd smelled strangers and was about to spill before she cut and milled the leader. That gal knows her cows!"

"She's crazy, too. Nan says it's not natural for a gal to dress like a man and ride astride like that. Nan's scared of her. Thinks she might be one of those funny gals who are queer for their own kind."

Longarm didn't answer, not knowing about Roping Sally one way or the other. The cowgirl spotted the break in the fence and, thinking in the saddle, swung the leaders for it with a slap of her coiled leather reata. Her two helpers swung in behind the stragglers without being ordered, and together, the three of them worked the little herd through the gap to join the others.

Roping Sally called out something to one of her hands and the man dismounted to repair the fence as Roping Sally loped her big buckskin their way, her long hair streaming from under her Stetson as she shook out a community loop from her coil. She was halfway to them as she twirled the braided leather rope above her head, letting the loop grow larger and larger as she came. Then she flicked her wrist and the loop dropped vertically in front of her like a huge hoop. The well-trained buckskin leaped through it without breaking stride as she twisted in the saddle and recovered her loop with a wild whoop of sheer animal joy.

Durler laughed and said, "Every time she does that I keep saying it ain't possible. How in hell does she do that without hanging up in her own rope?"

Longarm said, "It's not easy. Pretty as hell, though."

Roping Sally reined in near them, reeling in her reata like a fishing line with a series of blurred wrist movements and slapping the coil back in place neatly as she called out, "I found a stray I suspicioned was yours, Cal. Likely a half-weaned calf looking for his mama and halfway to town when he run into us. You gonna take my word on the weights this time or do we have to cut 'em out and run 'em over to your fool scales by the slaughterhouse again?"

Before the agent could answer, Longarm said, "We were just talking about that, Sally. New government policy. Uncle Sam's buying them by the head, now."

"Do tell? What's the offering price per head these days?"

"They're offering ten dollars a head for scrub stock. But seeing you've got some prime beef mixed in with those other cripples, how does fifteen sound?"

"Shit! I can sell 'em to the meatpackers at railside for more than that!"

"I know. Maybe you'd do better that way."

She grinned and said, "Might have known you'd wise old Cal up. When do I get my money? Ain't been paid for the *last* beef yet."

Durler said, "I sent the voucher weeks ago, Sally. You know how Washington is."

"That's for damn sure. I'd starve to death if nobody was buying my *good* beef. Say, Longarm, what are you doing in that army saddle? I thought you was a cow man."

"Used to be. Working for Uncle Sam on a government horse and rig these days."

"Hell, I wanted to see if you could throw a rope without hanging yourself. You want to borrow Buck?"

Longarm was about to decline, but he noticed a handful of young Blackfoot had drifted over to watch the sundown diversions.

He remembered the idea he'd had in the cigar store and nodded. By now one of the teenaged hands riding with Roping Sally had joined them and the girl swung out of her dally saddle as he steadied the buckskin for her. She walked over to Longarm with a swish of her chaps and said, "You can tie down if you've a mind to. My reata's a new one."

Longarm dismounted and walked around to the near side of the buckskin. He shot a glance at the girl's mount before he put a foot in the stirrup, muttering, "That's the way it's going to be, huh?"

He swung up in the saddle as the grinning boy passed him the reins and moved away. The buckskin took a deep, shuddering breath and exploded between Longarm's legs.

He'd expected it since noticing the white of the buckskin's rolling left eye, so he was braced for a dispute from the one-woman horse. Buck crow-hopped five or six times, saw he had a rider aboard, and started getting serious.

Roping Sally yelled, "Ride him, cowboy! Wahooooo!" as Buck and Longarm got acquainted. The buckskin shook himself like a wet dog at the top of every ascent through the evening sky and came down with the spine-snapping jolt of a serious bronc who wasn't afraid of sinking up to his knees in bedrock. The Indian kids were shouting now. Longarm didn't know if they were rooting for him or the horse as he noticed Buck was losing interest in killing him. He yanked his hat off with his free hand and started slapping it across the buckskin's face, grunting, "Let's get it all out of you, you old son of a bitch!"

But Buck had had enough. He was sensible as well as ornery and it's tedious to work up a sweat over a man who won't be thrown. Longarm saw that he had the buckskin under control and ran him hard once around the inside of the fence line to get the feel of him as he uncoiled a loop of reata. As he came by at a dead run, he whirled his medium-sized loop just twice to open it, and threw.

The dismounted Roping Sally crabbed sideways as she saw his intention but the leather loop came down around her head and shoulders anyway as she grabbed it, yelling, "You drag me and I'll kill you!"

Longarm let go the coil to keep from doing any such thing as he reined Buck to a skidding stop, whirled him around, and dropped to the earth with a bow of mock gallantry.

Roping Sally looked relieved and said, "I thought you were mad. I forgot to tell you old Buck ain't named after his color."

"It was sort of interesting. You want to do me another favor?"

Roping Sally disentangled herself from her own rope and coiled the other thirty-five feet in, clucking about the way he'd let the oiled leather lay in the dusty stubble before she asked, "What's your pleasure? I don't screw, if that's what you mean."

"You see them Indian kids watching? Cal, here, has been trying to get them interested in working cows. I thought maybe you, your hands, and me might show them how much fun it can be."

"I get your drift. What'll we show 'em? More rope work or some fancy cutting?"

"Let's just play it by ear. I don't have a saddle horn or rope, so I'll cut. You three throw some cows down for the hell of it."

He turned to Durler and said, "We're putting on a Wild West show for your kids, here. Why don't you talk us up? You might mention that working cows is almost as much fun as hunting buffalo was, when they had buffalo to mess with."

Durler laughed and said, "I got you, Longarm. You there, Short Bird! Come over here, I want to talk to you."

So, as the Indians watched, Longarm started cutting cows out of the uneasy, milling herd as Roping Sally and her two helpers went through the motions of roping and branding. Longarm enjoyed it as much as the grinning Indian kids, for Sally was a lovely thing to watch in the soft evening light as he worked with her. His army mount wasn't a good cutting horse, but he managed well enough, and every time he sent a steer running her way Sally roped it on the first cast. She roped underhanded, overhanded, and sideways, as if her reata was an extension of her fingers. She caught and stopped them by the horns, by either hind foot, and once she dropped a rolling loop in front of a young steer and grabbed him around the belly as he leaped through the hoop. Her dismounted helpers threw each critter she caught and hogtied it as if for branding. Longarm noticed they never got sloppy, like some hands, and threw a critter on the wrong side. He surmised that every animal she owned was branded on the left rump, the way well-tended cows were supposed to be. It was nice to see serious work. In his time he'd seen cows branded on the right side, either flank, or shoulder. Some old boys didn't seem to give a damn where they marked a cow, as long as they got done by supper.

It was getting darker and Longarm knew enough showmanship to call a halt before the audience got restless, so he rode up beside Sally and yelled, "That's enough! We've run fifty pounds out of this beef and if they're not interested by now, they never will be."

"Hot damn! You cut good, Longarm! What in thunder are you wasting time with that badge for? Any damn fool can work for Uncle Sam! Takes a *man* to work *cows*!"

"Oh, I don't know about that. I just saw a gal who could show Captain Goodnight a thing or two."

"My daddy wanted a boy. I just grew up as much of one as I knew how."

They rejoined Calvin at the gate and the agent was smiling as he said, "If they didn't enjoy it, I surely did. I still think some of those tricks aren't possible. My wife and I would be pleased to have you and your hands join us for supper, Miss Sally."

"That's neighborly of you, Cal. But we gotta get home. You can send me the receipt for these new cows when you've a mind to."

And then, without another word, she swung her mount around in a tight turn and was off across the pasture at a dead run. Her hands were a bit surprised, but they followed and the three of them jumped their ponies over the far wire without looking back.

Calvin laughed and said, "One thing's for sure, Longarm. Nan's wrong about her not liking men. I think you could have some of that, if you've a mind to."

"Hell, Cal, she chews tobacco!"

"I noticed. Sure built nice, though. I suspicion you touched her heart by catching her with her own rope."

Before Longarm could answer, an older Indian came up at a dead run on a painted pony, shouting, "Wendigo! Wendigo!"

It was the moon-faced Yellow Leggings. Durler called back, "What are you talking about? What Wendigo? Where?"

"North. Out on the prairie. Near the railroad tracks. Wendigo got Spotted Beaver! They just found him!"

"Spotted Beaver, the old man with that band of Bloods? What happened to him?"

"I told you! Wendigo got him! It was a bad thing they found. Wendigo killed Spotted Beaver and flew away with his head!"

"His head was taken, for sure," said Longarm, staring down soberly from the saddle at the god-awful mess that a dozen Indians stood around in the moonlight. It was too dark by the time they'd ridden over with Yellow Leggings to make out every detail, but it was just as well. The corpse spread-eagled on the grassy slope near the railroad right-of-way had been carved up pretty badly.

Rain Crow rode over, holding a coal-oil lantern in his free hand as he reined in beside Longarm to say, "No sign. I circled out at least a mile all around. You can see where Spotted Beaver's pony walked. You can see where it ran away. You can see where they rolled in the grass as they fought. That is all you can see. The Wendigo is said to walk the sky at night."

"I don't mean to question you as a tracker, Rain Crow, but a man on foot might not leave much sign in this buffalo grass."

"That is true. We don't know how long the grass has had to spring back from a careful footstep. But we are five miles out on open prairie. You can see where Spotted Beaver left hoof marks."

"A man can walk five miles in less than two hours, even walking carefully."

"True, but where would a human go? There is nothing north of the tracks for fifteen miles. We are twenty-five miles from the reservation line. Nobody came in to Spotted Beaver's campground. The Bloods knew something was wrong when his pony returned without him. They fanned out as they searched in the sunset light. If a man had been walking, they would have seen him."

"Suppose the killer was waiting out here, killed this man, then rode Spotted Beaver's mount and— No, that won't work, will it?"

"I have been thinking. The Bloods tell me the old man decided to ride out to look for medicine herbs late this afternoon. He told nobody but his own people, and they were all together when he was killed."

"Yeah. Hard to set up an ambush when you don't know where your victim's likely to ride. Maybe some old boy who just hates *any* Indian did it," Longarm speculated.

"You mean a white man? I have thought of this, too. The railroad tracks are not far. But the trains do not stop, crossing the reservation."

"So, while a mean cuss might snipe at a stray Indian from a moving train, he wouldn't cut off his head and mess him up with a carving knife, would he? I'm going to check their timetable, anyway. There might have been a work train out here this afternoon. Though I can't see how a whole work crew would stand by as one of 'em killed and carved an old man up like this."

"You don't think it was the work of the Wendigo, then?" Rain Crow asked.

"I'll be in a fix if it was. I never arrested a ghost before."

Calvin Durler rode over from where he'd been talking to some other Indians and said, "My folks are spooked pretty bad. They keep saying there is an evil spirit on the reservation."

Longarm said, "I won't argue about evil, but I'm not ready to buy a spirit."

"Jesus, they're still keening over Real Bear, and now this! We've got to put a stop to these killings, Longarm! What are you aiming to do?"

"Not sure. I reckon we'll just have to eat this apple one bite at a time. I'll have a word with any Indian who has a mind to talk about it. Then I'll run this body in for an autopsy, too, and see what the railroad has to say about track walkers and such."

"I guess we've done all we can for tonight, then?"

"No. You go on home and lock your doors and windows. I figure I'm just getting started."

Chapter 6

The old Blackfoot's face was painted with blue streaks and flickered weirdly in the firelight, and though he wore a shirt and dungarees, his long gray hair was braided with eagle feathers hanging down on each side of his narrow skull. He squatted near the fire in a pool of light as the others listened from the surrounding shadows of the open campfire. From time to time he shook the bear-claw rattle in his bony hand to make a point as he half-spoke, half-chanted, "Hear me! This place is not where men should live! Do you see buffalo about you? Do you see the skull-topped poles of the Sun Dancers? No! There is nothing here for us but white man's beef and who-knows-what in the iron drums of food he expects us to eat!"

Sitting their mounts beyond the firelight, Longarm and Rain Crow listened silently as the old man wailed, "In the Shining Times we ate fat cow! In the Shining Times we were *men*! In the Shining Times great Manitou smiled at us and our enemies wet their leggings at the mention of our name! But when the Blue Sleeves came we let them treat us like women. We let them tell us where we could live instead of fighting them like men! I say Wendigo has come among us because Manitou has turned his back on us in shame. I say we should fight again as men. I have spoken!"

Rain Crow started to translate, but Longarm hushed him, muttering, "I got the drift. Who's that other old one coming forward now?"

"He is called Snake Killer. Do you want me to tell them to stop?"

"No. Let them have their say. Nothing here's all that surprising."

Snake Killer was, if possible, even older than the man whose place he was taking at the fire. He wore one tattered feather with a scalp tip in his gray braids. His legs were bare, but he wore an old army tunic against the chill of the night. Longarm suspected that the tunic might have been issued to a Seventh Cav trooper, once. He could see where the arrow holes had been neatly darned over.

Snake Killer said, "Hear me. I do not count my coups, as all here know about my fight with the chief of the Snakes in the Shining Times. I agree this is a bad place for us. I, too, fear that

Manitou no longer smiles on us, but I think it would be a bad thing to fight the Blue Sleeves again. They beat us when there were only a few white men on the high plains, and now there are many. Many. I say we should go north, into the lands of the white she-chief, Victoria. In Canada there are not so many white men. In Canada there are still buffalo along the Peace River. There are other people like us on the Peace River, but I think we could beat them and take their hunting grounds away. It would be a good fight—better than fighting the Blue Sleeves for land they've already ruined forever."

Longarm swung his mount away and rode toward the agency as Rain Crow fell in beside him. The Indian policeman sighed and said, "They are just talking, I think. If you catch Wendigo in time they may not jump the reservation after all. Old Snake Killer likes canned beans and his bones are too brittle for the warpath."

"Yeah, but that same conversation's probably going on around a dozen fires tonight. Have any of Wovoka's missionaries been talking to your folks, Rain Crow?"

"You mean that Paiute prophet who makes medicine shirts and tells of ghosts helping us against the army? I chased one away a few months ago. I know how to read and write. I think a man who puts on a medicine shirt Wovoka says is bulletproof would be foolish. I have seen one. The medicine shirt was badly tanned deerskin with painted signs all over it. They said its medicine would protect the wearer from a soldier's bullets. But when I tested it with my knife it didn't turn the tip of my blade. That's when I chased the man away."

"But not before you decided his medicine was no good, huh?"

"Of course. I am what I am. I was too young to fight in the Shining Times, but my father took hair from two of your soldiers before they killed him. If I thought I could drive all of you back across the big water, I would do it. But I know I can't, so I am trying to learn. They say the Shining Times can never come again and I believe this. So I must be . . . I must be something new."

"Well, you're honest enough, and we'll likely always need good lawmen, red or white."

"It is almost a job for a real person. Tell me, is it true you white men count coup when you kill an enemy? I have heard it said yes and I have heard it said you just get drunk after a victory."

"You heard it partly right both ways, Rain Crow," Longarm

said. "Sometimes we hoist a few drinks to celebrate a job well done and the soldiers get medals if they've done something worth bragging about."

"I know what medals are. You wear them on your chest instead of your head. Have you ever heard of an Indian getting one of these medals?"

"Sure. The army's decorated some scouts for gallantry in action."

"I couldn't scout for the army. They never fight anyone I don't like. If they asked me to help them kill Ute or Crow, I would scout for them and win many medals. But they always want to kill our allies."

"Well, the killing's almost over, I hope. Save for some Apache holding out down near the other border, the army doesn't have much call for scouts any more. They've got a white scout over at the fort. You know him?"

"Jason? Yes. He is a good person, for a white man. I asked him why the soldiers were still there and he said he didn't know. He said he just goes where they send him. He said he didn't think the soldiers were mad at us anymore."

"Yeah. I'd say their officer is a pissant, though. He's bored and spoiling for a fight. I do hope if your folks decide to act foolish they'll jump north instead of any other way. Wouldn't take much to start that old lieutenant shooting."

They rode back to the agency, where Rain Crow said he'd stable Longarm's mount before going back to his own shanty. Longarm asked if he wanted a cup of coffee first and the Indian said, "No. The woman is nice to us, but she is afraid. Deer Foot says she thinks the agent's wife is going to run away from him one day. When this happens, I do not want to know anything about it."

Longarm said good night to the Indian and went inside, thinking of Rain Crow's notion. If the Indians saw it, too, he hadn't been as dirty-minded as he'd first supposed. Nan was fixing to run off with the first man who made her an offer and she was a pretty little thing. On the other hand, Calvin Durler was a decent cuss. Being a Christian surely could get tedious.

Inside, he found the Durlers seated at the kitchen table with a tiny white girl dressed like a sparrow. Calvin said, "Longarm, allow me to present you to Miss Prudence Lee. She arrived just after you rode off."

Longarm removed his hat as the agent added, "Miss Lee's

from the Bible Society. I keep telling her she'd do better in town, but she says she's come to bring the Gospel to our red brothers."

Prudence Lee dimpled prettily, considering how little there was of her, and said, "We were just talking about the ritual murders, Deputy Long. It's my intention to show the Blackfoot the error of their ways."

Longarm forked a leg over a chair and sat as Nan Durler shoved a mug of coffee in front of him without looking at him. He grinned and said, "The army's sort of showed them some errors already, Miss Lee. What do you mean by ritual murders?"

"Isn't it obvious that the medicine men have been sacrificing people to their heathen gods?"

"No, ma'am, it's not. I've been told the Pawnee used to make human sacrifices, long ago, but none of the other plains tribes went in for it, even before we, uh, pacified them."

"Come now, I know I'm a woman, but I know the terrible things they've done to captives in the past."

"Captives, maybe. That was torture, not religion. The two killings we just had were simple murder. The men killed were both on friendly terms with such Blackfoot as I've asked." He looked at Durler to add, "Rain Crow and I saw some old boys powwowing about a trip to Canada. You'd better see about issuing some rations and back payments."

"My God, I'd better let the army know if they're preparing to jump the reservation, too!" Durler said.

"I wouldn't do that. Not unless you want some dead Indians no Wendigo had to bother killing. Those boys over at the fort are bored and ugly."

Prudence Lee, having warmed to her subject, broke in insistently to ask, "What about the Sun Dance?"

"Sun Dance, ma'am?"

"That business of dancing around a big pole with rawhide thongs punched through living flesh. You can't tell me that's not a blood sacrifice!"

"Oh, bloody enough, I suppose. But we don't let 'em do that any more. Besides, you're missing a point. Indians think it's brave for a man to shed his *own* blood to Manitou. Other people's blood doesn't count as a proper gift."

"Brrr! To think of God's creatures living in such ignorance of the Word! Manitou is what they call their heathen god, eh?" Prudence asked.

"Well, Manitou means 'god' in Blackfoot, ma'am. I don't know how heathen he might be. Seems to me the Lord would be the Lord no matter what you call Him."

"Agent Durler tells me many of his charges speak English, so I'll have little trouble setting them straight. You did say I could use the empty house next door as my mission, didn't you, Mister Durler?"

Calvin shrugged and said, "If you won't go back to town. You won't be able to sleep there till we repaint the bedroom, though. Uh, you know what happened there, don't you?"

"Pooh, I'm not afraid of ghosts. My Lord is with me, even into the valley of death, forever."

Longarm wondered why she didn't say "Amen," but he knew better than to ask. He took out his watch and said, "Be more room here, if I took Spotted Beaver into Switchback tonight. I'll get there before midnight if I leave soon."

Durler asked, "Will the coroner be up at that hour?"

"Don't know. If he ain't, I'll have to wake him, won't I?"

"He isn't going to like it much," Durler cautioned.

"I don't like not knowing what killed Spotted Beaver, either. The railroad station's open all night and I'll have a few questions for them, too. I'll toss my saddle roll in the wagon and bed down somewhere along the way, once I'm finished in town."

Nan Durler grimaced and said, "You don't mean to sleep out on the open prairie, do you?"

"Why not, ma'am? It don't look like rain."

"It makes my flesh crawl just to think about it! It's so creepy-crawly out there at night!"

"I spend half my nights sleeping out on the prairie," he said. This wasn't strictly true, but he thought it might disabuse her of any notions she might have about his carrying her off to his castle in the sky. Even if he was wrong, he did intend to spend at least one night in the open. This place was too full of women for a man to sleep peaceably in, alone.

Longarm's luck was with him when he drove into Switchback about eleven that night. A lamp was lit over the coroner's office and the saloons were still going full blast.

He pounded on the coroner's door until the older man came to cuss out at him. Then he said, "Got another one for you, Doc. You don't get *his* skull, either. Somebody beat you to it."

He carried the stiff, wrapped form of Spotted Beaver into the lab and flopped it on the table as the coroner lit an overhead lamp. The coroner said, "Good thing I'm half asleep and my supper's about digested. What in hell tore this old boy up?"

"I was hoping you could tell me, Doc. What say you give him the once-over while I run over to the railroad station. I've got some trains to ask about, too."

He left the coroner to his job and walked the three blocks to the station, where he found the stationmaster dressed but asleep in a cubbyhole office under an electric light bulb. The man awoke with a start as Longarm came in, glanced at the wall clock, and said, "Ain't no trains due for a good six hours, mister."

"I ain't looking for a ticket. I'm a deputy U.S. marshal after some information. You have a train stopped out on the Blackfoot reservation this evening?"

"Stopped? Hell, no. There was a westbound freight around four and an eastbound crossing closer to six. No reason to stop, though, and both were on time, so they likely didn't."

Longarm took out a cheroot, stuck it between his front teeth, and spoke around it as he fished in his pocket for a match. "Someone killed an Indian near your tracks. I wondered if you might have some crewmen who lost kin at Little Big Horn or such."

The stationmaster shook himself wider awake and thought for a moment. "I know the boys on both crews. I don't think either of them would be mean enough to shoot at folks as they passed by."

"This jasper got off to work close up with a knife. How fast do your trains run through there?"

"Hmmm, the eastbound's coming downgrade a mite, so it'd be crossing the prairie there about forty-odd. Westbound might slow to twenty or thirty on uphill grades. I'm going by the timetables, you understand. So we're talking about average speeds. Be a mite faster going down a rise than up, but, yeah, I'll stick with those speeds. You want the names of the engineers?"

"Not yet. Looks like I'm sniffing up the wrong tree. While I'm here, though, do your trains run the same time every day?"

"Not hardly. Depends on what's being freighted where. We get a wire when a train's due in or out, but the timetable varies a few hours from day to day. Why do you ask?"

Longarm took a match from his pocket, igniting it with his thumbnail in the same motion, and touched the flame to his cheroot. "Man figuring to hop a slow freight would have to know when one was coming."

The stationmaster looked astounded. "Hop a freight on open

prairie? We don't run freights that slow, Deputy. Be a pisser to reach for a grab-iron doing more'n ten miles an hour, wouldn't it?"

"Yeah. Like I said, I'm likely in the wrong place."

Longarm left the man to sleep away the rest of his night in peace and went back to the coroner's.

The coroner couldn't tell him anything he didn't know already. Spotted Beaver had been killed and cut up, down, and crosswise. Except for the head, nothing important was missing. The coroner found nothing to tell him what had killed the headless trunk, though he muttered laconically, "None of that knife work did him a lick of good. If he was shot or bashed, the evidence left with his head."

"Could you say what was used to rip him up like that, Doc?"

"Something sharp. Wasn't a butcher's meat saw or animal teeth, but name anything else from a penknife to a busted bottle and I'll swear to it."

Longarm asked, "Can I leave him here with you for the night, Doc?"

"Sure. I'll put him away for you on ice. I know you're driving a long, lonesome ways, but they don't bother me all that much."

"I'm not worried about traveling with a dead man. Done it before in my time. Come morning, though, I aim to ship the remains to Washington for a real going-over at the federal forensic labs. I'll come back before high noon."

"I'll tin his internals in formalin for you, then. What do you figure I missed?"

"Likely not a thing, Doc. But it pays to double-check."

"I don't have the gear to look for obscure drugs or poisons, but you don't think he was drugged, do you?"

"Don't know what to think. Just covering every bet I can come up with till I hit a winning hand."

"Makes sense. How come you're making such a roundabout night of it, though? You could take a room over at the Railroad Hotel and get an early start, since you're due back anyway, before noon."

Longarm kept his true reasons to himself as he said. "I've got an appointment at the agency, come sunup. They're expecting me back tonight."

He said good night and left, going next to the saloon he'd busted up. The night man on duty didn't know him but a couple of the men who'd seen him come through the window wanted to buy him a drink. So Longarm let them, then stood a round in turn as he casually swept the crowd with his eyes from under the brim of his hat. Nobody seemed too interested in him. He told the two boys drinking with him part of what had been going on and repeated that he was heading back to the agency alone.

Then, having spread the word as much as he could without being too obvious, he left. He climbed to the buckboard seat and drove out of Switchback at a trot.

It was after two in the morning now, and the moon was low in the west, painting a long, zigzag chalk line of light where the black mass of the distant Rockies met the clear, starry bowl of the sky. It would be darker soon, and though he knew the mule could see well enough by starlight to carry them safely back to the agency, which wasn't now all that far, he had other plans.

They knew at the agency that he was supposed to be bedded down out here in the nothing-much. He'd told everyone in town who'd listen much the same thing.

He slowed the mule to a walk about three miles out of town and just over the horizon from the top windows of the agency. There was no wind and the night was as quiet as a tomb. Longarm looked up at the Milky Way arching palely against the night sky and muttered, "He-Who-Walks-the-Midnight-Sky, huh? If you're up there you'd best get cracking, Wendigo, old son. You're running a mite late of midnight."

He wheeled off the wagon ruts and reined in fifty yards away on the open prairie. The moon had dropped out of sight behind the Front Range now, and the outlined snow fields were dimming away. Longarm tethered the mule in its traces to a cast-iron street anchor and put an oat bag over its muzzle, saying, "You'll have to manage through the bit, old mule. Ain't sure how long we're staying hereabouts."

He threw his bedroll to the ground a few yards from the buckboard and spread it out in the darkness. He pulled up some bunches of dry buffalo grass and stuffed some under the weather tarp to make the bedroll appear occupied. Then he took kindling and some dry cow chips from the wagon bed and built a small night fire eight feet from the bedroll, moving back and keeping himself to the north of the little flickering fire as he moved back to the tethered mule and buckboard. He took his Winchester from the wagon boot, levered a round into the chamber, and hunkered down under the wagon.

A million years went by.

Longarm shifted quietly to a more comfortable position,

seated in the grass with his back against a rear wheel and the rifle across his bent knees as he chewed an unlit cheroot to pass the time and keep awake.

Another million years went by.

Somewhere in the night a coyote howled and once a train hooted far across the prairie. He muttered, "Must be a special. Stationmaster said the next train was due in six hours and that was two or three hours ago."

Then he heard something.

He didn't know what it was, or where it was coming from, but he suddenly knew he wasn't alone on the lonely prairie. He realized he'd stopped breathing and inhaled slowly through his nose, straining his ears in the dead silence all around.

A big gray cat was walking around in Longarm's gut for some fool reason; he told himself he didn't believe in ghosts. Nobody sensible believed in ghosts, but then, nobody sensible was sitting out here in the middle of nothing-much after making himself a target for whoever might be interested.

He heard the sound again, and this time he grinned as he identified it, muttering, "Man or devil, the son of a bitch is riding a pony!"

The sound he'd heard was someone dismounting, trying not to squeak saddle leather in the process, but not quite managing. Longarm had the sound located, more or less. Someone had reined in on the far side of the wagon ruts and climbed down for a more Apache-style approach than most found neighborly when coming in on a night fire.

Longarm rolled forward, shoving the Winchester into position for a prone shot as he stared into the inky blackness and listened for a footstep. Once he heard what might have been the distant *ting* of a spur on dry grass, but it was hard to tell. Whoever it was, was moving in like a cat. Longarm studied the stars along the skyline, and after a while, one winked off and on. He knew where the other was, now, but it was too far to do anything about. Another star went out and stayed that way. The jasper was standing there, likely studying the fire and what he could see of the bedroll. If he had a lick of sense he'd move a mite closer in. He was way too far out for a decent shot.

Then a distant female voice called out, "Longarm! Look out!" and a rifle flashed orange in the darkness near the vanished star. Longarm fired at the flash and rolled away from his own gun's betraying flame as, much farther off, a third gun fired, twice.

He heard the sound of metal on dry grass, followed by a groan and a thud. Longarm was under the tailgate now, so he rolled over once more and sprang to his feet, his Winchester at the ready.

The feminine voice called out again, closer, and Longarm heard the sound of running boot heels and jingling spurs as Roping Sally shouted, "Are you all right, Longarm?"

"Stay back, God damn it! I can't see a damn thing and I only shoot at one thing at a time!"

"I got him outlined against your fire and he's down! I'm coming in!"

Longarm circled wide. Then, as he got well clear of his night fire, he, too, could make out the inkblot on the grass. Another shadow stepped over it and kicked it, muttering, "There you go, you mother-loving, bushwhacking son of a bitch!"

As Longarm moved in cautiously, Roping Sally turned to the sound of his footsteps and said in a girlish tone, "He's dead as a turd in a milk bucket, old son! Who got him, you or me?"

"Maybe both of us put one in him, Sally. What in thunder are you up to out here?"

"I saw you come out of the saloon and ride off. Then I spied this jasper running for his pony like he aimed to go somewhere serious, so I sort of tagged along after him. I had him betwixt your fire and me when he dismounted, sneaky-like. So I did the same and, oh, Lordy, I thought you were in that fool bedroll!"

"So did he, most likely. Let's see who he used to be."

As Longarm knelt and turned the dead man over in the fitful glow, Sally said, "Hot damn! I might have known you were setting a trap for the bastard! Who was he, and how'd you know he aimed to follow you?"

Longarm muttered, "Shit—sorry, ma'am. His handle was Fats. I threw him off a train in the Denver yards and he said he'd remember me. I guess he did. As to knowing he was likely to follow me, I was aiming higher. You see his rifle hereabouts?"

"Over there to the southeast. Looks like an express rifle to me."

"Me, too. He was the one who took a shot at me in town the other day, damn it! Poor silly varmint tracked me all the way up here just because I made him look foolish one time. He had a younger sidekick, too."

"He followed you alone, Longarm. You reckon his pal is in Switchback?"

"Hope not. I've got enough on my plate up here. You hear mention of a new hand in the country called Curley?"

"Nope. There's a Curley riding for the Double Z, east of town, but he's been here for at least two years."

"Damn! I can't chance not watching for one more old boy with a poor sense of humor and I can't waste time hunting him down. I've got bigger fish by far to fry!"

"Tell me what the bastard looks like and me and my friends'll be proud to round him up for you," Sally offered.

"Can't do that, Roping Sally. No telling how many innocent drifters might get hurt if I turned you loose with a private posse!"

"Well, can I tell you if I see or hear tell of folks named Curley?"

"Sure, Sally. But just don't get excited before you talk to me about it, hear?" Longarm cautioned.

"I'll be sly as hell. What are we to do with this rascal here?"

"I'll put him in the wagon bed and see if they'll bury him for me someplace. Might be papers out on him, somewhere. He took things too seriously for a boy with a clean record."

"Hot damn! You mean I might get a reward for shooting him?"

"If there's anything like that, I'll see that you get the money, but you'd best let me take credit for gunning him, Sally. I don't want any of his friends dropping by to pay you a call some night."

"Aw, hell, I was aiming to brag on it some," Sally said disappointedly. "Lots of folks in this county treat me like a sissy!"

"You're all man, Roping Sally, but let's not build you a rep as a gunslick if we can help it. It can make for nervous nights. Believe me, I know!"

"I'll do as you say. Where you heading now?"

"Hadn't thought about it all that much. I doubt if anyone else is likely to creep into this web tonight. I gave my bed at the agency to a guest of the Durlers. Hmm, I'd best carry you and this jasper back to town and try for some shut-eye at the hotel."

"You can stay at my spread, if you've a mind to. It's just to the northwest of town."

"Uh, I figure to get up with the chickens, Sally."

"Hell, don't we all? You come on home with me and I'll fry you some eggs before we turn in."

Longarm didn't answer. Roping Sally punched him on the shoulder and asked, "What's the matter, are you scared of me?"

"Not hardly. But what'll folks say about it in Switchback?"

"Who gives a hoot and a holler? I don't keep any hands on my spread. The boys I was riding with before live with their folks in town and I hire 'em as I need 'em. Ain't nobody there but me and a mess of critters. I got dogs and cats, Shanghai chickens, a Poland China hog, and my remuda and herd keeping me company, but not one of 'em ever gossips about me worth mention."

Longarm laughed and said, "We'll talk about it along the way."

Chapter 7

Roping Sally's house was a large one-room soddy with a lodge-pole roof and a cast-iron kitchen range sharing space with a four-poster and enough supplies to stock a general store. They'd stored Fats in the smokehouse and put the mule in with Buck. Longarm sat at an improvised table made of planks laid across two barrels. He smoked as he watched Sally putter at the range with her back to him. He noticed that the seat of her pants was tight and worn shiny between the wings of her flapping chaps, and though she was a mite broad across the beam where she sat a horse, her waistline was as trim as if she'd been cinched up in a whalebone corset. The hickory shirt she wore was tight enough for him to see she wasn't wearing a corset, or much else, under it. She was one handsome woman—considering she chewed cut plug—but Longarm couldn't figure her out. He was either getting into something too good to be true, or just as likely, about to make a terrible mistake.

The girl turned with a grin and plopped two coffee mugs and a pair of tin plates down in front of him, saying, "There you go. Wrap yourself around those eggs before you tell me I can't cook."

"Uh, don't we use some forks or something, Sally?"

"Oh, Lordy, I'm so flusterated I clean forgot the silverware! You've likely suspicioned I don't entertain all that much."

He waited until she'd put some oversized cutlery on the planks before he said cautiously, "You told me, coming in, you didn't have any fellows sparking you."

"Hell, there ain't a man in Montana worth spit on a rock. Present company not included, of course."

"Sally, you can't tell me somebody hasn't tried," Longarm said skeptically.

"Sure they have. Sissy little things who have to sit down to pee, most likely. I knew they were just after my daddy's cows."

"Oh, you got a daddy hereabouts?"

"Dead. Got thrown and busted his neck, summer before last. He raised me to be a cowhand and he likely raised me right, for I've done right well here, without him. What's the matter with the eggs? You ain't eating 'em."

Longarm put a forkful of rubbery, overfried eggs in his mouth and chewed hard. He swallowed bravely before he shook his head and said, "You got 'em just right, Sally. I'm a mite tuckered after such a long, hard day, is all."

"Why don't we go to bed, then? Which side would be your pleasure?"

"Sally, I'd best spread my bedroll out in the wagon bed, out back."

"What in thunder for? I took a bath last Saturday. Besides, that fellow in the smokehouse tore shit out of your blankets with that old express rifle."

"Sally, how old are you?"

"I'm old enough, I reckon. My daddy and me ran just about the first longhorns north from the Powder River Range to this here territory and I shot my first Sioux before I lost my cherry!"

Longarm brightened and said, "Oh? I was, uh, wondering how soon we were likely to get to that subject."

"My daddy said I wasn't a virgin anymore when I told him about it. He was sore as hell, but there wasn't all that much he could do about it, since the cuss who cost me my cherry was long gone. You want to hear about it?"

"Not really. Just wanted to know where this trail was leading me. You take the right side and I'll take the left and we'll likely wind up in the middle. You want me to blow out the lights?"

"What for? There's stuff all over the floor and we'd likely bust a leg finding our way."

"Suits me. Most gals like to undress in the dark."

Roping Sally looked puzzled and said, "You reckon we ought to take our clothes off just to sleep two or three hours? It's going on four, and my old Shanghai rooster starts crowing any minute now."

"Well," Longarm said, "you're right about it being late, but I sleep better raw, so I'd best blow out the lights."

"I'll do it. You just climb over those boxes and I'll join you."

He did as she told him and had his boots off about the time Roping Sally doused the last lamp. He undressed, frowning and puzzled, then got under the covers as Sally climbed in on the other side, saying, "I took my britches and boots off, but I don't like the way these old blankets scratch when I don't wear my shirt."

Longarm reached for her and snuggled her head against his shoulder as he asked mildly, "You ever think of using sheets?"

"They just get dirty and torn up when I'm too tired to shuck my boots after a hard day's ride. What are you hauling on me like that for?"

"Don't you want me to cuddle you some, first?"

She moved closer and nestled her body into the curve of his as she said, "It sure feels nice. I like the way you run that hand up and down me, too. Feels like you're petting me right friendly."

Longarm slid his hand to her face in the dark, turned her chin up, and kissed her lips. Roping Sally's lips were a mite wind-chapped and her breath smelled like a tobacco shop, but she responded after a moment of hesitation. Longarm wondered why women always seemed to want to back off at the last minute after damned near running a man all around the corral to rope and saddle him. He kept his lips against hers as he moved the hand downward. Sally stiffened as he cupped her mons in his palm and rubbed her lightly through her shirttail. She rolled her mouth aside and whispered, "Are you getting dirty with me?"

Longarm was finding it difficult to keep his amazement concealed. He said levelly, "Honey, there ain't anything dirty about this. It's why the Lord made men and women different, is all."

"I don't know if you ought to do that, though. You're getting me all mushy and funny-like."

But she had her own free hand on the back of Longarm's, and when he asked if she wanted him to stop, she pressed it closer and murmured, "Don't know *what* I want. It feels nice as anything, but I ain't sure I ought to let you keep going."

"Sally, it's going on four, I got a long day ahead of me, and this palaver must cease. We've got no time for any more games!"

Suiting his actions to his words, Longarm cocked a leg over her, parted her ample thighs with his knee, and climbed aboard, moving her damp shirttail above her navel as he guided himself into her. Her matted pubic hair was wet with her own desire and though she was tighter than he'd expected, he sank full depth into her on the first thrust.

Sally gasped, "My God! What are you *doing* to me?"

He tactfully avoided a direct answer. "Could you maybe move your knees up some? You're tighter than a drum, and—"

"Oh, Lord, I'm *ruined*! I swear I think you're *screwing* me!"

Longarm frowned in the darkness, but this was no time to discuss the details. She began to respond with hard, rocking thrusts of her own, even as she sobbed, "You never told me you wanted to get dirty! This is terrible! How will we ever be able to look one another in the eye again, come daylight?"

"I'll stop if you've a mind to," Longarm lied considerately.

But Roping Sally dug her nails into his bouncing buttocks, spread her legs wider, and moaned.

Longarm figured she was one orgasm ahead of him by the time he stopped to get his breath back, still in the saddle. Roping Sally was breathing hard, too, but she sighed, "Oh, my, that was more fun than Saturday night after roundup! Can we do it again? I know you've ruined me forever, but now that I know what all the fuss is about I'm sort of getting the hang of it."

Longarm thought of himself as a patient man, but this was too much.

"Sally, what in thunder are you talking about? You're not going to tell me that old sad tale about being a virgin, are you?"

"I don't know what tale you're talking about, but if you mean to ask have I done it before, I ain't. You won't tell anybody, will you?"

"Honey, you told me you lost your cherry years ago and that your pa was pissed at the jasper who did it!"

"Oh, that was when our wrangler put me aboard a spooky bronc when I was maybe thirteen. I rode the bronc, but when I got off, my crotch was all bloody and Daddy was sore as hell. He said the ride had busted my cherry, and—"

Longarm's eyes rolled upward and he slapped his forehead with the heel of his hand. "Oh, Jesus! I see the light and I'm purely sorry, ma'am!"

"You ought to be sorry, you dirty old thing. You just screwed me and I'm a ruined woman, but to tell you the truth, I ain't all that riled. You want to do it some more?"

He stayed inside her, but didn't move, as he cleared his throat and said, "Sally, we've got to talk about this. I know a gent's supposed to do right by a lady and all, but I ain't the marrying kind . . . damn it! I had you down as a tough old cowgal!"

"I'm tough enough, I reckon. You don't think getting screwed is likely to turn me sissy, do you?"

"Not hardly, but . . . shit, I just don't know what to say."

"Are you sore at me? I know folks are supposed to be ashamed to see each other after they've been ruined, but you know what? I still like you, even after being dirty with you."

He kissed her tenderly, and said, "I like you, too, honey. I just ain't been down this trail too many times and I don't know what I'm supposed to say or do."

"Well, you've said we're still pals, and as to *doing*, I wish you'd either take that fool thing out of me or move it *right* some more!"

Longarm laughed and started responding to her mischievous thrusts. In a short while, it didn't seem all that big a fuss. Roping Sally might have been a late bloomer, but for a virgin, she caught on quickly.

Longarm was awakened at sunup by the smell of flowers and the sound of birds. The morning breeze was banging sunflower heads against the window over the bed and the chickens in the upwind henhouse stank something awful.

He stretched and the blond head cupped on his naked shoulder murmured, "Don't get up yet. The chores can go hang this morning. I want to hear some more of those facts of life you were jawing about before we went to sleep."

He scraped a thumbnail through the stubble on his jaw, ran a tongue over his fuzzy teeth, and sighed, "I've got to get back to my job, honey. Besides, I've told you all I know about the birds and bees and how you gals might keep from getting in a family way."

She raised her head shyly, stared at him in the wan gray light, and grinned, saying, "I can look you in the eye, anyway. Likely I ain't ruined after all."

"I told you it came natural, didn't I?"

"Yeah, but Daddy said folks jeered at ruined womenfolks. We'd best not tell anybody we've been screwing, huh?"

"I don't think we should do it in the streets of Switchback, but between us, we can likely whup anyone who jeers all that much. Why don't you catch a few more winks? I'll get something to eat in town before I start asking around about the fellow we shot last night."

"I am purely tuckered. When will you be coming back this way again? You *are* fixing to, ain't you?"

"Well, sure, if you want me to. I'm going to be right busy most of the day, but if I get the chance, tonight—"

"Hot damn! I'll take a bath, then. You were right about it being nicer with all my clothes off. Maybe I can find some sheets around here somewhere."

Longarm swung his bare legs out from under the covers and started to dress as Roping Sally watched. When he stood up to pull his tight riding pants up, she sighed and said, "Jesus, you're pretty. Did you get them shoulders roping cows or hugging other gals?"

"Little of both, I suspicion. You're built nice, too, Sally."

"I'm in fair shape from hard work and clean living, up to last night, I reckon, but these fool big tits of mine get in the way when I'm wrestling steers to the ground. You sure you weren't funning when you said you liked 'em?"

"I kissed 'em both, didn't I? Go back to sleep, now. I'll try to make it back around sundown."

He finished dressing and went outside. He got the stiff, heavy corpse from the smokehouse and threw it in the wagon bed, tossing a tarp over the late Fats before hitching the mule in its traces. Then he climbed up and drove out across the cattle guard to the road to Switchback in the crisp morning sunlight. Nobody saw him, thank God. He didn't know what he was going to do about Roping Sally and himself, but at the moment he had other things to worry about.

Chapter 8

Switchback kept early hours, so by the time he'd eaten breakfast near the railroad station, had a shave at the barbershop he found open across the street, and asked some more questions about the railroad, the coroner's office was open.

The coroner came out to lift a corner of the tarp as he asked, "What are you doing, starting a collection? I can tell you what killed this one without an autopsy. He was hit front and back with bullets. Either round would have been enough."

"I'm just reporting the killing to you for your county records, Doc. I'll see that he gets buried. You got the specimens for me to ship to Washington?"

"Canned his liver and kidneys along with the heart and lungs. You can have them any time you like. Are you sending them East on the noon express?"

"Yep. I'll see about getting the rest of the remains out to the reservation for burial this afternoon. Got another errand to do, first."

"You want to put this cadaver in my vault for now, or do you feel the need for company?"

"I'd take that kindly, Doc, if it ain't imposing."

"It is, some, but you'll impose on everybody if you leave him out in the hot sun under that tarp much longer. I'll get my helpers to tote him inside if you want to leave your buckboard parked here for a while."

Longarm thanked the helpful county official and headed for the land office. He found Agent Chadwick lounging in the open doorway and asked if he could use the federal telegraph line again. Chadwick nodded and led him back to the wire shack as Longarm filled him in on everything but Roping Sally.

Longarm sat at the desk and got to work on the wire. Chadwick, after a time, lost interest and went back out to the front office. It took Longarm over an hour to make all his inquiries and get some answers. When he had finished he got up and went to join the land agent. He found Chadwick just saying good morning to a surly-looking man in range duds. The land agent handed Longarm a cigar and explained, "That was old Pop Wessen. He's heard about trouble on the reservation and wants to file a homestead claim out there. Got sore when I told him it was a foolish notion."

"I wanted to ask you about that, Mr. Chadwick. What would

happen to all that land if the Blackfoot sort of, well, lit out for Canada or someplace?"

"You mean abandoned the land held in trust for them? Nothing, right away. I suppose the army would round 'em up and bring 'em back, in time, don't you?"

"Those the army left breathing. Would the land revert to public domain if it stayed empty long enough?"

Chadwick shifted his cigar and thought for a moment before he said, "It'd take a long time, but if Uncle Sam just couldn't get any Indians to live on that range for, oh, at least seven years . . . you know what? I don't *know* what the regulations are. I've got enough paper on the open-range questions I answer for white folks."

"Seems to me some of the Cherokee lands down Oklahoma way got taken by white settlers after the Cherokee picked the wrong side in the War. If those Blackfoot lit out and abandoned the reservation . . . hmm, seven years is a long time, ain't it?"

"I think I get your drift. You're suggesting someone's trying to run the Indians off, eh?"

"It's a natural suspicion, but planning on filing on abandoned land seven years up the road seems a right cool game for anyone with murder on their mind. You're sure there's no way anyone could get at that range sooner, huh?"

Chadwick puffed his cigar pensively. "Not as far as I know. Find out anything about that old boy you shot last night?"

"Yeah, he had his last name in his wallet. The nickname Fats fit the wanted papers on him. He was a gunslick for hire. New Mexico has a murder warrant on him and he's suspected in other parts of picking fights for pay."

"But you said you had a fuss with him in Denver."

Longarm nodded, slowly scratching the back of his neck. "I did. What I'm trying to figure, now, is whether he trailed me up here for personal reasons or was in town on other business, saw me, and decided to pay me back. I never told him I was coming to Switchback—I disremember saying so to anyone in Billings."

"You mean someone here in town might have sent for a hired gun and the rest was just dumb luck?"

"A man could take it either way. You have any ideas on who might be fixing to start a private war, hereabouts?"

Chadwick shook his head. "Not offhand. Save for the troubles out at the reservation, we ain't had much trouble up here lately."

"You issue range permits, don't you?"

"Sure. I register homestead claims and hire out government

grass on a seasonal basis. You know how most cattle outfits work. They claim a quarter-section with timber and water for the home spread, then range their cows on the open prairie all around. Uncle Sam's supposed to be paid a range fee by the head, but they cheat a lot."

"You hear tell of anyone fighting over range?"

"Nope, I ain't. The herds are building fast, since the buffalo thinned out, but most of the locals are friendly enough about it. They let the cows mix on the open range, work the spring and fall roundups together, and cut and brand neighborly. There's maybe a little friendly rivalry, but nobody's ever taken it past fists."

Longarm chewed thoughtfully on his cigar, then said, "Let's look at it another way. Cal Durler says he's been missing cows. Any others been having trouble along those lines, hereabouts?"

The land agent looked surprised as he asked, "Are we talking about rustlers, Longarm?"

"We're talking about what I call cow thieves. If some local stockman has been building his herd the sudden way, it might account for some of what's been going on. Cow thieves get shot a mite in these parts unless they have some guns to back their play. So a dishonest cattleman might hire some guns—or on the other hand, some neighbors who aim to put him out of business might do the same."

Chadwick nodded in understanding and blew out a stream of smoke before saying, "I've heard talk about the reservation herd losing strays. Some of the locals think it's funny as hell. That kid Durler has a lot to learn. I don't think anyone's really *stealing* his cows, but you'll have to admit an unbranded calf running wild along the reservation line might be tempting fate."

"Yeah, I've been trying to show him how to herd cows properly. But if you're right about the local cattle outfits, it's odd about those hired guns."

Chadwick shrugged and said, "That one you had to shoot was likely just passing through. Or maybe he was trailing you personal."

Longarm put a hand on the doorknob and said, "Maybe. I thank you for the use of your wire and I'd best be on my way."

"Don't mention it. Where you headed next?"

"Thought I'd drift around town and get the feel of things before I ship some stuff East at noon and get on out to the reservation. To tell you the truth, I'm sort of stuck for some answers."

Leaving the land office, Longarm walked across the dusty

street toward the saloon. In the shade of the overhang he found the army scout, Jason, talking to an older man with a tin star pinned to his white shirt. Jason thrust his bearded chin at the approaching deputy and called out to him. Longarm joined them on the plank walk in front of the swinging doors and Jason said, "Longarm, this is Sheriff Murphy."

As Longarm nodded to the lawman, Murphy said, "How come you didn't report that shooting you had last night, Deputy?"

"I did. The body's over at the coroner's. We had it out on the open range and I figured it was a county matter."

The sheriff fixed him with a hard look. "I like to know when folks get killed in or about Switchback, mister. I know you federals think your shit don't stink, but I'd take it kindly if you let us poor country boys in on things once in a while."

"Sheriff, I meant no offense. I truly thought the doc would fill you in, and as you can see, he did."

"Well, yeah, he did tell me about it, but—"

"There you go. I'll tell you what. Next time some old boy takes a shot at me, I'll run right over to your office. By the way, where is it?"

The sheriff jerked a thumb over his shoulder. "Down that-away, near the station house."

"That's settled, then. I hope you boys drink before noon. I see the bar is open."

Before anyone could answer, Jason shouted, "Down!" and pushed Longarm hard, as he dropped behind the nearby watering trough.

The first shot parted the air where Longarm had been standing and crashed through the boarded-over saloon window he'd broken the last time he'd been by. The second raised a plume of spray from the watering trough and spattered Jason with water as he shouted, "Up behind that false front! The hat shop next to the land office!"

Longarm had dropped behind a barrel he hoped was filled with something. He aimed his drawn .44 at the drifting smoke cloud above the building the scout had indicated and snapped, "I've got him spotted. Watch your head!"

Another shot from above the hat shop gave away the sniper's position behind the false front lettered HATS AND BONNETS Longarm figured the last S was his best bet, but he crossed both Ts with bullets as he fired three times. Jason popped up and sent an army .45 round through the pine boards as, somewhere, someone screamed and they heard the clatter of a rifle sliding down shingles and a loud, wet thud.

Jason said, "He dropped between the hat shop and land office, in that narrow slot."

Longarm saw Agent Chadwick peering out of his doorway and shouted, "Get back inside, Chadwick! Jason, you and Murphy cover me!"

Then, without waiting for an answer, he was up and running. He crossed the street in a zigzag run, flattened himself against the corner of the hat shop, and quickly reloaded as he got his breath. A woman stuck her head out of the hat shop and Longarm motioned her back inside with a silent, savage wave of his .44. Then he took a deep breath and jumped out, facing the narrow slot between the buildings as he fired for effect into it. He dropped to one knee under his own gunsmoke and took a long, hard look at the body lying facedown, wedged between the plank walls on either side. Then he stood up and thumbed more cartridges into his Colt as Jason ran across to join him, saying, "Murphy lit out. I think he ran into the saloon and just kept going. We get him?"

"Yeah. I owe you, Jason."

"Don't mention it. Lucky I seen the sunlight flash on his barrel as he was fixing to do you. Anyone you know?"

"They called him Curley. He was a friend of the one I got last night. I'll be surprised as hell if he don't have a record, too."

By now Chadwick had joined them, peeking around the corner to gasp, "Jesus H. Christ! How many of these hired guns do you figure we have in Switchback, Longarm?"

"Don't know. I make it two less, right now. I'll get him out of there in a minute. Right now I owe Jason, here, a drink. He just saved my ass."

Chadwick followed them to the saloon, as did the hat shop owner and a dozen others in the neighborhood who'd heard the shooting and wanted to steady their nerves.

The scout didn't seem to think he'd done all that much, considering, but he let Longarm buy, muttering something about the way the army paid folks these days.

As they leaned against the bar together, Longarm said, "It's lucky I found you in town. I mean, aside from what you just did for me. I've been meaning to ask some questions about the army's interest in the Blackfoot."

"Hell, they ain't all that interested, Longarm. Beats me why we're here. Likely Washington just figures soldiers've got to be some durned place if they ain't another."

"You been getting anything on expected Indian trouble?"

"From the Blackfoot? They were ornery enough, a few years back. Ain't lifted anybody's hair for a coon's age, though. They were rooting for Red Cloud back in '76, but only a few kids really rode with the Sioux. The old men kept most of the tribe back, playing close to the vest till they saw which way the cards were stacked. It's a small tribe, but they bled enough for a big one in the Shining Times."

"Were you out here then? You don't look old enough to go back to the beaver trade."

"I ain't. Came West as a hide hunter after the War. Knew some of the old Mountain Men, though. Most of 'em's getting on in years now, but my first boss hunter was left over from the Shining Times. Used to brag on a Blackfoot arrow he still carried in his hide."

"You ever hear mention of a breed called Johnny Hunts Alone?"

"Hell, I *know* him. He skinned for me five or six years ago, down by the Powder River. Wasn't very good at it, though. He was sort of a lazy, moody cuss."

"Damn! You're the first man I've met who can tell me what he looks like!"

Jason stared soberly at his drink and said, "Maybe. But he never done me enough harm to mention, Longarm. How important are the papers you might have on him?"

"I could lie and say I just wanted to talk to your old sidekick, but you just saved my ass, so I won't. Telling it true, I aim to take him in dead or alive on a murder warrant, Jason."

The scout shifted uncomfortably. "You're giving me a hard row to hoe. Johnny once talked some roving Sioux out of taking my hair."

Longarm shrugged. "I can't make you tell me, but—"

"But you can likely make me wish to God I had, huh? All right. As long as I was fool enough to allow I knew him, and seeing he ain't around Switchback anyway, he's maybe half a head shorter than me and looks like what he is—half white, half Blackfoot."

"Can't you do better than that?"

"He's only got one head, damn it. He's just another breed. Maybe younger than me and not as pretty. Oh, he does walk with a limp. I disremember which leg—he got shot one time. To tell you the truth, we never jawed much. He was a quiet, moody cuss, like I said. Never killed anybody while I rode with him, though."

"The limp's the only thing I don't have on my papers, so I owe you another drink. Chief Real Bear told us Hunts Alone was on the reservation."

"Maybe he is. I'm buying this round."

"You said he looks half white. The Indian police say they know all the breeds out there and none of 'em is him. You figure Real Bear could have lied for some reason?"

"Beats me. I didn't know the man. I've jawed with a few Blackfoot since they sent me out here, but I'd be lying if I said I knew any of 'em well."

"You talk their lingo?" Longarm asked.

"Not enough to matter. I'm pretty good in Sioux and I can make myself understood in the sign lingo all the plains tribes use. Blackfoot's sort of like Cheyenne, ain't it?"

"Just about the same. You said Johnny Hunts Alone talks Sioux as well as Blackfoot, right?"

"Oh, that old boy could powwow fierce," Jason said. "He'd have made one hell of a scout if he hadn't took to robbing and such. We figured he had something gnawing at him, but like I said, he was only after buffalo when we rode together."

Longarm picked up the fresh drink the bartender had put before him and said, "I'd like you to think about this before you answer, Jason. If you were to see Hunts Alone before I did—"

"I'd warn him," said the scout flatly. Then he added, "I'd tell him you were after him and give him a head start for old times' sake. Then I'd come and tell you true which way he'd lit out. I don't like being in the middle like this, but we're both working for Uncle Sam, so I'd do both duties as best I could. If that sticks in your craw, I'm sorry as all hell, but that's the way I am."

"A man has to stick by old friends, as long as he don't get crazy on the subject. Let me ask you one more question and have done with it. If I was to come on the two of you together, how big a slice of the pie would you be expecting?"

Jason took a swallow of his drink and said, "That's a pisser, ain't it?"

"Yeah, but I'd like an honest answer."

"Well, to be honest, I don't know. I can't see gunning you. I reckon I'd likely stand aside."

"That's good enough, Jason. Naturally, if you saw me coming before Johnny did, you'd likely mention my intentions to him?"

"Yep, I likely would. After that, the two of you would be on your own."

The officious Sheriff Murphy had circled back from wherever he'd hidden to take command once the smell of gunsmoke had faded away. Longarm was only too happy to leave him with the disposal of the bodies after wiring Denver where to send the reward for Fats. He knew Billy Vail would be discreet about bruiting Roping Sally's name and address about.

Longarm, as a federal employee, couldn't claim the reward for Curley. Jason said he didn't want blood money, so Longarm let Murphy put in a claim. If he ever got it, he'd likely brag on shooting outlaws into the next century, but what the hell—the poor idiot needed some brag to go with his badge.

Longarm hauled the mortal remains of Spotted Beaver back to the reservation for another interesting funeral. He arrived a little after one in the afternoon to discover some changes had taken place.

Prudence Lee had set up shop in the late Real Bear's house and was beating a drum and shaking a tambourine for some reason that Longarm didn't go over to find out. He joined Calvin and Nan Durler in the agency kitchen after giving the body to Spotted Beaver's kin.

He sat at the kitchen table and lit a cheroot as he told the Durlers about the interesting times he'd been having since last they'd been together. He didn't imagine they were interested in Roping Sally, but he told them everything else.

Calvin said, "That same fool calf busted out again this morning, but some Indian kids caught it and brought it back. Where in thunder do you figure that calf wants to *go*? He's got plenty of grass and water, damn it!"

Longarm thought before he answered. He had enough on his plate as it was; on the other hand, the answer to one question sometimes led to others. He took a drag on his cheroot and asked, "You feel up to hunting cow thieves, Cal?"

"Cow thieves? What are you talking about? Nobody *stole* the infernal calf. It just busted through the wire and took off on its own like it had turpentine under its tail!"

"You're missing other critters, ain't you? Come on, let's get Rain Crow and some other police and see what's eating your new calf. You got a good saddle gun?"

"Got a Henry repeater, but I ain't the best shot in the world."

"Don't reckon you'll have to use it, but it pays to have one along. Keeps folks from getting sassy when they see you're armed."

Nan Durler said, "You men can't leave me here alone. I'm coming with you."

Before her husband could answer, Longarm said flatly, "No, you're not. I don't mean to get your man shot, Miss Nan. Why don't you go next door and help Miss Prudence whang that drum? What's she doing over there, anyway?"

Calvin laughed and said, "Teaching some Blackfoot the meaning of the Word. They likely think she's crazy, but we don't have an opera house, so what the hell, at least it's entertainment."

Ignoring his wife's protests, the agent armed himself and followed Longarm outside. They saddled up, rode to Rain Crow's house, and got him and another Indian policeman called Two-Noses. Longarm didn't ask why they called him that. Two-Noses really only had the usual quota, but that one more than made up for the small size of the rest of him.

Longarm explained as they rode over to the pasture, "That new calf's not fully weaned, so he's likely looking for his mama. I figure we can turn him loose and see where he thinks she might be. Critters are good at finding one another."

Calvin said, "Roping Sally brought him to us. Do you think she held back on one of the cows we ordered?"

"Son," Longarm said, "you've got to learn to pay attention. When Sally and her hands drove that last herd in, they *told* you they'd picked up a stray from here along the way, remember?"

"Oh, you mean that calf's the same one?" Durler looked confused.

"Hell, weren't you even *looking* at them when she brought 'em in? Of course it was the same calf. Has a calico left rump as I remember."

"Then what you're saying is that the calf's mother was one of the cows recently stolen, and— Jesus, you must think I'm dumb."

"You're learning. Everybody starts out dumb. There's the herd up yonder and, yep, old calico-rump's over against the far fence, looking for an opening."

Longarm led his little band around the fenced quarter-section on the outside. As they came up to the wailing calf against the fence, he dismounted and pulled down the top wire far enough for the lostling to leap over it, bawling. By the time he'd remounted, the calf was making a beeline for the southeast horizon at a dead run.

The men followed at a discreet trot. From time to time the little runaway would slow to a dogged walk, getting its wind back, then run some more. Two hours later, and nine or ten miles from the agency, Durler said, "We're off the reservation."

Longarm said, "I know. He's making for that sod house, yonder."

As the four riders approached, a man came out of the soddy with a rifle and called, "You're on the Bar K, gents. State your business and state it sudden!"

Longarm and his companions reined to a walk but kept coming as Longarm saw the calf nuzzling a cow through the wire fence on the far side of the homestead claim. He smiled and said, "We're on U.S. Government business, mister. You've got about two eye-blinks to put that weapon near your toes before I shoot you."

The man hesitated as he considered the odds. Then he leaned the gun against the doorjamb and stepped away from it, complaining, "You got no call to threaten me, durn it! I'm a peaceable settler."

"I can see that, now. You likely didn't know that some of those cows that maybe strayed over here belonged to the reservation, huh?"

"What are you talking about? I ain't got no reservation cows."

"You've got one I can see from here, mister. For your sake, I hope you haven't run any brands." He swung around in his saddle and said, "Rain Crow, ride over there and cut out every cow that isn't wearing a Bar K on it. If you see any marked U.S., or anything that might have been U.S. at one time, give a holler."

The young Indian grinned and loped toward the fenced pasture with Two-Noses as the settler near the soddy protested, "I ain't had time to brand some of my critters, but I swear you got this all wrong."

A worried-looking woman peered out through the door and the man snapped, "Get back inside, Mother. I think these men are loco or something. They've as much as accused me of stealing!"

The woman ran out into the yard and got between Longarm and her husband as she wailed, "Oh, Lordy, don't you hang him, mister! I *told* him he was likely to get in trouble over them damn cows, but he ain't a bad man. Not really!"

Rain Crow rode back, still grinning. He said, "Fifteen head. Five U.S., one Double Z. The rest have no brands."

Longarm nodded. "Well, we'll take 'em all, then, after I thank these folks for their trouble."

The cow thief shouted, "Now, you just listen here!"

Longarm's amiable expression vanished without a trace as he turned toward the settler. "No, *you* listen, mister! I've got you dead to rights but I've got bigger fish to fry, so we're taking the cows and I'm letting you off with a warning. The warning is the next time I see you within a country mile of the reservation line, you are dead."

"I aimed to bring them branded cows in when I got around to it. I was rounding up and—"

"You've got a Double Z cow in there, too. You want me to tell them about it?"

"I was aiming to return that'n, too. The ones I ain't got to branding yet—"

"Are lost, strayed, or stolen, mister," Longarm interrupted. "You want to be friendly and call 'em strays, or are you just too foolish to go on breathing?"

"Damn it, half of them is really mine!"

"Not anymore. You're getting off light and you know it. Go ahead, Rain Crow, cut the fence and we'll herd 'em all back. I'll say we found the Double Z critter mixed in with our stock, next time I'm in town."

As the Indian started to carry out his orders, the man shouted, "You can't do this, mister."

Longarm said, "I just did, and, like I said, this lady's a widow woman if I see you near the reservation or have to pass this way again."

"Now all I have to do is find out who's selling booze to my Indians!" said Cal Durler, feeling pleased with himself as he and Longarm sat on the back porch of the agency after riding back with the purloined cattle.

Nan was in the house, putting together some vittles, and the mission woman was still beating her drum next door. Longarm noticed that Cal was fooling with a length of cotton clothesline as they talked. He said, "Your Indians are starting to take an interest in the herd. Old Rain Crow was tickled to hunt 'em down and sass a white man like that, but let's not get too cocky. Some cow thieves take their business more serious than that petty thief we just threw a scare into."

"Hell, let 'em come!" Durler said. "We'll dust 'em with number nine buck!" He got to his feet with the length of clothesline and started whipping it around through the air for some reason Longarm couldn't fathom.

He waited politely until the Indian agent wrapped it around

his own shins and was frowning down at the results before he asked quietly, "Are you trying to hogtie yourself, Cal?"

The agent grinned sheepishly and said, "It looks so easy when you fellows do it. What am I doing wrong, Longarm?"

"Don't know. What in thunder are you *aiming* to do?" Longarm chuckled.

Durler untangled the gray rope from his legs and answered, "I'm trying to learn to twirl a lasso, of course. What's so funny?"

Longarm got to his feet, saying, "You can't twirl a throw rope put together like that, Cal."

Durler held the length of limp clothesline out, saying, "I know I can't, damn it. Will you show me how *you'd* do it?"

Longarm shook his head as he took the improvised reata, explaining, "No mortal born of woman can twirl this thing, Cal. You've just made a slipknot for your noose. Every kid who ever played cowboy has made a creation like this. As you can see, they don't twirl for shit."

"Come on, I know there's a knack to it, but I've seen the way you old-timers do it and—"

"Damn it, Cal, you're not paying attention. You got any bailing wire?"

"Sure. There's a coil on that nail near the screen door."

Longarm spotted the coil of thin iron wire and stepped over to it, saying, "We have to do something about the way you hold a gun on a gent, too. That settler would have gone for you, had you been alone."

Durler watched as Longarm broke off about eighteen inches of bailing wire and then, not having any idea what the lawman was doing as he started fooling with the end of the rope, Durler said, "You told me you let him off easy because he was harmless, Longarm."

"No man is harmless. He just wasn't worth my time. Takes months to get a cow thief in front of a judge, so most folks just shoot 'em and the hell with it. I didn't think he was worth a killing. Not if he heeds my neighborly advice, at least."

"All right," Durler said in an exasperated tone, "what did I do wrong over there with my gun?"

Longarm finished wrapping the slipknot in wire before he said, "I'll get to guns in a minute. You see what I've done here? Your noose runs through what we call the *honda* on a throw rope. It has to be heavy, like the sinker on a fish line, if you want the rope to follow where it's aimed."

Longarm shook out a modest loop of the limp line and started to twirl it. "You see? The loop part's trailing after the heavy honda, the way smoke trails behind a locomotive's smokestack. Most folks think the loop's some sort of hoop, but it ain't. You don't twirl the loop. You trail the weighted honda and the rest just follows natural."

He suddenly reversed his wrist action, swinging the honda in a figure eight as the rope drew a pretty pattern in the air between them. Longarm said, "We call this the butterfly. You can't hardly catch anything with it, but it's good for showing off if gals are looking."

Durler laughed and said, "You know, I think I see how you're doing that!"

"There you go. Want to try her?"

He handed the rope to the agent and watched as Durler made a brave try. The loop stayed open for a few rotations and then, as Durler laughed in pleased surprise, wrapped itself around his waist.

Longarm said, "We'd best add some weight. Knew a Mexican fancy roper who used lead sinkers braided into his leather reata."

Durler handed back the rope and Longarm started wrapping more bailing wire around the improvised honda. As he worked, the agent said, "Let's get back to my gunmanship, Longarm. I thought I was pretty ornery-looking over at that sod house just now. Are you saying you thought I was bluffing?"

"Don't know if you were bluffing or not, Cal. The point was, you *looked* like you were trying to make up your mind what you'd do if that man pushed it to a real fight."

"Oh, hell, he was outnumbered four-to-one and you said yourself he was just a petty thief!"

"I know what I said. Know I won't be here if he should ever steal a cow from you again, too. Rain Crow looks like he's serious enough about such matters. So be sure you take him with you if it comes up a second time. He might have you down as an uncertain gunfighter, and even if he's wrong, such doubts lead to most of the trouble out here."

"Damn it, I wasn't afraid of him. If he'd made me use my gun, I reckon I would have."

"Back up and go over what you just said, Cal. You said you *reckoned* you'd throw down. Unless a man's *certain* he's out for blood with the first shot, he's better off not having a gun in his hands at all!"

Longarm finished wrapping the honda and twirled the rope experimentally, rolling the loop around him like a hoop as he turned on one heel, muttering, "This looks like I'm rolling it on the ground, but if you watch the wired knot, you'll see I'm not. Wish there was something to catch around here."

He handed the rope to Durler. "You fool with it for a while. I've got other chores to attend to. You got a survey map I can ruin?"

Durler took the rope but didn't try to spin it as he frowned and asked, "A map? I've got some maps of the reservation if that's what you mean. What do you mean about ruining one?"

"Pencil marks. I have to stop running in circles after this Wendigo critter. I'm going to mark out all the spots I've searched or know real well. Then I'm going to have a closer look-see at the blank parts. If I haven't found anything by the time I've covered the whole map with check marks, I'm in trouble."

Still holding the rope, Durler ducked inside and came out shortly with a folded survey map. He handed it to Longarm who sat on the steps and spread it out as the agent watched, idly twirling the rope. To Durler's surprise, the loop opened and began to spin easily as soon as he stopped concentrating too hard on his own wrist. He laughed boyishly as Longarm drew a loop of his own on the stiff paper and muttered, "If Johnny Hunts Alone, the Wendigo, or whomsoever is inside this circle I'm blind as a bat. Rain Crow's searched most of these outlying settlements, so— What's this *X*? About five miles north of the railroad tracks?"

Durler let the loop collapse and stepped over to stare down at Longarm's questioning finger. He shrugged and said, "That's an old, abandoned sod house. A white homesteader built it back in the sixties. Before this land was set aside as a reservation."

"What happened to the nesters? Government buy 'em out?"

"No. They were wiped out by Indians. My Blackfoot say they didn't do it. Others say they did. There's not much left of the place. Just some tumbledown sod walls and a few charred timbers."

"What about the well?" Longarm asked.

Durler looked puzzled.

"The what?"

"The *well*," Longarm repeated. "You can see there's no streambed within a mile. If they settled there, they had to have water, so there ought to be a well."

"Gee, I don't know, Longarm. I've only been out there once or twice. Don't remember seeing a well."

Longarm folded the map and put it away in a pocket, saying, "Ruined walls to cut the wind. Maybe water somewhere on the claim. Nobody living near it. Yep. I'll have a look on my way into town this evening."

"You're not staying here tonight? Miss Lee's moved into the house next door, so there's plenty of room for you, and Nan's expecting you for supper."

"Uh, I'll be staying in Switchback tonight. I'll likely be . . . investigating till right late."

"Hell, I'll be up past midnight, Longarm."

"I might be up even later. I'll hunker down in town."

"You're on to something that will keep you up past midnight?"

Longarm managed not to grin as he said, "I'll likely get some sleep, sooner or later."

Chapter 9

The abandoned ruins told their mute tale of frontier tragedy to Longarm's practiced eye as he left his mount grazing on the surrounding short-grass to poke on foot through the rubble. It was late afternoon and his shadow lay long over the weed-grown tangle of charred furniture and heat-scorched metal framed by the knee-high walls of rain-washed sod. With the toe of his boot, he gently kicked a baby's bottle, melted out of shape by fire, muttering, "Hope they had enough sense to send you away when the smoke-talk rose, little fellow."

A dozen spent brass cartridges lay in the weeds under what had once been a windowsill. They were green with corrosion now, but they still bore witness to the desperation of a long-dead stranger who'd knelt there pumping lead as hostiles circled out there on the open prairie. Longarm wondered if he'd saved the last rounds for his family and himself as the fire-arrows landed, quivering, in the woodwork.

There were no signs of recent occupancy in the ruins. Longarm circled out until he came to the deep, grass-filled depression where the well had been. The wooden well head had been hauled away. The earthen walls, unprotected, had caved in. Longarm walked over to his grazing horse, muttering, "Not so much as a dried turd. But at least we can likely write this place off."

He picked up the reins and mounted, shooting a glance at the low sun to his west as he swung the chestnut's head toward Switchback.

The sun was still up, but dyeing the prairie red by the time he passed a marker indicating he was leaving the reservation. The town was just over the horizon, but hidden by the scrap line where the prairie took a sudden step into the sky. Longarm spotted a distant rider a mite to his south. The rider saw him about the same time and swung his way, coming fast.

Longarm kept his mount to a steady walk, and as the oncoming rider waved a hat, he saw it was Roping Sally.

He shook his head and swung to meet her as Sally called out, "Yaaahooo!"

As she joined him, Longarm said, "I don't think you ought to be out here alone, Sally. I thought you'd be waiting for me at your spread."

"I was, God damn it! You promised you'd come at sundown!"

"You're wrong two ways, honey. I never promised and it's not sundown yet."

"Well, it's almost sundown and I was getting worried. Every time I let you out of my sight you get in a gunfight and I—I been hurtin' for you, damn your eyes!"

"Honey, we'd best get something straight. I've got a job to do and you're not my mother."

"Does that mean I ain't your gal anymore?"

Longarm muttered under his breath. Then he smiled and said. "Hell, you're the only gal worth having hereabouts. But I can't have you riding all around Robin Hood's barn after me. I want you to stay clear of this reservation, too. I've got enough on my plate without having to worry about you as well as the Indians."

"Hot damn! I didn't know you worried about me, too."

"Well, I do, out in these parts. You know there's some kind of lunatic running around out here at night, damn it!"

"I thought you'd shot all the rascals, honeybunch."

"Well, I didn't, and I'd rather be called late-for-breakfast than honeybunch. Those hired guns weren't who I came up here after. I've got one bad breed at least to watch for, and if Johnny Hunts Alone isn't the Wendigo, I've got a bad breed and God knows what else to catch. So you're to stay clear of these parts, hear?"

"If you say so, sweet darling," Sally murmured.

"Oh, Lord, that's worse than honeybunch!"

"Could I call you huggy-bear, then?"

"Not hardly. Where'd you come up with all the crazy names?"

"I been thinking 'em up all day. I suspicion I must be in love with you. Every time I think of you I get all fluttery. Let's get on home. I've took me a bath and bought me some fancy French perfume and, Jesus, I am purely horny as all hell!"

He noticed she wasn't chewing tobacco, either. God! How had he gotten into this fix? More importantly, how was he to get out of it without looking like, well, the miserable cuss he probably was?

They rode side by side through the gentle evening light as Roping Sally planned their future together. Longarm didn't try to stop her; it didn't seem possible. She'd know soon enough what a shit he was unless he got lucky and somebody shot him before it was time to move on.

A distant voice called Longarm's name and he turned in the

saddle to see Rain Crow riding after them at a dead run. He and Sally reined in as the Indian joined them, shouting, "Wendigo! Wendigo! He has taken another!"

"In broad daylight? Who, and where?" Longarm said, astonished.

"A boy called Gray Dog went out to hunt rabbit on foot. When he did not come home for supper his people searched. They found, him as we found Spotted Beaver. His gun was taken, along with his head. The other police and I looked for sign. There is nothing. Gray Dog was killed on the open prairie in broad daylight. There is no trail to follow."

"I'd best ride back. Sally, I want you to go on home and bar your doors till I come to you."

"Damn it, I'm riding with you! I'm a fair tracker and I can whup most men fair and square!"

"You do as I say, anyway," Longarm insisted. "What these Blackfoot can't track is likely tougher tracking than most stray cows, and whatever could take an armed Indian's head off in broad daylight ain't like most men."

"Honeybunch, I want to help!"

"You'll help most by locking yourself behind a good stout door. I don't work alone because I'm a hero, I work alone because I don't read minds, and when it's time to move sudden, I don't like to guess what a sidekick's likely to be messing up."

"You promise you'll come to me soon?"

"Soon as I'm able, Sally," he assured her.

"Do you really love me?"

The back of Longarm's neck reddened as, aware that the Indian could hear, he put out a hand to chuck Roping Sally under the chin and murmur, "I ain't all that mad at you, honey."

Sally's face lit up in a sparkling smile. "You get along home pronto, sweet love. There'll be a light in the window for you and I'm taking another bath!"

She trotted east as Longarm fell in beside Rain Crow, loping west. They rode a mile in silence, then slowed their mounts to a walk to rest them in the gathering darkness. The Indian said, "The moon will rise soon. Almost a full moon, tonight."

"Yeah. About that conversation back there, Rain Crow—"

"I wasn't listening. Sometimes I have trouble understanding what white people are saying. So I only listen when it might be my business."

"Sure you do, but if Washington ever allows you folks to

drink, I'll buy you one. How'd you find me, anyway? You came over the horizon like a rider who knew where he was going."

Rain Crow shrugged. "I tracked you, of course. Agent Durler said you'd ridden to the old homestead, so I looked for you there. I saw where you'd moved things in the ruins and walked over to the old well. I saw where you'd ridden east, so I followed."

"You're good, considering I've been riding over thick sod in dimming light."

"Oh, it is easier tracking on grass when the sun is setting. The long shadows help me see where trampled grass hasn't had time to spring back up. This time of the year many stems are dry enough to break off, too."

"What about in green-up time, when the grass is springy?" Longarm asked.

"Easier. When the prairie is greenest, the soil is softer. Even antelope leave hoof marks then."

"But you didn't find one hoof mark near that dead boy's body, huh?"

"No. The light was perfect for looking, too. The boy had left some broken stems behind him as he walked. The grass was trampled near the body, as if by a struggle. That was all. The others think Wendigo must have flown away."

"Maybe." The deputy stroked his mustache with a long forefinger. "Leaving aside notions like hot-air balloons and such, how do you feel about soft moccasins? I was wearing army heels out there by the homestead, and not trying to hide my spoor. Was this murdered kid wearing boots?"

"He wore the leather shoes the B.I.A. issues us. I see your meaning. Our people are not used to the white man's shoes, and in any case, they seldom fit right. Gray Dog may have scuffed more than a man in moccasins would have. But even so, Wendigo should have left *some* spoor!"

"Maybe he did. Meaning no offense, Rain Crow, a busted straw stem here and another one ten yards off ain't hard to miss."

"I will look some more, by moonlight. If we are lucky and there is summer frost before sunrise— Heya! Those people up ahead are gathered around the dead boy's body."

Longarm squinted against the sunset sky at the black knot of Indians on the horizon and made a mental note of where to mark it on his map. Then he heeled his chestnut and snapped, "Let's go, before they trample every goddamned sign away!"

Longarm and Rain Crow loped up to the site of the latest

killing and the deputy shouted, reining in, "Stand clear, damn it!"
He saw Yellow Leggings in the crowd and added, "Yellow Leggings, get these folks out of here!"

The Indian policeman shouted back, "These two are the dead boy's parents."

"All right, they can stay. Everybody else, vamoose."

He saw his orders were being grudgingly obeyed as he dismounted far enough away to avoid spooking his horse, dropped the reins to the grass, and walked over through the parting crowd. He looked down at the mess spread-eagled in the grass and muttered, "Jesus, I ain't seen anyone messed up like this since the War!"

The slim, broken body was that of a boy about fourteen years old. Longarm could tell it was a boy because the body was naked except for shoes and socks. The brown flesh was crisscrossed with gaping slashes and covered by buzzing bluebottle flies as well as caked blood. The kid's clothes hadn't been carried off; they lay around in bloody tatters. It was likely that the shreds of plaid shirt had identified the victim to his relatives. There wasn't any sign of his head.

Longarm saw Rain Crow was at his side, so he pointed his chin at a spatter of blood on a soapweed clump near the body and said, "You looked for blood on the stems farther off, right?"

"Of course. Anyone walking away with a cut-off head should have left a trail of blood, but we found none."

Longarm turned slowly on one heel, scanning the horizon all around before he muttered, "Could have headed out in any direction to start with. Due south would have run him smack into the agency. There's over thirty miles of nothing to the west before you reach some cover in the foothills over that way. A man can't walk that far on foot in a day, packing a severed head or not. East would take him smack into Switchback, where folks would likely ask questions about blood and such. I'd say we should look north."

He went back to his chestnut and remounted, after telling the grim-faced father standing by a kneeling, keening squaw that it was all right to move the body now. Longarm didn't intend to take this one to the coroner. It was beginning to look like wasted effort as well as needless hardship to the victim's kin.

Rain Crow and Yellow Leggings fell in at either side of him as he walked his chestnut slowly north, noting that the crowd had made a mess of the grass for yards in every direction. The sun was down now, but the western sky was bloodred and the big moon hung like a grinning skull to the east. They were riding over untrampled grass now, and the light was bright enough to see clearly by. Longarm spotted something shaped like a cartridge near a bird's-nest depression in the sod and reined in, saying, "What's that, by the rabbit's bed?"

Rain Crow said, "I see it. Coyote turd. Coyote found the nest empty and shit because he was angry."

Longarm allowed himself a subdued laugh. "Your eyes are better than mine, then, but I'll take your word for it."

"I dismounted the first time I saw it this afternoon."

"Oh, then that pony track up ahead must be yours. I was about to say something foolish."

"There is no sign this way. I searched for sign as far north as the railroad tracks and a mile beyond."

"You look for railroad ballast that might have been scuffed by a horseshoe?" the lawman asked.

"I got on my hands and knees and even tasted a ballast rock I thought might have been turned over in the past few hours. I made sure it was only displaced by a passing train, long ago."

The deputy's eyebrows shot up. "Do tell? How'd you figure all that by taste?"

"The fresh side of the rock tasted of coal smoke. The taste settles on the roadbed when the trains run in the rain. It rained two weeks ago. That was when the rock was turned over."

"You can tell a rock that was turned over half a month back?" Longarm asked, astonished.

"Certainly. Can't you? The trains lay a film of soot and dust on everything they get near. Everything near the tracks smells like burnt matches or spent cartridges. That is why the buffalo herds were split up by the coming of the Iron Horse. The animals are afraid to cross the tracks. Coyote, rabbit, and antelope will, if they have to. Wolf, bear, and buffalo fear the tracks. A few years ago we had a good buffalo hunt that way. We cornered a herd in a bend of the track and ate fat cow. The old men said we should let some of the buffalo live, but the younger men killed them all, anyway. They said it was foolish to leave them for the white hide hunters. I never ate so much in my life and I got sick." Rain Crow patted his stomach and rolled his eyes upward.

By now they were approaching the right-of-way he was talking about. The railroad followed the winding grade of an old buffalo trail, since the engineers who'd surveyed it had known that buffalo follow the lay of the land better than most surveyors could. The tracks lay mostly at grade level, with filled stretches as high as ten feet over low rolls and cuts through some rises.

Longarm rode his chestnut up a four-foot bank and reined in on the gritty ballast to stare up and down the line without dismounting. A line of telegraph poles ran along the far side, and though there was no wind near the ground, the overhead wires hummed weirdly overhead. He saw the black notch of a low railroad cut to the east, and as the two Indians joined him, he said, "Let's see how high above the tracks that cut bank is." As they walked their mounts along the ties he explained, "I've studied the timetables of the railroad. No way a man could jump even a slow freight out here from ground level. But if he climbed up on the rim of a cut, and had steel nerves . . ."

They reined in between the walls of earth on either side of the track and Rain Crow said, "I don't think so. The edge up there is not as high as the tops of the freight cars and it would be a ten- or twelve-foot leap even if it was high enough. Yellow Leggings, ride up to the north side and see if there are marks of running feet. I will check the south bank."

Longarm went with Yellow Leggings, figuring Rain Crow as the better tracker. But as he and Yellow Leggings dismounted to study the grass lip of the bank above the tracks, he saw that there was nothing to see. He called across to Rain Crow, "Any sign over there?"

"No, and the ground is barren in places from runoff. To jump off here with any chance would mean a dead run, with no hope for cautious footprints."

Longarm shrugged and said, "This was a low cut, anyway. If we could find something in the way of a higher jump-off point, not too far to walk on foot . . . hell, it's too damn dark to look for sign, serious. What say we ride back to the agency and study my map some more?"

Rain Crow called, "You go and we'll join you later. We know this range. As the moon rises, the light may shift and tell us something."

Longarm saw no harm in letting them have their head. So he climbed back aboard the chestnut and headed for the agency.

When he got there he found the Durlers and their guest, Prudence Lee, seated on the porch. He noticed that Calvin had his Henry across his knees as he sat on the steps, as if guarding the two women behind him in the porch rockers. Longarm tethered his mount to the rail in front and walked over to put a foot up on the steps as he filled them in on the little he knew.

The Durlers listened thoughtfully. Miss Lee said, "I've been talking to my converts. These heathens have Zoroastrian notions. According to Indian legend, the world's a battleground between Good and Evil and this Wendigo is like our Satan."

"We know that already, ma'am," Longarm said. He turrned toward the young agent. "Cal, the old ones were already jawing about a reservation jump afore this happened. We'd best wire Fort MacLeod and let the Canadian Mounties know they might have visitors."

"I'm trying to hold off, Longarm," Durler responded. "Some soldiers were by a while ago, asking about our troubles out here. I got the notion they wouldn't be all that put out to chase some Indians and maybe win some citations. Alerting the Canadian authorities would likely have to be cleared by Washington, who'd alert the army, and—"

Longarm cut in, "I know a Mountie at Fort MacLeod personally. I could send him a wire as one old drinking pal to another, wording it soft."

"Do you really think you have to? Nobody's jumped the reservation yet."

"And when they do they'll be headed for the Peace River country, scared and on the prod. Wouldn't be neighborly of us to let Queen Victoria's own Assiniboine get hit by U.S. Indians they weren't expecting. Them old ways the elders are jawing about includes bad blood between Blackfoot and Assiniboine going back before Columbus. Even if your folks came in peace, there'd likely be some fur flying along the Peace River."

"But if the army heard about it in time to try and head them off on this side of the border . . ."

The lawman nodded. "That's why I aim to word my telegram to Fort MacLeod careful. I'll say something about that breed I'm after being spotted in Canada or something. The Mounties will likely send out some patrols and they'll have at least a sporting chance of heading off such trouble as might be headed their way."

"I hope so. When did you figure to send the wire?"

"Later tonight, at the railroad station in Switchback. The wire I've been using at the land office is patched in to Washington, but the railroad wire's private. I wish Western Union was in business hereabouts. Makes life complicated, with either Washington or the Great Northern reading my mail."

"You don't suppose it's possible the railroad's behind this trouble, do you?" Durler asked.

"I've studied on that. Can't see how running off your Blackfoot could benefit the stockholders all that much. They've *got* their right-of-way over federal lands. Washington's stopped handing out big land grants for building new lines, and from the map, there's no place hereabouts to want a new line built. I've asked about the train crews, too. There's nobody riding through here regular with any reason to kill Blackfoot, unless he was crazy, and since there's at least a five-man crew on every train, odds are he'd have to be crazy with at least four sane men covering up for him." He shifted his weight and added, "I've considered someone hopping off and on from empty boxcars, too. But that last kid was killed in broad daylight. I know folks doze off from time to time in the caboose, but a man would be taking a big chance counting on grabbing for the side of a boxcar on the open prairie with the sun shining. And who knows when a brakeman's going to come walking along the top of the cars between the engine and caboose? Besides, there was only one train through this afternoon, and it passed *before* the boy was last seen alive."

Longarm took a deep breath. He wasn't accustomed to soliloquizing at such great length, and it tended to make him feel lightheaded.

Prudence Lee said, "The Indians think the Wendigo walks through the sky."

"Yes, ma'am. At *night*. I'm going inside for a spell, Cal. I want to study my map some more before I run over to Switchback. And, by the by, I think Miss Lee, here, should bunk with you folks in my old room."

Durler said, "Oh, I hardly think he'd hit this close . . ." and then his voice trailed off.

Longarm nodded and said, "That's right. Real Bear was killed in the same house Miss Lee's using for . . . whatever."

Then he mounted the steps, went inside, and back to the kitchen, where he lighted a lamp and spread his survey map on the table.

He marked the latest killing and put question marks on every railroad cut he could find on the small-scale map. There were a few contour lines, but the scale was too small to show every rise high enough for anyone to hide behind. He himself had once hidden from Apache behind a one-foot bump in the ground. A man in buckskins, lying flat behind a clump of soapweed, could be nearly invisible from as close as a quarter-mile on what seemed featureless prairie. The reservation was as big as some Eastern states, when you studied on it. He wasn't ready to buy a flying spook yet. Except for that hot-air balloon he'd seen at the Omaha State Fair, he'd never seen a man up there in the sky, either!

Prudence Lee came in and sat down across from him, saying, "That Indian policeman, Rain Crow, just rode in, Mister Durler is talking to him. I don't think he found anything."

Longarm started folding the map as the mousy little girl added, "I have a personal problem, if you have the time to listen."

"I'll listen, ma'am, but if it's about converting Indians I don't suspicion I know how."

"I face a moral dilemma. This is a privileged conversation, isn't it?"

"If you're asking if I repeat things, I don't."

"I supposed as much." She cleared her throat. "As you know, I'm duty-bound to uphold the commands of the Lord, but on the other hand, as a woman I understand her problem."

"*Her* problem, ma'am?"

"Nancy Durler's. I think she's about to run away from her husband."

"Did she tell you as much, Miss Prudence?"

"Not directly, but I know all the signs. You see I—I knew a girl, once, who ran away from a man she couldn't live with. She's tried to atone for her sin for years, but adultery is a terrible cross to bear."

"Oh? This, uh, other gal we're speaking of ran off with another man?"

"Yes. He deserted her in Baltimore six weeks later and I'm afraid, uh, she went a little crazy. She took to strong drink and, well, other men. I'm afraid she sinned rather badly."

"It's understandable, ma'am," Longarm said compassionately.

The girl continued, "Well, suffice it to say she found the Light in time to save her soul. You understand I only know a *little* of her story, but the way Nancy's acting reminds me of when . . . this girl was about to ruin her life."

"I'll take your word for it that another woman would know such things. But there's nobody hereabouts fixing to run off with Nan Durler."

"Oh, I thought . . . well, if she doesn't run off with anyone we know, it'll be someone, sooner or later. She doesn't just look coldly at her husband. She looks right through him, as if he wasn't there.

She's told me she hates it here and, Lord, I don't know what I'm to
do!"

"You might try minding your own business, no offense intended, ma'am. I like Cal Durler. I like his wife, too. If I knew
how to stop what might be happening, I'd be the first to try."

"Perhaps if you had a word with him, man to man."

Longarm smiled. "What am I supposed to say? 'Look here,
old son, your woman is fixing to light out on you?' He'd either
laugh or bust my jaw, and in the end, what could any of us do?
You didn't have a woman to woman with Nan yet, did you?"

Prudence shook her head forlornly. "I'm afraid it should only
light the fuse. My next-door neighbor . . . I mean the next-door
neighbor of this poor, sinful girl I told you about, tried to warn her
what a mistake she was making, and it only made her leave a couple of nights sooner than she'd intended to."

"There you go. There's nothing either of us can do. So let's
just hope it's a passing notion."

The deputy thought this might be a convenient place to change
the subject, so he asked, "How are you coming with your Bible
lessons?"

"I think the Indians are laughing at me behind my back. They
enjoy the music and coloring books, but they don't seem serious
about learning the Word," Prudence said, with a touch of disap-
pointment in her voice.

"Well, you've only been here a short while and at least it keeps
'em sober. If you really want to make friends hereabouts, spend a
little time buttering up the older squaws. Anyone can draw a crowd
of kids to a Bible meeting."

"I've invited everyone. But the adults are so cold and re-
served."

"I know. They're used to us taking 'em for fools. You might
start by asking questions, Miss Prudence. Most folks are proud to
share what they know with strangers. Asking a body a question
shows you think he or she might know something you don't."

"I see what you mean, but I don't know what sort of questions
I should ask."

"Ask the squaws about medicine herbs. Ask them how to cook
something."

"I tasted some Indian food. It was awful." Prudence wrinkled
her pert nose.

"Takes time to develop a taste for pemmican and such. But

asking a cook for a recipe beats complimenting her on her greasy stew and, hell, you don't have to *use* a Blackfoot recipe."

She laughed. Her little face was fetching in the lamplight as she said, "I'll try it. I'm not getting anywhere with that big drum I brought."

He grinned at her and excused himself to go out front and see what Rain Crow had to say. He found the Indian with the Durlers. Rain Crow hadn't found anything, as the girl had told him.

Longarm asked, "Where's Yellow Leggings? Did he go on home?"

Rain Crow shook his head and said, "No. I expected to find him here. We split up to search for sign and agreed to meet with you here for further orders. He should have ridden in by now."

Longarm looked at the moon and said, "Getting late. We'd best go see what's keeping him."

Calvin Durler opined, "Yellow Leggings has always been slow-moving. He's probably coming in at a walk. Why not give him a few minutes?"

"He's had a few minutes. We'll ride out and save him riding in all the way. Come on, Rain Crow."

The Indian waited until they were well clear of the agency before he asked, "How did you know I was worried about Yellow Leggings?"

"Didn't have to know. I worry enough myself. Any idea where your sidekick might have gone?"

"He rode east along the tracks to see if there was sign on any of the cuts you mentioned. I scouted north for a few miles until the poor light made me think I was wasting time. I thought he would be waiting for me at the agency."

Longarm didn't answer. They rode in silence until they regained the tracks and swung east. After a time they saw a pony grazing in the moonlight. Its saddle was empty.

Rain Crow said, "That is Yellow Leggings's pony." Then he called out, loudly, in Algonquin.

There was no answer, but somewhere in the night a burrowing owl hooted back at them mournfully.

Longarm followed as the Indian led, shouting for his friend. He felt as though something was crawling around in the hairs on his neck. He slid the Winchester out of its boot and held it across his thighs as they rode on. He heard a distant chuffing coming up behind them and warned, "Train's coming, Rain Crow. Let's swing wide so the locomotive won't spook our mounts!"

As the Indian ahead of him did so, Longarm saw his own shadow painted on the silvery, moonlit grass by the yellower light of a railroad headlamp. Rain Crow shouted something in his own language and moved forward at a dead run as Longarm followed. Then he, too, saw something up ahead, illuminated by the beam of the eastbound train.

The train overtook them and thundered by as Rain Crow dropped to the ground, shouting, "It's Yellow Leggings! Wendigo has him!"

Longarm's own mount shied as the scent of blood reached his flaring nostrils and Longarm had to steady him before dismounting. He joined Rain Crow by the dark mass on the ground and lit a match with his free hand. Then he swore and shook it out. He'd seen enough.

But Rain Crow took a little bull's-eye lantern from his saddlebags and lit it, cursing monotonously in Algonquin. He swung the beam over his dead friend's body and the trampled grass around. Then he said, in English, "It's like the others. No head. Not a drop of blood more than ten feet from the body!"

"The head could have been toted off in an oilcloth poke or something."

"Yes, but what does Wendigo want with their heads?"

"Wants to scare you, most likely. We're wasting time here. You know we ain't likely to find sign. Let's ride over to the next rise the roadbed cuts through. My map says it's twelve feet deep."

The Indian remounted and Longarm did the same. They were almost at the railroad cut when Rain Crow reined in and whispered, "Another pony. There, off to the south of the tracks."

"I see him. Looks like a big buckskin— Oh, damn you, Lord! You couldn't have let *that* happen!"

He loped over to where Buck stood, reined in, and almost sobbed, "Damn that gal! I *told* her not to come looking for me out here!"

The Indian said quietly, "Over there, near the tracks, pale in the moonlight."

Longarm raced his mount over, slid it to a stop and leaped from the saddle to kneel at the side of Roping Sally, or what was left of her. He didn't light a match. What he could see was ugly enough by moonlight. He pounded a fist hard against the sod by his knees and said, "We'll do right by you, honey. If that son of a bitch is on this earth within ten miles he's going to die Apache style!"

Remounting, he loped to the cut, rode up to the lip, and got down, calling, "Shine that bull's-eye over here, will you?"

Rain Crow did as he was asked, sweeping the rim of the dropoff with the narrow beam. After a time he said, "Nobody was up here when that train went by."

"Let's look over on the other side. A left-hander would have reached for a grab-iron from over there."

They rode down and across the tracks to repeat the same investigation on the north side of the track. The dry prairie straw betrayed no sign of blood or footprints, but when Longarm had the Indian swing his beam near his own boots, he saw that didn't mean much. The drained soil up here was bone-dry and baked brick-hard. The stubble had been grazed by jacks, judging from a rabbit turd he saw, and his own heels didn't leave tracks. Longarm took his hat off and threw it down, as he yelled, "All right, Lord! I've had just about *enough* of this shit!"

The Indian's voice was gentle as he said, "The woman back there meant something to you, didn't she?"

"God damn it, Rain Crow, shine that fool light somewhere else, will you?"

"I know what is in your heart, and there are tears in *my* eyes, too."

"Well, I won't tell on you if you don't tell on me. I got a bottle in my saddlebags. Before we go for a buckboard to transport the two of 'em, I figure we could both use a good stiff belt, don't you?"

"Indians are not allowed to drink, Longarm."

"I know. We're going to kill that bottle anyway."

Chapter 10

Longarm was still three-quarters drunk as he waited outside for the coroner to finish. He would have been drunker if he'd known how, but the numb anger in his guts had ruined his plumbing and the stuff was just going through without dulling the pain. It was bad enough to find a stranger's body mutilated and beheaded, but he knew he'd dream a spell of nightmares about that once-shapely body he'd intended to remember with pleasure.

A trio of cowhands came over to him as he sat on the wooden steps in the wan morning sunlight. One of them said quietly, "We ride for the Double Z. Is it true Roping Sally was killed by Indians?"

Longarm shook his head and said, "No. Whoever did it killed two Blackfoot in the process. I'd be obliged if you boys would pass the word about that. The Indians have enough to worry about without other folks after 'em!"

"We heard about them other killings, Deputy. Heard there's a Paiute medicine man out there, too, stirring up a rising."

"The Indian police know about the fool Ghost Dancer. They're keeping an eye on him. Blackfoot never had much truck with Paiute in the old days. He's just flapping his mouth in the wind, I suspicion."

"Army gent was telling us Washington's worried about this here Ghost Dancing. That Paiute cuss, Wovoka, has been down in the Indian Nation selling his medicine shirts, too!"

"There you go. None of the Five Civilized Tribes has risen. We've got all sorts of folks spouting religion in these parts, but that don't mean sensible folks have to take 'em serious. Have you boys been converted to Mormons? Are you fixing to build octagonal houses or vote the Anarchist ticket? Hell, we got a white missionary gal out at the reservation trying to sell the *Bible* to the Blackfoot without much luck."

"They say Sitting Bull's interested in Wovoka's new Ghost Dance notions."

The deputy stuck a cheroot between his teeth, but made no move to light it. "I wouldn't know what Sitting Bull's interested in, but he's way the hell over in Pine Ridge and he ain't a Blackfoot. I've been bedding down out at the Indian Agency, and if we

were fixing to have another war I'd likely hear about it before the
boys in the saloon."

Another hand asked, "What's this Wendigo shit they keep
jawing about? Did this here Wendigo kill Roping Sally?"

"The Wendigo is a spook. I'm betting on a flesh-and-blood
killer. I aim to get the son of a bitch, and when I do he'll likely die
slow, gut-shot and begging for another bullet, if I have my way."

"That's too good for the shit-eatin' hound! If *we* catch up with
him, he'll die even slower. We been discussin' whether to stake
him on an anthill smeared with honey or whether we should start
by stickin' his pecker in a sausage grinder first. Roping Sally was
a good ol' gal, even if she was too stuck up to screw her pals."

Before Longarm had to answer that, the coroner came out,
wiping his hands on his linen smock and looking cheerful, considering.

He nodded to the three cowhands and told Longarm, "We've
got a break, the last victim being white. Found a contusion just
below the severed vertebrae."

"You mean she was bruised on the back of her neck, Doc?"

"That's what I just told you. Looks like she was rabbit-
punched from behind, and if it's any comfort to you boys, I'd say
she never knew what hit her."

Longarm frowned and said, "Doc, she was on a tall horse and
likely riding at a lope! How in thunder can anyone rabbit-punch a
rider from behind like that?"

"Must have ridden up behind her," the coroner speculated.

"No, Doc, not a chance. We found the hoofprints where her
buckskin slowed after she left the saddle. That bronc was loping
when she fell. There wasn't another hoof mark within a mile."

"You must have missed something. I'm calling it like I read it.
Roping Sally was knocked off her buckskin by a hard blow from
behind, then slashed, gutted, and beheaded. The how and who is
your department. Maybe the Indians are right and this Wendigo's
some sort of *flying* critter."

"You don't believe that, Doc. If any man knew how to fly he'd
be too busy patenting the notion to go about killing folks. We're
likely missing his method, but flying ain't it. I've been meaning
to ask you something else about these killings, though. What in
thunder do you reckon he wants with the *heads*?"

"Beats me. Maybe he's taking up a collection."

"You said *you* collect skulls, Doc. I don't mean I suspicion you
of being the Wendigo, for I was impolite enough to ask about

where you were last night. I know about those papers you write for
the Smithsonian, too. But, leaving your own Indian skulls aside,
can you think of any other value a human head might have?"

The coroner scratched his head. "You mean a *cash* value? Not
hardly. I can get old skulls for five or ten dollars from the medical
supply houses. An interesting skull like Real Bear's might be worth
a little more to some museum. A white woman's skull? Maybe ten
dollars, cleaned and mounted properly. A man with a shovel could
ride out along the old wagon trails and dig up all the bones he
wanted without having to kill anybody. Hundreds of people died
and were buried in shallow graves moving West a few years back."

One of the cowhands nodded and said, "I know an old emigrant
burial ground just a few miles away. Every time it rains some bones
wash out of the ground where it's gullied some."

Longarm mused aloud, "No way the heads were taken to hide
the identity of anyone. We know who all the victims were. Wait a
minute—the killer never took Real Bear's head! He was skinned
instead of beheaded. How do you figure that, Doc?"

"Longarm, the man we're dealing with is a lunatic! How
should I know why he does the things he does? He'd have to be
crazy as a bedbug to do *any* of it!"

The deputy shifted his unlit cheroot to the other side of his
mouth, and chewed it pensively. "We both keep saying *he*, Doc. I
keep calling the Wendigo a 'he' because I've never met a gal that
ornery. Is there any chance I could be wrong?"

"You mean is the Wendigo a woman? You *have* been drinking
some."

Longarm pressed on, "Nobody's *seen* the Wendigo. A woman,
maybe smiling sweet, could get a lot closer to folks without arous-
ing suspicion of unfriendly intentions. That young buck Gray Dog
had a rabbit gun in his hand when he got jumped. Yellow Leggings
was *looking* for the Wendigo, and packing a carbine. Roping Sally
was riding armed and likely looking sharp about her. Not one of
those folks would have just waited for a strange *man*, red or white,
to announce his intentions."

"I see what you mean," the coroner said, "but a woman won't
wash. Not unless she was as strong as, or stronger than, most men.
Roping Sally may have been strong enough to cut those deep
slashes and sever a spine with one cut that way, but we know *she*
didn't do it. You fellows know any other tomboys like Roping Sally
hereabouts?"

The three hands shook their heads. One of them said, "Sally

was as big a gal as we had out here, Doc. She could have whupped any gal and likely half the men in the county."

"That's my opinion, too," the coroner agreed. "Longarm, your notion might work another way. What if all three victims met someone they knew? Someone they thought was a friend?"

Longarm shook his head. "The two Indians wouldn't have been all that close with anyone Sally might have. She got along with Blackfoot, but I doubt she'd have let one get the drop on her. Besides, we found no sign near any of the bodies. I'll allow a man could move across the grass on foot without leaving sign, walking creepy-careful, but wouldn't you ask questions if even someone you *knew* came tiptoeing through the tulips at you?"

The coroner impatiently waggled an antiseptic-smelling hand at the deputy. "Let's stay with *who* and leave the *how* alone for now. Can you think of anyone, anyone at all, who might have known all the victims too well for them to be suspicious?"

"Yeah, *me*," Longarm replied. "But I didn't do it. There's the agent, Cal Durler, but he has an alibi for a couple of the killings. So does Rain Crow. He was at my side when Roping Sally was killed."

"How can you be sure? You said he found you at the agency, told you he was worried about Yellow Leggings, and led you out to look for him. He could have killed his sidekick before he came for you. Could have killed the girl at the same time, as far as that goes."

One of the cowhands said, "Hot damn! Let's round that pesky redskin up and make him talk!"

Longarm laid a restraining hand on the man's arm. "Hold on! He didn't do it. He could have killed Yellow Leggings, but he was at the agency when the boy, Gray Dog, was murdered. As for Roping Sally, he didn't know she was riding out last night in the first place, and didn't have the time in the second. And even if my watch was wrong, I've ridden some miles beside Rain Crow and he leaves footprints like the rest of us mortals."

One of the hands asked, "What *was* Roping Sally doing out there last night anyway?"

"She'd said something about stray cows, last time I saw her," lied Longarm, adding quickly to change the subject, "I'm going over to the rail yards to jaw with the dispatcher. There was a train through, just before we found the bodies. Train crew might have seen something."

To his relief, the three cowhands stayed behind to jaw with the coroner about Roping Sally's funeral. Apparently the locals had taken up a collection to see her to the burial ground in style. It was just as well. Longarm wasn't of a mind to attend the funeral. He felt bad enough about the way he'd treated her as it was. He knew it hadn't really been his fault she'd ridden out there looking for him. He'd told her not to. On the other hand, if he'd kept his damned pecker in his pants . . . but what was done was done. Her soul would likely rest easier if he avenged her than it would if he just blubbered like a fool some more.

Longarm walked across the unfenced rail yards as a Baldwin switcher shunted a string of empties on to a siding. He spotted a man walking along the tracks toward the station with a sheaf of papers in one hand and dog-trotted after him, calling out, "Howdy! I'm a lawman!"

The man stopped and said, "I ain't. I work for the railroad and I got some cattle cars to move."

Longarm fell in beside him as the dispatcher walked toward a string of empty cattle cars down the line. He explained the situation and asked, "If somebody was leaping off and on your trains out yonder, would the boys in the caboose likely notice?"

The dispatcher answered, "The brakemen walk the whole train, setting the wheels for that nasty drop just west of here. How far out on the prairie are we talking about?"

"That rolling stretch just inside the reservation line. How long does it take to set the drags, headed east?"

"Well, each car has its own brake. The boys don't set every one unless they're loaded heavy, but the crews spend some time up on the catwalk on most trips."

"When would a fellow have the best chance of leaping for a passing grab-iron without being spotted?"

The dispatcher considered the question for a moment. "Headed west, he could likely climb aboard here in the yards and if he was in an empty reefer, he might leap off without busting any serious bones or being spotted. The train climbs for the Rockies without ever using brakes. Slows down some, topping rises. Yeah, getting aboard a train out there ain't that big a shucks."

"How about coming back? Could a man hop aboard without being seen, anywhere along the downhill grade?"

"He'd be one boss hobo if he could," the yardman chuckled. "Like I said, the crews start working the brakes at least twenty miles out. He'd have to pick his train ahead of time, too. A heavy freight would have a brakeman up on dang near every car. A train hauling back a string of empties would be his best bet."

"That train that passed me last night—the one I mentioned. Was it full or empty?"

"Empty. A string of gondolas coming back from delivering ballast to the new section they're building in the mountains. Only thing is, it was scheduled on an off-hour. Your man could wait out there a week for a line of empty gondolas. He'd have to be a railroader who knew the business, too. We run all sorts of mixed loads at odd hours. I keep trying to tell the front office this ain't any way to run a railroad, but will they listen?"

Longarm pulled the brim of his hat down to shield his eyes against the glare of the midmorning sun. "You said a boss hobo could do it. I noticed some cuts out there. If a man took a long run as a train was coming, then threw himself out a good ten or twelve feet—"

The dispatcher guffawed loudly. "He'd bust his fool head before a mile of freight ran over him. The only way you could do that in the dark would be to have a flat car or a gondola under you when you came down. You'd have to know where it was likely to be when you leaped, and like I said, pick a time when the brakemen wasn't walking along the tops of the cars."

"He couldn't grab the *side* of a passing cattle car or reefer?"

"In the dark, at that speed? Listen, mister, landing on your ass somewhere on a forty-foot flatcar bed would be bitch enough! Reaching for a passing grab-iron in the dark, ten feet off the grade, don't take hobo skills. It takes suicidal lunacy, and impossible luck to do it once. Twice is impossible."

Longarm nodded. "I'll take your word for it. How about hoboes, anyway? You have many riding your cars of an evening?"

"Naw, not this far west. Sometimes we give a lift to cowhands or Indians who ask polite. The stops are too far apart out here for the gents of the road."

"You'd notice, then, if the same hobo kept hanging about these yards?"

"Sure, and I'd sic the bulls on him. We got a real mean yard bull over at the roundhouse. His name is Mendez and he's a Mex or something. You want to talk to him about hoboes?"

"Later, maybe. Does he ride the trains or just work the yards?"

"Mendez is only a yard bull. We got some private detectives on the passenger trains, and the train crews deal with free riders on the freights. Mendez ain't on duty this time of the day, but he bunks over by the roundhouse with the switchmen and two kids he has helping him at night."

"I'll get around to them later. You'd know if they'd been having hobo troubles. Could you tell me the next time a string of empty flats or gondolas is due down from the mountains?"

"Nope," the yard man answered. "Like I said, they run this railroad off the cuff. Sometimes I'm lucky if they wire me a few hours ahead. Some night we'll have two locomotives meeting headlamp to headlamp in the middle of God-knows. Maybe then they'll listen to me."

Longarm frowned and said, "Hmm, a man using your trains to get about would have to be reading your orders over your shoulder, then, wouldn't he?"

"Just about. Who did you have in mind?"

Longarm leaned toward the man conspiratorially and whispered "He-Who-Walks-the-Night-Winds." Then he said pleasantly, "Thanks for your time," and turned and walked away across the yard, leaving the dispatcher to stare after him, scratching his head.

The murder of two Indians in one evening was bad enough. The murder of Roping Sally was something else. Any sign that the so-called Wendigo might have been careless enough to leave was obliterated as parties of hard-eyed cowhands and patrols of eager soldiers rode in circles all over the reservation for the next three days and nights. Calvin Durler was worried about possible misunderstandings between the races. Longarm was worried, too, but the possible bright side was that a reservation jump wasn't likely until things simmered down. The Indian police made sure the Blackfoot stayed close to home and Longarm spread the word in town that he'd take it personally if anyone shot a Blackfoot without one damned good reason. The fact that the Wendigo had killed Indians as well as whites helped.

The third evening after Roping Sally's funeral found Longarm seated on the agency steps, chewing an unlit cheroot, as the army scout, Jason, rode in alone.

Jason dismounted and joined Longarm on the steps, saying, "I've been ordered to find the Wendigo. Ain't that a bitch?"

"No reason you shouldn't try. Everybody in Montana's looking for the ornery son of a bitch. What happened to your dragoons?"

"Reckon they've had enough exercise for now. The lieutenant said he was reconsidering his options. That's what he calls drinking alone in his quarters. You aim to light that cigar or just gum it to death?"

"Been trying to quit smoking. What's your pleasure?"

"I thought maybe we could throw in together. I been all over this country and you know what I've found? I ain't found shit. You reckon this Wendigo's really a haunt?"

Longarm shook his head. "I reckon we're missing some simple trick. Whoever's doing it isn't completely crazy. The Wendigo's had enough sense to lay low while half the territory's out here looking for him. That leaves someone with a reason as well as some slick way of moving about."

"Well, the heat's dying down. You suspicion he'll be doing it some more?" Jason asked.

"It's not likely that he'll suddenly get religion and just quit. I figure his play is spooking the Indians, which he's done some. It'll take some more spooking to make them jump the reservation, so, yeah, he's likely planning his next move about now."

"You reckon there's a land grabber behind all this, Longarm?"

"That's an obvious suspicion, but I can't get it to wash. No way any of the local cattlemen could claim this land, even if the Indians light out and leave it empty."

"How about a buried treasure, or a mineral claim, or such?"

"Studied on that, too. The Blackfoot are spread out thin here. A man slick enough to get in and out without being spotted could dig up half an acre easier than he could kill folks watching for him. As to minerals, they've been looked for. The prairie soil's forty feet at the least to the nearest bedrock and it's been surveyed by Uncle Sam. There's some lignite coal beds to the north. Too deep to be worth mining and too poor to be worth burning, next to all that anthracite they have back East. Nope, there's nothing here but grass and water, and like I said, no way a white man could beg, borrow, or steal rangeland. The Wendigo is after something, but I'll be damned if I know what."

Jason scratched his bearded jaw and said, "I hear there's a powwow on the reservation tonight. You reckon the War Department might be interested?"

"You're welcome to come along, Jason. I'm riding over with Rain Crow, my Blackfoot deputy. He says one of Wovoka's Dream Singers is on the reservation. Rain Crow offered to run him off, but I said to leave the rascal be, for now."

"Them Dream Singers are pretty nasty, but it's your play. I'd go along if I thought there'd be some pretty squaws, but the old men will likely just be shaking rattles and talking sulky. So I'll pass on your offer and get on back to the fort."

As Jason turned to mount his bay, Longarm asked quietly,

"Before you go, would you mind if I asked you a sort of unfriendly question?"

Jason swung around and stared back thoughtfully before he shrugged and said, "Ask away. I'll let you know if I take it unfriendly."

"Where were you the night of the three murders, Jason?"

The scout laughed and answered, "At the fort. Lucky I can prove it, ain't it? I've seen how fast you can draw!"

"I had to ask. Didn't mean anything by it."

"I know you're just doing your job, Longarm. Hell, I won't even get pissed when you check my story at the fort. A man with nothing to hide has no call to get pissed, and, hell, you never mentioned my mother."

They both laughed. Longarm relaxed the hold he'd had on the derringer in his right coat pocket.

Jason asked, "Hear any more about Johnny Hunts Alone? Or do you suspicion him and the Wendigo might be one and the same?"

"I'll eat that apple a bite at a time. If they're the same gent, I'll catch 'em both whenever I catch one. If they ain't, I'll catch 'em separately. I've been asking about for a stranger with a limp. Nobody's seen any."

"Could be Johnny knows you're here and just lit out to other parts. As I see it, his only reason for hiding out here would be because you didn't know he could pass for an Indian. You get my drift?"

"Sure. Real Bear's the only victim who could have identified him. *You're* still breathing, too."

"What's that supposed to mean, Longarm?"

"If Johnny Hunts Alone killed Real Bear to keep from being given away, he'd have done better to go after a white man he'd hunted with than a mess of Indians and a gal who never knew him."

"I see what your meaning is and I thank you for the warning. Anyone out to skin *this* hombre and take his head had best be good at it, though. I know the breed on sight and I can get riled as hell when folks start cutting off my head!"

Longarm rose to his feet as the scout got up, remounted, and rode away with a friendly wave. Longarm was about to go into the house, but Prudence Lee fluttered out, and whispered, "Don't go in, they're fighting."

Longarm heard the sound of breaking crockery and a man's voice raised in anger through the open doorway. He nodded and said, "Maybe we'd best go for a ride or something."

"Oh, I'd like that. Calvin said something about riding out to an Indian ceremony, later. Could I go along?"

Longarm started to shake his head. Then he thought of his plan for enlivening the festivities and said, "It might prove interesting, at that, if a white gal was there watching."

Fair was fair, though. So he said, "Miss Prudence, I'm going out with Rain Crow and some other Indian police to make some folks feel foolish. I don't expect danger, but there's likely to be some cussing."

"Oh, it sounds exciting! Calvin said you were trying to expose the Ghost Dancers as frauds, and I'm very interested in Indian lore."

"Yes, ma'am. Some of such lore can tend to be a bit racy. You did say you were married once, didn't you?"

"Heavens, do you expect an orgy?" Prudence asked breathlessly.

"Ain't sure. I haven't been to many Ghost Dances. If I let you come along, you've got to promise to sit there poker-faced and not say anything, no matter what."

"I think I can manage that. If you'll help me with my sidesaddle . . ."

"We'll be taking the buckboard, ma'am. Indians don't laugh at wheels the way they do at white ladies riding funny. I'll be putting some bags of feed around the edges of the wagon bed. If there's trouble, I'll be obliged if you sort of flatten out behind 'em while the lead flies."

Chapter 11

It was sunset as the naked Ghost Dance missionary pranced up and down in front of the assembled Blackfoot elders gathered out on the prairie. His hair was long and stringy and his penis was painted red for some reason. He was about thirty years old and chanted in English as he waved the limp leather medicine shirt he held in one hand. His own Paiute dialect would have made no more sense to the Blackfoot than it would have to a white man, so as Longarm and the girl drove up to the edge of the crowd with Two-Noses and Rain Crow at either side, they could understand his meaning as he pointed the gourd rattle in his other hand at them and shouted, "Behold, the white man comes with a woman and two of his Blackfoot hunting dogs. Do not listen to their words, my brothers. The whites are ignorant of the message of Wovoka!"

Longarm reined in at a discreet distance, ignoring the sullen muttering from the crowd as he nodded to the missionary and shouted back, "You just go ahead and have your say, old son. We've come in peace to learn, not to dispute religion with a man of the cloth—if we stretch cloth to include red paint, I mean."

The missionary wiggled his hips, swinging his painted penis, but Prudence Lee didn't blanch as he and even Longarm might have expected. She sat prim and straight on the buckboard seat, looking at him like he was a bug on a pin.

He held the leather garment up and shouted, "So be it! Hear me, my brothers! Wovoka has blessed this medicine shirt! These others you see by the council fire are for your warriors. When the time comes for our dead ancestors to join us in a final battle for our lands, the bullets of the soldiers will not hurt you if you wear them!"

Longarm muttered, "Stay here, ma'am. Rain Crow, you see that nobody trifles with Miss Prudence, hear? I'm gonna mosey over and take a closer look and listen."

He climbed down and made his way to the front of the crowd, hunkering down politely on his heels and not saying anything as the Paiute shouted, "All our dead ancestors will come back from the Happy Hunting Ground to join us! All of them! The soldiers may be many, but think of our numbers if every Indian who ever lived rides at our side against the soldiers!"

Longarm called out, "Can I ask a polite question? I was wondering if you'd tell us what tribes Wovoka had in mind."

"Tribes? Wovoka makes no distinction, white man! Our Ghost Dances shall raise all the dead!"

"*White* dead, too? You mean these folks have to face George Armstrong Custer and his men *again*? If you don't mind my saying, Custer was a mean son of a bitch at Washita and some other places even before you boys killed him!"

"Don't mock me, white man. Wovoka's medicine is only intended to bring back dead Indians!"

"I suspicioned as much. Tell me, does he aim to raise the Crows, the Utes, the Pawnees?"

"Of course. Every Indian who ever was!"

The Paiute missed the worried muttering from some of the old men around Longarm. He was probably a stranger in these parts.

Longarm grinned and said, "That should be interesting. These Blackfoot get to kill their old enemies all over again, right?"

"No, when the dead rise, they shall rise as brothers. All the old fighting will be forgotten. Indian shall greet Indian, as his fellow man."

"That sounds reasonable. Wouldn't it save a lot of fuss if such whites and live Indians as are left just shook hands and called it quits right now?"

"You mock the message I bring. My brothers, here, are not taken in by your twisting of my words!"

"Now, that ain't fair. I ain't twisted word one. It was *you* who said they had to make friends with a mess of damn Pawnee. How about Snakes? Does Snake Killer, over yonder, get to keep his coup feather when his dead Snake brothers come to call? What if a dead Blackfoot pops out of the ground in the middle of some Crows? Does he shake hands with them, or run off with their ponies, like in the Shining Times?"

"If you won't let me speak, I will go."

"I'll be quiet, seeing as how you don't seem to know what your message is."

In the crowd behind him, someone snickered. Longarm didn't know if the laugh had been with him or at him. Neither did the Paiute. He waved the medicine shirt again and shouted, "As I was saying, your young men shall be immune to white bullets in these shirts."

Longarm asked, "How come? I mean, I don't doubt for a minute that those raggedy buckskins are bulletproof. What I don't understand is why in thunder you need live Indians to do your fighting if Wovoka has all these dead ghosts ready to fight the army?"

"The ghosts must know our people are sincere. Would you expect the spirits to fight for weaklings afraid to stand up for their rights?"

"I don't know what a spirit might do. I'd be scared as hell to charge a Gatling gun with nothing on but a magic shammy shirt, though."

"That is because you have a white man's heart. The medicine only works for those who believe."

"That sounds reasonable," Longarm said amiably. "Put the shirt on and let's see how it works for you."

"What do you mean, white twister of words?"

"Well, I thought, as long as you've got those magic shirts, and I've got a gun, we'd see how good your brag is. Put on the shirt and I'll bounce a couple of .44 slugs off it."

The Paiute's face clouded over threateningly, but Longarm thought he detected a quaver in the Indian's voice as he responded, "Are you threatening to kill me, white man? I have come in peace, unarmed. The Blackfoot have extended to me the protection of their hospitality!"

"Well, sure they have. I'm hospitable myself. I'd never in this world gun a man I thought was likely to die from it. But you said your shirts were bulletproof. So what say we have some fun?"

Longarm heard a murmur of agreement around him from the Blackfoot as the Paiute paled and stammered, "It would not be a fair test. I am not initiated as a warrior!"

The lawman allowed a larger-than-life expression of shock to appear on his face as he said, "You mean you're standing there telling all these folks to go to war, and you're not a proper soldier? Well, I *did* fight a war one time, and *I* ain't about to tell these old Dog Soldiers or Turtle Lances whether they should go to war or get married! Hell, I'm not ashamed to admit I never had the nerve to go through the Sun Dance as a full warrior. By the way, that's likely why I see no scars on *your* chest, huh?"

"We Paiute never danced the Sun Dance."

"I know. Never did all that much fighting, either, now that I think on it. Likely that's why Wovoka's so hot and bothered about another Indian war. It's the men who never fight that start our white man's wars, too."

An old Indian near Longarm muttered something in a jeering

tone and this time, when some other Indians laughed, Longarm knew they weren't laughing at him!

The Paiute licked his lips and said, "Don't listen to him, my brothers. Can't you see what he is trying to do?"

Longarm let a little scorn creep into his voice as he said, "I ain't doing anything but saying my mind. This may be a foolish time to bring it up, but I'll tell one and all I've fought Indians in my time. I mean, I've fought *real* Indians, not ghosts." He got to his feet, threw his hat down, and pounded his chest, shouting, "Hear me! I count coup! I have killed Dakota! I have killed Cheyenne! I have taken captives back from Apache and taken Comanche alive to be hanged by the government!"

Old Snake Killer asked in an interested tone, "How many Blackfoot do you count coup on?"

"None. I don't say this because of where I am and who might be listening. I say it because I wasn't here the last time you rose against the army."

"Would you have killed me, had we met in battle?"

"You're damned right I would have, unless you'd killed me first. We're both *men*, ain't we?"

Snake Killer smiled broadly. "Yes. I think it would have been a good fight. I like a man who says what is in his heart, too. But Wendigo—"

"The Wendigo has nothing to do with Wovoka's Ghost Dance, Snake Killer. I'm a white man, not a Dream Singer, so I'll not insult you by disputing about spirits. I just want to see this jasper's medicine shirt turn a bullet before any of your young men put one on to ride against the army!"

The old Blackfoot nodded and told the Paiute, "His words make sense. Why don't you put the shirt on and prove him wrong?"

The Paiute stammered, "I am not allowed to. Only a true warrior can wear the medicine shirt."

Old Snake Killer got to his feet, peeling off his old wool jacket to reveal the Sun Dance scars on his bony chest as he said, "I am a warrior. Give me the shirt."

Longarm swore under his breath. He hadn't planned on getting a *Blackfoot* at the wrong end of his Colt! The Paiute missionary saw the bind he was in at the same time. Slyly, he held the thin deerskin shirt out to the old man, saying, "Of course. Let us see what happens when the white man shoots you."

The old Blackfoot put the shirt on and stood there, his head cocked to one side in mild interest as he waited for Longarm to test his medicine. Longarm knew that if he killed the old man there'd be hell to pay. On the other hand, even though common sense indicated that he should back down, he knew what the Ghost Dancer would twist it into. He drew his .44, but said, "I have to think about this, boys. You see, I don't believe in this medicine!"

The Paiute jeered, "Go ahead and shoot him. Are you afraid? Behold, my brothers, the medicine is working! Snake Killer is wearing the medicine shirt and the white man can't shoot him!"

"Damn it, it ain't the same thing!"

"Yes it is! Wovoka says a man wearing the medicine shirt cannot be harmed by white man's bullets! Whether you shoot or not, the results are the same! Anyone with eyes can see this!"

Longarm had to admit that the Paiute had a point. The rascal knew he wasn't about to gun the old man and was twisting it to look like magic!

Then Prudence Lee was suddenly at his side. She held her hand out imperiously and said; "Give *me* the gun, Longarm!"

There was a murmur of surprise from the Indians. They were no more confused than Longarm. He said, "Miss Prudence, this gun is loaded with .44-40s and I told you to stay on the buckboard!"

"Give me the gun. I assure you I have no intention of shooting anyone with it."

"Then what's your play? You could miss without looking shameful, but they'd still say it was medicine, and—"

"Will you give me that damned gun and be still? You *know* I'm a missionary!"

Longarm let her take the gun by the barrel from his hand. She smiled prettily and held the grips out to the Paiute, saying, "The white man's heart is not strong enough to shoot at a friend, even a friend protected by your strong medicine. *You* will have to fire it at Snake Killer!"

The Paiute backed away, stammering, "Not I! It is wrong for me to shoot at a brother!"

Prudence Lee followed him, holding out the gun in grim determination as they circled the council fire. She was smiling sweetly as she insisted, "But what harm can come to Snake Killer if Wovoka's magic is stronger than a white man's bullets? Surely you know how to shoot a pistol, don't you? Heavens, I should think a man who preaches war would know at least a *little* about weapons!"

Most of the Blackfoot were laughing openly now. The Paiute stammered obtuse theology and the little female missionary cut him up and down and sideways with sophistries of her own until it became obvious that the naked Ghost Dancer had no intention of letting her hand him Longarm's revolver.

Presently, Prudence brought the pistol back to the tall deputy and handed it to him, saying, "Oh, dear, I suppose now we'll just have to take his word for it about the shirt! He doesn't seem to want to prove it one way or the other!"

Longarm grinned back at her as he holstered the .44 and said, "Yep, they'll likely have to try those bulletproof shirts without a demonstration."

Old Snake Killer asked, "If nobody wants to shoot at me, can I take this thing off? It's badly tanned and it itches."

There was a roar of laughter, and Longarm said, "Let's go, Miss Prudence. We'll quit while we're ahead."

He led her back to the buckboard and helped her up to the seat as Rain Crow leaned over in his saddle and asked, "Do you want me to run that Paiute off?"

Longarm said, "No. Don't make him look that important. This little lady just did quite a job taking the wind out of his sails and I suspicion that the more he preaches, the more they'll laugh at him."

"You may be right, for now. But what if Wendigo strikes again?"

"I see what you mean. But leave the Ghost Dancer be, anyway. If I don't stop the Wendigo pretty quickly, we'll be up to our chins in trouble, medicine shirts or no."

Longarm fingered a shiny new silver dollar as he stood in the saloon doorway scanning the bar in the dim light. Finally, he spotted the man he was looking for by the description the railroad workers had given him. The yard bull, Mendez, was a tall, lean man in a red checked shirt and peaked cloth cap. He wore an old Coet Navy .36 in a battered army holster and looked like he could use a shave.

Longarm bellied up to the bar beside him and said, "I'm a deputy U.S. marshal, Mr. Mendez. They told me over at the roundhouse that I might find you here."

Mendez shrugged and said, "I'm off duty. It's none of their business if I drink or not, on my own time."

Longarm noticed he had a slight Spanish accent. "What *are* you drinking, then?"

"I'm not. Already have a skinful and I have to work all night."

"I know. What's coming through the yards tonight?"

"Your guess is as good as mine. I think they're running a passenger train through about eight-thirty. They don't discuss the timetable with us greasers."

"Oh? The two boys helping you chase hoboes are Mexican, too?"

"One's a Mex. Other's Irish. I'm a South American, if it's bothering you."

"Seems to be bothering you more than me, Mr. Mendez. I have some friends who grew up speaking Spanish."

"I know, as long as they don't want to marry your sister, huh?"

"I figure who my sister might marry would be her own business. Did some lawman give you a hard time about your accent? Or do you just hate *all* us gringos?"

"*One* time might not have bothered me," the yard bull said bitterly. "It gets tedious being called a greaser after the first hundred times or so. Look, you don't have to butter me up to get me to cooperate. What do you want from me, Deputy?"

"I said it already. Trying to get a line on slow freights passing through the Blackfoot reservation at night."

"I heard someone might be shooting Indians from the passing trains. The roundhouse gang was talking about it the other evening. If any of 'em saw anything, they didn't let me in on it."

"I know you don't ride the trains. Can you think of anyone who might, aside from the regular crews?"

"Freight trains? Hoboes, if we let them. The insurance company says we're not to give rides to Indians any more. Damn fool Shoshone fell between the blinds a few months back and his squaw sued the line. Some free passes being given out, back East, but only to ride the passenger trains. Freight crews have enough to handle without some idiot getting in the way as they run the catwalk."

"Don't suppose any hobo could get by you, maybe late on a dark night in the rail yards?" the deputy asked.

"Sure, one could, once in a while. Play hell doing it regular, though. My boys and me have orders to dust their asses with rock salt, getting on or getting off."

"All three of you carry shotguns charged with salt, on duty?"

"Twelve gauge, double barrel, sawed off. I carry a sawed-off baseball bat, too. You want to hop a freight in my yards, mister, you'd better ask the dispatcher for permission, first."

"None of the caboose hands or maybe a friendly engineer could give a pal a lift?"

"Sure they could. I only check the cars for bums. I have a helper go up one side with a lantern while I ease up the far side in the dark to dust the rascals as they slip away from him between the wheels. I dusted one boy right in the ass that way a month ago and you should have heard him holler. But I don't ask who's riding the caboose or up in the cab. It's not my job."

Longarm tapped absently on the bar with the silver dollar in his hand and the yard bull added, "This sniper or whatever would have a hard time doing mean things from the cab or caboose, though, wouldn't he?"

"Yeah. I may as well tell you, I've wired about the country for suggestions about crazy people working for your railroad. Nobody thinks it likely a full crew of lunatics are working out here."

A worried expression appeared on the railroad cop's face. "You know about that colored boy I killed in Omaha, then?"

"Yeah. Nebraska says you got off on self-defense. You said that hobo pulled a knife on you, right?"

"He did, and he had two other niggers with him. They dropped the subject when I blew his face off. I warned him twice to drop the knife before I shot him, too, God damn it!" Mendez slammed a fist down on the bar.

"Cool down, old son! You don't have to convince *me*. You already got let off by a grand jury. I know you have a rough job."

"They fired me anyway. Said I'd overstepped my authority. Ain't that a laugh? They fire you if you let the bums ride and they fire you if you get in a fuss with 'em."

"There ain't no justice," Longarm commiserated. "I see you had no trouble getting another job out here, though."

"Oh, a railroad bull with a tough rep can usually get hired somewhere. I don't get paid as much, though, and the prices out here are higher than back East. If I had it to do over, those three coons could have driven the damned locomotive and I'd have looked the other way."

Longarm shook his head and said, "I don't buy that. The roundhouse gang has you down as a good, tough bull."

"Well, I'll get tougher if they don't quit calling me a Mex. I'm from Paraguay, not Mexico, and both my mother and father were pure white!"

Longarm nodded and said, "I suspicioned as much. How'd you get up here from such a far piece south? Merchant marine?"

"No. Worked for a British railroad down there when I was a teenager. Paraguay hasn't got that much in the way of railroading, but I liked it better than punching cows, so I followed the trade north."

"You've been here a spell, judging from the way you speak English."

"Hell, I fought in the War for Lincoln!" Mendez said proudly. "Least I could do to get back at Texas. The first time I was called a greaser was in Galveston and I haven't learned to like it yet."

Longarm promised never to call Mendez a greaser and left him alone at the bar. He walked to the land office to use the federal wire. After he'd reported his lack of progress and asked a few questions that nobody in Denver had answers to, he sent an inquiry to the Chicago stock market. As Agent Chadwick came in to join him under the telegraph batteries, Longarm said, "Beef's up a dollar and six bits a head and one of your battery jars is leaking."

Chadwick looked at the charred black spot on the blotter next to the telegraph key and said, "Cigar burn. Them wet cell jars are glass. They leak all at once or never."

"Doesn't it make you nervous working with all that acid up there?" Longarm asked.

Chadwick shrugged. "The batteries have to be somewhere. That's a pretty stout shelf."

"I'd have 'em on the floor if this was my wire shack. It's good to have a box of baking soda handy, too. Met a telegrapher who saved his eyes with baking soda, once, when a Sioux arrow shattered a battery jar in his face and spattered him with vitriol."

"You're a cheerful cuss today. How come you asked the current price of beef?"

"Still a cowhand at heart, I guess. I thought you'd be interested yourself, Chadwick. Seems only natural the land office out here would be abreast of converting grass to dollars."

Chadwick looked annoyed and said, "Stop pussyfooting around, damn it! You heard something about that trouble I had a few years back, didn't you?"

"Some," Longarm lied, adding, "I'd like to hear your side, Chadwick."

The agent smiled crookedly and said, "I might have known you were using the railroad telegraph for snooping around about us all. Did they tell you I was cleared of the charges?"

"I didn't suspicion you'd be working for Uncle Sam if he'd caught you with your pants down."

"Hell, everybody's pants were down when they gave away all that money to build the railroads West, back in the sixties. They caught Vice President Colfax making money on those watered railroad bonds, but I was only a clerk in those days. I never even got a crack at all they were giving away in the way of land grants and tax money. The only reason I was called upon to testify was that my boss was grabbing land right and left! I came out of it clean as a whistle, and believe you me, they had me on the carpet for days, going over everything I'd had for breakfast for a good seven years! They investigated my bank account and made me show 'em everything but my belly button. But what's the use of talking? You likely got my first-grade report cards from Denver when you wired 'em, right?"

Longarm laughed and said, "As a matter of fact, I never knew you were mixed up in that old financial mess till you just now told me."

"You didn't? What in hell are we raking it up for, then?"

"We're not. You are. Folks are funny that way. They get to jawing with a lawman and next thing they know, they're telling him about some gal they got in trouble once, or how much they hated their pa for whupping 'em. Had a fellow admit to incest once, and I never suspicioned him of more than murder."

Chadwick laughed and shook his head. "All right, you suckered me into revealing my dark past. Had it been a mite darker, I'd be smoking dollar cigars in my private railroad car instead of trying to live on a piss-poor wage, considering. Do you want the name of the lady I was sleeping with the night Roping Sally was murdered?"

"It ain't any of my business, but since you brought it up, Sheriff Murphy told me about it. Says you're likely to get killed if her *other* boyfriend finds out about it."

"Damn!" Chadwick exploded. "It's what I get for staying late! Who told Murphy, that old biddy next door?"

"He said he saw you himself, making his morning rounds. The old biddy next door was watching through her lace curtains when you came through the back yard just after sundown. I don't hold with small-town gossip much, but in a way she might have done you a favor."

"Jesus H. Christ! You don't mean you really had me under suspicion?"

"No more than anyone else in the territory. Let's get back to the price of beef. We're headed into a cattle boom after the droughts the last couple of years thinned the herds to where the price went up on such cows as are left. Everybody out here seems to want cows bad enough to steal them, lately. I've noticed the range here-abouts is getting overgrazed. Lots of spreads are overstocked, but they keep trailing longhorn north just the same."

"Jesus, are you still gnawing that same bone about someone stealing reservation rangeland from the fool Indians?"

Longarm nodded and said, "Ain't getting much marrow out of it, either. Seems odd that nobody's made an offer on damn near virgin range. The Blackfoot have maybe a hundred and fifty head grazing more than fifteen hundred full sections out there."

Chadwick shook his head wearily and insisted, "That's the B.I.A.'s problem. Who would you expect to make *me* an offer? I keep telling you I can't sell government land, damn it!"

Longarm said, "You do file claims and issue range permits, though. Yet you say no white man's approached you with any questions about all that grass going to waste."

Chadwick cut in with an annoyed snort to explain, "Hell, of *course* they've *asked* about it. But I've told everybody the same thing. Those Indian lands are not for sale, with or without Indians on 'em!"

"Could you give me a list of everyone who's interested in spreading out?" the lawman asked.

Chadwick frowned and said, "Sure, if I can remember 'em all. Let's go out to my office and I'll write down those I recall."

As he led the way, Longarm asked mildly, "Don't you keep books on such matters, Chadwick?"

"You mean, do I record the name of every man who stops me on the street to ask a fool question? No. I don't write down the dirty jokes I hear or the names of sons they seem to think I can get into West Point, either. People suck around a man in my position, Longarm. They seem to think I'm Uncle Sam in the flesh instead of his poorly paid hired hand!"

"But you don't take bribes, right?"

"I don't know. I've never had the chance. I remember how the man I used to work under retired rich, disgraced or not. It's been my misfortune to be posted to jobs that keep most men honest through no fault of their own."

He led Longarm out front, sat down, and started writing on the back of an envelope as he muttered darkly about the stupidity of people who thought he was Saint Nicholas. He handed Longarm a list of eighteen names and brands and said, "Here, this should keep you busy. Every one of these idiots has offered to buy at least a section of Indian land, should it ever be auctioned off."

Longarm scanned the list, noting that most of the names on it were those of local cattlemen with modest but growing herds and small home spreads. When Chadwick asked how he knew so much, he explained, "I haven't just been spitting and whittling since I came here, Chadwick. One time or the other since I got here, I've talked to just about everybody I've been able to get within a mile of."

"Any of them cowboys interesting enough to pester again?"

"Maybe. I'll keep this with my map and check them off as I get the time. Do you get any offers from bigger outfits, like the Double Z or maybe the Tumbling R?"

"Not that I remember. Why?" Chadwick asked.

"Takes a big outfit to afford hired guns, flying machines, and such."

"I see your meaning. Have you thought about the army?"

"Sure I have. They're spoiling for another go at the Blackfoot, and the War Department has observation balloons, too. But some officer out to start an Indian war to advance his career wouldn't have to use spooks. He'd just dream up some incident and start blasting away."

"If some soldiers were trying to frighten the Blackfoot into a jump, and knew the when and where of it . . ." the agent suggested.

"Too damned complicated. The second lieutenant out at the fort's ornery enough to frame up some excuse to kill Indians, but why shilly-shally about with Wendigos? If he had even one man in his command willing to murder for him, he'd just have the rascal scalp some passing white, and bye-bye, Blackfoot!"

"Yeah," Chadwick agreed, "the War Department's never been too subtle. How about the B.I.A., as long as you suspect your fellow federal employees all that much?"

"Hey," Longarm said, "it was you who brought up the War Department. But I've considered whether the Bureau of Indian Affairs might have a reason to scare their own charges off. They haven't got one. The minute the Blackfoot are gone, Washington cuts the funds allocated for feeding the tribe and, if there's one thing the Indian Ring doesn't cotton to, it's leaving money in the Treasury."

"Some of those funds tend to stick to fingers along the way, too," Chadwick observed. "It wouldn't make much sense for the B.I.A. to want to go out of business, would it?"

"Not hardly. Maybe now you see why I keep chewing the same bone over and over. It's boring the shit out of *me*, too!"

"So," the land agent said, "no matter where the trail seems to take you, it keeps leading back to a crazy man, or an Indian spook."

"I don't like those possibilities much. I'd best be on my way and see who else I can come up with."

Longarm left the land office and headed for where he'd tethered his chestnut in front of the saloon. He saw a townie nailing up a cardboard placard and paused to read it over the man's shoulder. It was an election poster, advising one and all to vote for Wilbur Browning for county sheriff. Longarm frowned and opined, "Seems to me your man is getting anxious, considering. The coroner tells me you've never held elections hereabouts, since there ain't enough county to mention."

The man finished hammering the last nail and said, "I know. Damned Indian reservation takes up most of the county and there ain't enough of us whites to matter. But that fool Paddy Murphy's not worth the powder to blow him up with. So we're fielding Browning against the shanty son of a bitch!"

"Browning's a rider for the Double Z, ain't he?" Longarm asked.

"Yeah, he shot a Texan in Dodge one time, which is more than Murphy can say. The territorial governor's given permission for elections and we aim to vote Murphy out."

"Reorganizing the unincorporated districts, is he? That's right interesting. They say anything about, uh, expanding the county, over at your party headquarters?"

"Hell," the man said, "we ain't got a headquarters. Ain't rightly got a party, either. But since Murphy's a Republican, the boys over at the livery who paid for these signs must be Democrats."

"Don't you know for sure? Seems to me a legal election has to register voters ahead."

"Shit, nobody in Switchback's all that fussy. We just aim to have us a real lawman. If Murphy won't be voted out polite, we'll just tar and feather the son of a bitch and ride him out on a rail."

Longarm cleared his throat and adjusted the brim of his hat. "Well, as I'm a federal man, it may not be my call to tell folks how to hold local elections. But you'll find elections work better if they're legal. How come folks are so anxious about politics, all of a sudden?"

"It's the killings out on the reservation. We keep telling Murphy he ought to do something about it and he keeps saying it ain't his jurisdiction. Wilbur Browning says he'll jurisdict the shit out of that Wendigo son of a bitch if we give *him* the job."

"The Blackfoot have their own police force out there. I suspicion they won't want your man's help all that much."

"It don't matter what they want. All these Indian rascals running about killing folks have everybody spooked. Seen some more damn Indians just this morning, coming up from the railroad station armed to the teeth."

A troubled look darkened the tall lawman's features. "Wait a minute," he said. "Are you saying men from other tribes are in Switchback?"

"They weren't Blackfoot. Don't know where they were headed. I ain't an expert on Indians, but one of the fellows over to the railroad said they were Sioux. They were dressed like white men, save for braided hair and likely needing a bath, but Wes Collins, who used to be in the army, allowed as how the lingo they were jabbering was Dakota."

"You couldn't say which way they rode, huh?"

"Well, they ain't washing dishes here in Switchback, or asking for a job as hired hands, so they likely went on out to the reservation."

"You say this morning, eh? They've got four or five hours' lead on me and I doubt they'll be reporting in to the agent. I'll tell the Blackfoot police about it and let them take care of it."

"How do you know you can trust your Indian police to tell you true about other redskins?"

Longarm started to say it was a foolish question. Then he reconsidered, shrugged, and said, "I don't."

Chapter 12

This time Longarm rode back to the reservation along the railroad tracks instead of taking the wagon trace from town. He didn't know what he expected to find, but he'd never ridden the entire stretch and it was possible that his survey map was missing a few details.

As he topped the rise, west of town, and started across the higher prairie rolling toward the distant foothills, a calico steer with a broken left horn stared wild-eyed at him for a moment and lit out, running. Longarm saw its badly worn hide and figured it for a queer. Sometimes something funny happened to a castrated calf and it grew up thinking it was a heifer. The range bulls thought so, too, and the poor spooked animal was all worn out from trying to get screwed. Some pissed-off bull had whupped it good for fooling him, most likely, and now it was ranging alone, too scared to let anything near it.

The range between Switchback and the reservation line was badly misused in this stretch, too. The native grasses had been overgrazed and the brush was getting out of hand along the railroad right-of-way. Prickly tumbleweed, both blowing and growing, formed dense windrows between higher clumps of sage and greasewood that had followed the tracks east out of the Great Basin beyond the mountains. Some of the brush was waist-high to a man on foot and getting too woody for even an antelope to browse. It was a hell of a way to treat a country, Longarm thought, but told himself not to worry about it. Nevertheless, he couldn't help wondering where it would all lead to. He was all for progress; the Iron Horse had opened up a continent to Europe's hungry hordes in his own lifetime, but couldn't people see there was a limit to what the land could take? The high plains had been grazed for thousands of years without being damaged by its indigenous wildlife. The longhorn probably didn't hurt the buffalo grass any more than the buffalo had, head for head. But the buffalo had kept moving, giving the grass time to grow back. The Indian had been willing to live the same way, drifting across the sea of grass from place to place. The white man's notion of staying put with his cows and crops didn't give the range time to recover. The ten inches of rain each season and the short green-up of the native short-grasses called for at least two years of fallow for every one grazed. At the rate they were overstocking, the cattle raisers would be raising more dust than cows in a few more years.

He kept an eye on the queer. It had stopped, and was staring at him from behind a clump of greasewood. The critter was mixed up enough between the horns to do almost anything, he knew. Cows grazing with others were usually neighborly enough, but loners, away from the herd, tended to get odd notions. When that messed-up calico didn't think he was a gal, he just might decide he was a Spanish fighting bull. That busted horn might make a nasty hole in his chestnut's hide, too.

Longarm rode on, pretending not to notice, the way one rides past a barking farmyard dog. Then, as he and the chestnut came abreast of the queer, it lowered its banged-up head, snorted, and charged.

"Son of a bitch!" muttered Longarm, swinging his mount in a tight circle to spoil the rogue's aim. Something ticked the brim of his hat as, behind him, a gunshot swore at him, too!

As the steer thundered by on one side, Longarm was rolling out of the saddle on the other, dragging his Winchester from its boot as he threw himself at the dirt. He landed on his side and rolled behind a waist-high clump of sage in a cloud of mustard-colored dust, ignoring the horse running one way and the steer the other. He rolled over again and rose on his elbows with the rifle trained back the way he'd come. The second shot tore through the sage where he'd landed, and spotting the gunsmoke wafting from some greasewood near the tracks, Longarm fired back, dropped lower and snaked at an angle toward it, cradling his rifle in his arms as he walked his elbows through the dust.

Longarm heard the pounding of hooves and turned his head to see the calico queer headed his way, its good horn down and plowing through the brush as it came!

He fired a shot into the dust ahead of the charging queer to turn it. The critter didn't even swerve, but Longarm's unseen attacker parted his rising gunsmoke with a bullet. The lawman pulled his knees up, dug his heels into the dust, and kicked himself sideways as the calico charged blindly through the space he'd just occupied, snorting like a runaway locomotive. Longarm landed on the back of his neck, somersaulted backward, and came up pumping lead in the general direction of the greasewood clump the shots seemed to be coming from. Then he dropped and rolled out of sight without waiting to see how good the other's aim might be. There were no answering shots. If he hadn't hit the son of a bitch, then his enemy was lying doggo, or had lost interest and was crawling himself.

There seemed to be no way to find out which, without catching a rifle ball in the head or attracting the attention of the crazy calico. So Longarm stayed prone in a clump of tumbleweed, propped on one elbow, as he took a fistful of loose cartridges from his coat pocket and thumbed them into the rifle's magazine. He risked a look to the west and saw that his chestnut had stopped a quarter-mile away and had begun to graze, as if nothing had happened. Longarm peered through a gap in the brush and observed that the one-horned calico was broadside to him now. The lunatic long-horn had its tail up and its head down, pawing the dirt with one hoof as it regarded something hidden to Longarm's left, closer to the railroad tracks. Longarm didn't think the calico had spotted anyone for sure, since it wasn't spooked or charging, but the calico had seen something, so Longarm started crabbing toward the tracks, keeping his head and ass down, moving as fast as he could. Before he reached the tracks, a double-header freight came over the rise between him and town, with both engines puffing, fore and aft. The one-horned queer lit out for Texas, bawling in fright. Long-arm heaved a sigh of relief and kept crawling toward the tracks as the ground vibrated under him in time to the pounding drivers of the double-header. He saw a brakeman staring down at him, slack-jawed, from the top of a car. Then the train was past and he was kneeling behind some tall, dried sunflower stalks with a reloaded rifle in his hands and not much notion where to point it.

He worked his way east along the railroad bank for four or five minutes until he reached a wooden culvert that ran under the tracks through the embankment. He saw where human knees had carried someone under to the far side and, swearing, threw caution to the winds and ran up and over. He dropped to one knee on the north side of the tracks, and swept the horizon with his eyes. Then he ran toward the edge of the dropoff, rifle ready. He sur-mised the bushwhacker had crawled through the culvert after that last exchange, jumped up as the train covered his movements, and lit out.

At the edge, he looked down the slope toward the outskirts of Switchback. There was nobody on the gently inclined, bare, eroded slope to the first fence line. The bastard who'd shot at him had made it to the cover of those railroad sheds and the shanties past them. Longarm considered strollling on down to ask anyone he met what they might have seen, but it seemed a waste of time. If anyone had anything to say, Sheriff Murphy would hear about it, sooner or later.

The deputy recrossed the tracks, and after some coaxing and cussing, got back aboard the chestnut. He rode on his way again without further incident, chewing an unlit cheroot as he dusted himself off and tried to puzzle out what had happened. If whoever'd shot at him was the same one playing Wendigo, Wendigo's methods weren't subtle. Could those others simply have been *shot*?

That might explain why the Wendigo took the heads. If he was trying to spook the Blackfoot with spirit killings, he wouldn't want corpses left about with bullets in their skulls. On the other hand, the sound of a gunshot carried for some distance, and nobody'd heard any.

Who was that fellow back East who said he'd patented some newfangled gadget that could silence the muzzle blast of a gun? There'd been a piece about it in *Frank Leslie's Illustrated Weekly*. A silenced rifle might explain a lot, but the shots just fired at him had sounded like a plain old .44-40. Even with a silencer, the Wendigo would have to be a fancy marksman to pick folks off in the dark from any distance. Luckily, whoever'd just been blazing away at him hadn't been too good a shot.

Aloud, he muttered, "Shit, a man picks up a lot of enemies packing a badge. Could have been just about anyone."

He passed a reservation marker where, though the locals trespassed their cows a mite along the edges, the brush began to thin out, replaced by the short-grass God had put there in the first place. The Blackfoot didn't have enough stock to graze this far from the agency. The prairie hereabouts was unspoiled. The land was tough enough to take the antelope and jack's occasional attentions. With the buffalo shot off, the virgin range was fat enough to seem indecent. Lots of last summer's straw was still standing. He'd have to tell Cal Durler it was time they either burned it off on purpose or had a wildfire from the sparks thrown by a passing train.

He followed the right-of-way, noting a couple of cuts he considered high enough for someone attempting to get aboard a train without a ticket, but when he took the time to investigate each one for sign, he found none. He came to the place where they'd found Roping Sally and swung away to head for the agency. All he'd learned was that someone was out to kill him, but he'd known that much before.

He found Nan Durler alone at the agency. She said her husband had driven Prudence Lee into town and added, "You should have met them on the road."

Longarm said, "Didn't come back by way of the wagon trace. Is Miss Lee leaving?"

"No, she said she had some shopping to do. They'll likely be back for supper in a few hours. What happened to you? You look like you've been rolling in the dirt!"

"I have. The dust'll brush out of my clothes, but I could use a bath and a fresh shirt."

"We've a washtub in the back shed you could use," she offered, "if you've a mind to. I'll boil some water and fetch you a towel and soap."

Longarm left his coat and gun rig on the bed in the guest room and lugged four buckets of pump water to the tub as the Indian agent's wife put two big kettles on the kitchen range. She served him coffee at the table while they waited for the water to heat up.

He noticed that Nan wasn't having any as she sat across the table from him. When he commented on this, she brushed a strand of hair from her forehead and sighed, "It seems all I do out here is drink that goddamn coffee. Next thing you know I'll be dipping snuff. I'm beginning to feel like one of those white-trash girls I used to feel so sorry for."

"I reckon it does get tedious out here for a woman alone, but you've got Prudence Lee to talk with, now."

"Good God, she's no more company than my husband! All either of them seems interested in are these infernal Indians! Prudence prattles endlessly about their heathen souls and Calvin's up half the night fretting about his balance sheets! You'd think it was *important* that they got his model farm working on a paying basis, for heaven's sake!"

Longarm took a slow sip of his coffee. "Well, it's likely important to Cal. He's got a heap of responsibilities out here for a man so young."

"So young is right! Sometimes I feel like I'm his mother. The trouble is, I never married him to be his mother."

"Well," he tried to console her, "you'll doubtless have some real kids to mother, sooner or later."

"With Calvin?" She laughed, a bit wildly. Then she stared at the spoon she was bending out of shape between her fingers on the table and muttered, "Not hardly. A woman needs a *man* to be a mother."

Longarm rose from the table, leaving half of his cup filled, and said uncomfortably, "Uh, I'll fetch my fresh shirt and such. Water's boiling now."

He went to his room and dug out some clean underwear before heading for the porch shed. He noticed Nan was still at the table, fidgeting with the spoon. He went out back and closed the shed door behind him before he remembered that he'd forgotten to pour the boiling kettles into his tepid well water. He hesitated, then decided he could get as clean in cold water.

He stripped, hanging his clothes on the nails Calvin had driven in the plank walls, and gingerly got into the tub, hunkering down in the well water, which was neither warm nor freezing. He lathered himself with the washrag and turned the water chocolate-brown with trail dust. It would likely dry somewhat gritty on him, but at least he wouldn't smell bad in his fresh shirt.

The door opened. Nan Durler was standing there with a kettle. Stark naked.

Her voice was calm as she said, "You forgot the hot water for our bath."

Longarm studied the brown water between his wet knees as he answered in a desperately casual tone, "*Our* bath, ma'am? This tub's a mite small for two and, uh, your man might think me a mite forward if he came home to find us like this."

"I told you they'll be in town for hours," she reassured him. "You just stay the way you are and I'll put a foot on either side and sort of sit down facing you. I think we'll both fit right nicely, don't you?"

"Nan, you're a married woman," he protested.

"Come on, you know you want me."

"What I want or don't want ain't the point. Your husband is a friend of mine," he told her.

"Would to God he'd be more friendly to *me*! I *need* it, Long-arm! I need a man inside me so bad I can taste it! Come on, we've got all afternoon. If you don't want to do it here, let's go back inside and do it right on the bed!"

She moved her blond pubis provocatively and laughed hysterically. "You can have me on the bed. You can have me on the kitchen table. I don't care where we do it, just so we do it, right now!"

"Ma'am, I wish you'd go put some clothes on. I'm done washing and I'd like to get out and put my pants on."

"You've got a hard-on, haven't you? You don't fool me with

that shy act! I'll bet you've lost count of the women you've had."

"Never occurred to me to keep a tally."

He saw she wasn't going to leave. So as she stood there, naked, watching, he got out of the tub, erection and all, and proceeded to dry himself off.

She sighed, "Oh, that's a *nice* one!"

Longarm tried to keep his voice level as he said, "I'd be lying if I said I didn't want to, for you are one handsome gal, even with your clothes on. But we'd best forget we had the notion, Nan. I know we've been acting sort of silly, but no harm's been done and let's forget it, huh?"

As he tried to dress she dropped the kettle and threw herself against him, bare breasts pressed to his naked chest as she wrapped her arms around him and insisted, "Just one time! I'm going crazy!"

"Yep, that's likely what's the matter with you, gal. Lucky I got a mite more self-control."

"Control? You must be made out of iron! What's the matter with you? Who would ever know?"

"*We* would, Nan. Maybe that wouldn't bother you, but I ain't done here, and I'd find it sort of difficult looking your man in the eye if I was to abuse his hospitality while his back was turned."

She suddenly stepped back, jeering, "What's the matter with you? Ain't I good enough for you?"

"Honey," he said gently, "I've bedded down with gals who couldn't hold a candle to you when it comes to looking pretty. But none of 'em were married to my friends."

"Oh, my, aren't we godly and pious today? Next, you'll have me down on my knees, repenting my wicked advances!"

"Not hardly. God is one thing, fooling with a friend's wife is another. I'm going to forget we had this conversation, Nan. But, if you don't like your husband, have the decency to just up and leave him. It ain't seemly for a pretty gal like you to carry on like this."

"I just need to be pleasured, damn it! I haven't been loved properly since I don't know when and it's only natural to do what needs doing!"

"Well, sure it is. But the only thing that makes us humans better than most other brutes is, well, that we *ain't* brutes. The Lord gave us common sense to go with our desires. So let's use some, and forget this whole thing."

"I thought a real man had to have all the loving he could get."

"No, a real man doesn't. A bull in the field, a dog in an alley, or a kid with a hard-on doesn't worry much about the who and how of it, but us grown-ups study on it before we go leaping at folks. I'll tell you the truth, I'm going to have hard-ons for a month over you, and I'll likely kick myself for being a fool someday, when I hear you've run off with a passing whiskey drummer or been caught with some cowhand. But when you bust this marriage up, it won't be with *me*. So, while my pecker will tease me over lost opportunities, my conscience will be clear." He stopped to catch his breath, amazed that he'd delivered such a long-winded sermon. He felt as self-righteous as a revival meeting Bible-beater, which he took as a sure sign that his resistance was breaking down.

"Oh, shit!" Nan exploded, "you think I don't know about that half-breed girl and you?"

"Don't know what Miss Two-Women might have said while you and she were jawing, ma'am. So I'll not defend myself, save to point out that I never met anyone she was married to."

"You . . . bastard!" she shrilled, turning from him to flounce out of the shed. She looked as nice going away as she had facing him, and Longarm sighed wistfully as he buttoned up his shirt.

"Damn fool," he told himself, "she'll likely play that trick the Egyptian's old woman pulled on Joseph in the Good Book and tell Calvin I tried to screw her, anyway!"

That was something to ponder as he finished dressing. If Nan tried to revenge herself on him by playing Potiphar's wife, Cal would likely come after him with a gun. Damn. Maybe he'd been too hasty, as well as mean to his poor pecker. A man could get killed either way and she'd purely had one nice little rump!

He finished dressing and decided to let Nan cool a while before he went back inside. He went down the back steps and walked over to the corral. He didn't have anything to do there, but at least if he was out here where the Indians in the other houses could see him with his pants on . . .

Then he grinned as he spied a dot on the horizon and recognized it as Calvin and Prudence driving back from town. They were two hours earlier than Nan had expected them to be. He hadn't just been decent; he'd been goddamned lucky.

Prudence Lee had purchased a box of vittles in Switchback along with her other supplies. She insisted that everyone eat at her house that night, the house Real Bear had been murdered in. Longarm didn't go into the bedroom, but he hoped it had been cleaned up since last he'd seen it. The front room was cluttered with a big bass drum and religious pictures she'd cut out and tacked to the whitewashed walls. The two women went out to the kitchen to fuss over the tinned food she'd brought from town while Longarm and the Indian agent sat on the porch steps, smoking as the sun went down.

Longarm mentioned the strange Indians he'd heard about in town and Calvin said, "I know. Rain Crow said he'd try to find out if they were staying with anyone out here."

"Isn't he with those Blackfoot that the Paiute missionary's visiting with?"

"No, not if I can believe Rain Crow. Tell me something, Longarm. You know Rain Crow as well as, or better than, I do. How far would you trust that boy?"

"About as far as I'd trust most, I reckon. Why?"

"I get the feeling he's hiding something from me. He doesn't seem at all interested in catching whoever's been selling whiskey to his tribesmen; the other day, I was sure I smelled some on his breath."

"That was likely my fault," Longarm said. "I shared a bottle with him the night we found Yellow Leggings and Roping Sally."

"I'm not talking about that far back. I think he's been drinking recently."

"Maybe he has. I had a couple of drinks this afternoon. You reckon I'm fixing to scalp you?"

"It's not the same. You and I are white men."

Longarm took a drag of smoke and blew a thoughtful ring before he nodded and said, "I know. When Indians get drunk, they sing funny. Most white boys sing 'O'Riley's Daughter,' or 'The Girl I Left Behind Me,' when they get falling-down drunk. Can't make head or tail out of those Indian songs."

"Come on," Durler said. "You know how many drunken Indians have gotten in trouble."

"Yep. Some Indian drunks are mean as hell. But the meanest drunk I ever met was a trail boss called Ben Thompson— No, come to think of it, I met a jasper called Doc Holliday last year, who was even meaner. I do so wish they wouldn't let mean fellows drink, don't you?"

"You're funning me, but it's no laughing matter. I'm not supposed to let my Indians get at firewater."

"Hell, *you* ain't been serving it to them, have you?" the deputy asked.

"No, but if it's on the reservation—"

"There can't be all that much of it, or, if there is, your Blackfoot hold their liquor better than most folks in Abilene or Dodge. You've got enough on your plate just trying to make cowboys out of them. Try and make *sober* cowboys out of anybody and I'll show you an easier task, like walking on water or feeding the Blackfoot Nation on loaves and fishes."

The Indian agent sighed and said, "I know you think I take my job too seriously. Nan says I worry more about my Indians than I do her. But, damn it, somebody has to worry about them. They're like children. If someone doesn't help them, they're as doomed as the buffalo!"

Longarm shook his head wearily and said, "You're wrong a couple of ways, Cal. They ain't kids; they're folks. Likely not much smarter or dumber than the rest of us. As to 'the poor Indian, fading away like the snows of yesteryear,' there are more Indians now, counting breeds living as whites, than there were when Columbus found and misnamed them."

"That's crazy, Longarm!" Durler said. "Why, there's hardly an Indian east of the Mississippi and this whole territory used to be Indian land until—"

"Until we took it all away from them and packed them tighter on these reservations," Longarm interrupted. "I'm talking about population figures, not land. Before we crowded them, they were wandering hunters or small farmers, scattered in bands of maybe thirty-odd souls hither and yon. Little Big Horn never would have happened if the far-flung bands hadn't been snowballed into a real army-sized gathering of the clans. You started here with a fair-sized reservation for Blackfoot, right?"

"Of course," the agent agreed.

"Only now, you've got Bloods and Piegans on the same land, and if I know the B.I.A., they'll be shipping you stray Shoshone and leftover Flatheads any day now, as the cattle country expands with this beef boom. I wouldn't worry about 'the noble savage' fading away on you, Cal. He's having kids like everyone else, and getting sardined on such little land as we see fit to set aside for him in odd, godforsaken corners."

"All right, what would you do, Longarm?" Durler asked.

"I'd start by treating them like *folks*. I'd give them full citizenship and leave 'em the hell alone."

"You can't be serious! Why, right this minute, the Apache are running around killing folks and—"

"I'd make Indians obey the law, like everybody else," Longarm cut in. "If a white man or a colored man kills somebody, we call it murder. When an Indian gets mean, we make a policy."

Durler said, "Well, I don't make the policy, and you've got to admit these Blackfoot aren't enthusiastic to learn about herding or farming."

"Why should they be?" Longarm asked. "If you were in jail and some nice warden told you he aimed to teach you a trade, would you stop thinking about busting out?"

"I see your point. But, like I said, I don't make the policy. So there ain't much I can do about it, here."

"Sure, there is. You can ease off and ride with a gentler hand on the reins. I've smelled some sour mash on a few breaths since I came here, but what of it? Last mean drunk who came at me was as white as you are. I'd worry more about catching the Wendigo and holding the tribe this side of the border than I would about sociable drinking."

Before they could argue further, Prudence Lee came out to tell them supper was served.

The missionary was a good cook, but the meal was uncomfortable for Longarm. He found himself facing Nan Durler across the table, and while her eyes stayed on her beans, Longarm couldn't help wondering what she'd been saying in the kitchen to Prudence. He'd learned a long time ago, the hard way, that women were even worse than men about kissing and telling. For all the fretting and fussing about so-called fallen women, he'd noticed fallen women bragged like anything about all the men they'd fallen with. Prudence Lee said something to him, so he risked a look her way. The missionary woman met his eyes innocently as she repeated her request that he pass the salt. But that didn't mean much; Nan hadn't let on she'd known about him and Gloria Two-Women, until she'd tried to seduce him in the bathtub.

He wondered what Prudence Lee would say if he asked to sleep on her couch; not that he was about to ask her such a foolish thing. There was no way he was going to get out of spending another night under Nan Durler's roof, without it looking odd as hell to her husband.

"Someone just rode up outside," said Calvin Durler, breaking in on Longarm's worries.

Longarm said, "I heard it. Sounds like an unshod pony. One of your Blackfoot, I suspicion."

The two men excused themselves from the table and went out on the porch. Rain Crow was sitting his pony in the last rays of the sun. He called out, "I have found the Paiute Ghost Dancer. He told some people he was going off alone to make medicine. He told them he was calling on the ghosts in a place where Indians had fought a good fight. When I thought about it, I knew where the place had to be."

Durler looked blank, but Longarm nodded and said, "That abandoned homestead. It's the only battleground of the Shining Days on this reservation."

Rain Crow nodded and said, "Yes. Long ago, the Indians won there. The legends say the white settler fought well before they overran him. The Paiute must have thought to meet the ghosts of those who fell in the old fight. Instead, he met Wendigo!"

Both white men looked surprised and Rain Crow nodded. "Yes, the man was dead when I found him. He was wearing his medicine shirt, too, but it did no good. Perhaps Wovoka's medicine was only meant to protect us from white people."

Longarm raised an eyebrow and said, "You sort of *grin* when you tell your tale, Rain Crow. I didn't know you found the Wendigo so infernally funny!"

"Wendigo is not what I'm laughing about. When I first found the Paiute out there, I was very frightened. But it came to me, riding in, that the Wendigo didn't want a no-good white man's Indian like me. He came for a Dream Singer who said the spirits were his *friends*."

Chapter 13

It was dark by the time Rain Crow had led Longarm and Calvin Durler out to where he'd left the body. But the Indian had his bull's-eye lantern and Durler had brought a big coal-oil lamp from the house.

The Paiute Dream Singer's beheaded cadaver sat propped against the sod walls of the old house in what was left of his pathetic buckskin medicine shirt. The garment had been slashed to ribbons, too, and the dead man's entrails lay in his lap.

Longarm left the others to fiddle with the body as he circled the entire site with Rain Crow's bull's-eye, sweeping the prairie sod with the beam carefully and walking slowly. Then he shook his head wearily and walked back to join the others, saying, "I can see where the Paiute came in. I can see where Rain Crow came and went. I found some fresh rabbit shit, too. That's all the sign there is."

Durler shook his head and said, "We're in trouble. I was just getting used to your notion about the railroad right-of-way."

The lawman nodded. "I know. I like it, too, but we're a good three miles from the tracks this time. If he wasn't riding that rabbit, he must have flown in and out on a magic carpet."

"It's black as a bitch out here, Longarm. Are you sure you couldn't have missed something?" Durler asked.

"Not a hell of a lot. We've had some wind since I was out here last."

Durler asked what that was suppposed to mean. Before Longarm could answer, the Indian snorted in annoyance and said, "There has been no rain. The dry grass is dusty. Don't you people *look* at the earth you think you *own*?"

Longarm explained, "There's a film of dust on the north side of nearly every stem and blade. Nobody's been over this ground for at least a full day. When was that last north wind, Rain Crow? About this time last night?"

"Later than this. You read sign well, for a white man."

"There you go, Cal. You've got two expert opinions against the simple scientific fact that what we're saying isn't possible."

He shined the bull's-eye beam near Durler's boots and added, "You see where you just walked through this dry straw, Cal?

According to all the rules of evidence, before we got here, two men came in and only one rode out. If I didn't know Rain Crow had good alibis for other such killings, I'd have no choice but to arrest him. I'd have no trouble, selling it to a grand jury, either. Anyone can plainly see no other human being came within a country mile of this dead Paiute before *we* got here!"

Rain Crow protested, "I did not do it! What kind of a fool would kill a man and leave his own sign? If I wanted to fool you—"

"Hold on, old son," Longarm cut him off. "I'm not accusing you. Just reading the sign as it was left for me. Hell, I know you could have dragged some brush through the dusty grass or maybe left some false sign, if that had been your notion."

"I don't like to be accused, even in fun. Everyone knows I did not like the dead man. If you keep talking like that, the people will say I killed him!"

Durler asked, "You think that was the intention, Longarm? To somehow frame Rain Crow for the killing?"

The deputy pulled at a corner of his mustache. "I don't know. Whoever killed this poor medicine dreamer had no way of knowing who'd find the body. As far as that goes, the ants and carrion crows might well have picked this old boy clean before *anybody* ever found him. We're way the hell and gone out on the prairie and— Son of a bitch! *That* doesn't make sense, either!"

"What doesn't make sense, Longarm?" Rain Crow asked.

"The Wendigo's *reasons*. Up to now, I've been working on the notion that these spooky killings were to scare the Blackfoot. All the others were killed and messed up where they'd be found quickly. This poor bastard might never have been found at all. It looks like pure, crazy spite work, after all! You'd best see about getting this body back to the agency for burial. I hope you boys won't take it unfriendly, but I'm riding into Switchback, straight from here."

"You think the killer's in Switchback?" said the agent.

Longarm shrugged. "Don't know where he is. Don't even know how the son of a bitch got in or out of here. Might know more if I could ask some questions. As you see, that Paiute ain't talking much."

Leaving the two of them to dispose of the remains, Longarm mounted and rode for Switchback in the dark. He didn't really have his next moves planned, but at least this got him out of spending the night at the agency, and somebody might have noticed something unusual.

The moon was rising as he rode down the slope into the dimly lit streets of Switchback. It was still early and a rinky-tink piano was playing "Garryowen" in the saloon. Some old boy had probably requested it after reminiscing about old times. The Seventh Cav had marched to Little Big Horn to the strains of that old Irish jig and every time someone said "Indian" in Montana, some fool was bound to bring up Custer.

The land office was closed, but the railroad station wasn't. He tethered his chestnut and went in to send a progress report to Denver, knowing Billy Vail was likely having a fit. Then he asked the railroad telegrapher, "When was the last train in from the west, this afternoon?"

The telegrapher said, "There was one about noon. Eastbound passenger express will be coming through in an hour or so. It don't figure to stop here, but we can flag her down for you if need be, Marshal."

Longarm shook his head. "Ain't going anywhere. Just asking about your timetable. Was that noonday train a slow freight, with flatcars and such?"

The telegrapher frowned. "Flatcars? Don't think so. It was a fast freight, bound for Chicago with live beef. I could ask Dispatch if they were deadheading any flats."

"Don't bother. What I had in mind was no cattle train high-balling downgrade."

He took out two cheroots, offered one to the telegrapher, and thumbed a light, muttering, "Damn! Just as I was hoping I had it figured, the son of a bitch went and busted all my bubbles!"

"I thank you for the smoke, Marshal. But I don't know what the hell you're talking about."

"Neither do I. Is your yard bull, Mendez, patrolling out back?"

"He should be. Old Mendez drinks a mite. If you don't find him, you'll find one of his sidekicks. Be careful about creeping up on 'em sudden, though. That one Irish kid is quick on the trigger as well as a mite hard of hearing. Come up on him sudden and—"

"Never mind. No sense in poking around dark tracks at night, spooky yard bulls or no. You could likely tell me if there was a work train, or something slow like that, fixing to leave the yards tonight, couldn't you?"

"I could, but there ain't. Next slow freight headed west will be at ten tomorrow night. Empty cattle cars, due in from the East. They'll be dropping 'em off for loading, all up the line and through the night."

"Anything coming east? Say around midnight?"

The telegrapher picked up some dispatch flimsies from his table and consulted them before he nodded and said, "Yeah. Here's a string of flats, lowballing through as the other orders allow it. Flats empty from unloading telegraph poles, over in the Great Basin sage country. There's a midnight passenger train using the tracks, first. Then the lowballing empties will likely poke on in."

Longarm thanked his informant, and leaving his mount where it was, moseyed over to the saloon to drink while he studied on where he'd spend the night and what in hell was going on.

In the saloon, he found Jason, the army scout, talking to the piano player, who'd stopped playing "Garry-owen" long enough to wet his whistle. Jason waved Longarm over and said, "I owe you a drink, don't I?"

"Don't know who's ahead, but I'll take it."

As Jason ordered another shot for himself and a glass of Maryland rye for Longarm, the deputy asked, "Was that old cavalry tune your notion?"

"No. I just got done explaining to the professor, here, about this being a time for other songs. How soon do you figure your Blackfoot out there aim to make their move for Canada?"

"You can tell your soldier boys not to bank on any medals this summer. Somebody killed the damn fool who was trying to talk them into it."

"Do tell? Some friends of mine likely made a long trip for nothing, then. We *are* talking about a Paiute named Ishiwatl, ain't we?"

"I don't know the bird's name well enough to say it, but that sounds close. You say somebody was looking for him?"

"Yeah, out at the fort. A posse of Crow lawmen just arrived with a warrant for his arrest. I was fixing to bring 'em out to the reservation, come morning. You say somebody shot him?"

"That's close enough. He's deader than hell. These Indian police looking for the Dream Singer would sound like Sioux to folks, wouldn't they?"

"Reckon so. Crow and Sioux both talk Dakota. Why do you ask?"

Longarm chuckled and explained, "You've just handed me the first good news I've had all day. I heard there were some strange

Sioux hereabouts and I've had the Blackfoot going crazy trying to locate 'em on the reservation."

The barkeep brought their drinks and they downed them in silence. Longarm ordered them each another, and Jason said, "I'll tell the Crows they can rest easy when I ride back to the fort later tonight. That Ishiwatl was one bad Paiute, to hear 'em tell it. Now, if someone would just shoot that damn Wovoka himself, we'd likely have some peace and quiet. What was the killing about? More of that Ghost Dance shit?"

"Sort of. You might say Ishi-whatever got into a theological dispute with the Wendigo."

The scout whistled and said, "Another one of *them* things, huh?"

The piano player asked, "What's a wendigo?"

Longarm said, "I wish I knew, Professor. Jason, you're a professional tracker. How would you cross maybe two or three hundred yards of dusty stubble without leaving sign?"

"I'd ride around it. There's no way to *jump* three hundred yards."

"That's the way I see it. When are you heading back to the fort?"

"A couple of hours, maybe. Came into town for some tail, but the professor, here, tells me French Mary's been rented for the night by a big spender off the Double Z. I was just fixing to try my luck at Madam Kate's. You want to come along?"

"Not tonight. French Mary's the little redhead with the saucy mouth, ain't she?"

"Yeah, and she does use it nicely. But I can't wait around all night for that damn cowboy to get done and, anyway, I got delicate feelings. Don't like to kiss a gal right after she's been . . . well, you likely know why they call her French Mary."

The piano player said, "There's a new gal at Madam Kate's who ain't been used all that much. They say she ain't more than sixteen or so and still likes her new job."

Jason laughed and said, "There you go, Longarm. What say we go over there and get her while she's hot?"

"You go, if you've a mind to," Longarm said. "I've got other fish to fry."

"What's the matter, don't you like tail, or are you too proud to pay for it?" the scout gibed.

"Hell, everybody pays for it, one way or another. I've just never liked cold cash transactions," Longarm said.

"Shit, whores are the only honest women I've ever met," Jason observed. "I'd far rather give the gal the two dollars than shilly-shally about with 'nice girls' who wind up with your money anyway."

"Like I said, we all pay, one damn way or another, and I've often said to myself it makes more sense to just slap down the cash right off. I suspicion I must be a sissy."

Jason laughed, and before they could continue their discussion, the land agent, Chadwick, came in to join them. Or, rather, to join Longarm and the professor, for he didn't know Jason, except by sight. The scout, as if inhibited by the other federal man, finished his drink and left in pursuit of carnal pleasure.

The professor went back to the piano to play "Drink To Me Only With Thine Eyes," for some reason, and Chadwick said, "I have a wire for you here, someplace."

He took a folded scrap of paper from his frock coat and handed it to Longarm, who read:

WHAT'S HOLDING UP THE PARADE QUESTION STOP YOU
ARE OVERDUE AND NEEDED HERE STOP REPORT TO
DENVER AT ONCE STOP SIGNED VAIL

Chadwick said, "I could open up and send a reply for you." But Longarm shook his head and answered, "He's likely not in his office and you're closed for the night and God knows how long, remember?"

"Won't you get in trouble, ignoring your superior's orders?"

"Hell, I'm already in trouble," Longarm laughed.

"No notions about those killings last week yet?"

"*Had* some. They blew up in my face this evening when the Wendigo hit again."

Chadwick looked astonished and gasped, "Jesus! You must be joking!"

"Nothing funny about it. This one was *really* spooky. The others were almost impossible to figure, but this time the Wendigo outdid himself. Killed another Indian in what must have been broad daylight, then sashayed off at least three miles to the nearest cover, without leaving a single sign coming or going."

"Good God, I can't understand it!"

"That makes two of us. But I made a promise not to leave here until I caught the son of a bitch. So I'll likely write Marshal Vail a letter in a week or so."

"I don't envy you. Where are you staying tonight, the agency?"

"Nope. Figured to bed down here in town after I ask around some more."

"You're welcome to stay at my place," Chadwick offered. "I stay up late and I've got a spare room you can use."

"That's neighborly of you, but no thanks. It's early yet, and while I'm asking questions about this job I'm on, I might get lucky and meet somebody prettier than you. No offense, of course."

Chadwick laughed and said, "Stay away from Madam Kate's. They say a couple of her gals give more than tail. The doc's been treating one of 'em for the clap, and he says there ain't no real cure."

Longarm thanked him for the warning and left. He went to get his chestnut and mounted up, then sat there, fishing out a cheroot, as he pondered his next move.

He knew he didn't have a next move. He was chasing himself around in circles to avoid another sparring match with Nan Durler. He rode slowly along the street toward the end of town where Roping Sally's spread had been. The spread was still there, just outside of town, of course, but somehow he didn't feel like it was there anymore. Had he really ever spent that wild night, just up ahead where the lights of Switchback faded into blackness? It seemed as if it had never happened. The poor woman was hardly cold in her grave and he remembered her as if he had known her long ago, before the War. *You've got nothing to feel guilty about,* he told himself firmly. What was done was done and the only duty he owed Sally was to find her killer. He was only feeling fretful because someone had made a fool of him. It seemed like everyone in Montana had him figured for a fool and it was getting tedious.

He rode on into the darkness toward Sally's, running the whole thing through his head again, once more stumbling over the impossibilities of this whole infernal case. He slowed his mount, knowing he really didn't want to pass the dark, empty cabin where he'd slept with what he now remembered as a beheaded horror. Maybe he'd just hunker down on the prairie someplace. . . . "Damn it!" he swore. "There's a feather bed and a warm breakfast waiting for you out there. And you've done nothing to be ashamed of!"

He reined in and swung his mount's head toward the west, his mind made up to ride back to the agency and brazen it out. As he turned, something sounding like bird wings, *big* bird wings, fluttered past his head and snatched off his Stetson!

Longarm threw himself to one side, grabbing for his saddle

gun as he heard the thing coming through the darkness again! He
rolled out of the saddle and landed in the roadside ditch as it flew
over him, flapping.

The chestnut had been spooked by the sound, too, and ran off a
few yards, snorting nervously, as Longarm crouched in the grassy
ditch with his rifle at port, ready for anything.

But nothing happened. He stayed frozen and silent as he
strained his ears. He stayed that way for a very long time. For
though the moon was rising now, it was still nearly pitch-black
around him and that thing had swooped at him like a diving eagle who'd known where it was going!

Could it have been an owl? Too big. No owl he'd ever heard
had flapped as loud and mean as that. For that matter, he couldn't
remember ever running into an *eagle* that size! He'd been attacked
by an eagle as a kid, trying to collect some eggs for some foolish
kid's reason, and the sound of its angrily flapping wings had been
a pale imitation of whatever had just snatched off his hat!

He was still wondering about it when the moon pushed an edge
above the horizon and he could see the pale streak of the road better. The road was empty. The overgrazed weeds lay ghostly gray
around him for at least a hundred yards, and there was nothing
there to see.

After a while, he rose slowly to his feet and walked over to his
hat, where it lay in the road. He examined it for talon marks, and
finding none, put it on. Then he clucked soothingly to the chestnut
and caught the reins. The horse was still nervous, but he soothed it
and remounted. He kept the saddle gun across his thighs as he resumed his way west toward the agency.

It took him a while to get there, this time. The rising moon kept
telling him he was alone as he slowly rode across the prairie, straining his ears for the sound of those mysterious wing beats. But,
though there was nothing to see and not a sound to be heard out on
the lonely range, he kept swinging around to look behind him.

Longarm spent the morning at the fenced quarter-section, showing a bunch of Blackfoot kids how to twirl a throw rope. By the
time he saw that their interest was flagging a bit, he had two of
them getting the knack of a passable butterfly and at least five
who could drop a community loop over a fence post one out of
three tries. He called a halt to the lesson. If he hadn't gotten them
at least curious about roping, by now, they weren't like any other
kids he'd ever met.

As he ambled back toward the agency buildings, one of the older boys fell in beside him to say shyly, "The white man's rope tricks are fun, but my father says the ways of the cowboy are not our ways."

Longarm said, "I don't mean any disrespect for your elders, Little Moon, but your daddy likely doesn't know that the art of roping was invented by Indians. Us American hands learned roping from the Mexicans, who learned it from the Aztec, Chihuahua, and such."

"You're making fun of me! There were never Indian cowboys before you people came here!"

"Nope. No white cowboys, neither. The cowboy was born when the Spanish horsemen got together with the Indian hunters who roped deer and antelope, down Mexico way. The vaquero, buckaroo, or cowboy owes as much to the red man as the white. Down in the Indian Nation, there are some Cherokee and Osage cowboys few men could hold a candle to. Jesse Chisholm, who blazed the Chisholm Trail, was a Cherokee."

"Oh, we know about the Five Civilized Tribes," Little Moon said scornfully. "They are not real Indians. My father says they live like white men."

"Your daddy's right about that point, Little Moon, but I doubt if the Cherokee would agree that they weren't real Indians. In their day they were wild enough, and the Osage lifted their fair share of white folks' hair in the Shining Times. All in all, though, the Five Tribes, Osage, and such Comanche as have taken to herding longhorns are living better than you Blackfoot, these days."

The boy walked head-down, pondering, before he shrugged and said, "I don't know. I think it was better in the Shining Times, hunting the buffalo and Utes."

"Maybe," Longarm concurred, "but those days are gone forever. As I see it, you've got two choices ahead of you, Little Moon. You can learn new ways for the new times coming, or you can sit out here on a government dole, feeling sorry for yourself while the rest of the world leaves you behind."

"Wovoka says more Shining Times are coming. If all of us stood together, we could go back to the old ways and—"

"Wovoka's full of shit," the deputy cut in. "I hope you won't take it unfriendly, son, but you could gather every tribe in one place, armed and mounted, and one brigade of cavalry would be pleased as punch to wipe you out. What happened on the Little Big Horn was a fluke; old Custer only had about two hundred green troops with him. The army has new Gatling and Hotchkiss guns now, too. So at best, that gives you *three* ways to go. You can learn to make your own money, or you can take the little money the B.I.A. might dole out as it sees fit, or you can just go crazy with the Ghost Dancers and die. Meanwhile, you might work on what I just showed you about roping. You've got to loosen up and remember to swing the loop twice to open it up before you throw. Your aim ain't bad, but your throwing is too anxious."

Leaving the Indian youth to ponder his own future, Longarm walked past the agency to the back door of the cottage Prudence Lee was staying in. As he mounted the back steps to knock, she spied him through the screen door and opened it, saying, "I was just brewing some coffee. I'm afraid your suggestion about asking for Indian recipes turned out pretty dismally!"

He joined her in the kitchen as she waved him to a seat, explaining, "You forgot to tell me Indians put bacon grease instead of sugar in their coffee. Uncooked white flour dusted over canned pork and beans is rather ghastly, too!"

Longarm chuckled and said, "Lucky they didn't serve you grasshopper stew. The grasshoppers ain't all that bad, but the dog meat they mix in with it takes time to develop a taste for."

Prudence paled slightly. "Oh, dear, I did eat some chopped meat boiled with what I hoped was corn mush. You don't think—?"

"No, I was funning. They only eat stuff like that when they're really hungry, and old Cal's been seeing to it that the rations are fairly good. There's nothing wrong with Indian cooking. It's just that they have different tastes. I've met some who hated apple pie, and Apache would starve before they tasted fish. Some tribes look on eating fish the way we look on eating worms."

She grimaced as she put a cup of coffee in front of him and said, "I wonder if I'll ever get used to conditions out here. The Bible Society never told me what it would be like."

"They likely didn't know. Folks back East have funny notions about this part of the country. It ain't the Great American Desert Fremont said it was. It ain't the Golden West of Horace Greeley. It's just . . . different."

"I'm trying to adjust," she said with a sigh, "but I'm beginning to see how it might drive some women, well, strange."

He wondered if she was talking about Nan Durler, but he didn't ask. He said, "I came by to ask a favor, Miss Prudence. You were fixing to hold some sort of powwow here this evening, weren't you?"

"If you want to call it that. I've invited some of the women over for a class in infant care."

"I'd be obliged if you could leave 'em to their heathen ways with kids at least one more night, Miss Prudence. I've told Rain Crow and the other reservation police I want a tight curfew after sundown. Some of the squaws would be riding home in the dark, even if you were to cut 'em loose early. The moon won't be up before nine-thirty tonight, and I aim to have every Indian tucked in good by then."

"Oh, are you expecting trouble from those Ghost Dancers again? I thought the man behind it was just killed."

"Yes, ma'am, and what killed him might be on the prowl tonight."

"Oh, dear, then you do think the Wendigo may strike again tonight?"

Longarm shrugged. "Don't know. Don't aim to leave any man, woman, or child out alone on the prairie after dark, Wendigo or no. I'm going to have to ask you to spend the night next door with the Durlers, too. Rain Crow and Calvin will be sitting up all night with the doors locked and guns loaded. The Wendigo's been making me look like a fool—partly because I've been one. From now on, I ain't waiting for him to hit so I can chase him around like a bloodhound with nose trouble. I'm making sure, no matter how he's doing it or when he's figuring to do it again, that there won't be anybody out there in the night for him but *me!*"

"You can't hide an entire Indian tribe from that madman forever!"

"Don't aim to hide 'em forever. Just until I catch Mr. Wendigo."

"But even if the Indians cooperate, the reservation's so *big*! How can you hope to intercept anyone or anything out there in all those miles of darkness?"

"If I knew that, I'd know the Wendigo's methods, reasons, and likely who it was. Getting every possible victim out of the Wendigo's reach is the best first bite I've come up with. So, like I said, you'll help a heap by bunking down with the Durlers until it's safe for you to stay here all alone."

She sipped her own cup of coffee thoughtfully, and though she finally nodded, her voice was worried as she said, "I'll do it, but I won't like it. You know they've been fighting like cats and dogs next door."

"They'll be keeping company manners with you and Rain Crow

listening, Miss Prudence. They weren't fussing when I came in last night."

"You should have heard them earlier! These walls are thin, and if there is one thing I can't abide, it's hypocrisy— What's so funny?"

Longarm wiped his grin away and said, "I'd be out of a job if everybody suddenly took to being truthful. We're all a mite two-faced, Miss Prudence. I know we ain't supposed to be, but I reckon it's just human nature to keep our true feelings hidden."

She stared at him oddly and licked her lips before she brazened, "Well, *I* certainly try to be truthful in my dealings with everyone!"

"I know you try, ma'am. But tell me something. When's the last time you asked the lady next door why she was fussing with her man?"

"That's different. Hypocrisy's one thing, rudeness is another!"

"Maybe. But lies are what we call *other* folks' falsehoods. When it's *our* turn to bend things out of shape we generally have a more angelic reason." He sipped his coffee and added, "I suspicion the lies we tell ourselves are the biggest whoppers of them all."

Her eyes blazed defensively as she asked, "And just what sort of lies are you saying I tell myself, sir?"

He smiled gently and answered, "I never accused you, ma'am. It's funny how the less I accuse folks, the more they seem to want to tell me. I'm in a nosy line of work, so I'm probably better at reading the silences between folks' words."

"In other words, you're just fishing? Well, you can just fish somewhere else, then. For I've nothing to hide."

He nodded as if in agreement and sipped some more coffee. He didn't really give much of a damn about such secrets as a little sparrow-bird spinster-gal might have. He wasn't getting paid to find out what had driven her to reading Bibles for a living. But wasn't it a bitch how it spooked folks when you backed off just as the questions were getting close to home?

Prudence Lee said, "I suppose you think I'm as silly as poor Nan Durler, in my own way. But that really was another girl I was talking about."

"What girl was that, ma'am?" Longarm asked innocently. "The one back East who ran off on her husband? I'd almost forgotten about her."

"I'll bet you have. I'll bet you have a whole crazy story cooked up about my atoning for some dark, secret sin. But you're wrong. It was only a girl I knew, one time."

He nodded and said, "I know. Her story reminds me a lot of Madam LaMont, down Denver way."

"Who's Madam LaMont? She sounds like a—you know what!"

"Yep, that's what she was. Ran the most expensive parlor house on State Street, for a while. The poor old gal was atoning for a terrible mix-up."

Prudence looked shocked. "*Atoning?* Is that what they call being a prostitute, these days?"

"Well, some folks have odd notions on the subject of atonement. You see, Madam LaMont came West as a bride, back in the Pikes Peak Rush before the War. Her name was something else then, of course. Her husband was a preacher. He freighted her and a mess of Bibles to the gold camps, aiming to wash the sins of the miners away. The gal was likely fond of him, for they seemed happy. Then the preacher vanished, as did a gold camp redhead at the same time, who was said to be no better than she might have been."

"Heavens, the poor girl was deserted by her husband for a dance-hall girl?" She shook her head sadly.

"That's what she suspicioned, and it sort of jarred something loose inside her head. She took to drink and then, since it beat taking in washing, she started pleasuring men for pay. She must have been good at it, for the next thing anybody knew, she had the biggest fancy house in Denver. I reckon she was trying to get as far from the preaching trade as possible. But like I said, it was all a mix-up. Her husband hadn't done her wrong at all."

Prudence's eyebrows knit in confusion. "Indeed? But you said he ran off with this redhead!"

Longarm nodded. "That's what everybody thought. But a few years later someone found the redhead working in a house in Abilene, alone. Then, a short while later, some prospectors found the skeleton of a man down an abandoned mine shaft. Nobody ever figured out if he'd been robbed and thrown down it, or if he'd just fallen in, wandering about in search of souls to save."

"My Lord! You mean it was the woman's missing husband?"

"Yep. There were some shreds of clothing clinging to the bones and he was still packing the Bible Madam LaMont had given him with a sentimental inscription on the flyleaf. When they brought it to her, she went a mite crazy."

The girl gasped, and her hands flew up to press on either side of her face. "Oh, what a terrible story! To think that poor girl abandoned herself to a life of sin because of a ghastly mistake about an innocent man!"

Longarm reached out and patted Prudence's arm. "Well, it came out all right in the end. Madam LaMont ain't in that line of work anymore, but while she was, she got as rich as Croesus. So she lives in a big brownstone house on Sherman Avenue with her new husband, these days. He's rich, too, as well as understanding. They're both right happy and the madam still helps fallen women, orphans, and such. In her own way, she's likely done more good than she ever could have as the wife of a poor wandering preacher."

Prudence Lee tried not to smile as she said, "The moral of your tale is a bit grotesque, but I think I see it. Are you suggesting I'd do more for these Blackfoot by opening a parlor house on this reservation?"

"Not hardly. They've already got a mess of gals and a saloon. Old Snake Killer's cooking sour mash over at his place, judging by the smell. Don't tell Cal Durler, though. He frets about 'em drinking."

"Oh? And you approve of drunken Indians?" Prudence asked with a frown.

"Don't approve of drunken anybody. But they're less likely to get poisoned on their own home-brewed corn than they are on trade whiskey. Saves 'em money, too. You see, some men are going to drink, federal regulations or no. I figure it's better if they stick to cheap, pure bootleg, and confine it to the reservation."

"I won't tell on them, but I must say your ideas on law and order are rather cynical," the missionary observed.

"I'm a peace officer, ma'am. My job is keeping the peace, not pestering folks about what they do in the privacy of their own homes. Trouble with nitpicking over laws is that those fools in Congress write so many of 'em. When you get right down to it, everybody could be arrested if we enforced every law ever written. Lucky for us all, few lawmen have enough time or eyes at keyholes."

Prudence laughed. "I'll remember that the next time my secret lover comes to call on me with his wicked leer and French postcards." Her face reddened fetchingly at her daring little joke. She paused, gazing down into her coffee cup. When she had regained her sobriety, she looked up and continued, "Meanwhile, I've a

Bible class to teach. How soon do you think it will be safe for people to move about out here again?"

"Don't know. I'm leaving in a few minutes for Rabbit Gulch. That's a water stop, up the railroad line to the west. If I start this afternoon I should make it to the foothills in plenty of time."

"You're riding off the reservation in the *other* direction? What do you expect to find in Rabbit Gulch?"

"I'm not sure. But all I've found in Switchback is a lot of dead ends."

"Heavens! Do you think it's possible the Wendigo has been working out of another town we've never thought of?"

"Anything's possible, ma'am. And as you see, I *have* thought of it."

Chapter 14

The eastbound train of empty flatcars left Rabbit Gulch late. Nobody working for the railroad seemed to care when or where it arrived, as long as it didn't get in the way of paying traffic.

The moon had worked its way clear across the sky and was shining down now from the west. The rolling sea of buffalo grass all around was ash-gray, with occasional pitch-black clumps of soapweed here and there. Anything darker than the dry grass in the moonlight would be visible, if it was big enough and moving.

Longarm rode hunkered down in the shadow of the boxcars behind the locomotive, facing backward with a string of six flatcars between him and the caboose. His chestnut was in one of the empty reefers. The brakemen in the caboose had been told not to come forward across the flats until it was time to crank the brake wheels, just west of the grade into Switchback. Longarm hoped his orders would be obeyed. Anybody he spotted on the rocking planks back there was in trouble.

The train passed through a railroad cut and Longarm tensed as the flats he was watching were plunged into darkness by the shadow of the banks. Then he saw that he was still alone out here in the middle of the night. He was going to feel foolish as hell if he'd ridden all that way for nothing. Worse yet, he knew he only had one chance with this plan. He'd boarded the train in Rabbit Gulch at the last possible moment, but once they reached Switchback, one of the crew was bound to blab about the lawman's sudden interest in railroading. He'd known enough about human nature not to bother telling them to keep this ride a secret. He had to assume the secret would be out, after tonight, whether it was or not.

They ran through another cut, with no results. That didn't mean much. The son of a bitch he was laying for had nearly fifty miles of leeway out here. Besides, if he'd jumped off the westbound a couple of hours earlier, he'd have found nobody outdoors to play with, and not having any real reason to cover his tracks tonight, might not even be waiting for this train. A footprint here and another sign there wouldn't mean a thing in court, unless there was a victim found nearby.

"If I was him," Longarm muttered, "I'd walk back along the tracks as soon as I discovered the Indians were all holed up for the night. I'd suspicion someone was on to me and want to haul ass out. On the other hand, I'd have quit after Roping Sally's murder had the whole territory stirred up and looking for me, too."

He spotted something loping along beside the train to the north and stiffened. Then he saw it was only a coyote pup having fun, and after a while the animal dropped back out of sight. The train was doing about twenty on the open stretches, a bit slower up the grades. A coyote or a horse could run alongside easily enough for a quarter-mile or so. A man afoot would have to grab hold on a grade, or drop down from a cut. Yeah, he could relax for a few minutes along this stretch.

He stood and stamped his booted feet to ease his cramped thighs, then hunkered down again, bracing the Winchester across his knees as he chewed an unlit cheroot and mused, "Killing that Paiute just don't *fit*, even leaving aside the distance and the missing sign on that dusty grass. Unless the others were killed for no good reason at all, that Ghost Dance missionary was playing right into the hands of—whoever. If *I* was the Wendigo, I'd have killed almost anybody else first. Between the killings and that fool Paiute shaking his rattles, the tribe was just about ready to jump. Well, let's study on it that way and see who'd most want that Dream Singer dead."

Longarm suddenly brightened and said, "Hell, that's got to be it!" as the train chuffed through another deep cut. Then the flat-cars were rolling along in the moonlight once more and Longarm saw he was no longer alone.

An ink-black blob crouched on the planks, two cars back. Longarm rose slowly, the boxcar behind his back concealing his own dark outline, as he studied the form that had dropped from the rim of that last bank. It looked like a human being, sort of. It was on its feet now, and moving his way, as if seeking the same shadows he'd been hiding in. It walked peculiarly, on great big blobby feet, but a sudden shift of the moonlight flashed on the holstered gun it wore. It moved to the break between cars and leaped across, landing as quietly as a cat in that funny footgear. Longarm waited until it sort of danced the length of another car, jumped the gap, and was coming his way, before he called out, "That's close enough! Freeze in place and grab for some sky, friend!"

The Wendigo threw himself prone on the weathered planks and a blaze of gunfire answered Longarm's voice as a bullet slammed into the bulkhead of the reefer at his back. The shot was too wild to get excited over, so Longarm said, "You've had one free shot, you silly bastard! Now drop that fool gun and behave yourself!"

The Wendigo fired again at the sound of Longarm's voice. The round ticked the tail of Longarm's coat. So he swore softly and fired back. The Wendigo's head jerked up like he'd been punched in the jaw. Then, moaning like a wounded bear, he rolled away from the pistol he'd let fall to the planks and Longarm grunted, "Oh, shit!" and ran to grab him before he could fall between the cars.

Longarm didn't make it. Up in the cab, the engineer had heard the shots and was slowing down. But the Wendigo had fallen under the wheels!

Longarm jumped off, landing on one hip and rolling over twice in the grass beside the track as, up on the train, a brakeman yelled out, "You want us to hit the brakes?"

"Hell, yes!" shouted Longarm as he got to his feet, rifle at the ready. Then the train had rolled on, its squealing brakes hardly slowing it until the caboose was winking its red lights at him from half a mile away. Gingerly, Longarm walked over to the tracks, shining silver in the moonlight. He found one leg on the ties, with its foot wrapped in rope and straw-filled burlap. It had been sliced off by a wheel above the knee.

Longarm fished a match from his coat pocket and thumbnailed it alight. The gentle night breeze from the mountains blew it out, but not before he'd spotted the trunk a few feet to the west. He sighed and said, "Jesus, we had so much to *talk* about, too!"

The brake boss was trotting back from the halted caboose with a wildly swinging lantern, calling out, "What happened? Did you get him?"

Longarm said, "Your train helped. Wheels tore off his head, one arm, and both legs as he bounced along the ballast under it. Bring that light over here, will you? I suspicion that's his head against that rail, there."

The brake boss stopped and raised the lantern. Then, as the puddle of light swept over the battered human head lying on its bloody left cheek against a rail, he gagged and gasped, "My God! It's that Mex, Mendez! The yard bull from Switchback!"

Longarm said, "He wasn't a Mexican. He was from South America, where they rope cows different." He bent to remove something from the belt of the mangled yard bull's torso and held it up, explaining, "You call this thing a *bolo*. The gauchos use them, down there in Argentina. You hold this leather thong, whirl her around your head a few times, and let her go. These heavy balls spread out as she goes *whoom-whoom-whoom* through the air at you. He threw it at me one night, and it sounded like a big-ass bird."

"I know what a bolo is. But what in thunder was he out here throwing it at folks for? He's supposed to be tending to business in the Switchback yards!"

"Yeah, he let folks know he kept unsteady hours. Likely pretended to drink more than he really did, so his two kid helpers would cover for the times he wasn't where everyone thought he was. Nobody notices a railroad man getting on or off a slow freight. So he'd ride out here, drop off, and lie in wait like some beast of prey for anyone who came by. Then he'd hit them from behind with that bolo, rip them up and behead them, and just wait for another train going back. He didn't walk much, and he did it carefully in those big padded sacks tied over his boots."

"I can see how he got about. But why was he doing it, and what in thunder did he take those heads for?"

"Well," Longarm said, retrieving his hat from the ditch beside the roadbed, where it had landed when he jumped from the train, "I was aiming to ask him the why of it, but as you see, he doesn't have much to say now. The reason he took the heads with him was to keep us from seeing them. When the bolo thongs hit someone about the neck, the heavy balls spin in and hammer hell out of their heads and faces. Then, too, carrying off the heads was sort of spooky. You might say he was in the trade of being spooky, and I don't mind saying, he scared hell out of *me* a few times!"

The brake boss shook his head and said, "Mendez, the yard bull. Who'd have ever thought it! You reckon he was crazy, Deputy? A man would have to be crazy to do what he done, right?"

The deputy slapped his hat against his knee, raising a little puff of dust, then reshaped it with his hands and replaced it on his head, dead center. "Maybe. I'll know more after I figure out *why* he was doing it."

The coroner couldn't tell Longarm anything he might not have guessed about the cause of the Wendigo's death, but the papers had to be filled out, so, leaving the coroner to deal with the mangled remains, Longarm got on the federal wire at the land office. This time, the results were more interesting.

As he finished and rejoined Agent Chadwick in the front office, Longarm said, "Mendez had a record a mile long. He told me about killing a colored hobo in Omaha, but he left out some union-breaking activities and some questions the Saint Joe police wanted to ask him about a lady he left in his room when he checked out sudden, owing rent."

Chadwick asked, "Really? What did she say he'd done to her?"

"She didn't. Her throat was slit from ear to ear. Saint Joe thought maybe Mendez could explain this to them, but as you know, it ain't likely he'll be able to."

"But you've made the point that the man was a killer and at least a little crazy. So let me be the first to congratulate you."

"Congratulate me? What for?"

"What for? Why, damn it, you've solved your case! You caught the Wendigo and everyone can breathe easy again!"

Longarm took out a cheroot and lit it, saying, "Hell, it's just getting interesting. Did you know Mendez didn't savvy telegraph codes? I tapped out a message to him on the bar one day, and he never blinked an eyeball when I said a dreadful thing about his mother. He was a moody cuss, too."

"I don't follow you, Longarm. The man was a railyard bully boy, not a dispatcher. He wasn't supposed to know Morse code. Oh, you mean about the railroad's schedules, right?"

"Somebody had to tell him ahead of time when the slow trains were running across the reservation. He had no call to hang around the dispatch sheds, either."

"Boy! I'm glad *my* wire's not connected to the railroad's! I expect you'll be checking on that, right?"

"Already did. Our federal line's not tied in with the railroad's. I hope you understand I've got a job to do."

"I'm getting used to the idea. What did your friends in the Justice Department say about that scrape I got into a few years back?"

"Oh, you were telling me the truth. They said your boss had been a crook but that you'd had no way of getting at the missing money even if you'd aimed to."

"Thanks, I think. If you're not arresting me, these days, who *do* you have in mind for the Wendigo's confederate?"

"I'm keeping an open mind on that. It's possible Mendez had some other way of knowing the schedules. It'd take forever, which seems a mite long, to check out every switchman and train crewman who might have gossiped about who was running what to where. While I was using your wire, I got in touch with my boss. Marshal Vail says he's pleased about the Wendigo, but he's still pissed off at me for not catching that rogue half-breed, Johnny Hunts Alone."

"You know, I'd forgotten all about that."

"Denver didn't forget. The warrant I pack on Hunts Alone was the only reason I came up here in the first damn place. You might say this crap about the Wendigo, Mendez, or whomsoever was a side issue."

Chadwick laughed and said, "Some side issue! You scattered the poor bastard from hell to breakfast!"

Longarm smiled. "Well, he wasn't too tidy while he was alive. I'm sorry I shot him, though. He died too sudden, and before he could tell me some things I wished to know."

"You still think he had a motive, then? I mean, a sensible motive a sane person might understand?"

"There's no big mystery to that part of it. Mendez was a killer by nature and a bully by profession. He was playing Wendigo to run the Blackfoot off their land."

"Damn it, Longarm, we've been over that till I'm blue in the face from explaining. There's no way anyone can claim that Indian land. I not only looked it up in the regulations, I wired Washington to see if there'd been any new rulings on the subject."

"Do tell?" Longarm raised an eyebrow. "What did Washington say?"

"The same thing I've been telling you. Even if this particular reservation was completely abandoned for a full seven years, the land's been set aside in trust for the Blackfoot Nation."

"In other words, as long as one Blackfoot's still living anywhere in the country, no white man can claim an acre of that range?"

Chadwick rolled his eyes heavenward and said, "Not even if the Blackfoot ran up to Canada and took an oath to Queen Victoria. I checked that out with headquarters while I was at it. As wards of the state the Indians are not allowed to sell, give, or even throw away a square foot of their land, once it's been allotted to them."

Longarm asked, "What about some other tribe being given an abandoned reservation?"

Chadwick looked blank. Then he went to the bookshelf and started rummaging through a buckram-bound book of regulations, muttering, "I can see it, in *time*. But that couldn't be what the Wendigo, or Mendez, had in mind."

"Why not?"

"Hell," Chadwick said disgustedly, "you know how slowly the

government works. And even if the B.I.A. did assign some other tribe the lands, what good would it do any white man?"

He opened the book to the regulation he'd been looking for and nodded, saying, "Seven years with no other claims, as I thought. Besides, even if another bunch of Indians were brought in, what would it mean to a white cattleman? I agree, all that ungrazed range might tempt almost anyone who might have hired Mendez, but as I keep trying to tell you, there's no way on earth they can *get* it!"

As he put the book back, Longarm asked, "Let's try it another way. What if someone were to just *hire* the range? Doesn't the government charge a modest fee per head for running cattle on public lands?"

"Certainly. Collecting range fees is part of my job."

"All right. What would it cost me, per head and season, if I came to you for a grazing permit on those reservation lands?"

Chadwick reached for his bookshelf, hesitated as if lost, and turned to say, "I don't know. You'd have to ask Durler, the Indian agent."

"I have. He doesn't know how to *rope* a cow, either. I thought the Land Agency had the final say on all government lands not being used for anything else."

"We do and we don't. You know about interservice rivalry, Longarm. The B.I.A. would never release grazing rights to us."

"Doesn't your office hire out land in the Indian Nation, down Oklahoma way?"

Chadwick frowned and said, "I'll have to ask about that. It's my understanding the Indian Nation's a special case. As you can see, I don't have any B.I.A. regulations here. Doesn't Durler have a library of his own out at the reservation?"

Longarm sighed, "Yeah. I've been looking through those fool books, too. I never was good at Latin and they seem to have been written by some old boys who never learned enough English to matter. Durler says he doesn't know what the Wendigo wanted, either. Do you think he's telling me the truth?"

Chadwick blinked in surprise before he asked, "Jesus, do you think the Indian agent himself might have been behind the killings?"

"Somebody was. I've been going with the notion that Durler doesn't know too much about stealing money from the government yet."

Chadwick laughed and said, "It takes a while. I'm still working on my education. By the way, how long have *you* been in the service, Longarm?"

Longarm chewed his unlit cheroot and answered soberly, "Seven or eight years. They haven't caught me stealing from them yet."

"That makes two of us. Us little fellows never get to put our hands in the cookie jar, do we? You have to know those thieves in Washington pretty well before they let you at the pork barrel."

Longarm didn't answer, so Chadwick continued, "I don't know Durler all that well, but I'll stick my neck out and say he's probably as honest as most of us field men. If he was thinking of pocketing bribes for granting range fees to any local cattleman, he'd be foolish to run his own Blackfoot off."

Longarm frowned and said, "Keep talking. How *would* a crooked Indian agent go about getting rich at his job?"

Chadwick hesitated. Then he shrugged and said expansively, "Hell, we all know how the Indian Ring worked it under Grant. They didn't chase Indians *off* reservations. They crowded 'em *in* like sardines. If Durler was a crook, he'd want all the Indians out there he could get!"

"How do you figure that, Chadwick?"

"Jesus, I thought you said you'd been reading the B.I.A. regulations!" Chadwick said impatiently "The B.I.A. gets money from Congress to take care of them. The money in mistreating Indians is in skimming off part of the government allotments for food, clothing, medical supplies, and so forth."

"Then the more Indians an agent has to work with, the more loose change there is to sort of lose in the cracks?"

Chadwick laughed a bit enviously as he nodded and said, "There you have it. If *I* was a crooked Indian agent, I'd have ten times as many Indians out on that reservation. Then I'd divert about ten cents on the dollar and retire rich!"

Longarm nodded as if in sudden enlightenment and agreed, "You'd make more that way than selling range permits for a side bet under the table, huh?"

Chadwick sighed in open envy this time as he said, "Oh, God, yes. Cows only eat grass. There's no way to fiddle with the price of beans and white bread, feeding cows. They don't wear shoes or sleep under blankets, either. I'll bet that agent Cal Durler replaced is living in a big New York brownstone now."

Longarm frowned and said, "Back up. Are you saying the agent young Cal replaced might have been a crook?"

Chadwick grew suddenly cautious as he answered slyly, "I don't want you to quote me about a fellow federal man, but it's common knowledge he was a Grant appointee. His name was McBride and the new reform administration threw him out on his ass as soon as they went over his books."

Longarm ripped a piece of yellow paper from a pad on Chadwick's desk and wrote the name down before he asked, "Was this McBride ever charged with anything, or are we only funning?"

Chadwick said, "I told you I have no real evidence. No, they did not put him in jail. The way I heard it, they let him resign peaceably, after he had some trouble explaining why he was collecting rations for three times as many Indians as there were in all Montana Territory."

"They get a federal indictment on this McBride jasper, or is all this just suspicions?" Longarm asked, folding the piece of paper and putting it in his pocket.

"Oh, you know half of Grant's boys, including Grant, were never out-and-out *arrested* for stealing half the country. I'll allow the old general, himself, was just a fool who trusted too many old friends after he was president for a while. President Hayes has been taking things back gentle. Just firing or transferring boys caught with their fingers in the till."

"I know. I've only been allowed to arrest half the crooks I've run across in my travels. Crooked or honest, politicians like to sweep old scandals under the rug. I reckon stealing from the taxpayers is a trade secret. I'd better have a few more words with the Justice Department on your telegraph, though. Some of what you just told me is interesting as hell."

Chapter 15

When he was finished at the land office, Longarm went to get his chestnut at the livery near the railroad station. He put off his intended return to the reservation when he spotted a trio of morose-looking but well-dressed Indians, hunkered on the station platform with their backs braced against the wall.

He walked over to them, flashed his federal badge, and asked, "You boys wouldn't be the Crow policemen from the B.I.A., would you?"

The leader of the trio nodded and said, "I am Constable Dancing Pony. You must be the one who killed the crazy man who killed the man we came here to arrest."

"I'm sorry you boys came out here for nothing," Longarm apologized. "Since you're headed home, can I take it you don't suspicion any other Ghost Dance activity out at the Blackfoot reservation?"

Dancing Pony shrugged and said, "The Paiute we were after was the only one reported in the territory this summer. We are going to Pine Ridge to talk to Sitting Bull. The Sioux are more interested in Wovoka's nonsense than the other Plains tribes. The death of Ishiwatl seems to have nipped it in the bud here. That crazy white man did a good job in killing him."

Longarm asked, "Did you boys by any chance have a look around out there?"

"Of course. The army scout, Jason, led us over to the old homestead where the Ghost Dancer was killed. Some Blackfoot said you had buried the fool. But from what we have been told, he answers the description on our warrant, so the case is closed."

"Maybe. I've got another warrant on a Blackfoot breed named Hunts Alone. He's said to be hiding out somewhere around here."

Dancing Pony nodded. "The scout, Jason, told us this. We did not meet every Blackfoot on the reservation. The Crow and Blackfoot are not friends. But those we met seem to be pure-bloods."

"Did you talk to the Blackfoot policeman, Rain Crow?"

"Yes. He seems a good man, for one of *them*. He does not have white blood."

"What made you think I thought he wasn't a good man?" Longarm asked, frowning.

"He is one of your suspects, isn't he? If I had been in your place the night the Ghost Dancer was killed, I would have said Rain Crow did it."

"He told you about the way the sign read, huh? Lucky for Rain Crow the Wendigo turned out to be another man."

"Yes," the Crow agreed. "Any other lawman would have arrested Rain Crow for the killing. They told us the crazy man wore straw-filled sacking on his feet. I think that might have hidden his tracks, most places. But I don't see how he crossed fresh dust without leaving sign. Can you tell me how he did it?"

"No, and since Mendez is dead, he can't, either."

Dancing Pony stared thoughtfully into Longarm's eyes for a long, hard moment. Then he smiled thinly, and said, "You intend to write a few loose ends off, then?"

Longarm ignored what seemed to be a leading question, saying, "*You* have the power to arrest any Indian for murder, Dancing Pony. Do you intend to take Rain Crow in for some serious questioning in the near future?"

The Indian chuckled and answered, "No. If somebody took advantage of the other murders to get rid of a dangerous troublemaker, even if I could prove it, I don't think I would want to. If one of our people would only kill that damned Wovoka, before he stirs up more trouble . . ."

"I see we're in agreement on some things, then. I'd say that the Wendigo was just one clever son of a bitch, wouldn't you?"

Dancing Pony studied Longarm for a time before he said, "You have a good heart for a white man. We shall remember your name." Then he added, "Since the case is closed, will you be leaving with us on the train?"

"Not hardly. I still haven't caught the man I was sent up here about." He might have added that he hadn't really closed the books on the Wendigo, either, but he didn't. Other lawmen tended to get in the way sometimes, since his own methods were inclined occasionally to bend the rules.

Saying good-bye to the Indians, Longarm got his mount from the livery and rode out to the reservation. As he tethered the chestnut behind the agency, Prudence Lee came out of her own place and motioned him over with a worried look.

Longarm joined her in the shade of her back porch, touched the brim of his Stetson, and said, "Ma'am? You look like you've just met up with a spook."

"Calvin Durler's out looking for you, with a gun! Thank God you didn't meet him on the wagon trace!"

"I took a shortcut across the open prairie. What do you mean, a gun?"

"It's that Nancy! She told him something about you and he's half out of his head with rage! I only heard the loud parts when they were shouting about it half an hour or so ago, but she seems to have said you, uh—you know."

Longarm swore under his breath and said, "I never. I reckon you must suspicion it too, huh?"

Prudence shook her head emphatically. "No. If I thought she was telling the truth, I'd let him shoot you. I told you she was going crazy. What are you going to do about it?"

Longarm shrugged and said, "Nan will have been watching from her back window the same as you, so she knows I'm here. Cal will ride clean into Switchback and they'll tell him I rode out. We'd best go inside your place."

"You're welcome to hide with me, of course, but if I could have a talk with Nan before he gets back—"

"No. I want you where I can keep an eye on you. I've run into crazy-jealous husbands before, and there's only one way you can handle them."

"Good heavens! You don't mean to kill the poor boy!"

"Not if I can keep him from killing me some other way."

"Oh, my God, I shouldn't have told you! I can't have a dead man on my conscience!" Prudence cried in dismay.

"Well, had you left me in smiling ignorance you might have had two. He'd have had the clean drop on me, and since I don't take kindly to getting shot, I'd have likely gone down shooting back. Let's go inside while I study my next move."

"Can't you just ride out?" Prudence asked.

"Nope. Ain't finished hereabouts. Oh, I could hide out for a day or so, but it'd make my job tedious, and in the end, he'd likely catch up with me when I wasn't set for a showdown. I think it's best we get it over with as soon as possible."

He led her inside and started piling furniture against the wall facing the agency next door, saying, "I hope he doesn't just start shooting through the wall when Nan tells him I'm in here, but you never know. When we see him coming, I want you flat on the floor behind this stuff."

"Oh, my God, I don't believe this is happening! I must be having a bad dream! You can't mean it, Longarm! You can't just ambush that poor boy like this!"

"Miss Prudence," he said, laying a firm hand on her shoulder,

"I ain't all that happy about it myself. You do as I say and I'll do what I have to. He'll be coming back before the sun sinks enough to matter."

Longarm was right. It was an hour before sunset when Calvin Durler rode in at a lope, his pony lathered and his face red with rage. He swung out of the saddle with a double-barreled shotgun in his free hand and ran into his own house, shouting.

A few minutes later he was out the back door again and headed next door, yelling, "I know you're in there, you son of a bitch! Come out and fight like a man!"

There was no answer. Calvin strode, grim-faced, toward the back porch entrance, all caution thrown to the winds as he searched for the man his wife had accused. He stopped a few paces from the roof overhang and called again, "Don't hide behind a woman's skirts, you bastard! If you won't come out, I'm coming in! Defend yourself, sir!"

And then a loop of throw rope dropped around his head and shoulders, snapping tight to pin the enraged husband's elbows to his sides as Longarm, standing on the roof above, yanked hard.

Durler was lifted off his feet, sputtering in surprised confusion, as Longarm ran the length of the eaves and spilled Durler on one side. Then he dropped to the ground, still pulling the rope. He dragged Durler, kicking and screaming, away from his fallen shotgun, then came in hand over hand down the rope, and as Durler struggled to rise, kicked him flat, jumped on top of him, and proceeded to hogtie him with the pigging string he'd been gripping between his teeth.

The back door flew open and Prudence Lee flew out, shouting, "Don't hurt him, Longarm! It wasn't his fault!"

Longarm finished binding his victim securely before he looked up with a grin, and still kneeling on Durler's thrashing body, he said, "I told you I'd try to take him without gunplay, ma'am."

The other back door opened and Nan Durler peered out, looking almost as confused as her husband. Longarm slapped Durler a couple of times to gain his undivided attention before he said calmly, "She wasn't expecting to have to repeat her fool story to both of us, Cal. Let's see if she was trying to get *you* or *me* out of the way, huh?"

He called out amiably, "Which one did you think it would be, Nan? I know you were pissed at me, but on the other hand, you likely figured I could take your man. I know divorce is frowned on, but wouldn't it have been more Christian?"

Nan ducked inside without answering, but her husband grunted, "Get off my back, God damn you! You're killing me!"

"Not as dead as she figured I would be. What in thunder's wrong with you, old son? Even if you bought that fool tale she must have told you, did you really think you had a chance against me? Meaning no offense, the last time I rode through Dodge, Ben Thompson and John Wesley Hardin both stayed out of my way."

"You just untie me and let me at a gun, you son of a bitch, and we'll just see how good you are!"

"I know how good I am, Cal," Longarm said calmly. "Likely your wife does, too. I don't aim to let you up till you've had time to reconsider a mite. You've been fighting with her for days. Ordinarily, I don't ask what married folks are fighting over, but she's been talking about leaving you, hasn't she?"

There was a long silence before Durler said grudgingly, "That's between me and her. She said you trifled with her while my back was turned, God damn you!"

"Well, she's a handsome woman and I'm no saint, so I can see how you might have been fool enough to buy that shit. But you missed a point or two. If I'd been at her while you were out tending your chores, don't you suspicion she'd have sort of wanted to keep it a secret? Most gals do. How'd she get you so riled? Did she say I had a bigger prick?"

"You bastard! How did you know that?"

"I'm a lawman. This ain't the first time I've run across such action, though I've usually been the arresting officer. Ain't it a bitch how gals get us poor idiots to fight with that old taunt about our peckers? I don't care if you believe this or not, but Nan ain't in a position to say all that much about my anatomy. She only saw me once in my birthday suit and it wasn't up enough to mention."

From the sidelines, Prudence Lee gasped, "Mr. Long! I'll thank you to remember I'm a lady!"

"Can't be helped, ma'am. This is man talk. You'd best go inside if it's too rich for your ears."

She didn't move. Interested in spite of himself, Calvin Durler asked, "She saw you naked? When was this?"

"When she came in on me as I was taking a bath. She likely meant to scrub my back or something."

"She told me you'd had her in our own bed. She said she'd tried to resist, but you were so strong and she was so weak, her flesh betrayed her into going all the way."

"Sure, she told you that," Longarm said. "Next to being told the other man is bigger and better, nothing steams a man like hearing it took place in his own bed. She didn't miss a trick, did she?"

"God damn it, she *must* have been telling me the truth! How could any woman admit to such a thing if it wasn't true?"

"To get her husband killed, most likely. Just *think* a mite, damn it. Even if I was fool enough to trifle with a man's wife under his own roof with miles of open country all about, why would I take even more of a chance than I had to? Hell, you've given me a guest room with a lock on the door, old son! Don't you think I'd have sense enough to use it for my wicked seductions, if such was my intention?"

Durler said, "She told me you caught her in our room, making the bed, and—"

"Damn it, she makes all the beds at the same time," Longarm interrupted. "Besides that, if I was some sort of mad rapist, Miss Prudence, here, has been all alone at my mercy without a husband to protect her. Ain't that right, Miss Prudence?"

The missionary blushed and stammered, "What are you saying? We've never been improper together!"

"There you go, Cal, and meaning no disrespect to your woman, this single gal, here, is no uglier. Well, never mind. The point I'm aiming at is that I'd be too foolish to be let out without a keeper if I'd been fooling with a married-up woman under her own roof with a good-looking single gal alone next door."

Prudence Lee added, "I can assure you, Calvin, Mr. Long has been a perfect gentleman the times we've been alone, and come to think of it, he's been alone with me more often than with Nan."

Longarm asked, "Can I let you up now, Cal?"

"Well, maybe I won't shoot anybody just yet, but I've got a lot of questions to ask everybody hereabouts!"

Longarm untied his wrists and ankles and helped him to his feet as Durler muttered murderously, "Somebody's been trying to pull the wool over my eyes, God damn it."

"I know. Why don't we all go over to your place and have us a powwow with your woman?"

But when the three of them got to the agency kitchen, they met Nan Durler with a packed carpetbag and a defiant look on her face. Durler said, "Honey, we've got to talk about this situation."

But his wife snapped, "I'm through talking, you mealy-mouthed nitwit! If you were any kind of a man at all, you'd have killed him for what he did to me!"

"He says he didn't do it, Nan."

"I don't care who says what to anybody!" Nan Durler exploded. "I'm taking one of the ponies into Switchback. You can pick it up at the livery. I'm going where men know how to do *right* by a lady!"

She swept grandly out, and as Durler followed, pleading, Longarm caught Prudence by the elbow and murmured, "Stay here with me and let 'em have it out."

"I don't want her to tell him more lies about you. I've never met a woman with such an evil tongue!" Prudence said with righteous indignation.

"I have. I'd say her mind's made up and she's leaving peaceably. Her notions on collecting a government pension as the widow of a federal employee didn't pan out, but she's on her way East and he won't be turning her around."

"Oh, good heavens! I didn't even consider a pension! So that's why she wanted you both to fight!"

"Only partly. Since Cal ain't listening, I will confess she did try to get me to do what she said, only I wouldn't, and she was likely moody enough about it to not care all that much which of us got buried. Since she never figured she'd have to repeat her fool tale under cross-examination, I suspicion she's given up. He'll be fool enough to tag along all the way to town, but she's getting on that train. Her jaw was set for a long trip elsewhere."

"Well, he's well rid of her, I suppose," Prudence said. "But what's to become of her?"

"Don't know. Don't care. She'll find another man, or failing at that, take up the trade she was likely born for. I doubt she'll become a missionary."

Prudence Lee's eyes narrowed as she snapped, "Just what was *that* supposed to mean, sir?"

"Just funning."

Longarm was drinking alone in the Switchback saloon that night when Jason joined him at the bar. Jason said, "Heard you took a room at the Railroad Hotel."

Longarm said, "Just for the night. I'll be pulling out for Denver in the morning."

"Oh, you finished here?" Jason asked, surprised. "I thought it might have something to do with that domestic trouble out at the agency."

"Jesus, news travels in a small town, don't it? The back-fence gossips must have had a lot of fun when Durler's old woman left on the evening train."

"I heard something about her leaving him. Surprised *you're* leaving, though. When I rode in to see the Crow police off, they said you had some loose ends left hereabouts."

"There's loose ends and there's loose ends, Jason. Sometimes, in my trade, it pays to leave a few be. The Wendigo killings have stopped, and I can't find Johnny Hunts Alone. Meanwhile, there's more work waiting for me back in Denver and my boss is getting moody about it."

"I see. So we'll likely never know how Mendez pulled off some of it, or why, eh?"

Longarm said, "Oh, I got the Wendigo's moves nailed down. Like I suspicioned, he was using the railroad and those burlap boots to get on and off the reservation. Killed his victims with that South American bolo, and you know the rest."

Jason scratched at his thick-stubbled jaw. "Damned if I do! What about that Ghost Dancer, killed miles from the track, or old Real Bear, murdered right next door to the agency? No tracks near there, were there?"

"Mendez never killed those two," Longarm explained, "The Ghost Dancer was killed by . . . never mind. The point is, the Indian who got rid of a troublemaker before he could get the tribe in hot water did everyone a favor, and what the hell."

"What about the old chief?" Jason asked, puzzled.

"Oh, that was Johnny Hunts Alone. Real Bear had recognized and turned the rascal in. So he butchered the old man and skinned him. You said the breed was once a hide skinner, remember?"

Jason snapped his fingers. "That's right, and Real Bear's head wasn't cut off, either!"

"There you go. Mendez was sent to follow up on the first spooky killing when the Dream Singers started scaring folks about the Wendigo. The idea was to scare the Blackfoot off all that open range. Mendez was a hired thug. Don't know if the grisly trimmings were his idea or not. He didn't have much imagination. Kept pulling the same fool tricks till I caught him."

Jason frowned and said, "Wait a minute. Loose ends are one thing, but this is ridiculous! You say you think Johnny Hunts Alone killed Real Bear, but you've given up on catching him?"

"I'd catch him if he was on the reservation. But he ain't. He likely lit out shortly after killing the informer. His only reason for being in these parts was to hide out. With the Justice Department, army, Indian agency, and all combing the reservation for the Wendigo—"

"I follow your drift. He's likely in Mexico by now. But what was that about someone putting Mendez up to those other killings?"

The deputy laughed softly. "Ain't it obvious? Mendez didn't kill folks as a hobby. He did it for money. He was hired to run the Blackfoot off a huge stretch of virgin range. None of the big cattle outfits would be in a position to claim or buy the land, once it was deserted, but they don't *buy* open range in the first place. They pay a fee per head to the government to graze it. Cal Durler says he's had lots of offers, but he turned them all down. Says he was offered a few bribes, too." Longarm reached for a cheroot, lit it, and mused, "Had the Blackfoot run to Canada as planned, the B.I.A. would have fired Durler as deadwood."

"Then who would they go to with an offer on the grazing rights?" Jason asked.

"Land office, of course. Bureau of Land Management has the say on all federal lands not occupied by anybody."

"You mean Chadwick could lease out grazing rights on Indian lands?"

Longarm nodded. "Sure. He says he can't, but I checked with Washington and he has the power to lease even your army post, if it ain't being used by anybody. The grazing rights are leased on a yearly basis. Land office can grant the rights to the White House lawn if President Hayes ain't there to object."

"Kee-rist! Don't you see what that means, Longarm?"

The lawman took a long drag on his cheroot and blew out a thick column of bluish smoke. For a moment, he watched it thin out and spread to merge with the pall already floating in the thick atmosphere of the saloon, then he said, "That Chadwick ain't up on his regulations? Or that he'd have been in position to line his pockets if the Blackfoot had deserted all that land?"

"Good God Almighty! Ain't you going to arrest him?" Jason asked.

"I'd like to," Longarm said. "But on what charge? Mendez is dead, so he can't be a witness. There's nothing I can prove. But what the hell, the killings are over and he'll be too scared to try again, so I'm closing the books on the case."

Jason drained his glass and held his finger up to the bartender for another as he growled, "That's raw as hell, Longarm! Can't you see Chadwick was behind it all? You know how big cattle spreads take care of government men who can grant 'em grazing rights while keeping smaller men off the free grass!"

Longarm nodded morosely, and agreed, "Sure, I know. But I can't touch the rascal. It's no crime to be a mite confused about his land office regulations. Not in court, anyway. He was never on the reservation or anywhere near the victims, so what am I to do about it?"

"By God, if it was me wearing that badge I'd *shoot* the son of a bitch!" Jason said vehemently.

"I've studied on that. The man's a federal official with powerful friends. Wouldn't be legal for me to just up and gun him down like the dog he is. But like I said, he likely won't try anything else. He was mixed up in another scandal a few years back and it took him a long time to get up the nerve to have another go at the pork barrel. So he'll retire poor but honest. It happens that way, once in a while."

Jason grabbed his fresh drink peevishly and snapped, "I thought you had more sand in your craw! Ain't you even gonna have harsh words with him over all he did to them poor folks?"

Longarm shrugged. "I could lecture him some, but he'd just laugh at me. He's had time to cover his crooked tracks better than his hired Wendigo ever did. No, I'll just leave polite and peaceable. I'm only a deputy and he's got some powerful pals in higher circles. One thing I've had to learn the hard way, Jason, is that the big shots never get caught."

"Jesus, you call that justice?"

"Nope, I call it the facts of life. I've got enough on my plate with the *little* bastards they send me after." He took out his watch and consulted it before he added, "I've got some wires to send at the station and a ticket to buy. If I don't meet up with you again, it's been nice knowing you, Jason."

Leaving the scout to brood about it over his drink, Longarm left and walked over to the station. He went inside, then out the far door to the dark tracks. He moved west along the railroad right-of-way until he came abreast of an alleyway cutting behind the storefronts of the main street. Then he drew his .44 and moved slowly down the alley toward the back door of the land office.

He took his time deliberately, but he'd reached the back fence when he heard a fusillade of gunshots, followed by a ghastly scream!

Longarm nodded and moved in slowly and cautiously. The screams were still going on as he kicked in the back door and moved along the dimly lit corridor in their direction. They were coming from the telegraph lean-to.

Longarm heard the front door slam, so he entered the shack. Agent Chadwick was rolling on the floor in a puddle of blood and steaming battery acid, his hands covering his smoldering face as he wailed, "Oh, Jesus! Mary, Mother of God, I can't stand it!"

Longarm placed one boot on a dry spot, holstered his .44, grabbed one of Chadwick's booted ankles, and hauled him clear of the vitriol and broken battery glass, saying, "Don't rub it in, you stupid son of a bitch!"

He dragged Chadwick along the corridor, leaving a trail of smoldering carpet in their wake, and kicked out the front door to drag the screaming land agent out into the street. People ran from every direction as Longarm hauled Chadwick through the dust to a watering trough, picked him up by the belt, and plunged him full-length into the water, soaking his own arms to the elbows as he did so. He called out, "Somebody run for the doc and stand clear of that splashed shit. Even mixed with water it's strong enough to peel you alive!"

He glanced around for Jason, but the scout wasn't part of the crowd. Longarm shrugged, and since Chadwick seemed to be drowning, reached in for a handful of his hair and pulled his head up. As he did so, the hair came off in his hand and the land agent's head banged against the soggy end planks, out of the water. He was screaming again now, so he'd probably live for a while, the poor bastard.

Longarm turned to the bartender from across the way and said, "Tell the doc somebody put a bullet in his gut, then shot out the battery jars above him. He's likely done for, but ask the doc to try to keep him alive till I get back."

Someone asked, "Where are you going, Deputy?"

Longarm said, "To arrest the man who did it, of course. A favor is a favor, but the law is the law, too."

He caught up with the scout in the livery. They were alone there, since the stable hands were up the street, attending the evening festivities around the dying land agent.

Longarm said, "'Evening, Jason. Going someplace?"

The bearded scout smiled thinly and said, "I was wondering why my saddle was missing. You came by here and hid it before laying for me over at the saloon, huh?"

"Yep. I owe you for pushing me out of the way of a bullet, so I hope we can settle this peaceably."

"I notice you haven't drawn. Don't reckon you could see your way to just let me ride out? You know that skunk had a good killing coming to him."

"You killed him better than most Apaches might have managed. I reckon blood is thicker'n water, even if you killed old Real Bear after he recognized you. Since you had nothing to do with killing those other Blackfoot, and they were your kin, I sort of figured you'd go for Chadwick, once I told you he'd been behind the Wendigo bullshit. I want you to listen sharp before you go for that gun at your side, old son. I'd rather take you in alive, but I'm taking you in, not for what you did to Chadwick, but for those other folks you robbed and killed as Johnny Hunts Alone."

"I might have known you had me spotted. Can we talk a spell before we slap leather?"

"I've got time. If you're trying to tell me you've gone straight as an army scout, forget it. I've sent some wires and there's no scout assigned to Fort Banyon. You knew it was a quiet post and just rode in with bogus orders you'd typed up under a carbon paper. That drunk C.O. out there never gave enough of a damn to check, and since you only aimed to stay a month or so, you had till next payday before anyone might have asked for confirmation. I'm surprised the Crow police didn't tumble, though. Few army posts have scouts assigned between campaigns, and when they do, it's usually a local man who talks the local tribe's lingo. I know you said you didn't talk Blackfoot, but of course you do. That part about talking Sioux was clumsy, Johnny. Got me wondering why you were scouting in Blackfoot country. Saying you didn't know your way around the reservation was foolish, too. A real scout would have known the country like the back of his hand, or there'd be no point to the War Department's hiring him in the first place!"

"You gotta admit I can pass for pure white," Jason-Johnny said proudly.

"Sure you can. That's what mixed us up, at first. They sent me looking for a Blackfoot, *on* the reservation, not a white scout right next door. Old Real Bear forgot to put that part in when he got word to us you were in the neighborhood. But as you see, I figured it out. Once I knew you weren't a real scout, the rest just sort of fell into place. Nobody'd be working as a scout just for the hell of it, and you *are* sort of dark, once folks get suspicious."

Johnny Hunts Alone nodded and said, "I still say you had dumb luck. Had that son of a bitch, Chadwick, not used my killing Real Bear to start a war of his own . . ."

"That's right. I'd have likely run in circles for a few days, found out no breed answering your description was on the reservation, and decided he'd just lit out after killing the old man. But as you see, it didn't work out that way. I had you spotted soon enough, but I didn't know if you were the Wendigo, so I left you to one side until I caught Mendez, and you know the rest. If you'd oblige me by unbuckling that gun belt, gentle, I'd be willing to take you to Denver without putting you in irons. Like you said, I owe you."

The half-breed shook his head and said, smiling broadly, "Can't hardly see my way clear to do that, Longarm. I reckon it's you or me, huh?"

"I wish you wouldn't make me kill you, old son."

Hunts Alone laughed a trifle wildly, and staring hard at the holstered .44 at Longarm's side, went for his own.

There was a bright orange blaze of two rapid shots and Johnny Hunts Alone staggered back against the wall of a stall as the horse behind him whinnied in terror. The half-breed slid down the planks, leaving a trail of blood against them as he sank to his knees, his own gun still undrawn and his eyes riveted on the grips of Longarm's holstered sixgun. He shook his head and muttered, "What the hell—?"

Longarm took the little brass derringer from the side coat pocket he'd fired through and explained, "I was covering you with a double-barreled whore pistol all this time, Johnny. You said you wanted to talk, so I let you. But I've had men draw on me in the middle of an interesting conversation, so . . ."

"Damn it, that wasn't *fair*, Longarm! I thought we were going to settle this like gents."

"You had your chance to come peaceably. I gave you a better chance than you did when you hit old Real Bear from behind, and while we're on the subject, that last bank clerk you gunned was unarmed. But we're wasting time with this fool talk, Johnny. How bad did I hit you? The doc's right up the street."

"I'd say you killed me," answered Johnny Hunts Alone judiciously as he removed a blood-slicked hand from his chest and studied it calmly in the dim light.

Longarm said, "I'll be taking that gun before I go to fetch help, Johnny. You just rest easy and try not to move about."

But as he drew his .44 and knelt to take the gun from the kneeling man's hip, the breed suddenly vomited blood and fell forward on his face. Johnny Hunts Alone's body twitched a few more times, then lay very still. Longarm felt for the pulse on the side of his neck and said aloud, "You were right, old son. I purely put at least one round where it counted, didn't I?"

The man stretched out in the stable litter didn't answer.

Longarm hadn't expected him to.

Longarm knelt a while in silence, wondering why his gut felt so empty. It was all over. He'd done the job he'd been sent to do and he had done it damned well, in all modesty. So why did he feel so shitty?

It wasn't that he'd just killed another man. He'd gotten used to that part. It went with the job. He'd given this poor jasper the chance to come with him peaceably and politely, and where in the U.S. Constitution did it say a lawman had to treat a wanted killer fairly?

No, he didn't feel guilty about killing Johnny Hunts Alone. He'd owed the man for saving his ass that time, but the breed had only been acting natural when he spied that gun barrel trained on them from across the street. Nobody was all bad. The man he'd just killed had likely been decent to his friends and good to his horse, too. Had he been given more of a break than he'd asked for, he'd be riding out about now with a dead lawman lying here, and not feeling all that sorry about it.

As to tricking Hunts Alone into killing the one man the law couldn't touch, Longarm thought that had been right slick, if he said so himself. He'd file it that he'd gunned Johnny after tracking him from the murder of a government official and there'd be no scandal worth mentioning. It was all as neat as a pin. Perhaps he was feeling sad because, no matter how many of them died, poor Roping Sally would never come back with her tomboy smile and rollicking rump to brighten up a tedious world.

He got to his feet again, brushing the stable dust from his knee with his hat, and stepped outside.

More sightseers were running to the sound of the more recent shots and Longarm saw one was Sheriff Murphy. Longarm said, "Take charge of the body in there, will you, Murph? By the way, there's a reward on the cuss. I'll write you up for an assistment, if you want."

"Why, that's neighborly as hell, Longarm. But who in thunder did you shoot this time? The doc says Chadwick's done for!"

"I didn't shoot Chadwick. The man who did is inside, dead. You'll find he's that jasper who said he worked for the army,

Jason. His real name was Hunts Alone and he was a Blackfoot on his mama's side. Now you know as much as I do and I've got other chores to tend to."

Leaving Murphy in charge at the livery, Longarm jogged up the street to where Chadwick lay naked on a wagon tarp near the watering trough. The coroner looked up brightly and said, "You're delivering 'em fresh these days. This poor cadaver's still breathing. No need for an autopsy, though. The cause of death was a bullet through the spleen and a shower of battery acid. I just knocked him out to ease his way out of this world. Before he went under, he said something about a double-cross."

"He likely thought one of the folks offering him bribes was spooked about it. Did he mention any names?"

"No, and he won't. Even if he'd lived—I mean for the night—he'd have been in too much pain to talk sense. Those third-degree acid burns must smart."

The deputy marshal pulled at a corner of his John L. Sullivan mustache. "Hell, I wanted him to confirm a few things. No way to bring him around for a minute or two?"

"I'll try."

The coroner started to give the charred body an injection. Then he shook his head and said, "He's gone. Maybe I gave him a mite more morphine than I should have."

"I reckon it was your Christian duty, Doc. I can see the bones in his face and the eye holes are still smoking."

"Yeah, it was a hell of a way for any man to die," the coroner agreed.

Longarm shrugged and muttered, "Oh, I don't know. All things considered, I suspicion the mother-loving son of a bitch got off easier than he deserved!"

A man in the crowd marveled, "Jesus, Deputy, when you hate, you hate *serious*, don't you?"

Longarm swept the crowd with his cold, gray blue eyes as he nodded and said, "Yep, and you might spread the word that I'll be back if anyone ever, ever raises another finger against my friends out at the Blackfoot reservation!"

He assumed, as he walked away, that they'd gotten his message. If they hadn't, what the hell, he'd meant every word.

Chapter 16

It was another midnight by the time Longarm reached the agency after one last, tedious ride out to fill Calvin Durler in on all that had just taken place.

He found the young Indian agent in a chair next to the kitchen table, sprawled facedown across it and out like a light. There were no bullet holes in Durler, but a jar of white lightning stood on the table near his snoring head, three-quarters gone.

Longarm considered shaking him awake, but decided not to. Drunken young men whose women had just lit out on them tended to be testy, even when they were able to hear you. So Longarm snuffed out the kitchen lamp to keep the poor kid from cremating himself and stepped outside.

There was a light in Prudence Lee's window, but it was late. He thought maybe he'd just light out and the hell with it. If Durler had any questions they couldn't answer for him in town, he could write to Denver when he sobered up.

But Prudence must have heard his chestnut's hooves, for she popped out on the porch to hail him, saying, "I was so afraid you'd leave without coming by to say good-bye. Is it true you're finished here?"

"Yep. I've returned the hired mule and buckboard to the livery, made arrangements to return the army's horse to Fort Banyon, and I've bought a through ticket to Denver. My train pulls out tomorrow."

"Oh? Then surely you intended to spend the night out here?"

"Not hardly. Calvin's drunk as a skunk and it gets tedious listening to folks blubber about lost love. I've got a room in town for the night—or what's left of it."

"The least you can do is come inside and sit a spell," Prudence said. "I'm so confused about all that's happened, and I'd love to have you explain it all to me."

Longarm shrugged and followed her inside, where a pot of coffee was already boiling on the stove. She'd likely put it on as soon as she'd heard him ride in.

He sat down at the table and said, "Well, I've told this tale so many times I'm sick of it, so I'll make it short and sweet."

Which he did, between draughts of Prudence's strong coffee, up to the events of the previous few hours. When he had finished,

Prudence Lee said, "So the Wendigo business was all a ruse to drive the Indians away to Canada, right?"

"Yep. Almost worked, too," Longarm said, taking a sip of coffee.

"But you were waiting for the Wendigo on the train. The fact that the Ghost Dancer was murdered miles from the track never fooled you?"

"Heck, no. I could see right off who did it. When you read two men going in and one coming out, and don't believe in ghosts, there can only be one answer. Rain Crow tracked the Ghost Dancer down and killed him for being a troublemaker. Then, when he saw he might have exceeded his authority a mite, he tried to make it look like the Wendigo had done it."

"Are you going to have to arrest Rain Crow?" Prudence asked, a troubled look in her eyes.

"No. By now he's figured out what he did wrong. Had he just up and shot the jasper, as a lawman trying to make an arrest, there'd have been no crime to report. I suppose I could get picky about it, but I'm not of a mind to. I could make a fuss about Snake Killer's homemade liquor, too. But I'm a peace officer, not a man to cause trouble for peaceable folk. Besides, I see Calvin's got a jar of Snake Killer's medicine next door, likely helping him get through the first troubled nights. So I ain't putting anything about firewater in my official report."

As she poured him another cup of coffee, he said, "That's about the size of all that's happened, Miss Prudence. I'll just drink this and be on my way."

"Don't you think we'd be more comfortable on the davenport, out in the other room?" Prudence asked.

"If you say so, ma'am."

He followed her into the parlor, where he noticed that she didn't light the lamp as they sat down together. She waited until he'd swallowed a few sips before she said, quietly, "I'll be going into town myself, in the morning. Would you take me with you?"

"You leaving for good or just shopping, ma'am?"

"For good. Why do you ask?"

"I've returned the hired buckboard. I could ride you postern on the chestnut, if it was just a shopping expedition. Packing you and all your gear on one horse, though, is another story, I'm afraid."

"I won't be taking much. Just my personals, in one bag. I noticed when Nan left that a woman can carry all she really needs in one neat bundle."

"What about your big bass drum, Miss Prudence?"

She laughed oddly, and said, "To hell with the big bass drum! I'm so tired of beating it I could scream!"

Not meeting her gaze, Longarm asked, "Don't you want to be a missionary anymore, ma'am?"

"I never wanted to be a missionary, but what was I to do? I don't know how to play one of those new typewriters, I'm not pretty enough to be an actress, and I don't know how to walk a tightrope in the circus."

"Now, those are purely interesting trades for a lady, ma'am. Are you saying you just took up reading Bibles because you needed a *job*?"

"Of course. It was that or . . . work I'm not ready for. I was rather desperate when I checked into that home for wayward girls, and when they offered me a position as a missionary . . . well, damn it, what was I to do? Work in a fancy house? I may have strayed, some may have said I was fallen. But, damn it, I never fell *that* far!"

"I see." Longarm nodded sagely. "That gal you were telling me about—the one who ran off with a rascal who deserted her? She was you all the time, right?"

"Of course. Don't tell me you didn't have *that* figured out!"

Longarm winked. "The thought sort of crossed my mind, but it wasn't my business."

"So now you know. And I don't mind telling you it's a load off my mind! I was getting so sick of playing Little Miss Goody."

He chuckled and said, "A little Goody ain't all that bad, taken in moderation. If you're giving up on being a missionary, what's your next goal—learning to play a typewriter after all?"

"Anything would be an improvement over reading the Bible to a lot of people who just aren't interested. I thought I'd get back to civilization with the little I have left and . . . I don't know. That story about Madam LaMont had a moral, all right. I noticed that while she was atoning, she got *rich* at it."

Longarm drained the cup, placed it on the floor, and leaned back to observe, "You ain't as wicked as you'd have to be to take up that line of work, honey. Don't be so hard on yourself."

"What makes you so sure I couldn't be . . . one of those women?"

"You ain't cold-blooded enough. There's a poor, lonesome fool right next door, with a good income, and he's ripe for the plucking. A wicked lady would be over there right now, helping him forget his troubles while she taught him to leap through hoops. A gal who was willing to sell her favors could take that idiot for every cent he had and make him wire home for more!"

"My God! The thought never crossed my mind!" Prudence gasped.

"There you go. You just don't think like a dance-hall gal. You'll likely wind up an honest woman in spite of yourself."

She laughed and said, "You have a wicked imagination. Now that you've pointed it out, I can see how I could trap poor Calvin without, as you put it so bluntly, selling anything at all."

"Yep, he'd likely marry up with you if you took him under your wing. Old Cal's the marrying kind."

"Well, I'm not a mother hen and if I was I don't think he'd be my cup of tea. Nancy was an awful girl, but I could see how living with such a wishy-wash could drive most women to distraction. I don't know why I'm telling you this, but I ran away from a husband who was twice the man Calvin is!"

Longarm shifted his weight and observed, "He'll likely find some gal in Switchback. Word gets around quick about a lonesome cuss with a good job. Besides, he ain't that bad—just has some growing to do. He's already learned to ease up on the Indians and brand his livestock. He'll make some gal a good man, provided she ain't as particular as yourself."

"Could we please drop Calvin Durler? A body would think you were trying to marry her off to the nearest thing in pants! Maybe I am particular, for a woman of my age and looks, but when I *am* ready to try again, I shan't make the same mistake. I was a teenaged silly and my mother was after me to marry the boy next door and . . . no, the next time I'm going to have a much better notion what I'm getting myself into!"

"Pays to shop around a mite, eh?"

Prudence sighed, "I suppose you could put it that way. I've wasted some of my best years on a nice boy who bored me to distraction; I've made an awful fool of myself with a no-account handsome devil, and for a while, acted so crazy I hardly remember what it was like. Now that I've seen I'm just too . . . well, *healthy* to give my remaining good years to mission work— Heavens, what am I saying? Why am I baring my soul to you like this? And is that your *arm* around my shoulders, sir?"

Longarm gently drew her closer, and observed, "Lots of

folks seem to tell me things they hadn't intended to. Gal I knew once, said it had something to do with my not getting all excited in the middle of a quiet conversation. As to why I'm holding you friendly, I reckon I'm cold or something. I'll stop if you want me to."

She reached up to clasp the big hand cupping her shoulder as she sighed, "It does feel comforting, but you're to go no further. Just because I've let down my hair a mite is no reason to get ideas. I may be middle-aged, and not much of a looker, and I've told you far too much about how weak I've been, but—"

"Slow down! You're talking silly. You can't be thirty yet, you know you're a right pretty little mouse, and friends don't take advantage of each other's weaknesses."

"Oh, you're just saying that," Prudence scoffed. "I'll admit I'm not deformed, but 'fess up—you wouldn't have your arm about me if I hadn't confessed to being a fallen woman, would you?"

"I might have hesitated if you'd stuck to beating drums for the Bible Society, but as for being fallen, I suspicion you haven't fallen as far as you might have aimed to. Most of us have more lust than nerves. We've been brought up to think a lot of things that are only natural must be wicked. Somehow the people who wrote the rules got the funny notion that anything that felt good had to be bad for us."

Her reply, if she had one, was muffled against his lips as he gently pulled her closer and kissed her. She responded, started to struggle, then moaned in pleasure and started kissing back.

Longarm put his free hand against her firm little belly, felt that she wore no corset, praise the Lord, and started moving up. Then he decided what the hell, and slid his hand down between her thighs and began to stroke her gently through her cotton twill skirt and whatever was under it.

She gasped and twisted her lips away from his, pleading, "No! I don't want to!"

"Sure you do. Don't you think I can read the smoke signals in your pretty brown eyes?"

"Oh, I'm so bewildered! My body's saying one thing, but my head tells me this is wrong. The Bible says it's wrong!"

He noticed she wasn't pulling away all that vigorously, so he massaged her through the cloth and soothed, "Go with your body, honey. Anyway, if you really want to talk religion at a time like this, don't you reckon the Lord would never have made us like we are, or let us be together like this, if He was so dead set against it?"

Even as she stopped struggling and opened her thighs to his caress, she protested, "Damn it, you know that's pure sophistry!"

He grinned and said, "Yeah, ain't that a bitch?" as he picked her up and carried her into the bedroom, observing, "We could wrestle on that damn horsehair some more, but it ain't civilized, and all these fool clothes are in the way."

"What are you *doing*!" she exclaimed, even as she helped him with the hooks and eyes while he was undressing her. He gently stripped her to her shift and high-button shoes as she half-struggled, half-cooperated on the mattress. Then he popped a few buttons of his own, got most of his duds out of the way, and was mounting her. She sobbed, "Oh, I never should have told you about my past!" as she wrapped her thighs around him and gripped his naked buttocks with her leather-clad ankles. He moved them into a better position and started thrusting harder as she rolled her head from side to side and gasped, "Oh, this is terrible! What must you think of me?"

"I think you're more wondrous than an army in its banners. You want me to take it out?"

"You do and I'll kill you! I think I'm . . . oh, Jesus! I *know* I'm coming!"

Later, after they'd taken time to catch their breath and get rid of all the remaining clothing, Prudence held him in her arms, nibbling on one ear, as she purred, "Will you take me with you to Denver, darling?"

He said, "I'll take you to the moon if you want, but maybe I should have explained a few things."

She placed a finger to his lips. "Hush, don't spoil this moment, darling. I know you're not the marrying kind." She chuckled and added, "As a matter of fact, I'm not sure I am, either. Not for a while, at least. There's so much of life I seem to have missed out on. God, you must think I'm terrible!"

"No, I think you're one of the few sensible gals I've run across lately. I'll take you with me at sunup and we'll just sort of drift with the tide till—"

"No plans, dearest. I know better than to hold you to foolish promises and, well, you seem to have started something, for *I* don't mean to be held to any, either!"

She saw he wasn't going to answer and chuckled. "You're not sure if you like that or not, are you? I suppose most girls you do this with fall madly in love with you?"

"I like it best when there's less fool talk and more action," Longarm said.

She laughed as he remounted her. She responded to his first thrust, saying, "My heavens, Nan Durler really told the truth about one thing. If this be carnal depravity, I like it. I didn't mean to offend your manly pride, dearest, but I *told* you I was weak-willed."

Longarm laughed, too. He started moving faster, thinking, *Yeah, this is what every old boy says he wants—a pretty little thing that moves her tail like a saloon door on payday, with no strings or tears in the cold, gray dawn.* By jimmies, he'd take her to Denver and hold on to her for a spell! Then, as he paused, once more sated for the moment, Prudence sighed, "Roll over on your back and let me do it my way."

"I'm still up to it, honey, and I like to do things my way and I'm bigger than you!"

"My, yes, in every way," she purred. "But please let me get on top. Pretty please with sugar on it?"

So, having shown he was still the boss, sort of, Longarm rolled his back against the mattress as she took her own way with his flesh. As he suddenly laughed, she paused and asked with a frown, "What's so funny? I didn't think I was all that ridiculous with my old shimmy off!"

He laughed again and explained, "I was thinking of a gal I met, maybe a million years ago, who said I'd never meet up with another half as good."

Prudence Lee arched her petite torso back to grasp his bare ankles and brace herself on locked elbows. Then she hooked a heel in each of Longarm's armpits and began moving her tiny pelvis in a manner he found impossible as well as delicious. He gasped, "You're purely fixing to bust me off inside you, but don't you dare stop!"

"Was that other lady right in her assumption you'd never meet her match in bed, darling?"

Longarm grinned up at the gamin face smiling back at him between a pair of bouncing cupcake breasts and answered, "Honey, she was as crazy as a bedbug! Every other gal I've ever done this with was just practice for tonight. You are the very best I've ever had and that's the truth!"

That was what he liked most about women. No matter how good the last had been, each time he found himself a new one, it really did seem that she was the best he'd ever had. So no matter how often he said it, he was always telling the truth.

GIANT-SIZED ADVENTURE FROM AVENGING ANGEL LONGARM.

BY TABOR EVANS

2006 Giant Edition:

LONGARM AND THE
OUTLAW EMPRESS

2007 Giant Edition:

LONGARM AND THE
GOLDEN EAGLE SHOOT-OUT

2008 Giant Edition:

LONGARM AND THE
VALLEY OF SKULLS

penguin.com

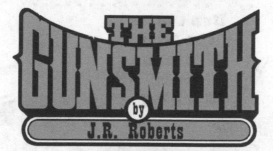